REGENCY IN COLOR

VOLUME 1

GABRIELLE CARR   HILDIE MCQUEEN
ELISE MARION   JESSICA CALE

THANK YOU FOR DOWNLOADING OUR COLLECTION

Dearest Reader,

The authors bringing you this collection are so excited to present Regency romance as you've never seen it before. In our Regency world, women of all shades are desired and cherished, and men of all backgrounds can be lords, dukes, and anything else that the imagination brings to mind. In this first volume, our tales will take you on a magical journey through Vauxhall Gardens in London on the night of a masquerade.

We hope you will enjoy the historical references, the setting, and of course, the romance.

With love,

Gabrielle, Hildie, Elise, and Jessica

DESIGNING HIS DUCHESS

GABRIELLE CARR

"Never try to emulate them. Their friendship is as false as their words are flattering. They call you the OBA (ordinary ball companion)." Lady Juliana Drake swallowed the cruel truth in the Duke of Hersthire's words. She was the misfit of Society. But not for long. With fierce determination and a plan--of sorts--she intends to shed the horrid moniker, and she'll use the Duke to do it. Surely, the devilish rake had taken off enough fashionable dresses to know how to help her pick one out.
All she has to do is keep from undressing him first...

CHAPTER ONE

LONDON

JUNE 1817

To take Lord Emsbury's money, or not to take Lord Emsbury's money? That was the question Colin Lewis Francis Latham, Duke of Herstshire, contemplated as he glanced through eyes half-cast from too much drink and a fair bit of indifference, at the young earl across the card table.

At some point during the game of faro they'd been playing with the three other gentlemen, whose names now escaped Colin, the conversation had turned to who would win in a bare-knuckle match between Tom Molineaux and Tom Belcher. From there, it had spiraled into boasting of each gentleman's sporting prowess, and finally into Lord Emsbury wagering ten pounds that he could withstand the hardest blow to the face Colin had to offer.

The scrawny man's skeletal face begged to differ.

Pearls of sweat glistened on Lord Emsbury's forehead,

subverting his weak performance of confidence. He discreetly dabbed at the offending moisture with the cuff of his dress coat, no doubt hoping Colin's inebriated brain would keep him from noticing the slight act of apprehension.

Colin did notice.

Which was why he currently deliberated whether or not to hold the young man to his foolhardy wager. Plus, he rather enjoyed his membership to Brook's. He could very well imagine having it revoked after boxing the future Duke of Willfolk. Then again, Colin was no longer a second son. He was the bearer of a title many generations older than Lord Emsbury's and possessed a fortune many times larger. For that reason alone, his membership would remain secure.

That settled it.

Colin emptied the remainder of his fourth—or was it his fifth—glass of brandy in one gulp. If the young man wanted to squander his inheritance on frivolous gambling, who was he to deny him the privilege?

He removed his coat and draped it over the back of his chair. "This won't be pleasant, but you look like a weeper, so I'll give you half strength," he said, his voice slightly slurred. His bleary gaze took in Lord Emsbury once more. "Maybe half of half strength," he amended.

Lord Emsbury stood. A cherry hue crept from beneath his cravat up over his pale face. "You wound me, sir," he said, his head held high. "I have more strength of character than to sob after taking a *measly* punch, even if to the face."

The corner of Colin's mouth curled. He hadn't missed Lord Emsbury's emphasis on the word measly, and for it, his respect for the young earl grew. A man who maintained such a haughty bearing even as he quaked in his boots was either brave or a fool. Although one could argue those were two ways of describing the same character trait.

Colin unbuttoned the cuffs of his shirt and rolled up his sleeves. He inclined his head to Lord Emsbury. "Apologies. Let us prove your rugged constitution so that we can return to our card game."

"Yes, let's."

Lord Emsbury marched around the table and stopped before Colin, arms stiff at his side, back fire-iron straight. He angled his head to the right, presenting the left side of his face for its impending punishment.

Men left their tables, and others poured into the gaming room, gathering around to watch the spectacle. They pushed close until Colin barely had room to cock back his arm.

"I have two that Lord Emsbury goes down," someone in the crowd shouted.

"Three for me," another added.

"Three that he loses consciousness."

A stifled collective laugh rolled through the gathered men. More bets poured in, shouted from every direction. If he weren't so far in his cups, Colin might have felt bad for Lord Emsbury.

Unfortunately, the brandy did what it was supposed to—numb his soul and shut off his humanity.

Colin rolled his shoulders then lifted his fists, ready to get on with it. He squinted, attempting to turn the three blurry Lord Emsburys into a single, more solid one. His target a little more in focus, he drew back his right arm and swung, using what his drunken brain gaged to be much-reduced force—although whether his perception mirrored reality was debatable.

"How odd," Colin mumbled to himself.

Instead of pain emanating from his knuckles, there was a constricting, dull ache in his forearm. Colin looked at the pained area. A brawny hand latched onto his arm in a grip so tight its fine, black hairs stood out against the contrasting milky-white knuckles. Colin followed the line of the arm up to the face of its owner.

His lips spread into a wide, lopsided grin. "Ah, Hamon, my old friend."

Richard Clarke, the Earl of Hamon, was one of Colin's closest friends since their time at Eaton. Hamon returned the greeting with a scowl that made most delicate young ladies quiver, and most men mousy versions of their formerly lion-hearted selves. But Colin had known Hamon since the time his adolescent bladder couldn't hold its contents through the night, thus nullifying his fear of the other man. Even the portion it would be wise for him to maintain during moments such as these.

Colin used his free hand to pat Hamon on the shoulder. "I was in the middle of winning a few pounds. How rude of you to interrupt."

Hamon shook his head at Colin, disappointment hewn into each crease in his brow. He released Colin's arm but kept his hands poised at his side, ready to intervene again if necessary. "More like saving you from your idiocy. Come along. It's time to go."

The gathered men grumbled amongst themselves, not appreciating the thwarting of their entertainment. They dispersed, many complaining about all the ways they could have spent the assured winnings they would have received from Lord Emsbury's defeat.

Lord Emsbury's shoulders slackened, his entire body nearly convulsing as he sighed in relief. He quickly scurried back to his seat, collected his chips, and relocated to another card table.

"Go?" Colin pulled a peevish face, sloppily shaking his head. "Nonsense. I still have several more hours of gambling left before retiring for the evening. It is still evening, is it not?"

Colin stepped around Hamon, heading back to his table. The large quantities of alcohol he'd consumed made his movements slow, giving his friend the advantage. Hamon quickly blocked his escape. He retrieved Colin's discarded coat, hat, and gloves and held them out to him.

"Your grandmother awaits you at Torridune House. After returning from Lady Alborn's ball and finding you not at home, she sent a footman to my townhouse asking me to retrieve you. Needless to say, we both knew there were only two places you would be at this hour."

Colin stepped back, pinching the bridge of his nose to ward off the impending headache that, as of late, always followed the mention of his grandmother. "If Lady Herstshire is at home, I have many, many, many more hours of gambling left. And why do you still not possess the ability to tell her no?" He shot Hamon a bleary-eyed, withering glare. "We've been friends for far too long for you not to have learned how to do so from me. It must be nearly midnight by now. Your excuse was built into the inappropriate hour for calling on a person to ask for favors."

Hamon lifted a nonchalant shoulder. "Because unlike her ungrateful grandson—that would be you—I know the value of a caring maternal figure, seeing as how I grew up without one. Thus I respect her and have no qualms assisting her plots to mold you into something resembling an upstanding gentleman, when and where I can."

Colin made a noise somewhere between a grunt and a snort. Some friend he had. Hamon had abandoned him in favor of becoming his grandmother's champion. The treacherous lout. He should have never invited him home over the school holidays.

"Look at you. Using guilt to try and sway me. You grow more like her by the minute. I forbid you from visiting my grandmother for at least a fortnight. Maybe two."

"And I chose to ignore you. Now let's go." Hamon thrust Colin's garments out with more force, his stony expression leaving no room for further arguments.

Colin snatched the offered items and clumsily put them on. "I am coming with you only because you've ruined my mood. Now I must seek the company of a more agreeable, and preferably more buxom, companion to revive my spirits."

Hamon didn't reply. He stepped to the side and swept an arm out, prompting Colin to precede him. Colin eyed his friend suspiciously as he passed. If his grandmother awaited him, there was no way Hamon would allow him to do anything other than go straight to her. His silence generally preceded a diabolical maneuver that forced Colin to do as he bade.

It was no surprise to Colin that his carriage awaited him right behind Hamon's when they stepped out of Brooks. No doubt, his driver had been given strict instructions to bring Colin straight home. Fortunately, Colin didn't economize when it came to paying his staff, which had the marvelous effect of making them very loyal and swift to carry out his requests. Including swallowing their timidity and ignoring the threats against their lives that Hamon had a habit of issuing to deter disobedience.

Stepping up to the coach, Colin paused in front of the door held open by a footman and looked at Albert, his devoted and trustworthy driver. Albert inclined his head, a conspiratorial glint in his eyes. A devilish grin pulled at the corner of Colin's mouth—he'd meet no opposition to overruling Hamon's instructions. He'd be burying his face in the exquisite Miss Catherine Griffith's Cupid's kettle drums soon enough.

Colin turned to Hamon, working to keep the glee of winning this clash of wills from his expression. "I believe this is where we part ways old friend. Enjoy the remainder of your evening." A hint of gloating entered his voice. "I know I shall."

Hamon crossed his arms over his chest, his expression neutral. "You'll go straight home then?"

"Not a chance," Colin scoffed.

Hamon's lips curled into a humorless smile, his visage

turning fiendish. "I hoped you'd say that. This is for your own good."

Before Colin could work past his inebriated confusion to form a coherent response, Hamon cocked back his fist and punched him in the face. Clearly, he'd learned a thing or two from his lessons at Gentleman Jackson's boxing academy. Colin crumpled to the ground. Hamon's command to Albert to take him home followed him into the darkness.

CHAPTER TWO

C olin slowly emerged from his slumber, immediately wishing to plunge back into the nothingness of sleep. Throbbing spasms rippled from the back of his head, along his scalp, until they exploded behind his eyes. He squeezed them shut. The tight skin around his left eye pulsed with sharp, stabbing pain. He touched the no doubt bruised, swollen area, and hissed.

"Oh, good. You're awake," a familiar imperious feminine voice said.

Colin groaned, fighting off a new pain located auspiciously close to his arse. "Hello, Grandmother. Did you watch me while I slept?"

"More like watched over you to make sure you didn't leave this world while you slept. The way you poison your body with alcohol I wasn't sure how you'd fair. I've been here a short while. If you didn't wake soon, I planned to rouse you. By force if necessary."

"I don't doubt it."

He opened his eyes, rotated his head on the pillow, and took in the petite woman perched in a chair next to his bed. She glowered at him. Her frigid eyes, as clear as a cloudless blue sky, assessed him in the critical way of a disappointed parental figure.

Even at the age of one and sixty, it was clear to see why his grandfather had snatched her off the marriage mart only two weeks into her first season and made her Lady Herstshire. Her delicate, classically beautiful features made her the envy of most women and the desire of most men. Features she'd passed on to Colin's mother, who had passed them on to him. Ones he took advantage of at every opportunity. He had no qualms admitting to anyone who asked that his reputation as one of the biggest rakes in London was well deserved.

Lady Herstshire stood, placed her sewing in her vacated chair, and came to sit on the edge of his bed. She flicked the bridge of his nose, right between the eyes, sending a new explosion of pain shooting through his skull. She positioned her hand to do it again, but Colin quickly blocked his face from her assault.

"Ow! Would you stop that?"

"If you wish to act like a child, I will punish you like one."

"Hamon punished me well enough last night. I can assure you of that."

"That is true enough." She gently ran a finger around the wounded area of his face, her expression softening. "You've been asleep for so long, I almost feared he'd hit you too hard." Then as if it had only been a fleeting figment of his imagination, the tenderness vanished. She straightened and folded her hands primly in her lap, her glower back in place. "Though it is a shame that you needed to be struck in the first place to get you home."

The dip in her inflection and the thin layer of censure underlying her words were so well done that if he were a different man, he'd feel shame—quite possibly even some remorse—for his behavior. As it were, he was not that sort of man, and the monsters haunting his every waking moment made it hard for him to want to be.

"You may no longer speak of Hamon," Colin brooded. "His roles as my best friend and your pseudo-grandson are terminated henceforth. The insidious bas—fiend is no longer welcome in my presence."

Lady Herstshire shook her head, casting her eyes up to the heavens. "Give me strength." She met his gaze again, her eyes a wall of steely determination. "My daughter, your mother, suffered in agony to bring you into this world. For what? So you could squander your life on drinking, chasing skirts, and evading your responsibilities?"

Colin laced his fingers over his stomach, an unbothered smirk forming on his lips, making him look every bit the smug, uncaring cad. "You know, the more you use that particular tactic to invoke guilt in me, the less effective it becomes. Besides, I have it on good account that my coming into the world was a rather smooth affair."

A streak of pink blossomed over Lady Herstshire's cheeks. "Oh, hush now. It's not proper to discuss such things with your grandmother."

"As you wish," he said, raising a shoulder dispassionately. "Although, I can't let this moment pass without reminding you that we wouldn't be discussing it if you'd give up your campaign to sway me with guilt. It will never work."

"Then tell me how I can get through to you." She fumed, an undercurrent of frustration and distress in her voice.

Her hands balled into fists, then relaxed. She released a long, weary exhale, her posture hunching and her forehead wrinkling, making her appear as unsure and out of control as Colin felt.

He wanted to reach out and place a hand over hers in comfort but couldn't bring himself to do it. He hated being the source of so much vexation in her life. Although she was tough on him, he never doubted she did everything out of love. But exercising his self-control, and presenting himself as a moderately decent gentleman, was becoming a more grueling feat of strength each day.

She placed her hand over his, her gaze boring into his, pleading for understanding. "I worry about you as any grandmother would. Within the span of a year, you've come back from war, lost your father and brother, and inherited a title and the burden of responsibilities you were never meant to shoulder. That is a lot for any man to deal with."

"Yes, it is," he whispered.

"And I've barely seen you shed a tear, let alone properly grieve. All you do is drink, gamble, and keep company with women of questionable moral character. I'm afraid that one of these days, your pain will drag you into darkness you can't escape from."

Colin said nothing. He slumped farther into the pillows. Her words struck a secret chord in his heart that he tried his best to avoid. She was right about the darkness, although it had possibly already ensnared him in a mental prison he'd never escape from.

Either way, the truth in her words was something he did not wish to face.

He slipped his hand from beneath hers and donned his best imitation of an unencumbered smile. "I promise I will try and do better."

This act must not have been as effective as he'd hoped. She silently searched his face, probably hoping to find something that would make her believe his vow. After a moment, she nodded, short and without much conviction.

"Yes, well, your first step toward that end can be making sure you are dressed and in attendance at Lady Devonford's ball this evening. You've slept through the night and most of today, so you should be more than recovered from your night of debauchery. If not, I will have Cook whip up one of her concoctions to help you mend faster."

Colin pulled a disgusted face. "I will never be so foxed as to need one of those ever again. Drinking that vile brew once was more than enough, I assure you."

"If that is your choice, so be it. Either way, you are to be there this evening." Her warm palm cupped the side of his face. "It is time to put away your juvenile antics and act like the respected member of society that you're supposed to be. You are no longer a second son. You are the Duke of Herstshire, and with that comes specific obligations."

"You are right. I will be there. I swear it."

"Thank you. Well, I must be going. I'll be visiting with Lady Chamberson if you are in need of me."

"Have a lovely time. And make sure to save some gossip for another day."

She straightened, smoothing her hands over her dress. "A lady never gossips. She merely informs her friends of things they should be aware of. For their protection, of course."

"Ah yes, my apologies. Thank you for doing your part to protect the vulnerable moral fiber of the *ton*." Colin sat up and kissed her on the cheek.

Lady Herstshire demurely tilted her chin down, her honey brown lashes lowering, performing the part of a humble, benevolent member of society better than any stage actress. "I do what I can."

They both laughed. She kissed his cheek, then gracefully rose from the bed, and departed the room.

Left with only his thoughts for company—ones he greatly wished to evade—Colin tossed back his coverings and slung his legs over the side of the bed. The shock of his feet meeting the ice-cold wooden floor sobered him up better than any of Cook's draughts ever could.

Before he'd made it to the looking glass, Mr. Lewis, his valet, entered carrying a pitcher of warm water. Colin inspected his reflection, taking the generous growth of fine hair over his cheeks and jaw, the puffy darkness under his eyelids, and the streaks of red mixing with the blues of his eyes, giving them a violet hue.

His grandmother was right. He couldn't keep carrying on the way he had. The effects of excessive alcohol consumption and continually dwindling hours of sleep were beginning to take their toll.

The time to stop running from his pain had come. Perhaps finding a respectable wife would provide the solution he sought. Stories of former rakes reformed by a good woman's love were a favorite among the scandal sheets. He wouldn't require love in his marriage. His affection would always belong to the woman whose heart he'd broken several years ago. But perhaps the influence of a polite, well-bred young lady would provide the motivation he needed to make his actions match his desire to be a better man.

"Tell me, Lewis, do I look as bad as I think I do?" Colin asked.

"Probably worse, Your Grace," Mr. Lewis replied without missing a beat. He placed the pitcher next to the washbasin, then headed to the armoire to begin setting out Colin's clothing.

Colin's chest rumbled with his laughter. "Good to know."

Mr. Lewis had entered his family's employ while Colin was still in leading strings. The older gentleman never veered from the truth, even to spare Colin's feelings, which was why he held him in the highest esteem and never doubted his loyalty.

"Well," Colin said, turning away from the glass. "I believe you have your work cut out for you today. Lady Herstshire has demanded my attendance at Lady Devonford's ball this evening, and I must look my best. I do believe she plans to introduce me to every eligible young woman of marriageable age, and for the first time, I don't plan to argue with her about it."

Mr. Lewis's eyebrows rose. "Does this mean we shall have a new duchess soon?"

"If all goes well, hopefully, yes."

"Then let us make haste whipping you into shape. You almost look as bad as the day you stumbled home after spending a week with that French actress."

Colin doubled over and laughed outright. "What a week that was," Colin said, his dreamy voice far away. He stared off, lost in his wickedly delectable memories of his provocative week with Brigitte, which might or might not have included another woman. That part—as well as most of what had happened—was hard for him to recall clearly. He cleared his throat, coming back to the present. "If I look as bad as that, then you are in trouble, old man."

"Yes, I know, my lord."

"Well, let us begin. Perhaps with a good shave."

"As you wish, Your Grace."

Colin glanced at his reflection again while he waited for Mr. Lewis to collect his shaving instruments. Tonight he'd begin his search for a wife. That should be easy enough. As long as he continued avoiding *her*. The woman he was never meant to love, but always would. It had come to his attention recently that she'd made her debut this season—the reason as of late he'd preferred to lurk about his club instead of attending social functions.

But what could go wrong if they happened to see each other again? What happened between them was a long time ago. They could be civil now. Couldn't they?

CHAPTER THREE

P eople.

So very many of them.

Too many of them.

Miss Julianna Abigail Drake strangled her fan between her clenched fists until the polished steel guard sticks bit into her palms through her gloves. She should have it held open in her left hand, using a delicate wrist motion to wave it gently, allowing the mother-of-pearl to catch the candlelight and sparkle like jewels.

An open fan in a lady's left hand signified she desired a man to come and converse with her. At least that was so according to the rules of subtle flirting her aunt, Lady Roxburrow, had drilled into her every day since her uncle, Viscount Roxburrow, had declared Julianna must either come out this season or be cut off.

In no uncertain terms, he had made it very clear his charity toward his younger brother's only child had reached its end. Julianna needed to either find a husband or . . . Well, she much preferred not to think of the alternative.

Which was why she now stood at the edge of the dance floor

at Lady Devonford's ball, wishing she were back in her room in front of an easel with paint splattered over her hands and arms up to her elbows. Or that she was anywhere else, for that matter.

But wishing and hoping never changed anything.

She released her grip on her fan and forced her stiff arms to her sides. Currents of nervous energy relentlessly flowed through her limbs, making her want to move, walk, run, or do something—anything—other than stand about waiting for a man to look past the sea of beautiful debutantes and notice her. She smoothed a hand over the skirt of her dress, touched her pinned, thick midnight curls, and then the silk at her throat.

Lady Roxburrow leaned in until her lips nearly touched Julianna's ear and hissed, "Touch your fichu one more time, and I swear I will yank it from around your neck. No man wants a woman who fidgets so much."

"Yes, Aunt," she replied softly, removing her hand from the kerchief wrapped around her shoulders and tucked into the front of her bodice.

Over the years, Juliana had learned it was best to keep her responses short whenever whispering was necessary. Because of her hearing impairment, she struggled to gauge her volume. Especially when she wanted only her conversation partner to hear—and not the over-eager aristocrats who would happily ruin her to elevate themselves.

"I'm horrified that the viscount even allowed you to wear it," Lady Roxburrow continued. "It's covering your entire neck and cleavage. We women are afforded few tools of the physical variety with which to capture a man's attention, and you are hiding your most valuable one."

If she weren't on the edge of crumbling under the stress of being at this ball, Juliana might have laughed at the vehement offense in her aunt's voice. As if Juliana's choice to wear a fichu was an affront to the lady herself.

Why did it matter if she chose to show a little less skin than what was considered fashionable? The more skin she showed, the more self-conscious she became. The more self-conscious she became, the more awkward and clumsy she became.

Juliana resumed her vise-grip on her fan, silently praying for an escape from her aunt's presence. To her great relief, the answer came shortly thereafter in the form of Lady Eleanor Phillips. She'd had the pleasure of meeting the lovely young woman at whichever ball she'd been forced to attend several nights ago.

"Good evening, Miss Drake and Lady Roxburrow," Eleanor said, dipping into an elegant curtsy Juliana could only dream of executing someday. "I hope the two of you are well this evening."

"I am, thank you," Lady Roxburrow replied first.

Juliana shifted her position to read Eleanor's lips better. A trick her father had taught her, in case she ever missed hearing a portion of a conversation. It had saved her many times from embarrassing herself in noisy, crowded places such as this.

"I am very well, Lady Eleanor." Juliana attempted a curtsy with considerably less success. "Thank you for inquiring. I hope you are, as well."

Eleanor placed a feather-light hand to Juliana's forearm and smiled. Perfectly gracious. Perfectly . . . perfect.

"As I told you before, it's Eleanor, please."

"Very well. Eleanor."

"Excellent." She turned her smile on Lady Roxburrow. "With your permission, I would love to take a stroll about the room with Juliana."

"Yes. Goodness, please do," Lady Roxburrow blurted, hardly able to contain her excitement.

Juliana didn't doubt that her aunt probably wished some of Eleanor's charm would rub off on her. Or at the very least, elevate her prestige by association.

"Thank you. We shall be back shortly." Eleanor looped her arm through Juliana's.

"No, no. Take your time."

Eleanor dipped her chin in farewell, then led Juliana away from her aunt. A kindness she would be forever grateful for.

"Thank you. I don't know if our acquaintance has been long enough for me to tell you this, but you rescued me from a rather unpleasant discourse about the many ways I am lacking. All of which my aunt thinks will lead to me falling into spinsterhood."

Juliana bowed her head ever so slightly so she could steal glances at Eleanor's lips. Luckily, their closeness and the way Eleanor annunciated every word helped her hear most of the conversation without needing much assistance.

"Spinsterhood," Eleanor groaned dramatically. "The fate all young women of society dread above all else."

Juliana grinned. "Not I. If I could, I'd love to remain unmarried. I'd travel the world and deepen my studies of art and painting."

"You are a painter? Are you a good one?"

"If it doesn't sound too arrogant, I like to think I am."

Eleanor waved a dismissive hand. "Since arrogance is a trait only men are allowed to partake in, I'd never assign it to another woman, especially a friend, even if it were true. But if you have a talent, there is no shame in saying so."

"Thank you." Juliana's cheeks warmed. Praise, no matter how small, was something she'd never fully known how to accept. "If I could trade my skill for your grace and amiability, I would. As much as I wish it were otherwise, life as a self-sufficient painter is not a possibility. And I possess none of the talents necessary to acquire a husband and run a household— yet it is the only realistic future available to me."

"Practice is the key, my dear. For years, my mother made my governess force me to curtsy in front of a mirror until my knees practically gave out."

"How dreadful." Juliana shuddered, thinking about such a childhood.

"Very." A shadow flickered across Eleanor's face, dampening her cheerful disposition. As quickly as it had come, it was gone. "I am grateful to her, though. I wouldn't be the favorite of the season otherwise."

"Excellent point."

Juliana couldn't argue with her about that. Nearly every man in attendance had clamored to claim a spot on Eleanor's dance card as soon as she arrived. While Juliana's dance card still had many available spots left, Eleanor's had filled within minutes.

Perhaps if her parents had provided a stricter foundation in social decorum, she'd have a better chance at finding a suitable husband. Then again, nothing about her parents, or the way they raised her, had been traditional. Her British father, the second son of the former Viscount Roxburrow, had fallen in love with her mother, a free woman of color on the Island of Jamaica. He'd never once thought twice about marrying her and bringing her home to England. His family's displeasure meant next to nothing compared to his unending love for her mother, who had loved him just as fiercely.

Their love had spilled over onto Juliana, who had adored them just as much. Losing them was the hardest thing she'd ever endured.

Shaking off the memories of the past, Juliana refocused on Eleanor, hoping she hadn't missed something requiring a response. "If you don't mind . . ." the rest of the words dried up on her tongue.

Her head snapped up. She searched the surrounding crowd for the source of the voice she thought she'd never hear again. The one she never had trouble picking out, even in the loudest room.

She stilled when she spotted him.

Colin. Duke of Herstshire.

The man she'd foolishly loved with the fervor of a hopelessly naive girl.

It was him. Standing with a group of his peers, captivating them with every word he spoke, as he'd once done to her.

Her heart rattled in her chest, searching for a dark hole to dive into for protection.

She'd been concentrating so hard on Eleanor's lips and listening to their conversation that she hadn't noticed the direction Eleanor had been leading her.

Straight to him.

He watched them approach in that intense way he had that always made her feel like he wanted to devour her very soul. Like he could see into her heart and pluck out her deepest secrets. While it used to excite her to be known so fully, now it terrified her.

Being known by him had left her vulnerable to him.

Being vulnerable to him had left her crushed by him.

As they came closer, he excused himself from his group and turned, his full attention on them. Or more so, on Juliana.

"Good evening, my lord," Eleanor greeted him, dipping into another impeccable curtsy.

Juliana remained frozen, every muscle in her body drawn taught. Instinct screamed for her to run across the ballroom, out the front door, and not stop until she was safely nestled in her carriage, on her way home.

"Good evening, Lady Eleanor," Colin responded to Eleanor, although his eyes never left Juliana. "Miss Drake."

The deepening of his voice and the way his posture relaxed when he said her name, raised the hairs on the nape of Juliana's neck. It was as if he were remembering the easy, uninhibited relationship they'd once shared. And moreover, enjoying every memory.

Eleanor's questioning gaze flicked between Juliana and Colin. Their familiarity couldn't be missed by anyone paying a modicum of attention. How much of their history should she tell her new friend?

"I hope you are well, Your Grace," Eleanor continued, cutting through the tension surrounding their small circle.

Colin tore his eyes away from Juliana. "I am. Are you?" As soon as the polite platitude fell from his lips, his rapt attention centered on Juliana once again.

While the sting of being ignored had lost its bite for Juliana, it was probably a new, highly unpleasant experience for Eleanor. Juliana wanted to feel bad, but truthfully, she didn't. It was nice being the object of a man's desire of once—even if it was Colin's.

Eleanor's smile tightened. "Yes, I am very well, Your Grace."

"And you, Ju . . ." Colin peered at Eleanor. The corners of his lips turned down. "Miss Drake. Are you well this evening?"

Could it be he wished they had a private moment? She must be going mad because, for a moment, she wanted to be alone with him as well.

What would he say to her?

What *could* he say?

There weren't enough apologies in all of London to rectify the way he'd treated her.

"I . . ." She couldn't do this—pretend as if a painful history didn't exist between them. It did. And so did the tears, broken promises, and shattered dreams. Juliana moved to walk away, but Eleanor's arm tightened around hers, holding her in place.

She studied the other woman, her brow creased in confusion. Eleanor stared straight ahead at Colin as if purposely avoiding eye contact with her. What was she up to?

"If I may be so bold as to speak on her behalf." Eleanor beamed, her visage overly sweet. She patted Juliana's arm a little too forcefully to be friendly. "Miss Drake was informing me of how grateful she was that I rescued her from the stern attention of her aunt. Lady Roxburrow doesn't understand Juliana's

23

shyness and how it contributes to her desire to remain on the outskirts of fashion. Some women aren't as confident in their appearance as others, and that is perfectly acceptable. Plenty of gentlemen love a more homely woman. Wouldn't you agree, my lord?" She finally looked at Juliana. "Did I speak up enough for you, my dear? I've been informed you have a slight problem with your hearing."

Eleanor's voice was so loud that not only did Juliana hear her clearly, so did everyone around them. Juliana snatched her arm back, breaking Eleanor's hold. The betraying remarks bludgeoned the little confidence she'd managed to muster at the start of the evening. So much for her hopes of having a friend with which to brave the perils of the season.

Tears stung the back of her eyes, but she kept them at bay.

"Though the duplicity of your words is not lost on me, I shall address you as if it was," Colin growled, low and dangerous. "You are correct. I do think Miss Drake is a stinkingly beautiful woman, and I'm sure plenty of other men do as well. Now, if you will remove yourself from my presence, I would be much obliged."

Eleanor's mouth flopped open, then closed. If being ignored was a new concept for her, being put so thoroughly in her place was not something she'd thought within the realm of possibility. She thrust her chin in the air, spun on her heels, and stormed off without another word.

The urge to bolt and never show her face in public rode Juliana so hard she couldn't enjoy Colin's expertly executed rebuff. She moved to flee in the opposite direction from Eleanor, but Colin's warm hand clasped onto her wrist, halting her retreat.

"Are you well?" he asked quietly, making sure to move his lips slowly for her to read them. Not that she needed him to. Juliana had long ago memorized every movement and shape his lips could form.

She didn't reply. Couldn't reply to him. He was her enemy. The man who had encouraged her affections, then trampled them beneath the hooves of his horse the day he'd ridden away from her. Se loathed him for having the audacity to show concern for her now. And why she was ashamed of herself for wanting leap into his arms and take the solace she hoped still awaited her in them.

Misunderstanding her silence, Colin released her, then held his hands up in front of his stomach and discreetly made the sign they'd made up a long time ago, to ask how she was feeling.

"Don't do that," Juliana hissed. "I heard your question. Release me at once. People are beginning to stare."

Damn him.

Using their secret language. He had no right!

Colin obeyed her command and dropped his hands to his side. His voice gentled. "Pay no attention to what Lady Eleanor said. And never think you have to emulate her and her ilk. Their friendship is as false as their words are flattering."

Juliana hugged her middle in a feeble attempt to protect herself from the emotional bruising she didn't have the strength to take. A new wave of anger flared within her. At Eleanor, at society, at him, and at herself for longing to have his touch soothing her once again.

"You would know a lot about the falseness that can be found in flattering words."

"Do not let our past keep you from heeding my warning. She is not to be trusted. I heard her gossiping with her friends about you the other night at the theater."

"Why would I be important enough to be a topic of conversation for Lady Eleanor and her friends? What did she say?"

Colin uncomfortably shifted his stance and slid a hand beneath the lapel of his coat. "She called you an OBA. It means 'ordinary ball companion.' Someone she can keep nearby at social functions to make herself look better in comparison. She said you were her 'infallible plan to gain a husband.'"

Juliana inhaled a sharp breath. The depths of human cruelty would never cease to shock and appall her.

"Thank you for your honesty, Your Grace." She hated the tremble in her voice as she spoke.

"Juliana—" He reached for her again. His hand stopped, suspended in the space between them when her wintry glare sliced through him.

"Don't waste your concern on me. If you truly are capable of feeling such emotion on my behalf. Our last encounter left me very doubtful of that."

"I'm very sorry," he said so low that Juliana didn't hear it, only saw the shape of his lips issuing the apology.

His pained expression almost made her want to accept it.

"Don't be, my lord. You have taught me to be much more judicious when assessing the character of those with whom I chose to associate. You know, with your reckless disregard for the feelings of others, you and Lady Eleanor are made for one another. If you will excuse me, I must be going."

Juliana hurried off, giving him no chance to respond, or see her tears fall.

COLIN'S HEART shattered a little more with each step Juliana took away from him. He'd hurt her yet again. As if the first time didn't haunt him enough.

How could he make this right? Should he even try?

He was supposed to be finding a wife, not hammering more nails into the coffin of a dead love.

He needed to leave.

He needed a drink.

CHAPTER FOUR

J uliana sat on the sofa in the drawing-room, poking her fingers again and again as she attempted to practice the needlework that Lady Roxburrow insisted upon filling the time with while they waited on callers. Not that any gentleman paid her a visit. She was damaged, and everyone knew it. A fact Lady Eleanor made very evident last night.

Lady Roxburrow paced in front of the unlit fireplace, tightly wring a kerchief through her clenched fingers. She finally stopped walking and sagged dramatically onto the chair opposite of Juliana.

She tossed her head back over her seat's edge and pounded on the chair's arm. "What are we going to do?" she moaned, shaking her head from side to side. "We're more than halfway through the season, and you're no closer to finding a match than you were at the start."

"You could ship me off to France and settle me in a small cottage in a remote village," Juliana said, keeping her voice neutral as if she hadn't spent countless hours plotting her escape from London. "I won't need much to live off of, and soon after I'm gone, people will forget I ever existed. The shame of me will be lifted from your family name."

"Do not jest, girl. This is serious."

Juliana placed her needlework aside, relieved to have an excuse to be rid of it. "I know, and I'm not."

She truly wasn't. After last night's debacle with Colin and Lady Eleanor, Juliana had absolutely no intention of ever showing her face in society again. Spinsterhood was no longer a possibility; it was an inevitability. Come what may, she would never put herself in a position to be so thoroughly humiliated ever again.

"I think it's a perfect solution. We both know I will not secure a husband. I truly won't need much to live on, and eventually, I might be able to earn enough with my paintings to no longer require anything from you. I just need a chance."

Lady Roxburrow leaned forward, her rigid finger jabbing the air between them. "Now, you listen here. Lord Rox—"

A quick rap on the door halted the rest of what promised to be another of Lady Roxburrow's long-winded speeches about a woman's duty to find a husband, give him an heir, and run his household.

The butler stepped into the room and announced, "Pardon me, my lady. There is a caller here for Miss Drake."

Juliana and Lady Roxburrow exchanged stunned glances.

Recovering first, Lady Roxburrow asked, "Who is it?"

"The Duke of Herstshire."

Juliana choked on air. Apparently, her hearing had gone from poor to unreliable because there was no way Colin was currently at her townhouse, requesting to see her.

Lady Roxburrow hopped out of her chair with a lithe swiftness Juliana hadn't known her usually sluggish form possessed. She hurried over and stood behind Juliana. In what Juliana assumed as meant to create a picture of a loving guardian encouraging her ward, Lady Roxburrow placed a hand on her shoulder.

"Hurry off then," she said, shooing the butler out of the room. "Send him in."

"Wait! No!" Juliana objected a little too late. The butler had already quit the room.

"Hush up, girl," Lady Roxburrow hissed. Her grip tightened on Juliana's shoulder. "You better be on your best behavior."

Juliana's stomach clenched, then collapsed in on itself when Colin walked through the door. The walls closed in on her, gradually squeezing the air out of the room.

He strolled in, his long strides erasing the distance between them a little too quickly. In the light of day, he looked as handsome and sinful as Lucifer himself. The sapphire-blue of his dress coat made his eyes glimmer like twin jewels. His—

Wait.

Juliana brushed the fog of infatuation aside and looked at him with sober eyes. His now wrinkled dress coat was the same he'd worn last night. Dark smudges underlined his eyes, which had a suspiciously glassy quality to them. His hat sat crooked atop his ruffled chestnut hair. And a light shadow covered his chin and jaw.

He hadn't been home.

"Good afternoon, ladies," he said, his voice slightly slurred.

He's foxed!

"Good afternoon, Your Grace," Lady Roxburrow crooned, ignoring his disheveled condition. "We are so happy you came to visit. To what do we owe this great honor?"

"I came to speak with Ju . . ." He cleared his throat in a blundering attempt to cover his slip. "Miss Drake. I came to speak to Miss Drake. If you would allow me the privilege."

"Certainly!" Lady Roxburrow crooned. "I was just telling Juliana what a lovely day it is. Perhaps the two of you would like to take a walk?"

"That sounds like a splendid idea." Colin turned to Juliana and bent at the waist, keeping his eyes cast down. "Miss Drake, would you do me the pleasure?"

No.

No.

Never again would she give him another second of her time.

"Of course she will," Lady Roxburrow answered before Juliana could declare her true feelings. "Up, up, up."

Juliana ignored Lady Roxburrow's prompting, staying stationary a moment longer, frowning at Colin. A sharp pinch on the back of her arm from Lady Roxburrow coerced her into motion as the overtone of the room reached peak discomfort.

"It is a lovely day. A brisk walk does sound divine," Juliana preened, her tone teetering on the edge of mockery.

She dipped into a curtsy, which ironically was one of the best she'd ever executed, then lead the way to the front door. Colin and Lady Roxburrow followed silently behind, the latter casting apologetic smiles at the former.

Juliana noticed while she retrieved her gloves and shawl that Lady Roxburrow didn't do the same. "Would you like—"

"I hope you don't find this too inappropriate, my lord," Lady Roxburrow rushed out, cutting Juliana off. She pressed the tips of her fingers to her forehead. "But I've been feeling under the weather. Would you be willing to go without me? I trust you are a man of honor, and the two of you will be in public so no one can claim anything untoward occurred."

"I find that perfectly acceptable."

"Excellent."

Juliana thrust her hand into her glove with unnecessary force, her lips pressed into a thin line. Lady Roxburrow's ruse was so wispy thin she might as well have saved herself the trouble of thinking it up. She could have spared them all the triviality and told him, "take my niece, and do what you will with her."

Despite her blatant objection to being forced to promenade in public with him, both Colin and Lady Roxburrow ignored her silent protests and carried on as if nothing were amiss.

"After you, Miss Drake," Colin said, stepping aside to allow Juliana to precede him out the door.

"Such a gentleman," she sneered.

"The two of you enjoy yourselves," Lady Roxburrow said, waving after them.

Juliana marched out down the steps and took a sharp right onto the road, not stopping to wait for Colin. She kept up a brisk clip in hope that the pace and his drunkenness would lead to him giving up and allowing her to go home.

He jogged up to her, quickly closing the distance between them. Once beside her, he kept pace with her easily.

Damn his long legs and natural athleticism.

Juliana slowed her steps. There was no point tiring herself out when her attempt to spite him had failed.

"Why are you here?"

Colin stopped and stepped to the edge of the walkway. He took hold of Juliana's hand and made her pause as well. A jolt of miserable joy exploded in her heart. She stared at their entwined hands, mesmerized and in agony over how wonderful this small gesture still felt, and the revelation of how much she missed it.

Colin followed the direction of her gaze and quickly snatched back his hand. "Apologies." He stepped directly in front of her, as he'd done many times in the past to make sure she could fully see his lips. "I know without your aunt's prompting, you wouldn't be speaking with me now, so I will keep this brief. After I present my proposition to you, I will escort you home if you still wish to be rid of me."

Juliana folded her hands behind her back. "Very well. What is your proposition?"

31

"First, I'd like to apologize for last night. Although well-intentioned, I made a bad situation worse. I'm sorry."

"I accept your apology because propriety dictates I must," she said coolly. "Please continue with your proposition."

"I would like to help you find a husband."

"You'd like to what?"

In what world did he think that would be a good idea? The man who broke her heart, proposing to help her marry another.

His brow furrowed in concern. "I'm sorry, did I not speak clearly enough? I confess to recently consuming a generous amount of alcohol, which might be causing my speech to slur."

"No, my ears picked up the words emitting from your mouth, but they were so absurd my brain can't comprehend them."

"What is so absurd about it?"

Where should she begin? The list was so vast she couldn't decide. Of the many reasons, though, the most important was that she still loved him. The thought of him trying to pawn her off on another man broke her heart anew and made her feel more foolish. Her flame still burned for him, while his love had extinguished a long time ago.

But why? Why did he want to embark on this foolhardy mission? The question clung to the roof of her mouth, refusing to leap forth into existence because she didn't know if she were strong enough to hear the answer.

"How will you help me find a husband? And more importantly . . . Wh—Why do you wish to do so?"

Colin bowed his head like a petulant boy giving an account of his misdeeds in front of an incensed governess. "Because I owe you that and so much more. I can never fully make up for treating you so horribly in the past. But I can help you secure a pleasant future."

Juliana jerked as if she'd taken a right hook to the heart.

Repentance—not love. He wanted a clear conscience, no doubt, so he could move on and marry some flawless young lady without contrition of how he'd left things with Juliana.

She crossed her arms over her chest, a volcano of resentment bubbling up inside her. She might as well hear the rest of his outlandish plan. To learn what he thought wrong with her and how he planned to fix her so she could make a match.

"And how do you propose to help me procure a husband?"

"I will teach you how to be more desirable."

Juliana's mouth fell open. Her head snapped back, then tilted to the side as she regarded him with revulsion. "I do believe I am more offended now than I was last night."

Colin held up his hands in surrender. "Apologies. My mind is not performing at an optimal pace right now."

"Evidently."

"What I meant is that I will teach you what will attract a man's attention. Any man. You will have your pick of proposals."

It was possible that her pride might not survive much more of this conversation. He had admitted she was undesirable and wanted to help her become so to attract someone else's attention. The insult was almost too much to bear.

"I will never have my pick of proposals. I know next to nothing about running a house, nor do I want to. My skin is several shades too dark for most men's tastes. And my hearing is subpar at best. No respectable gentleman of any note will want me when he can have a perfect, unblemished English rose."

Colin had the nerve to become indigent. His cobalt-blue eyes sparkled with disappointment and ire as he said, "Don't speak so poorly of yourself in my presence ever again."

Juliana sneered in derision. "You're the one who thinks I need to be fixed to secure a marriage contract."

"That's not—"

"I like myself as I am. Truly I do. But I prefer to remain realistic above all else. And you know, did it ever occur to you to ask what I want before concocting this ludicrous scheme? Whether or not I wished to marry? What if I wanted to travel the world and become a painter?"

He removed his hat and raked a frustrated hand through his rumpled hair. "You're being unreasonable. I thought you said you are realistic above all else," he mocked. "With what money will you do this traveling?"

"I don't know. Maybe I'll become a working woman," she tossed out haughtily. Her lips thinned into a scornful smirk. "Or a harlot. Use men like you who can't resist an upturned skirt to pay my way across the continent."

Colin's eyes narrowed into hard slits. "The devil, you will! I'd kill every man who dared to touch you."

Juliana scoffed at his show of possessiveness. The man was insufferable. "So you'll help sell me off to one man, but won't allow me to do so to whomever else I choose? How chivalrous of you."

"You are twisting my words. I came here with good intentions."

"Yes, and hell is full of them," she shouted.

"Damn you, woman!"

Several onlookers had slowed their pace or come to a complete stop to watch their spat. Quarreling with the new Duke of Herstshire in such a public scene would create a new hurdle to her matrimonial crusade. Arguing wasn't a very ladylike behavior. Her aunt would have her head for it later, but Juliana cared not.

Juliana's scowl deepened. "There's the callous blaggard I knew was under all those good intentions."

"Why are you being so difficult?"

"Because you don't deserve to feel better about what you did to me," she hissed. An irritating crop of tears formed on her lashes, but she wiped them away angrily. "You asked me to run away with you to Gretna Green, but didn't show up the day we were supposed to leave. I waited all day. I waited hours after the sun had set. In the darkness. Alone. You abandoned me. I will never give you my forgiveness. You can never redeem yourself from that."

Juliana spun around and broke into an unladylike run.

Why here?

Why now?

Of all the times Colin could have shown up over the years, why did it have to be now, when she was trying to navigate her uncertain future. He was ruining everything. Dredging up emotions she didn't have the time or desire to confront.

She'd be damned if she took his help, even if it meant a life of spinsterhood. Anything would be better than groveling to that scoundrel.

JULIANA DRAGGED her weary body up the last few stairs and internally cheered when she saw the door to her bedchamber. The emotional strain of fighting with Colin had stolen all of her physical energy. She felt as if she could crawl beneath her covers and sleep for an eternity.

"You ca—t be se—ous? Bar— Crom—l?"

Lady Roxburrow's disgruntled voice carried from the open door of her sitting room. Juliana couldn't make out exactly what she was saying, and normally she'd never listen in on their conversation, but something propelled her forward. She stopped outside the door and listened closely. Her vantage point gave her a clear view to read their lips, though neither of them could see her.

"He's nearly three times her age. She'd be miserable."

"She'd be fed and provided for. That's all that matters," Lord Roxburrow countered sternly.

"But—"

"No arguments. I've given you time to do it your way. I let her have a season, bought her a new wardrobe to prance around in as if it would make any difference. The girl is deaf and from distasteful origins. No one wants her."

"She's not deaf. And your brother married her mother. She is a legitimate subject of the Crown. There is nothing distasteful about that."

"You know what I mean."

"Surely, there must be another option. Perhaps I can speak to—"

"You can waste your breath speaking to whomever you choose, but it will not change my decision. At the end of the season, if she is still unwed, as I know she will be, she will marry Baron Cromwell, and we will be done with her."

"Very well," Lady Roxburrow conceded.

Baron Cromwell? Lord Roxburrow intended to marry her off to that miserable old man?

She doubled over, placing one hand on her knee, the other clutching her stomach. Her entire body began to tremble. Bile rose in her throat, forcing her to work to swallow it down continuously.

Rumors abounded about the way Baron Cromwell had mistreated his first wife when she'd failed to produce an heir. Some even suspected foul play in her demise.

Juliana would rather die than marry that villain.

Or—She could humble herself before Colin and accept his offer.

She needed to lie down. Juliana crept away and hurried to her room, but not quickly enough.

"Juliana," Lady Roxburrow gasped, catching her as she opened her door.

Their eyes met over the distance, one set filled with guilty remorse, the other with anguish. Both of them understood the helplessness of the other. Juliana stepped into her room and quietly closed the door, severing the tether of understanding all women of marriageable age understood: your life was not your own.

CHAPTER FIVE

The mid-afternoon sun shone brightly in the clear sky above, casting its warmth to the assembly of people below. Ladies promenaded around the Earl of Missenden's beautifully curated garden, occasionally stopping to say hello to an acquaintance or commenting on a particular bloom's vibrant color. Their parasols served to be more of a fashion accessory than a necessity since although it was sunny, the temperature remained rather pleasant.

It was as close to a perfect day as anyone could ask for.

Yet Colin stood among a group of very eligible, very eager young ladies and their chaperones, absolutely miserable.

They fluttered their lashes at him over their gracefully flapping fans and tittered at just the right volume whenever he could muster the wherewithal to utter something witty. Their mothers listed off their accomplishments, some of which were rather extensive. If he wished, he could propose to any number of them and be talking over the details of a marriage contract within the hour.

So why couldn't he pick the low hanging fruit and execute his mission to find a suitable wife?

A pair of luminous brown eyes, as sweet as chocolate candies, floated in from his memories. They used to stare at him as if he were Helios. Powerful enough to make the sunrise and set. The picture slowly expanded, bringing into focus Juliana's brilliant smile, which he used to be able to conjure with a few offhanded words.

How things had changed.

Now everything he said was wrong. All of his actions were scrutinized for sinister intentions. It was all his fault, and he hated himself for that.

Imbecile.

Inconsiderate.

Inappropriate.

In the light of the new, sober day, Colin regretted everything about his rather ill-advised offer to Juliana. She was right. He hadn't thought twice about what she wanted. He'd charged in like a bumbling knight in dented armor, attempting to save a damsel he hadn't ascertained *wanted* to be saved.

The paradox of it all was that he did not wish to see her wed to someone else. The thought of another man enjoying Juliana's affections brought forth unbridled jealous wrath that bordered on lunacy. He could almost visualize his fist repeatedly striking the face of her undetermined husband.

He'd wanted to do something for her. To give her something she needed or help her reach a goal she longed for. It was a pity he'd forgotten that the best place to begin when attempting to help someone achieve an aspiration was first to inquire what their desires were.

Next time he'd . . . No, there wouldn't be a next time. He had so thoroughly botched things with Juliana he'd be surprised if she ever allowed him within a yard of her ever again. "What do you think, Your Grace?" Miss Manning asked, from beside him.

"What? I—" Colin scoured his memory for the last several seconds of Miss Manning's inane chatter, attempting to figure out the question he was supposed to provide the answer to. His search came up empty. He hadn't paid attention to anything the petite slip of a girl had said for the past several minutes. There'd been something about gardens, or curtains—perhaps card games, or something equally as uninteresting.

"I beg your pardon, but I admit I missed your question. Would you be so kind as to repeat it?"

"Of course, Your Grace." A pink flush bloomed on her cheeks, now aware he hadn't been listening. "I merely asked if you'd be attending the masquerade at Vauxhall Gardens at the end of the week."

"Ah, yes. Unfortunately, I will not be in attendance at that particular gathering."

"Pity. I was rather hoping we might run into each other there."

Colin noted the intense, meaningful glint in her eyes as she spoke. She held his gaze for a moment longer than was proper, then coyly dropped her lashes until they brushed her cheeks. Colin had partaken in more than enough liaisons to understand the subtle message in her words and actions.

Many a lover had enjoyed a late-night romp in the vast gardens at Vauxhall. Even if he were interested in such a tryst, he had a strict rule about not compromising marriage-seeking young ladies. The consequences could quite literally be death or life as a fugitive. No matter how magnificent the experience, giving a girl a green gown was never worth meeting an aggrieved father or brother at dawn.

This was his cue to leave.

"Indeed." Colin glanced over her shoulder and pretended to notice something in the distance. "If you all will excuse me, I see an old friend I'd like to catch up with."

He inclined to each lady in turn, then hustled off with no particular direction in mind.

THAT DAY, Juliana spotted Colin sitting in a chair on the Earl of Missenden's lawn, in front of the string quartet performing one of Ignaz Pleyel's compositions. The musician was so well known that even without a single musical bone in her body, she could distinguish his style when she heard it.

He sat with his ankle propped on his knee, his fingers tapping the rhythm of the song on his boot. Where she lacked musical talent, Colin mastered any instrument he decided the learn. He could make the strings of a violin weep in devastatingly beautiful agony or sing a melody fit for the angels.

She missed hearing him play. The day he'd proposed, he'd arrived at her family home in Kent and set up a picnic in the yard in front of the drawing-room window so her mother could keep watch. While she enjoyed the cheese, strawberries, and other refreshments, he had pulled out a violin and played a heart-melting tune that he'd written for her. If she hadn't already been madly in love with him, she definitely would have fallen victim to the emotion after that.

A wave of overwhelming sadness and loss crept from the corner of her heart, threatening to submerge her into despair. Before the dark emotions could take hold, she put one foot in front of the other, marching forward with her plan.

She lowered herself onto the empty chair next to Colin, who immediately turned his head in her direction. He gawked at her, dazed and confused as if he saw a phantasm come to life from the pages of a Gothic novel.

Juliana took a deep breath to steel her resolve. She leaned in, closer than what was considered appropriate but necessary to make sure she could engage him in a whispered conversation. "I accept your offer."

Colin's brows knit together, his head angling slightly to the side. "Pardon?"

Her jaw clenched. Did she truly have to remind him of the conversation they had a day ago? She glanced over her shoulder at Lady Roxburrow, a stone's throw away, chatting with several other chaperones keeping a watchful eye on their charges. A reminder of why she had to secure Colin's aid, no matter the blow to her dignity.

She faced forward, focusing on the musicians. "Your offer to help me find a husband. I accept."

Colin turned his head and looked at the side of her face. He watched her silently. His usual indicator that he wanted her full attention to make sure she heard him. She reluctantly rotated in her seat just enough to see his lips.

"May I ask what has caused your sudden change of heart?"

"I've learned that my circumstances are much direr than I first thought." She twiddled her gloved thumbs, needing a release for her anxious energy. "It is imperative I find a husband by the end of the season, else I may suffer a fate worse than any imaginable."

"I see." He looked as if he wanted to say more but didn't.

"Let's not dwell on it. How should we proceed? What great tricks do you plan to teach me that will elevate my value on the marriage mart?"

He stroked his knuckles under his chin, his expression thoughtful. After several seconds, a roguish grin spread across his full lips. Juliana's pulse quickened. She could never resist his mischievous smiles and the adventure they promised. Perhaps this wasn't the best idea. He'd broken her once—she couldn't set herself up to be broken again.

Colin sprang to his feet and offered his bent elbow. Juliana hesitated, then looked at Lady Roxburrow once more. She stood and tucked her hand into the crook of his arm. She had no choice.

Marriage to Baron Cromwell frightened her far more than her feelings for Colin.

"Before we begin your lessons," he said as he led them away. "I'd like to apologize for calling on you in such a slovenly condition. I've been asking for your forgiveness more than ever before. For some reason, I can't seem to conjure the right words anymore when I'm with you."

"I'll accept your apology if you tell me why you drink so heavily. You also appeared to be rather far in your cups at Lady Devonford's ball. I have a feeling that is a common condition for you now."

"It is. More than I prefer."

"Why?"

"Because it silences the nightmares and dulls my grief."

"From your brother and your father's deaths?"

"Among other things, yes."

"I'm sorry I never got to send my condolences."

"As I am sorry that I did not send you mine when your parents passed."

"Thank you. I miss them every day."

"I can empathize. I miss them my father and brother, but Robert, most of all. He should be the Duke of Herstshire, not me. Sometimes I feel guilty enjoying the privileges that were meant for him."

"There is nothing to feel guilty about. You didn't wish for your brother's death or covet his title while he lived. It happened, and there is nothing you could have done to stop it. The best thing you can do now is to create a legacy for your family, and the title, which he and your father would be proud of."

"Thank you. Your words are the first I've heard in a long time to give me comfort."

"They are but the truth."

"Which makes them all the more special." He cleared his throat. "Let us begin your instruction. Lesson one. You must show that you know how to have fun."

"That makes no sense."

"It makes perfect sense. No man really wants a dull, boring wife that it is a chore to come home to. You must show these gentlemen that you know how to enjoy yourself and will bring happiness into their lives."

"How do you propose I do that?"

"By playing a game. In our case, that game." He pointed into the distance, where a row of targets on the edge of the open lawn had been assembled in front of the tree line. A bow and quiver of arrows were set up several yards away, in front of each target.

"Archery? I'm not very good at it."

"Lesson two. Confidence. Always have faith in yourself. Most men don't expect their wives to be perfect, as we hope you'd extend that courtesy back to us. However, there is nothing more appealing than a woman who has the confidence to try something new."

"Very well. I can make a valiant effort."

"I know you and I have both changed from the individuals we were when we . . . when were better acquainted, but I know you have a well of courage within you. You once raced me head-long through the forest, dodging branches and jumping your horse over stumps." His smile widened as he recalled the memory.

"Only because you challenged me and I wanted to impress you," she replied, recalling that rather invigorating day. "You made me daring."

Her smile dimmed, as did his. It was true. Colin had made her want to experience many new things with him. His departure, followed by the death of her parents, had left her so shattered she'd forgotten that side of herself once existed.

No longer.

She would reclaim her confidence and use it to better her

life. Starting with giving her all to learning and implementing Colin's instructions.

They stopped next to an empty set of equipment. She released his arm and withdrew an arrow from the quiver.

"You will have to remind me of the proper technique," she said, adding a boost of enthusiasm to her tone. "I'd hate to misfire and launch one of these at your rather large feet."

Colin followed her lead to leave the gloominess of the past behind; his expression once again brightening. "As would I. I'd have to take spinning a young lady around the dance floor until she forgets how rakish I am out of my collection of seduction techniques."

Ow.

Juliana resisted the urge to flinch. She had no interest in hearing about the tricks he used to lure other women into his bed. A slight flush crept up over Colin's face, the realization of his blunder dawning.

This was going to be harder than either of them had thought.

He cleared his throat. "What I meant was—"

"So I place the arrow here, then pull back the bowstring and aim. Is that correct? Or am I missing something?"

"You are missing many things. Hold the bow in your left hand and the bowstring in your right. Nock the arrow here, then lift and aim."

She did as he instructed.

"Good." He stepped up behind her, lifted her right elbow, and then moved her left arm down a fraction.

Juliana gasped when his hands moved down and encircled her waist. He twisted her hips, then tapped her thigh.

"Widen your stance a little."

She swung her head in every direction, checking if anyone watched them. Thankfully, the number of people on the archery range had dwindled, and those that remained paid them no attention.

"Watch where you place your hands," she attempted to whisper.

Colin's head snapped up. "What was that?"

Juliana stared into his eyes, then dropped her gaze to his lips, now mere inches away from hers. Colin's eyes darkened, sensual awareness causing the affable instructor to give way to the carnal man who'd once made her think he wanted her more than anything else in the world. The air around them shifted, charged with memories of youthful stolen kisses and the new, matured curiosity of what could be.

"Ahem." Lady Roxburrow strolled toward them, a raised eyebrow and knowing grin trained on the pair.

Colin jumped back as if Juliana had suddenly turned grown snakes from her head that could turn him to stone.

"Good to see you again, Your Grace," Lady Roxburrow cheerily greeted him.

"Lady Roxburrow." He folded his hands behind his back and bowed. "A pleasure. I hope you are well this afternoon."

"I am. Thank you for asking." Her gaze volleyed between Juliana and Colin. " It was kind of you to instruct my niece so *thoroughly* in the art of archery. However, I fear we must make our rounds before leaving."

"Juliana is a dear and old friend. I am always delighted to assist her when, and how, I can."

"So it would seem. Will we be seeing you at the Fansworth's ball tomorrow evening?"

"I will be in attendance, so yes, I hope we do run into each other."

Her eyes lit up. "Very good. You have a lovely day."

"You as well, Lady Roxburrow." He turned to Juliana and bowed. "Juliana."

"Goodbye."

Once she'd turned her back on him, Juliana lightly touched her fingers to her lips. Would Colin have kissed her if Lady Roxburrow hadn't interrupted? How did she stop herself from wishing he had?

CHAPTER SIX

Colin spotted Juliana as soon as she entered Lord Fansworth's ballroom. He watched her follow Lady Roxburrow to the edge of the dance floor, in a prime position to allow any passing gentleman to see Juliana if he wished to ask her to dance.

Her golden yellow gown accentuated her smooth, copper complexion, giving it an ethereal glow in the dim candlelight. His amusement soared at seeing the fichu wrapped securely around her shoulders and tucked into the bodice of her dress. He might have to repeat his lesson on confidence tonight.

Like the true artist she was, her focus immediately strayed to the elaborate floral chalk design drawn onto the wooden floor. He could almost feel the restraint she called upon to keep herself from bending over to get a closer look. He made his way around the room, wanting to be closer to her.

To his absolute relief and delight, Juliana smiled at him as he approached. He hadn't been sure what her reaction to him would be after the moment they had shared yesterday.

All he'd been able to think about since was how close he'd come once more to the bliss of her soft lips on his. That unsure hopefulness reflected in her big brown eyes, hinting that despite what happened, a part of her might still want him as much as he still wanted her.

He hadn't allowed himself the indulgence of expecting that she could forgive him. But now, the door of possibility had been cracked, and he wanted to ease it open further to see where it could lead.

"Lady Roxburrow." He bowed, then lifted her hand to his lips. "You look mesmerizing this evening." He employed every ounce of charm he possessed in his greeting. If there were a chance of something more developing between him and Juliana, he'd make sure to do things properly this time. Starting with gaining the approval of her guardian.

"Thank you. You're too kind."

"With your permission, may I accompany Juliana during this next dance?"

"You most certainly may," she beamed. "She'd be delighted to dance with you, my lord. Wouldn't you, Juliana?"

"I would."

"Thank you."

Lady Roxburrow placed a hand on the small of Juliana's back and all but shoved her into Colin's arms. He took Juliana's left hand in his right and ushered her away. They assumed their place among the other couples, and then he drew her close for the next waltz. Although considered scandalous when it first reached Britain's shores, Colin adored the dance. Its main draw being, of course, that he could hold Juliana against him and speak softly in her ear.

"Are you ready for lesson three?" he asked.

"Yes, oh, wise tutor. I am ready for whatever you have to teach me."

They both laughed. A joke. Good. She was becoming comfortable with him again.

"Lesson three," he said, his voice imperious like a high-handed schoolmaster. "Men want what they cannot have, which is why mothers keep their daughter so heavily guarded. The temptation of the forbidden is hard for any man to ignore. This dance will increase your allure tenfold."

"What does the jealousy of men have to do with our dancing?"

"It is an offshoot of the principle 'men want what another has.' Dancing with me makes other men curious to know what about you has captivated me. Look around. People are already beginning to watch us, wondering what it is I am whispering to you."

Juliana glanced about, taking in the men and women huddled about the room, their attention riveted on them. Several groups of young men had gathered at the edge of the dance floor, nodding and whispering to each other while their eyes tracked Juliana's movements.

"It seems your assertion has merit."

"It helps that I have a reputation as a bit of a scandal's rogue. They are all saying to themselves, *'good heavens. Herstshire is shown an inordinate amount of interest in Miss Drake. He hasn't been able to keep his eyes off her since she arrived. She must have the power of the heavens hidden beneath her skirts to get that scoundrel to behave.'"*

Juliana laughed so hard she choked, followed by a short coughing fit.

"Now they are wondering if they too should employ such an unladylike laugh to garner my favor."

"It's your fault for making me laugh so hard. And they are saying no such thing."

"Mark my words. They are."

They shared another laugh, an experience Colin hadn't realized he missed so much. Seeing her smile and laugh so freely made him want to do all in his power to make sure her joy never faded.

He loved her. Always had and always would. If he could figure a way out of this ruse of wanting to help her find another to marry, he would. But just because she laughed with him didn't mean she would forgive him.

He held back a flinch when she stepped on his toes yet again. "You are rather graceful, you know."

"No, I'm not. I've stepped on your toes at least twice already."

"Very true. However, my words were an example of lesson four. Flattery."

"You mean, lying to a person to make them feel better about their inadequacies?"

"No. I mean, occasionally slipping a compliment into a conversation to make your partner feel more at ease. Despite putting on chauvinistic airs, most men have had the same meager sense of self-worth since they were wobbly kneed whelps cowering behind their mother's skirts."

"Does your proclamation of the male population include yourself?"

He gave her a lopsided grin. "Most assuredly. One snub from you and my world will fall to pieces. I'm one disparaging comment away from crawling into a corner and sucking my thumb."

Juliana laughed again, loud and unrestrained. More. He needed more of that effervescent sound.

"You give my thoughts of you too much importance," she said between her tittering.

He placed their joined hands over his heart. "Never."

"More flattery?"

"No. The truth." He sobered. "What you think of me truly matters more than anyone "else's opinion ever could."

"Then, why?" She searched his face for the truth. "Why didn't you show up?"

"Because—"

"Pardon me, Your Grace," Lord Emsbury's scratchy voice called from beside them.

Juliana jumped in Colin's arms. She must have been so engrossed in her conversation with him that she hadn't heard Lord Emsbury approach. Even Colin had not noticed when the music stopped.

He cut his hard scowl to the other man. He should have knocked the young lad unconscious when he had the chance, so he'd be too scared to speak to him, let alone interrupt him.

"Do you mind if I steal Miss Drake away for this next dance?" Lord Emsbury asked, either not understanding or not caring about the dangerous glare Colin directed at him.

The next time they ran into each other at the club, Colin would finish what they started.

He begrudgingly released Juliana and took a wide step back. "It would be rude of me to say so, even if I did."

The idiot had the nerve to laugh. "You have quite a sense of humor, my lord."

"So I'm told." He quickly bowed to Juliana, then stormed away, leaving her to *practice* the lessons he'd imparted on her.

"STARE ANY HARDER, and you just might run the risk of affixing that scowl on your face permanently," Hamon said, sauntering up beside Colin.

He flicked his gaze to his old friend briefly, then resumed brooding in the shadows and watching Juliana dance with another partner.

"Thank you for that rather witty observation, but since we both know I am in a foul mood, maybe we can skip to the part where you tell me what you're doing here?"

"This is the social season of London. Can't I be out enjoying a lovely evening of dancing and good company?"

Colin scoffed. "You don't dance. You think the marriage mart is a blood sport for ambitious mothers and their conniving daughters. And you're generally a recluse, so no, that cannot be your intention. My grandmother sent you to spy on me, didn't she?"

Hamon gave him a hearty pat on the back, an annoying smirk on his irritatingly pleased face. "More or less. I've been tasked with gathering and reporting news on how your search for a wife is going. I thought I'd have to return without any promising updates, but it appears I was wrong. Are you officially pursuing Miss Drake again?"

"No."

Hamon regarded Colin as if he'd been knocked upside the head and lost his good sense. "Why the hell not? You look ready to tear Bixby's arms from their sockets for touching her. As you did when she danced with Emsbury and Shefield. Your feelings for her have not waned."

Colin crossed his arms over his chest. His shoulders hunched, and he turned slightly away from Hamon, grumbling to himself.

"Because I don't believe in pursuing the impossible. Gaining her forgiveness is the closest thing to it. She told me so in no uncertain words."

"That's just her hurt and anger talking. I saw the two of you laughing together on the dance floor. Go and grovel. Plead your case, and I'm sure she will forgive you."

"I have no case to plead. My father asked me to choose between her and my inheritance, and I chose the latter. Little did I know I'd end up with the whole damn coffer anyway, so my choice would be moot."

"You were young and a little obtuse. We've all made mistakes. And you didn't do it completely out of selfishness. Without that money, you wouldn't have been able to take care of her. You did what you thought was best for both of you."

"It doesn't matter why I did it. I let her go, and now I can never have her back."

Hamon placed a comforting hand on his shoulder again. "Never is a fallacy, my friend. Every problem has a solution. The question is, are you smart enough to find it?"

Colin mulled over Hamon's words. The hope they provided was so tangible and so tempting that he could almost reach out and touch it. The weighty chains of insecurity kept him from giving in.

"What if I tell her how I feel, and she spurns my affections and ends our acquaintance for good? I can't lose her twice."

"Then, I will be here to help you continue. Without action, the result is guaranteed. Nothing will change."

He could not deny the truth in what Hamon said. If only it weren't so hard to follow through on it.

"Where are you going?" Colin asked Hamon, who'd begun walking away.

Leave it to his friend to toss out a monumental challenge, then merely stroll away.

"To request a dance with Miss Drake. Just because you refuse to pursue her doesn't mean I have to."

"Make one inappropriate advance toward her, and all the years of our friendship won't be enough to keep me from flogging you to death."

"Noted. Now, if you will excuse me. I have an enchanting young beauty to woo."

Colin didn't move to stop him. Of all the men in attendance, he trusted Hamon the most with Juliana's honor and knew his friend wouldn't attempt to seduce her. His loyalty ran so deep that he might even spend the time dancing with Juliana advocating Colin's shining attributes.

Colin focused on Juliana once again. Would a groveling apology work as Hamon claimed it would?

Watching her smile up at her dance partner, he knew that if he was going to try, it had to be soon. His window of opportunity was steadily beginning to close.

CHAPTER SEVEN

Lady Roxburrow fanned her hand in front of her face, the other perched on her ample him. She heavily breathed as if she'd just participated in a vigorous sporting event instead of hosting two gentlemen in her parlor. "Gracious me. Two callers. I do believe our luck is starting to turn around."

She sunk onto the sofa next to Juliana, plucked the book from her hands and used it as a fan.

Our luck. Juliana grinned at Lady Roxburrow's association of her own success or failure to whether or not she found a husband. After all, it would only be Juliana who had to choose between living on the streets or wedding a brutish ogre.

"Thanks to the duke," Juliana admitted. "As much as I hate to admit it, I owe him a great debt."

"I watched the two of you as you danced last night, as did everyone else in attendance. You were radiant. The way he looked at you was so . . . intense. Is there possibly any interest there?"

"No." She looked down at her hands. "He is only trying to rectify a great wrong he committed against me several years ago. Nothing more."

Lady Roxburrow stopped fanning herself and sat straighter. She gave Juliana her full attention. "Ah, he is the young man you fancied yourself in love with when you were what, seventeen."

"Yes, that is him."

"You two had planned to run off together, did you not?" There was no judgment in her tone. More, an almost motherly curiosity.

"Yes. My mother knew of our intentions, but Father disapproved. He thought the previous duke looked down upon our family and refused to allow me to marry into a family that might treat me poorly. We planned to elope in Gretna Green. I waited for Colin all day, but he never showed up. I didn't get so much as a letter explaining why he didn't come. Last week at Lady Devonford's ball was the first time I've seen or spoken to him in four years."

Lady Roxburrow placed a comforting hand over Juliana's. "Have you asked him?"

"No. Well, yes. I started to ask him last night, but we were interrupted before he could answer."

"Maybe you should try again."

Juliana extracted her hand from beneath her aunt's, withdrawing from the optimism Lady Roxburrow inspired in her. "What would be the point? It won't change what has passed."

"True. Although, it could change your future." Lady Roxburrow lifted Juliana's chin. "Listen, deary. I know I have been pushing you relentlessly this season, but I promise it is because I care about you. There aren't many avenues available to women for us to support ourselves. You are a very talented artist. I wish you could pursue your studies further. That, however, is not the reality of your situation. Even if you don't achieve a love match, I want you to find a husband who will take care of you and treat you well. Marriage can be a long, unpleasant journey with the wrong type of man. Do you understand?"

"Yes, ma'am."

"Good."

"Thank you. For everything." For the first time since she'd come to live with her aunt and uncle two years ago, Juliana reached out and wrapped Lady Roxburrow in a hug.

Shocked, Lady Roxburrow hesitated but then returned the affectionate gesture. They held each other, silently giving and taking much-needed love and support.

"No need to thank me," Lady Roxburrow said, her voice a little watery. She finally pulled away and sniffed several times. "I'm going to lie down for a bit. Why don't you go out into the garden and enjoy the day?"

She gave Juliana's hands a quick, reassuring squeeze, then stood to leave.

"That sounds like a splendid idea. If it is all right with you, I think I'd like to take Charlotte and go to the park."

"Wonderful. Enjoy yourself."

Juliana picked up the book Lady Roxburrow had discarded onto the small table next to the sofa and followed her out of the parlor. After Juliana found Charlotte, her lady's maid, and informed her of their outing, she'd gather up her art supplies so she could draw while sitting under a tree.

Hyde Park was a well of inspiration for creativity. She grew more excited the longer she thought about what inspiration awaited her today.

"I'M ALWAYS amazed by your talent."

"Oh!" Juliana jumped. She caught herself right before accidentally running a long charcoal line through her drawing. "Colin. Make more noise next time."

Despite her chastising, she was happy to see him. She'd never admit it aloud, but she had missed his company more and more when they were apart. He sat down on the blanket next to her and lounged against the trunk of the wide oak tree.

"So, you wish for me to come to visit you again?" he asked, raising an eyebrow.

"You know what I meant."

He leaned closer to get a better look at her paper. She pressed the pad against her chest, blocking his view.

"You know I don't like anyone seeing my pictures until they are finished."

"And you know I think your work is superb, no matter what stage of completion it is in."

She grinned, a more frequent occurrence since he'd returned to her life. "Why are you here? Do you have another lesson for me?"

"No, I don't have a lesson for you, although I have it on good authority they are working. You had two callers today, I believe."

"How do you know that? They just left a little more than an hour ago."

He shrugged and crossed his ankles. "I have my sources."

"Are you spying on me?"

As mad as it sounded, the prospect of Colin keeping tabs on her incited a swarm of flutters in her belly. Men only kept track of the women they cared about.

"How am I to know if my instruction is working if I don't keep abreast of what men are saying about you? Besides, I don't have to try too hard to find out. Men at the club flap their lips more than a gaggle of women."

"Fine. I will accept that as a suitable answer. For now." She placed her sketchbook on the blanket, away from Colin. "Since you're here, I wanted to know if I can expect to see you at Vauxhall on Monday for the masquerade?"

"I'm afraid not. They will be performing a reenactment of the Battle at Waterloo. Seeing it once was more than enough."

"I understand."

Colin sat up, bent a knee, and leaned his elbow against it. "There is a reason I'm here. Something else I wanted to talk to you about."

"You sound so serious. Are you setting me up to be the conclusion of a joke?"

He rubbed the back of his neck. His leg began to bounce—something wasn't right. He was so nervous. Dread began to slither through her chest and up to her ear, whispering all the hurtful things he could say.

"No. Though what I have to say is of a serious nature. And I admit my nerves are starting to get the better of me."

"Is everything all right?"

"Yes, yes. Don't be alarmed. In fact, what I have to say is a good thing. At least I hope it is."

"What is it? Spit it out."

He grabbed both of her hands in his. "I love you, Juliana. I've never stopped loving you. I didn't show up that day because I was young and foolish, and I've spent every day since regretting my decision."

Juliana's mind went blank. He'd never stopped loving her. So he had loved her while he had left her waiting for him to carry her off and start a life together? He'd chosen to abandon her while he loved her. The thought was more painful than if he said he'd fallen out of love with her.

"What was the reason? The real reason you didn't show up that?" she asked, her voice void of emotion.

"My father didn't approve of our match."

"Yes, nor did mine, which is why we were going to elope. What was your reason?"

"Robert told him about our plans. I'd packed my bags that morning and had the carriage readied, I swear." He paused, giving her time to absorb his words.

The whisper of panic became a clanging alarm so loud she

could barely hear herself think. His words had begun to fade into an abyss of internal, crackling noise. She lifted her shaky hands and signed the question she needed to know the answer to.

Why?

Colin replied, using both his hands and voice, "My father was waiting by the door when I was ready to leave. He said he wouldn't stop me, but if I left, he would cut me off and take back my inheritance."

"Money," she choked out. Her chest shook with the force of her sobs. He'd abandoned her for money.

"No! It wasn't about the money. I didn't want my inheritance for myself. I knew that I couldn't take care of you if I didn't have a penny to my name. When we made the plan, I thought once we returned married, my father would have to accept you. I didn't know he would cut off my inheritance, or I would have thought of a different plan."

Juliana shot up off of the blanket, leaving everything behind, and sprinted off. Needing as much space between them as possible.

"Miss Drake," Charlotte called after her.

She didn't stop.

"Juliana! Wait," Colin shouted. He raced after her.

Juliana spun around and pointed her finger at him as if wielding a sharp blade. "Don't."

It was all she could manage, but Colin understood. She took off again, leaving him behind. This time, he didn't follow.

CHAPTER EIGHT

Juliana milled around through the gardens at Vauxhall, unable to enjoy any of the beauty surrounding her. People dressed in elaborate costumes, smiling behind their feathered masks, danced, drank, and ate their fill. She'd watched the acrobatic performance with mild interest, then left Lady Roxburrow under the pretense of needing fresh air.

In truth, she wanted to leave.

She hadn't wanted to come at all. After crying for three days, she looked far from her best. Charlotte did the best she could to cover the puffiness under her eyes, but even her paints and a mask couldn't hide the sadness in them.

Colin hadn't called on her since revealing why he hadn't come for her. She'd searched for a glimpse of him at each social function Lady Roxburrow had forced her to attend since then. There was never any sign of him. He might very well have left London for all she knew.

Left her.

Again.

Tonight her heartbreak felt especially burdensome. Finding a secluded spot among the tall shrubbery, she dropped onto a marble bench to sulk. She snatched off her mask and set it down, closed her eyes, and cradled her face in her hands.

"What have I done?" she asked aloud.

"Juliana?"

Her eyes flew open, but she kept her face hidden in her hands. Too afraid to look and see that the voice was a cruel trick of her imagination. She slowly lifted her head.

Colin.

He was here.

He'd come for her.

Her heart flipped in her chest. It wanted to crawl up her throat, stand on the edge of her tongue and confess its unending devotion to him.

"What are you doing here?" Of all the more eloquent things she could have said, that was the trite question her mouth settled on.

"I love you, Juliana. I had to come. I had to try one last time. I'd never forgive myself if I didn't."

Tears pooled on Juliana's lashes, then spilled silently down her cheeks. It took strength for him to stand before her. She understood how much now. She'd worked up the courage to seek him out countless times. Each ending with her nerve crumbling to ash before she made it out the door.

He walked forward, cautiously at first, then seeing she did not object he quickly closed the distance between them. He knelt in front of her, close but not touching her.

"Juliana, I was foolish. I was a coward. I made a choice that affected the both of us, without consulting you. I couldn't bear to see your face shrouded with disappointment when I told you we couldn't marry, so I abandoned you. A shame I shall have to live with for the rest of my life. You've always made me feel as though I was enough. I didn't want to face the truth that I wasn't. That I couldn't give you everything you deserved." He took both her hands in his and kissed each of her knuckles.

"Please forgive me. Please, I beg you. Let me taste happiness one more time. I swear I will live each day until I die making you feel like it was worth it."

Juliana opened her mouth to speak, but no words came forth. Her throat worked, swallowing down tears of elation. Instead of using words, she threw her arms around his neck and pressed herself against him. She kissed him deep and hard. Channeling all her love and dreams for their future into the action.

Colin wrapped his arms around her and held her tightly to him. They kissed until she couldn't breathe. She pulled back, cupping his face between her hands.

"I love you! Colin, I love you so much. You were right. We wouldn't have been able to survive without your inheritance. I wish you would have discussed it with me, but I understand your fear. I forgive you."

"Marry me."

"Yes. With all my heart, yes."

Colin pulled her in for another searing kiss. Her hands traveled up his back until they burrowed into the soft strands of his hair. They kissed until Juliana felt as if she were in danger of bursting into a glorious flame of passion and need. She groaned in protest when Colin broke the kiss. He moaned low in his throat, his breath coming in ragged spurts, and then set her at arm's length.

"We must go before I lay you down on the grass and take liberties I am not yet entitled to."

"I can keep a secret," she purred.

The corner of his mouth lifted into a sensual grin. "It appears you didn't need my help at all, making a man desire you. Keep saying things like that, and you will learn how much I do."

A mischievous, wanton woman she hadn't known existed within her came to life wanting to accept his challenge. Colin had been the only man she'd ever desired. To learn how brightly his passion burned for her was a temptation like no other.

She nipped his ear with her teeth. "I'm a quick study."

He shuddered. "No!" He held her away again. "We will do this the honorable way even if it kills me. I will apply for a special license tomorrow."

"If we must." Juliana pouted playfully. It was a heady power to affect him so. "Let us return before Lady Roxburrow becomes suspicious and searches for me."

"Excellent idea."

Colin leapt to his feet, then helped Juliana up. She dusted the specks of dirt and grass from her dress. He held out his arm, which she gladly accepted.

As they began to walk, fireworks exploded in the sky above. Juliana looked up and marveled at the beautiful rainbow of colors decorating the night. It was a rather perfect ending to the moment.

Suddenly, Colin stilled. His entire body stiffened, and his muscles drew taught.

Juliana examined his form but could find nothing wrong. "Is something the matter?"

He didn't answer. She placed a hand over his heart. It thudded furiously. Pearls of sweat formed on his forehead. Another round of fireworks exploded in the sky. His body jerked.

Understanding dawned on her. He had mentioned not wanting to come tonight because of the battle reenactment. The sound of the fireworks must resembled cannon fire, and this was some sort of reaction to it.

Juliana's heart both shattered and swelled with a new surge of love. He came tonight, knowing the possible suffering that awaited him.

She wrapped him in a hug and lowered his head to rest on her shoulder. She ran her hand over his back in a soothing motion. "You're safe. You're with me. Juliana. I won't let anything harm you."

His arms slowly came up and latched onto her. His fingers dug into her dress until the pressure was almost painful, but she didn't complain. She held him in her arms, repeating the words of comfort.

"You're safe. I won't let anything harm you. I love you."

They stood like that until a few minutes after the fireworks ended. Finally, his body relaxed.

"Thank you. I—" he began.

Juliana placed a finger to his lips. "I love you. All of you. That is all that needs to be said."

Colin took her hand once more and placed a kiss against the back of it. They walked back toward the festivities, both lost in their love and gratitude for the other. Colin was the love of her life. The man who needed her as much as she needed him.

The day of their marriage couldn't come soon enough.

***

Colin's heart flipped over, standing in front of his wife. He lifted his hand to watch the gold band on his left ring finger gleam in the candlelight. Adrenaline rushed through his veins, anticipating what was to come next.

Juliana wrapped her arms around his neck, a shadow of hesitation in each movement. She kissed him softly at first, but soon passion flowed from her lips with the fierceness of a woman who knew what she wanted and had come to claim it. Gone was the innocent, self-conscious girl he'd courted long ago.

Colin kissed her back, trying to convey all the remorse, guilt, and promise of change in his heart. He held her tight against his body, savoring every second of the moment. She felt so good in his arms.

Their hands roamed over each other, exploring, remembering, and learning more about each other's bodies. Her lips were as soft as he remembered. Her kisses still fierce, yet more mature. More confident. She slid her hands into his hair, then yanked on the stands, causing a slight burning in his scalp.

Bloody hell!

She was driving him mad.

Too soon for his liking, Juliana broke the kiss. She placed her hands on his chest, blocking his efforts when he tried to capture her lips again. "I'm not sure what to do next."

The corner of Colin's lip curled into a sensual grin. "I'll teach you."

He took a small step back. He didn't want too much space between them. Having her so close was like regaining a piece of his soul he hadn't known he'd lost. He'd be damned if he let anything come between them again.

Slowly, sensually, he began unbuttoning his shirt, exposing his naked chest one unhurried inch at a time. She watched him. He spread his legs wider, feeling like a king under her sensual admiring stare. Her eyes narrowed with the hungry delight of a predator observing their prey. A knowing grin spread across his lips. So, she liked what he had to offer?

Juliana crushed herself against him, devouring his lips in a carnal kiss that set his blood on fire and made the wonder of the universe flash before his eyes. Colin locked his arms under her thighs and lifted her up his body. Her hands dug into his hair, pulling, and inciting the wild erotic yearning only she'd ever had the power to create in him.

He carried her to the bed, holding on to his waning control. He needed to be inside her. Connected in the most intimate way possible. Hearing her scream his name. Watching her give herself to him, confirming she was his forever.

"More," she said in a breathy purr. "I need more."

Colin made quick work of removing their clothing, gravitating back to her lips to steal kisses between each piece. His body pulsed with the need to touch and be touched by her. He needed more. As if reading his mind, or maybe needing the same thing, Juliana grabbed his hips, drawing his body against hers.

Everything about her felt so good. He gently lay her onto the bed. She slid across the mattress, never taking her sultry gaze off him. Her hips swayed in slow, tantalizing, graceful movements as she crawled to the center. She was trying to stop his heart.

Colin took in every detail of her tempting body. His throat constricted, his heart stopping, then thrumming in an uneven rhythm as a thought came to mind. "You're perfect. Everything I've ever wanted. I can't think of a single thing about you I'd change."

To his surprise, her seductive expression faltered. He hadn't expected her to preen under his praise, but he hadn't expected to see... fear? No, he must be mistaken.

As if to prove the idiocy of that thought, she folded her arms around his neck and drew him close.

Lips inches apart, she issued a command, completely erasing his doubt. "Kiss me."

Colin happily obliged her request. Their lips melded together, sucking, nipping, and giving everything the other offered. He pushed her back on the mattress, cherishing the warmth of her soft skin against his. With one long, tortuously slow stroke, he pushed himself inside her.

He stopped when sunk all the way in. Juliana moaned beneath him. Her warm exhale caressed his face, making it hard to hold back from spilling inside her right then and there. Perfect. He'd been a fool to think he could ever live without her. His world wasn't complete without her.

"Colin."

The low, husky way his name rolled off her lips set his blood on fire. He lifted his head to look into her dark brown eyes. "Yes, love?"

"I don't know what, but I think something else is supposed to be happening right now."

His chest rumbled with his laughter. "Yes, love. I should move my hips."

Putting them both out of their misery, and plunging them into a sensual bliss, he rocked his hips back, then slowly forward again. He moved slowly at first, to keep the night from ending too soon, then increased his speed until he thrust into her with a powerful, almost animalistic desire. This is what she did to him. She made him want to give up control. To worship her. To follow her wherever she led him. To give her the world and make every one of her dreams come true.

Juliana purred beneath him, not holding back her pleasure. He continued rocking his hips, watching the ecstasy flicker across her alluring face. Her body tensed, the pleasure building inside her, pushing her closer and closer to the edge.

"Colin!" she moaned. "Oh, Colin. This feels so good."

"That's it," he coaxed. "Let go for me, love. Show me how good I make you feel."

Her face twisted with desire, her skin flush from the heat surrounding them. Colin held on to the waning fragments of his restraint, refusing to give in until she did.

"Oh. Colin. Colin!" She screamed her release, her body shuddering with euphoric bliss.

Colin finally let go, spilling himself into the heaven between her thighs. Spent, he rolled to the side, careful not to fall on top of her. Four years. He'd kept himself from this bliss for four years.

Damn fool.

He gathered Juliana into his arms, hugging her against his chest. She snuggled close and tucked her head under his chin. He held her, stroking a hand up and down her back until her breathing became even and shallow as she fell asleep.

Everything about the moment felt right. Juliana might not be perfect, but she was perfect for him.

"I love you," he whispered into her hair before closing his eyes and following her into sleep.

***

Through the fog of sleep, Juliana swatted the air in front of her face, trying to get rid of the nuisance tickling her nose. It vanished for a moment, then returned. She whined, wishing the bothersome cretin would leave her to sleep in peace. She swatted it away again, only to have it return seconds later.

She reluctantly peeled open an eye and found her overly cheerful-for-so-early-in-the-morning, husband perched on the edge of the bed, with a feather in his hand.

"Oh good. You're awake."

They'd only been married for a day—although a very glorious day—and already she wanted to kill him. He'd kept her up half the night with his insatiable desire, then he had the audacity to wake her.

"No, I am not. Leave me alone."

"I'm afraid my excitement won't let me do that, my sweet."

"Why can't you and your excitement find some other poor creature to bother? Leave me. I need to rest."

Juliana cringed when a blast of cold air swept over her. The fool man had snatched away her covering.

"How dare you?" She sprang up, kneeling on the mattress like a vengeful harpy.

Showing that he had a modicum of intelligence, Colin backed away from the bed, his hands—one still holding the blasted feather—in the air. "Listen, my sweet—"

"Don't you my sweet me after what you just did."

"You mean this?" Colin tickled the feather against her nose, then backpedaled from the bed and sprinted out the door.

Juliana stayed unmoving on the bed for several beats, too

shocked at the juvenile antics of her husband. Her shock slowly transformed into indignation, then ire.

"Why you little..."

She hopped off the bed and took off running after her husband. Several servants gasped as she ran by. Seeing their new duchess running through the house in her nightclothes probably wasn't something they ever expected to see, let alone on her second day in residence.

Apologies would be given later. For now, she had to find and murder her husband.

She spotted Colin a short distance ahead, darting through an open door at the end of the hall. She chased after him and burst into the room, alert and watching for whatever trick he had up his sleeve.

"There is only one door and—" she began, issuing her threat when she spotted Colin on the other side of the room.

Juliana released a shocked gasp, her hands flying up to cover her mouth. In front of Colin was a blank canvas upon an easel, with several more canvases piled next to it. A small table next to it held an assortment of brushes and paint in almost every color she could think of.

"Colin. Is this for me?"

He gave her a satisfied grin. He'd won the medal for the Most Thoughtful Husband in London, and he knew it. "Who else would it be for? There is no other lady I've promised to make happy for the rest of her days."

"I'm happy. So very happy. Thank you."

Juliana ran over to her husband and flung herself in his arms. Colin caught her with ease. She rained kisses over every inch of his face. Colin's warm, jovial laughter wrapped around her like a second hug. He gave her a quick kiss, then placed her back on her feet.

"I have one last surprise or you," he said, stepping backwards.

He unbuttoned his shirt, one tantalizingly slow button at a time with each step he took. Juliana watched him, the new carnal hunger he'd awakened in her last night making her want to chase after him again. This time to topple him over and have her way with him.

When his shirt was completely undone, she took a step toward him, but he held up his hand, stopping her movement.

"Sorry, my sweet, that will have to wait for later."

"How do you know what I planned to do?"

"I can see it in your eyes," he teased. "If I let you have your way with me, you'll miss your next surprise."

"What might that be?"

He made quick work of discarding his trousers, then finished walking over to the arrangement of cushions covered in red velvet fabric on the floor in front of her easel. He laid down, then propped his head on his hand and bent one knee, exposing every seductive inch of his manhood.

"I remembered that you once mentioned wanting to take a live model class. There is no way in bloody hell I'd ever let you paint another man naked, but you are more than welcome to paint me. In any position you want me."

Juliana couldn't help herself. She laughed so hard she doubled over, placing her hands on her knees. This man. This wonderful man was all hers.

"Laughing at man while he's naked before you is not a usual response."

"I love you. How very much I love you."

A twinkling laugh still issuing from her lips, she rushed over and threw herself onto her husband. "For now, I want you on the bottom. We'll discuss further position later."

"As you wish." He pulled her in for a long, hungry kiss. "I live you make you happy."

Yes, he did. He made her very, very happy.

ABOUT THE AUTHOR

Gabrielle Carr is the author of Regency Romances featuring casts of diverse characters, that are full of heart, hope, and happily ever after.

THE ALLURE OF A REFORMED RAKE

HILDIE MCQUEEN

She's as determined to pursue him as he's determined to keep his distance.

After a heartbreaking debacle, Thomas Sullivan decides to give up his roguish ways and become celibate. A test comes sooner than later upon meeting the lady of the house's companion, Mary.

Mary Asher is not sure why the handsome new driver tries to avoid her at all costs, when he obviously finds her attractive. She decides to find creative ways to get time alone with him.

CHAPTER ONE

BERKHAMSTED, ENGLAND 1818

The sound of her footsteps echoing as Mary Asher made her way down the corridor reminded her of the years she spent at a boarding school in London. Now as a companion for a lady, she lived in a gorgeous immense home in the country town of Berkhamsted, which was a full day's ride from London.

Instead of taking tea, as was the custom for her and her mistress, Vivian Yarnsby. She went to the kitchen to have tea with the newly hired cook.

Vivian was recently married, and therefore needed the upmost privacy. It was only when she and her new husband, Alexander, emerged that Mary's duties began.

Like the rest of the house, the kitchen was huge. Mary strolled in to find the cook, Moira and housemaid, Lottie, already sitting at a small table with bowls of porridge.

"I see you started without me," Mary teased as she filled the kettle with water from a pitcher and placed it atop the stove. She then stirred the pot of porridge and filled a bowl for herself. "It is a most beautiful day is it not?"

Moira gave her a knowing look. "Did you spy a certain someone outside?"

Pretending not to hear, Mary continued. "I hope it will be warm enough to begin work in the flower garden."

"I see you took special care with your hair today," Lottie added. "The style suits you."

Ever since she'd mentioned thinking the estate coachman, Thomas Sullivan, was handsome, the women had been relentless in teasing her about him.

And although she did wish to speak about the very attractive man, she kept any new thoughts to herself, for the time being.

It was rare that she had an opportunity to see or speak to Thomas as he only came to the house to eat. Other than a polite response to questions, while he ate, Thomas maintained a professional, and polite distance from everyone, except for Harold, Moira's husband.

"I have not spoken or seen him since yesterday," Mary said. "He is very quiet."

Moira laughed. "I do enjoy hearing the both of you talk. Between your island accent and his Irish brogue, listening to the conversation is quite entertaining."

When the door to outside opened, the three women went silent. Thomas entered and looked at each of them in turn, eyes narrowing. "Good morning ladies."

With a rather dreadful snort, Lottie chuckled and looked down to her bowl and mumbled. "Morning, Thomas."

Doing her best to avoid eye contact with Moira, Mary nodded at Thomas. "Good Morning Thomas. The porridge is very good today."

"Sit," Moira instructed and went to the stove. "Let's get some food in you. Need to get full. I hear our employers plan to go into the village today. I assume you will be taking them."

Thomas sat across from Mary, removed his hat, and placed his hat on an empty chair. "Yes, I will be going. If you require anything, I can fetch it for you. It will give me something to do while I wait for them."

Moira slid a bowl in front of him and returned to pour tea into a cup. "As a matter of fact, I do have a list," Moira exclaimed. "I haven't asked Harold to take me to the village market since my hip is bothering me," she said, referring to her husband, the estate groundskeeper.

When Lottie nudged Mary's arm, her spoon fell onto the tabletop with a thump and porridge splattered, some landing on Thomas' sleeve.

"I'm so sorry," Mary sputtered. Grabbing her napkin, she wiped at his sleeve, which made the stain grow. She gave up and glared at Lottie.

"I didn't mean to hit your arm so hard," Lottie explained. "It's just that I was going to point out that you are going into the village as well."

Mary's fingernails scraped the tabletop when she grabbed the spoon. She turned to Lottie. "Why would it require you to push my arm so hard?"

"Because," Lottie said, and once again, hit her on the arm, this time not as hard. "it's a bad habit." A wide grin brightened her freckled face. "You and Thomas will be in the village. At the same time," she added unnecessarily.

If there was a way to become invisible, Mary wished it to be then. She should have never told them that she admired him. Although Moira wasn't as obvious with her comments, Lottie had absolutely no control.

"I will be accompanying Miss Vivian. Where she goes, I go." Mary tried to avoid eye contact but ended up looking at Thomas. "And yes, Lottie, you are correct. Thomas and I will be in the village at the same time, along with Mrs. Yarnsby and her husband."

Thomas lifted his green gaze to hers but remained silent.

When their gazes met, she fumbled with what to say. "This is my first time visiting the village. Is there a dressmaker?" It was a stupid question as she was an accomplished seamstress and had no need for anyone to make clothing.

Thomas nodded. "Aye. It's a good-sized village. Plenty of shops, you'll see."

Moira gasped. "Oh goodness, I should have planned this better. I had forgotten that it is your first venture into the village. You won't know anyone, and neither will Mrs. Yarnsby."

Not knowing why Moira was so alarmed, Mary gave her a puzzled look. "There is no need to make a fuss. I will be living here for a long time, and there will be plenty of time for us to explore on our own. Today, I will be accompanying Mrs. Vivian while she visits with the constable's wife and whatever else she wishes to do."

"Since Mr. Yarnsby grew up here, he is very familiar with the village. I'm sure Mister Yarnsby will ensure Mrs. Yarnsby will learn where everything is. Therefore, you will as well," Lottie said with a sigh. "He is most handsome, is he not?"

"Lottie!" Moira said, motioning with her hand toward a counter. "Go fetch water to boil and put more firewood into the stove. I must prepare breakfast for Mr. and Mrs. Yarnsby."

Mary took a spoonful of porridge and ate it. It was hard to keep from stealing a glance at the quiet man across the table from her. She peered up, pretending interest in the window behind him.

His shorn, light brown hair had just a hint of auburn, the same for his eyebrows. There was a shadow of a beard on his jaw, which looked to be a shade darker. His eye color seemed to change between green and blue, she supposed they were hazel if one were to describe them.

Taller than her by half a foot, he had the masculine build of a man whose work required physical effort. She would not describe him as astonishingly fetching, but he was handsome in

THE ALLURE OF A REFORMED RAKE

an understated way. If asked, she would call him attractive. Yes, that was it. Thomas Sullivan was very attractive.

"Excuse me?" He studied her. "Who do you refer to?"

Her eyes widened. The annoying habit of mumbling when she thought often got her into difficult situations. "Err... I was thinking that Lottie is right. Mr. Yarnsby and Miss Vivian make an attractive couple."

Thankfully, Moira interjected. "Oh, they do, and so well suited."

"Indeed," Lottie, who'd yet to get up, added.

Thomas ate the rest of his breakfast in silence and then stood, put his bowl on the counter, and walked out. It was as if he'd rather be anywhere but around people.

"Do you think he is shy or just does not care for our company?" Mary asked, looking toward the now closed door. "Certainly, seems in a hurry to leave our company every morning."

"Rarely asks for a second serving," Moira said. "He does linger at times."

Lottie huffed. "Only when you are here alone, Moira. He must dislike either me or Mary."

"It does not matter," Mary said, standing. "I best see about preparing for the day. First I will inspect the garden."

Wrapping her shawl around her shoulders, she went out to look over the garden area. It was only ten days that she'd come to live at Woodhall, and the size of the huge home still astonished her. Upon turning to the back of the house, where the garden was, she stopped in her tracks, finding Thomas.

He stood with his head bent and hands clasped against his chest, as if in prayer. Like most Irish, he was probably a devout Catholic. Mary turned to leave just as Moira's huge orange cat made its way to the kitchen for its morning bowl of milk.

Despite her attempt to avoid the animal, the cat weaved around her legs. Mary did her best to walk away to avoid being seen by Thomas and unfortunately lost her balance when the cat continued its pattern around her ankles.

She fell to the ground on all fours. "Crumpets, George," she hissed at the cat, who sat at the doorstep and glared at her. "Bad kitty." While Mary scrambled to stand, the wind blew her shawl over her head, so she couldn't see.

"I will help you up." Thomas took her left arm and pulled her up to stand.

Fruitlessly she tried to be graceful by pulling her shoulders back and lifting her head high. Unfortunately, once again, her shawl was blown up and ended draped on her head like a kerchief.

When she yanked it off, her hair tumbled from its pins.

"My goodness. This is not how I expected to start the day," Mary said, breathlessly as she did her best to smooth her hair, as the shawl kept sliding off her shoulders. Finally, she gave up and blew a breath. "Thank you, Thomas."

Lips pressed together, he nodded. "Were you headed somewhere?"

"Yes. Yes, I was," she replied, wondering why he remained. The man always hurried away from any room she entered, and now when she wished him to go, he suddenly became interested in what she was doing.

"I was about to inspect the garden. I did not wish to disturb your prayer time, so I was about to leave." She motioned to George, who scratched at the back door. "Then the cat tripped me."

"I see," he said and glanced to where he'd been standing. "It looks as if it were once a very well-maintained garden. Hardly any weeds."

"Yes, well, I do believe Mr. Yarnsby had his staff keep it in good order." Mary took a step toward the garden, astonished when Thomas walked alongside.

"My mother loves gardening," he said.

"Is that so?" Mary replied, astonished at his willingness to share something with her. "My grandmother did as well. Of course, Jamaica has wonderful year-round weather, which lends itself to growing plenty of things."

"Were you born there?"

Mary smiled at the memory. "Yes, in Jamaica. My father, who is English, brought mother and me to live in London when I was very young. Thankfully, we have returned several times to visit grandmother. The last time was only about three years ago."

They fell silent as Mary walked through the walled area. A few plants, she recognized as flowers were just beginning to sprout. There were several trellises that stood bare, waiting to be draped with whatever would be planted at its base. Along the top of the wall, clay pots of various sizes were lined in. In each one, a different herb seemed to have been recently planted. She guessed by Moira or Lottie.

Not wishing to continue any type of conversation, Mary took inventory of the space, committing to memory where she'd plant what. The garden was on the north-facing side of the house, which meant, it would get sun most of the day.

George the cat strolled past her and gracefully jumped atop the wall to sun himself. Its large green eyes pinning her with daring.

"I do not think he cares for me," Mary murmured. "I have always liked cats, but this one may prove to be a challenge."

Thomas moved to where George sat and rubbed the cat's head. "I think he prefers to be left alone. Cats are fickle creatures who do not need our validation."

"Very true," Mary's lips curved. It was strange in a way to have such a superficial conversation with the Irishman. Despite the fact Thomas avoided her most days at the moment, he seemed perfectly comfortable, alone with her in the garden. When George lifted its head for Thomas to continue to scratch, she wondered if the reason the cat allowed it was because they were kindred spirits.

Both seemed to be fickle when it came to others.

"I best go see about preparing for the trip into town," Mary said turning away. She hesitated for a moment and then turned to Thomas. "Don't forget to get the list from Moira."

At his nod, she hurried inside.

VIVIAN YARNSBY, her mistress, was a beautiful young woman, whom Mary adored. Recently married, Vivian glowed with happiness. She and her husband, Alexander, were a love match, which in Mary's estimation was the best kind.

Mary, who'd been Vivian's companion for almost ten years, enjoyed seeing her mistress' excitement at the start of every day. In her opinion, it was only a marriage of love that brought on such anticipation and enjoyment of life.

Now as they settled into the carriage, Vivian leaned forward and peered out the window for a long moment. "I'm both excited and nervous about this trip to the village. I have no idea who anyone is.

Mr. Yarnsby had decided to ride ahead on horseback so he could then ride to the Torrington's estate. When very young, he'd been taken in by Duke and Lady Torrington. He'd grown up with their son, William, with whom he owned several businesses.

The passing landscape was dull, as winter had yet to fully end and all the trees were bare. The sky was grey, giving the impression that it would snow at any moment.

"I am sure you will enjoy meeting the constable's wife and the other ladies who have invited you for a visit," Mary said hoping it was true.

Vivian covered Mary's hand. "I am so glad you are with me. I tried to get my sister to come with me," she said referring to her sister Clara, who was married to Viscount William Torrington. Although to be fair, Clara lived a lot further from the village, which would mean several hours of travel there and back.

"I look forward to meeting whoever works for the constable's family. Hopefully, both of us will make new friends," Mary said assuring her mistress.

Vivian let out a breath. "You're right of course, it is time that I do things on my own. I am a married woman after all and must forge ahead."

Less than two hours later, the village came into view. Much larger than Mary expected, it was situated between sloping hills on one side and farmland on the other. Horse drawn wagons traveled the narrow roads and people hurried into buildings to avoid the chilling wind.

They passed several shops, the shingles informing them there was a shoemaker, a baker, a butcher shop, a candlemaker and an apothecary.

"There is a seamstress and tailor shop," Vivian said pointing. "Interesting."

"*The White Elk*" tavern commanded one corner of the square, across from it a church.

They arrived in front of a wooden two-story house and Thomas brought the horses to a stop. When he opened the door, Vivian leaned forward. "What are their names again?"

"Constable McAllister and his wife Ann," he replied in a flat tone. Vivian must have noted Thomas' lack of inflection because she gave him a puzzled look. "You don't care for them. You must tell me why."

Thomas shrugged. "The man doesn't matter to me one way or another."

At his lack of further explanation, Vivian sighed. She took Mary's hand. "Time to meet Ann McAllister."

Mary slid a look to Thomas, as he helped them from the

carriage, his gaze forward, not making eye contact. When his hand cupped her elbow, it was a light and fleeting touch.

Her mistress looked to Thomas once again. "Alexander tells me you wish to meet with the priest today. Just ensure you are back here in a couple of hours."

Thomas nodded. "Yes Ma'am. I must also purchase items for Moira."

"Very well," Vivian replied. "We will be about the village square shops."

THE CONSTABLE'S WIFE, Ann was a thin woman, who wore her dull brown hair pulled back in a rather austere style. It was hard to tell the woman's age, but since there was no gray in her hair, Mary guessed she was younger than she appeared. Along with her, were two women. Both of them seemed older, but again, it was hard to tell by their dull dresses and lack of enthusiasm.

Mary felt sorry for Vivian having to spend time with the drab women, as she was led to the kitchen where she was to wait. A plump woman welcomed her introducing herself as Donalda. "I am so glad to see new people arrive and live at the estate. It has stood empty for so long." Donalda slid a cup in front of Mary. "Drink please."

It was hot cider, rather sweet and delicious. "What is this? I must get the ingredients to Moira," Mary exclaimed.

"Honey and winterberries," Donalda said. "There is a beekeeper just outside the village. His honey is in high demand, because of its delicious sweetness. Ensure that you and your mistress send your coachman to fetch some. Hammond, the beekeeper, is a rather unpleasant man. It's best to not expose yourself to his sour disposition."

Just then a young woman entered. Her gaze swept over Mary and she went to a cupboard without speaking.

Donalda studied the younger woman for a beat. "Nettie this is Mary, she..."

"I know who she is," Nettie interrupted and looked to Mary. "I've never seen anyone like you before."

It was not the first time someone deemed themselves above her, because of her mixed heritage. Instead of a reply, Mary turned her attention back to Donalda. "Is there anything I can help you with, while I wait. I do not wish to interrupt your work."

Donalda glared at Netty and pointed to a tray set up. "It's ready for you to take," she told the sullen girl, who picked it up and hurried out.

"She was taken in by the Constable and his wife after her parents died. She's never been a pleasant one," Donalda told Mary. "Best to give her wide berth."

A pattern was emerging. Seemed Donalda excelled in seeing who to avoid. "Have you lived here long?"

"My entire life. My husband works at the mill, my daughter, who walked you back here, and I have worked for the family for many years."

When Donalda's daughter came for her an hour later, Mary has been helping the cook make bread. Time had passed rather quickly, but obviously not for her mistress because Vivian practically raced from the house.

Vivian looked around. The carriage remained, but Thomas was not there. "I need fresh air. We should walk about a bit."

"The visit was shorter than I expected," Mary said.

Vivian shuddered. "It seemed never ending to me. The conversation was stilted and awkward. Almost as if they measured every word, careful about what to share. Strange really."

"I was given dire warnings to stay away from a beekeeper and the constable's wife's maid, Nettie."

They chuckled.

The walk into the village square was short, and Mary was thankful for the opportunity to see everything the village had to offer.

Her mistress read a shingle. "I am curious to know if everyone in this town is so dour?" She opened the door, and both slipped inside.

Immediately, the aromas in the apothecary enveloped them. Mary took a deep breath of the aromatic air.

"I have heard about you," a pretty woman entered from a back door and left it partially open. "Welcome to Berkhamsted."

Unlike others they'd met so far, this woman welcomed them. A smile on her lips, the shopkeeper told them about every herb and oil in the shop. She explained the benefits of drinking some of the herbs in teas. As the woman spoke, Mary found it very informative, and it gave her an idea of what new herbs to plant in the spring garden.

"You must try my tea," the woman said motioning to a small table in the corner. "What you smell upon entering is my chamomile tea. A special blend of it and lavender make it a perfect combination for many ailments. Her eyes twinkled. "Drink it in the evening, and I guarantee you a good night's rest."

Indeed, the tea was flavorful, and the visit turned out to be enjoyable. The shopkeeper told them which other shops to visit and about the sellers that came to sell their wares at the town square several days a week.

In the end, they purchased several bags of herbs and oils, promising to return soon. Once outside, Vivian looked to Mary. "I forgot to ask her name. Wait here for me. I won't be but a moment." She handed Mary her small bags and went back inside.

Mary walked to the end of the building and looked to the village church. There out front was Thomas speaking to the vicar. It seemed as if the clergy did most of the talking, while

Thomas nodded. It was curious to her that the men would have so much to discuss. Perhaps they'd known each other for a while.

If she remembered correctly Moira had said Thomas was new to the area as well, having arrived just after Mr. Yarnsby's father had passed.

"What is so interesting?" Vivian asked coming up. "Oh, there's Thomas and Father Matthews. We should give them a few moments before going closer. I would like to thank the vicar once again for agreeing to marry Alexander and I on such short notice."

As they walked toward the men, Thomas looked in their direction and then began to walk toward them. Vivian held a hand up motioning that he did not have to leave.

Upon approaching, the priest greeted them warmly. "Mrs. Yarnsby, I am hopeful that you will be attending Sunday services soon," he said with a smile. The man had graying on his temples and bright blue eyes. Instantly Mary liked him.

When he looked to her, Mary held her breath, not sure what he'd say. "What about you Miss. Do you attend services with your mistress?"

"I do, Father," Mary replied. "I look forward to your services."

Seeming satisfied, the priest turned to Thomas. "I have been speaking to Thomas regarding his calling."

"Calling?" Vivian asked, looking to the driver. "Thomas, do you feel called to becoming a man of the cloth?"

Thomas looked to the vicar and then his gaze lowered to hers. He frowned. "I am not sure as yet."

"Neither Alexander nor I would hold you back from it. Please know that if you feel compelled to join the church, we are not an impediment."

"Thank you, Ma'am," Thomas replied.

The clergy walked with them back to the carriage, speaking

to Vivian, who invited him for a meal the following day. Much to the delight of the clergy, who obviously enjoyed attending meals at different homes.

A silent Thomas took the parcels from Mary, and walked beside her, his face turned just away enough to let her know he did not wish to have a conversation.

Mary on the other hand had questions, so she decided not to be put off by his demeanor. "Have you known Father Matthews for long?"

He shook his head. "Only since arriving here seven months ago. He is who helped me find employment at the Yarnsby estate."

"I see," Mary replied and started to ask another question, but Thomas hurried away so he could open the door for Vivian.

When she reached the carriage, the vicar took her hand and assisted her up and into the carriage.

"I find this situation quite intriguing," Vivian said, looking at her. "Why would Thomas even consider joining the priesthood when it's obvious he is not prepared to be fully celibate?"

"Why do you think he is not prepared?" Mary asked, truly interested in the response herself. "One can only hope that a large portion of the decision would be done with counsel by the vicar."

Vivian gave her a knowing look. "I will only say that Thomas looks at you in a way that seems quite contrary to someone preparing for priesthood."

"I'm sure you are mistaken," Mary said, but smiled. "Do you really think so?"

"Positive," Vivian replied with conviction.

CHAPTER TWO

The entire drive back to the Yarnsby estate, Thomas went over and over in his head the conversation with Father Matthews. It was the third time he'd met with the priest to discuss the possibility of joining the priesthood. Each time, the priest had been adamant, that it if was his calling, he would know without hesitation.

A part of him figured it was his part in someone's death that drove him. However, guilt being the driving factor was not a good reason to join the church. In that moment, Thomas felt compelled to wait and allow time to make things clearer.

Thankfully, that day the priest had not been as insistent to know what his decision was. Instead, Father Matthews brought up why Thomas had moved there and asked about his life prior to coming to Berkhamsted.

Although there was plenty to tell him, Thomas did not feel ready to reveal everything. There were days when he wished to relieve himself of the burden of what he held inside. It was the right thing after all, as a Catholic, he should confess the sins of his past that he carried with him.

Long before arriving, he'd spoken to the priest at the church where he'd grown up but stopped short of confession.

His roguish ways of the past, had come with a price, not only was a woman dead, but he'd hurt many people. What he'd considered fun in the past, he was now deeply ashamed of.

Thomas' father often said that the burden of guilt was sometimes the hardest punishment one could live with.

And yet, despite the looming cloud, over his head, that rarely dissipated, Thomas wasn't sure he was prepared to speak about it to Father Matthews. The hesitation was perhaps a sign he wasn't truly ready for or right for the priesthood.

Then there was the new situation, the appearance of a beautiful woman, the likes of which he'd never seen before. Mary Asher.

Her brown skin was so distractingly beautiful. With a combination of amber colored eyes and midnight black hair, she was like a rare alluring jewel. Then there were the additional distractors of plush lips and sensual husky voice.

Thomas shook his head and inhaled deeply. A feeling of calmness came over him whenever he was in Mary's proximity. Of course, she barely noticed him, which was understandable. Mary was like a part of his employer's family, and he a mere coachman.

UPON ARRIVING AT THE HOUSE, he helped Mrs. Yarnsby from the carriage. The beauty gave him a soft smile. "Thank you, Thomas. The drive home was delightful."

"I ensured to go a different route so you could see different landscapes," he admitted.

When he turned to help Mary out, his breath caught at the sight of her. There was a softness about her that brought out a protective nature. At the same time, her quiet strength gave him pause. Unlike women he'd met before, Mary didn't seem to have a problem speaking her mind, nor did she come across as a wilting flower who fawned over his looks.

If he were to be honest, she intimidated him a bit.

"Thomas?"

He turned to find Moira standing with a hand on her hip. "Harold wanted me to tell you to come to the stables as soon as you return."

Moira's husband, Harold, the groundskeeper and overseer of the estate, was a fair man when it came to work duties and responsibilities. Thomas admired the man and had become close to him since arriving.

Thomas drove the carriage to the stables and began unhitching the horses just as Harold walked out. The man helped him lead the horses into the stalls so that they could be watered and fed. "How did they do?"

"They worked well as a team. If I hadn't known that they'd never been together, I would not have guessed. They became a bit restless while we waited for the ladies, so I took them around the village. Once that was completed, they settled," Thomas informed Harold.

"I am glad to hear it," Harold replied, his expression somewhat pensive.

Thomas studied the man. "Is something wrong?"

"Two men came here earlier," Harold said, looking toward the house. "They asked about you by name. I didn't tell them you worked here, only that I knew you and that you came by sometimes to do work."

A chill traveled up Thomas' spine. "Why did you not tell them I worked here?"

"I got a strange feeling about them. They did not seem friendly at all." Harold studied him. "Seems to me they have some sort of grudge, by the way they said your name. With disdain."

"Did they give you their names?"

Harold shook his head. "No."

Glad that he'd taken a different route from the village, Thomas could only give thanks to heaven for it. If they had come across them, he had no idea what could have happened.

Thomas shook his head. "Can you describe them?

The older man frowned in concentration. "English, dark hair and eyes the same. They came in a wagon being pulled by one horse." Harold made a motion with his right hand down the side of his cheek. "One had a scar on his cheek, as if he'd been cut."

At once, Thomas knew who they were. He hung his head, letting out a long breath, his stomach clenching in frustration. "I will tell you," he said.

"Go on, son. Sit down," Harold said, motioning to a pair of stools at the opposite side of the stable.

They sat and Thomas let out a long breath. "I was a wee lad when I came to England from Ireland, we settled in the south. Growing up I had a good life. My father bought some land and farmed it. My mother is an accomplished seamstress and was soon in high demand in our village. Because my parents did well, my sister and I never wanted for anything."

He looked into the man's eyes. "Unfortunately, I took advantage of the fact the young women of the village considered me handsome and a good catch. Soon I gained a reputation for being the town rogue."

"I can imagine your parents did not care for it."

Thomas nodded. "My father put me to work, did his best to keep me in hand. Mother, well, mostly she prayed." His chest constricted. "One day I met a young woman named Catherine. She was quite pretty and... willing. After knowing her for several weeks, she began demanding I marry her. I was a cad and told her I never had any feelings for her."

At Harold incredulous look, Thomas continued. "It was

94

cruel. I said it because I wanted her to dislike me and not keep making demands."

"When did this happen?" Harold asked.

"Almost two years ago." Thomas let out a breath. "She sobbed and begged me to stay with her. I refused. The following week, she was dead. Drowned."

Harold shook his head. "Her family blames you."

"Of course. I do believe it was my fault. Her brothers let it be known they would kill me. It was then, my father insisted I go away. I didn't wish to run, but my parents insisted I leave. I am not sure how they came to find me here."

"Do you think she drowned herself because of you?" Harold asked.

Thomas shrugged. "I heard rumors that she and her parents had a horrible row. One overheard her father tell her he wished her dead. Those are just rumors. My mother was told she was involved with another man while with me. I am not sure if it is true or they hoped to ease my burden of guilt."

"What are you going to do? Do you wish to leave?"

Thomas shook his head. "I am not running any longer. I will face them."

Harold was thoughtful. "I agree, it will not end until you clear things with them. I pray they will listen to reason. I am sure if they go into the village and ask, they will be told you work here. Depends on how many people know you by name."

"I go to the village often, it will not be hard for them to find out I am the Yarnsby's driver."

"There is nothing to do but wait. I will speak to Mr. Yarnsby. Unfortunately, he may consider it too dangerous for his wife that you remain."

His stomach tumbled at the thought of having to start again. He managed to save most of his earnings mainly because he was unsure how long he'd remain at each job he managed to acquire. "I understand. May I speak to him first?"

"Yes, of course."

MARY WASN'T at the supper table when Thomas and Harold joined Moira and Lottie that evening. It was not unusual as she often ate with the Yarnsby's.

"Thomas, how was your venture into the village today?" Moira asked. "Where are the things I asked for."

"I left them in the carriage. I will get them."

"Eat first," Moira said. "The food is getting cold."

After the meal, he retrieved Moira's items as well as the parcels for Mrs. Yarnsby and Mary. He then went through the foyer to find a place to leave the parcels, the ladies had acquired in the village. There was a side table and he placed them on there with care.

Deciding it was best to get things over with, Thomas went to Mr. Yarnsby's study and stood at the doorway.

The man sat at his desk scribbling notes in a ledger and looked up sensing him. "Good evening Thomas."

Since first meeting Alexander Yarnsby, Thomas had liked the man. Unlike most wealthy people, he didn't hold himself above them. Before marrying, he'd eaten meals with the staff in the kitchen, claiming to not like eating alone in the dining room. Now he prayed the man's humanity would help in his situation.

"Sir, I have a problem that I wish to speak to you about, if you have the time."

"Of course," Yarnsby motioned for him to enter the study. The room was bright during the day and at night, one could see the stars, as one wall was all windows.

He waited for his employer to round the desk and to sit in a chair opposite him before beginning.

"What is it Thomas?"

The dryness in his throat made Thomas clear it. "Men came here looking for me today. They asked Harold if I worked here and he denied it because he got a bad feeling about them. I am not sure what they plan, but I fear it is not good. They will return to look for me, I am sure of it."

"Who are they?"

He hung his head for a moment, hating to have to admit to his roguish ways and the consequences, once again. "Brothers of a woman, whom I had a relationship with."

"I see," Yarnsby replied. "Am I to assume she was compromised, and they seek for you to make things right?"

He met the man's gaze and nodded. "I am not proud of my past and how little I considered the impact it had on others. Unfortunately, there is nothing I can do that can ever repair any damage in this case."

"What happened?"

He took a deep breath and swallowed. "She drowned, and her family says it was done on purpose, as she was broken-hearted over me not wishing to continue the relationship."

Yarnsby stood and looked out into the night. "It is not your fault. Her act, if it was indeed because of you, was her choice."

"How can I make her brothers understand that?" Thomas said. "I do not blame them for how they feel. And I do feel responsible. If someone did the same to my sister, and as a result, she took her life, I would want revenge, whether justified or not."

They remained in silence for a long moment; finally, Yarnsby turned to him. "How dangerous are these men?"

"In all honesty, I grew up knowing them and never saw any kind of hostility between them and anyone. I shouldn't have allowed my parents to convince me to leave my home. Running gave them a stronger impression that I am responsible for what happened."

"They were worried about you," Yarnsby said sitting again.

"If I was in your place, I would feel the same. In all honesty, this conversation makes me think about my past as well. Although I did my best to keep relationships from becoming too deep, there were several times, breaking away was tough."

"I understand if you ask me to go. I do not wish to put you and Mrs. Yarnsby in harm's way."

"I surely doubt it will come to that," Mr. Yarnsby said. "Perhaps, we should find the men and speak to them directly. It may be the only way for this to end and for you to stop looking over your shoulder."

Relief swept over him, and Thomas lowered his shoulders at sharing the burden. "I agree."

Mr. Yarnsby met his gaze. "You have not been in my employ long, but already I can tell you are a good man. I have no doubt that if you could repair things with this woman, you would."

"Thank you, Sir."

Thomas made his way out to the stables to check the horses one last time. He'd promised Harold to do so, so the older man could go to bed early as he'd been complaining about back pains.

Thankfully the full moon allowed plenty of light so Thomas could see. Once inside the stables, he lit a lantern and hung it on a hook.

The horses were restless, making soft noises at his presence. In the nearest stall, the horse pawed the ground, the animal's eyes wide. "What's the matter?" Thomas said in a soft tone. "Is there a wee beastie about that makes you nervous?" He stroked the animal's nose. "Let me look."

Just as he reached the stall door, movement caught his attention. Two men appeared from the shadows blocking the entrance to the stables.

"You can't run this time Thomas Sullivan," one of them said.

He looked to one and then the other. "I heard you were here earlier. Can we talk?"

"We didn't come here to talk. But to make things right. You killed our sister, and now you will pay with your own life."

The familiar faces were twisted in fury, both seeming to enjoy the moment. Thomas knew it would be hard to win against both. One perhaps, but not two angry men.

"As I told you back then. I regret what happened. Your sister seemed to understand why we could not continue the relationship. She was sad, but I do not believe to the point of killing herself."

The eldest brother sneered. "Our sister is dead. You killed her."

It was of no use to attempt to convince them otherwise. Thomas blew out a breath and prepared to defend himself.

CHAPTER THREE

H ard and fast knocks on her door made Mary hurry from the bed. It was dark outside, the sun barely peeking past the horizon from the feeble light that came through the window.

"Mary," Lottie said, opening the door. "Come, hurry."

"What is it," Mary asked, as she grabbed a robe, jammed her arms through the sleeves, and tied the sash around her waist. Together they hurried down the corridor to the rooms where the others slept.

"Keep quiet, we don't wish to waken Mr. and Mrs. Yarnsby," Lottie whispered. "This is dreadful."

Puzzled when they went to a door and Lottie pushed it open, Mary looked to the maid. "Whose room is this? Please explain to me what is happening?"

Moira took her hand and pulled her into the room. "Thomas is dying. Harold found him in the stables this morning."

At the words, her stomach sank, and her chest constricted. "Was he stomped by a horse?"

She went to the bed only to recoil at the sight. Thomas was unrecognizable. His entire face was bloodied and swollen. Both eyes were swollen shut. He lay shirtless atop a bed, his bloodied hands down on his sides.

"Go get the water," Moira said to Lottie. "Mary, help me tear these sheets into strips."

Lottie raced from the room and returned, lugging a pot of water. She poured it into a basin. "I will put more water to boil."

"I knew they'd return, but didn't think it would be so soon," Harold said. "They must be found and charged."

As much as she wanted to understand what happened, Mary kept quiet. It was more important to concentrate on doing what she could for Thomas.

She approached the bed and studied him calmly, although her hands trembled when she felt his sides. "A broken rib or two," she said methodically. "His jaw may be broken as well." She ran her hands down the sides of his face pausing at his throat to feel a pulse. "His heart is beating, not strongly, but steady."

She then felt his stomach. He was cool to the touch. Although she'd been taught the basics of caring for injuries, as her mother had been a midwife, she'd never seen someone so battered and bruised.

"They left him for dead," Harold said as Moira neared and began cleaning his face. "I'm riding to town to alert the constable."

"One of us should inform Mr. Yarnsby," Lottie said. "He needs to know."

'Once I finish cleaning his wounds and get a good idea of how badly he is, I will do it," Mary assured her.

Bowls of bloodied water and cloths were taken only to be filled again as they cleaned away blood and bandaged what they could. Thomas finally came to just as the sun rose, moaning but not able to speak.

Mary had wrapped his head, a bandage keeping his mouth

closed. They were going to have to help him drink until his jaw healed.

Just as they began to bandage his tattered hands, he lost consciousness once again.

"I will go speak to Mr. Yarnsby," she said looking to the others. "Is there anything I should say happened?"

"He was beaten by two men," Harold said. "I am sure of it. They came looking for him yesterday."

As soon as Mr. Yarnsby opened the door to his bedchamber and saw her expression, he seemed to know what happened. "Is it Thomas?"

"Yes Sir, he's been beaten badly."

The man hurried down to the room where they'd placed Thomas. He entered and immediately dispatched Harold to the village to seek a doctor and the constable. He then asked that Clark, a young man, who worked as gardener be sent to Lark's Song, his friend's estate to inform them he would not be going there that day.

In the meanwhile, he went to Thomas's bedside and took inventory of the beaten man. "They took no mercy," he said quietly.

"No, they did not," Moira replied wiping a tear. "The poor man. How could someone do this?"

"I will inform Vivian and will try to keep her from coming here." He looked to Mary. "Will you come with me?"

As they made their way back to his bedchamber, Mary had to ask. "Do you know who did this and why?"

"I do. He spoke to me yesterday about it. Neither he nor I considered it would happen so soon. It is nothing to worry about as far as anyone else's safety. The attackers had only Thomas in mind."

As she expected as soon as Vivian was dressed, she hurried to help with Thomas. They took turns keeping cool cloths on his forehead because a fever took over and he vacillated between being drenched in sweat and shivering from being cold.

"I have never seen someone injured so horribly," Vivian said to Mary when they'd been left alone with Thomas. Moira and Lottie had gone off to cook a meal for the family.

None of them had much of an appetite, especially with the constant smell of blood that filled the room.

It was several hours later, that not only the doctor and the constable arrived, but also Father Matthews.

The priest hurried into the room with the doctor. "I should administer last rights," he said with a sad expression. "I will come and fetch you when I am done," he continued, sending Mary and Vivian out.

They went to the foyer just as Mr. Yarnsby and Harold went into the study with the constable. Vivian looked to Mary. "Do you know anything?"

"Only that your husband was aware that someone was looking for Thomas and that we should not worry about our safety."

Both looked to the closed door. Vivian blew out an exasperated breath. "We should ask Moira what she knows. Harold did speak to those awful men."

As soon as they entered, Moira shuffled over with bowls of steaming food, motioning for them to sit. "This is horrible," she said and wiped away a tear with the hem of her apron. "Just horrible. That poor boy."

"Who are the men who harmed Thomas?" Vivian asked.

Moira looked to the doorway, as if expecting to be overheard. "They are from the town where Thomas grew up. He told Harold that a woman he'd been involved with died, and he is blamed for her death. Apparently, she drowned herself."

"Scorned," Vivian said. "Goodness. I cannot imagine anyone wishing to die over a broken heart. But I suppose it happens."

Mary frowned. "These men, who blame Thomas and came

to seek revenge. Am I right to assume they are the woman's relatives?"

"Yes," Moira said. "Brothers. This is why Thomas has been meeting with Father Matthews and considering the priesthood. To atone for what he considers a horrible sin."

"That is absolutely ridiculous, and I will inform him so once he recovers," Vivian said. "One cannot just choose to become a priest. The priesthood is a calling."

"I agree," Moira said. "But the boy feels horrible about it."

"And he should," Mary interjected. "Men come and go as they please, ruining women without a second thought. Episodes like this happen because of it. I do not agree with what the woman or her brothers did, but I think it should serve as a warning for roguish men."

At both the women being struck silent, she released a breath. "That said. I feel badly for Thomas and plan to care for him until he recovers."

"Thank you, Mary," Vivian said. "I am sure your presence will give him incentive to heal faster." At Vivian's smirk, Mary gave her a droll look. "The man is barely conscious, and you think he would give care to who is in the room?"

"I do."

The sounds of voices were followed by Vivian's sister Clara rushing into the room. "William is with Alex and the constable," she informed them referring to her husband. "I had to come and ensure you are well and to help."

The Humphries were like family to Mary. She'd been with them since very young, hired as a companion for the quietest of the three sisters when she was fifteen and Vivian just ten. Now almost eleven years later, she could not fathom life without them.

Clara hugged her sister and then rushed to Mary and did the same. "How is he?"

THE ALLURE OF A REFORMED RAKE

"Very badly hurt. In and out of consciousness," Vivian said. "He is unrecognizable."

"Oh dear."

Mary and the sisters went to the sitting room to wait for the doctor to emerge.

Father Matthews finally appeared and told them the doctor would only allow Lottie in the room since Thomas was bereft of clothing.

Lottie traveled back and forth between Thomas's room and the kitchen doing the doctor's bidding, her expression glum. Meanwhile, Moira boiled water and emptied the basins as needed.

While Vivian told Clara what she knew, Mary fetched tea for them and poured. Time passed slowly, with Lottie giving them updates of what she understood went on in the room.

When Thomas regained consciousness, the constable was hurried into the room. But he came out soon after because Thomas once again fell unconscious.

It was late in the day that they all sat down for a meal, the priest remaining in the room with Thomas.

As they ate, Mr. Yarnsby insisted the doctor tell everyone about Thomas' status. The man explained what Mary already knew. Thomas had broken ribs and a broken jaw. He'd acquired quite a few injuries to his back and stomach, which worried the doctor. Both the doctor and the priest would remain for the night. The constable, on the other hand left so he could gather men and search for the attackers.

That night, Mary went into Thomas' room to ensure he was still alive. Each time he slept or was unconscious. Honestly, she couldn't tell the difference.

What she did know was that he was not doing well and hung on to life by a thread. The doctor entered behind her, his concerned gaze going to Thomas. "I will stay here tonight. Get some rest Miss."

In truth, she was afraid to leave. Terrified that sometime in the middle of the night Thomas would pass away and she'd never see him again. It was strange that after living there for just a short time, she'd only had two short conversations with him, but had somehow felt a connection of some sort with him.

It could be that Vivian's notion that Thomas found her attractive had given her illusions, or that he was so very handsome. Either way, it felt as if what transpired between them was only a beginning.

"Please send for me if anything happens. I will get up early and come, so you can get some sleep." Mary neared the bed and took one of Thomas' bandaged hands in both of hers. She leaned closed to his ear. "Get rest Thomas. I will be back in the morning."

She then reluctantly left the room, her stomach in knots. At seeing the kitchen alight, she went in. Moira, Harold and Lottie sat around the table with cups in hand.

"Ale?" Moira offered and Mary nodded. She fetched a cup and poured from the pitcher in the center of the table. They sat in companionable silence, none wishing to leave in case something happened, and they'd not be nearby.

"He seemed to have regained some color," Lottie offered.

"How could one tell?" Moira asked. "His entire face and body is covered in bruises."

Lottie shrugged. "At least his fever lessoned."

"It did," Mary said.

"You DO NOT HAVE to stay here," Thomas informed her three days later, his words sounding muffled since his jaw remained bandaged. "I can take care of myself." He was sitting up, his back against the pillows and once again in a bad mood.

Mary ignored him. With bandaged hands and unable to

open his mouth properly, he required assistance to eat. He'd refused almost every meal, until Moira threatened to have Harold and the gardener hold him down as she poured soup down his throat.

His face remained bruised and he still had trouble breathing, but at least he felt well enough to argue.

"It's potato soup," Mary said as she lifted the bowl and dipped a spoon into it. "Moira ensured it's creamed so you don't have to try to chew." Understandably, he was embarrassed to not be able to feed himself. The stubborn man had tried to feed himself several times and ended up throwing the bowl across the room when he'd dropped the spoon or spilled the food.

She pushed the spoon gently past his lips, feeling self-conscious at the proximity. He kept his gaze away the entire time while taking each spoonful and waiting for the next.

"Father Matthews is to return today. He was reluctant to leave. Seems to have taken quite a liking to you," Mary said as she fed him another helping. "Otherwise, it will be a quiet day. The Yarnsby have gone to Lark's Song for the day."

Thomas swallowed. "Why is Father Matthews returning. I don't require constant company."

"Have you always been this disagreeable?"

He looked away to the doorway, obviously considering throwing her out. If not for his bruised ribs and injured ankle, she figured he'd not remain in the room. "I do not mean to be so cross," Thomas said in a quiet voice.

"You are in pain, not able to eat and trapped in this room. I understand," Mary told him. "If I were in your shoes, I would probably be unpleasant as well."

"I apologize."

"No need. Finish eating. Perhaps we can see if Harold can help you go outside for a bit."

He met her gaze for a long moment. Despite all his injuries, his eyes were clear. The directness of his look made her insides quiver. The way Thomas made her feel was something she was not used to.

"You look much better," Father Matthews exclaimed from the door. He gave Mary a warm look. "I am glad you, Moira and Lottie are taking such good care of him."

For some reason, his comment annoyed Mary. It was as if the vicar took ownership of Thomas. She smiled and stood. "He is getting stronger every day."

She wanted to add. "And therefore, you do not have to keep returning," but she didn't.

Instead, Mary stood and looked down at Thomas for a moment before leaving. At the doorway, she turned to see that the priest had sat down and began praying over Thomas who glared up at the ceiling.

"Is it wrong of me that at times I find Father Matthews a bit irksome?" Mary asked Lottie.

Lottie giggled. "He seems a good sort. Most times, men of the cloth do look down on others, but I suppose they have a right to."

"No, they do not," Moira replied. "We are all equal."

THE DAY WENT by rather quickly despite Vivian being gone. Father Matthews had left after dinner.

As darkness fell, Harold went to check on Thomas and ensure he was ready for the night. Mary drank ginger tea with Moira and Lottie.

"Its best that we all get some rest," Moira said with a yawn, we have a busy day tomorrow.

Mary trudged to her bedroom, which was on the same floor as the others, but on the opposite side of the house. Her room was rather lavish compared to most staff. She'd grown accustomed to having nice accommodations since London, where she and Molly, Clara's companion shared a room much like the Humphries sisters themselves had.

As Mary slipped into bed, she couldn't help but wonder what kind of conversation transpired between Thomas and the priest.

No one thought Thomas should go into the priesthood. Perhaps it was time to put him through a test. Since he was recovering, Mary had a reason to see about him regularly, and there would be no questioning her being alone with him.

Her lips curved as a plan came to mind.

CHAPTER FOUR

Knocks sounded.

Thomas called out for whoever it was to enter, and Mary came into the room instantly making it seem brighter. Her lips were curved as she carried a tray and placed it on a table that had been set up for him next to the table.

Thomas cringed inwardly at the idea of moving, but at the same time he was tired of being on his back.

Ten days since the attack, his ribs were finally allowing him to sleep through the night. Still sharp pains continuously roused him when he moved the wrong way.

"You look better," Mary said meeting his gaze. "Your bruising doesn't seem as bad today." She studied his face and he looked away, not quite sure how to take her perusal.

Had she always been so beautiful in the morning? How could he not remember? Then again, he'd gone out of his way to avoid her. For the first time in a long time, a woman made him feel alive. Every ounce of his body came to life around her.

Sunlight streamed into the room when she pulled the curtains aside. Then she pushed open the shutters allowing the frigid air in. "I know it's quite cold, but I am a firm believer in airing out rooms where someone is ill."

In the new light, he admired the long lines of her neck and deep rich color of her wavy hair. Instead of the usual bun at her nape, today she wore her hair in a looser style. The top pulled back from her face and the rest loose to her shoulders.

"I'll help you to sit." She neared and wrapped her arms under his. "Push up." A floral scent tickled his nose and he realized it was her hair.

Thomas grimaced in pain when she pulled him up to sit. As hard as he tried to keep from it, a groan escaped when she released him, and he fell back against the pillows. "I feel like an old man, barely able to move without hurting."

"Let's put this blanket over you to keep the chill away." Mary lifted the quilt and brought it to the bed, and then spread it over his shoulders. Meeting his gaze, she seemed to assess if he was comfortable. The ever-present soft smile took his attention until he had to drag his gaze away.

"Thank you."

Mary pulled a chair closer so that she could sit next to the bed to help him eat. "The morning Harold found you, we thought you would not live. You looked to be dying." She looked away. "That you have pains is not surprising. It could have been a lot worse."

He almost told her the pains in his abdomen and back were almost horrible enough to make him wish for death. Instead, he took shallow breaths waiting for the pain to subside.

Mary touched his hand. "I remember once this woman was very heavy in her pregnancy had taken a fall. The poor thing, her ribs and back were injured. She had to go through labor, and I cried with her at the horrible pain she endured to bring her child forth."

His own pains forgotten at thinking of the woman's predicament; Thomas could not imagine how the woman would have withstood it. "What happened to her?"

Mary lifted the cup to him so he could hold it with both hands and drink. It was a warmed cider that had been sweetened by honey. Hungry, he guzzled it. "Very good."

"The woman delivered a healthy baby boy," Mary said taking the cup and placing it on the side table. Since four fingers on his right hand had been broken, he had to use his left hand. He guessed the men had stomped on his hands when he was passed out. Thankfully, other than very sore, his left hand was not as damaged.

She arranged the tray over his lap, and he lifted the spoon awkwardly with his left hand, using his thumb and forefinger.

Mary continued. "As soon as the baby was born she became very ill. Mother wrapped her ribs and saw to her back. It was a long hard time for the young mother, but she did recover." She watched as Thomas ate for a moment. "It was the first time I've ever seen a man taking care of a child alone so well. Her husband was adamant that he'd care for the child while his wife recovered and did an admirable job."

She chuckled softly. "I am talking your ear off. Tell me. How do you feel today?"

If he were to be honest, he could listen to her talk for hours. Mary had a soothing voice that lulled a listener in.

"Harold is going to help me dress so I can go out to the stables. I cannot take remaining indoors any longer," Thomas informed her, feeling childish at complaining, but at the same time, it was honestly how he felt.

"I don't blame you," Mary said. "If I had to remain indoor for so many days, I would go mad. Let me help you." Taking the spoon from his hand, she slid it into the porridge and lifted it to his lips.

For some reason her proximity and focus on his mouth

seemed intimate. Much more than someone nursing someone who was ill. This was so different, almost sensual.

He could only open his mouth wide enough for the spoon to fit, not entirely in, but far enough that the contents would spill into his mouth.

When her eyes met his for a moment, it was as if all the air left his lungs. Thankfully, she looked back to the bowl to get another spoonful and it gave Thomas time to get his bearings.

Whatever was the matter with him? Then again, it had been a long time since he'd been alone with a woman and one so beautiful. She smelled like a field of flowers that he could lay upon and rest.

"Thomas? What happens?" Mary gave him a quizzical look. "Should I fetch someone?"

Blinking, Thomas realized he'd been lost in his thoughts. He hoped Mary would not realize it was her he thought about. He cleared his throat. "I'm fine. Just had a bit of a twinge down my leg and took a while to go away."

She looked from his face to his legs under the blankets. "I think it is a good idea that you go outside. Perhaps being in bed so long is affecting your ability to move your legs."

"I can move them," he demonstrated by bending one and then the other.

Mary seemed delighted. "Good. I am glad." She took the tray and empty bowl from his lap. Taking a small cloth from the tray, she went to the basin and wet it. Then she returned to him and wiped his face.

This time his body went on full alert. His stomach tumbled, chest tightened, and his throat went dry. "You don't have to do this."

Once again, she smiled at him, this time the effect was hard to hide. He shifted and rearranged the blanket across his lap so that it bunched.

The beauty's lips parted as she continued with tasks that

kept her much too close. "I am well aware, but I feel badly that you have no one to care for you. I will be available until you can do for yourself."

His gaze fell to her full lips, the thought of pressing kisses to her pillowy mouth made it hard to keep from reaching for her. "Thank you."

"I enjoy it. Now, I will fetch Harold so he can help you." Mary then leaned forward and kissed his left cheek. Thomas turned his head and kissed her fully on the lips. The kiss lingered just a moment longer before Mary pulled away with an unreadable expression.

"It's best I go see about fetching Harold."

"You certainly have better coloring this morning," Harold said as he walked in. "Moira insists that I get you up and out of this room."

Thomas nodded. "I like the idea. There's nothing wrong with my legs, no reason, other than it hurts to move." He chuckled when Harold laughed.

It was a slow walk to the stables, which gave Thomas pause as he entered. Despite bothersome aches, he managed to help feed the horses.

In the distance a buggy neared and he knew it was Father Matthews. A part of him didn't want to talk to the man that day. At the same time, it was best to get counsel from the priest, who'd always been kind to him.

Harold neared. "He sure is persistent."

"What do you mean?" Thomas asked, meeting the older man's gaze.

"I understand you are exploring the idea of priesthood. However, a decision as important as that should be yours and yours only. I know he means well, but he should give you more time to think on it without his constant influence."

"He means well," Thomas replied.

They waved as the priest neared and Thomas stood from the stool he sat on. Father Matthews smiled broadly, making quick inventory, his eyes moving from his face down to his feet. "I am certainly pleased to see you out," Father Matthews exclaimed as he climbed down from his seat.

"There is much to thank our Lord for today," the priest continued as he neared and held out his ring for Thomas to kiss. Harold grunted and went back into the stables.

"You didn't accompany your wife to church on Sunday," the priest called after Harold, who ignored him.

Thomas motioned to the house. "It's much warmer in the kitchen."

"Before we go in, I wish to have a word in private." Father Matthews pursed his lips. "The reason I am here today is that the constable wishes you to return to the village with me. It seems they've captured the pair who beat you."

The news caught Thomas by surprise. "What will happen to them?"

"If you identify them as the assailants, they will be jailed or hung. They did leave you for dead." The lack of empathy in the priest's tone took Thomas by surprise.

"They are misled in their thinking, and yet acted maliciously. I do not condone them to be killed. I have known the men since childhood..."

"They allowed grief to lead them astray to commit a sinful act," Father Matthew's interjected. "It is out of your hands either way as you have already told their names and they've been caught. You coming to the village is only a formality."

Thomas closed his eyes and let out a breath. "Very well. Although I am not sure I can travel so far yet. The constable will have to wait a few more days, I'm afraid."

It was much later that Thomas was able to get away from Father Matthews, who needled an invitation to remain for the night. The priest was currently in the parlor, in a chair before the fireplace, snoring contently.

He'd not seen much of Mary, other than that morning, as she'd joined the Yarnsby and Father Matthews for dinner in the family dining room.

Thomas wanted to search her out, but his body protested quite vigorously to moving about so much. Reluctantly, he trudged to his bedroom stopping at the end of the hallway to wait for his ribs to stop aching.

"If you faint, you will only cause more harm," Mary's voice fell over him like a warm breeze. The slight accent coupled with a natural hoarseness was like a soothing balm to Thomas' senses.

He looked up to meet her gaze. "I overdid it today. Once I got out of the bedroom, I didn't rest once."

"Mmmm." Mary studied him for a moment. "I will help you get inside."

HE DIDN'T REQUIRE help getting into his room, in actuality, her putting her arm around his back hurt. The need for her touch pushed away all good sense and he leaned into her. "Thank you."

They walked clumsily into the room and he walked to a chair. "I'd rather sit than spend more time than necessary in bed."

"Very well, but you seem a bit weak. Are you sure?" Mary asked, her face much too close for comfort. If it wasn't for the fogginess in his brain from her proximity, he would have taken a bit longer to consider his words and actions.

"Why did you allow the kiss?" Thomas asked. "I don't look my best at the moment."

Seeming to be taken aback by his directness, Mary looked away frowning. "I wanted it to happen long before your attack."

This time it was Thomas who was startled. "You did?"

"Yes," she said with a mischievous sparkle in her eye. "Perhaps your aloofness and the fact you are constantly in a bad mood caught my attention."

She'd called him aloof, which in his mind meant unapproachable, exactly the façade he'd been hiding behind since leaving his home.

"Sometimes there's a reason why a man must keep others at bay."

Her lips pursed in thought, taking his full attention. "I understand that perhaps the past has brought you to make certain changes in your life. I hope that you will find peace once the attackers are brought to justice."

Instead of lowering to the chair, Thomas remained standing. "I am not sure they should be punished. It is punishment enough to have lost their sister."

"It is a decision they made knowing the possible consequences. The fact they remained nearby attests to it. Why didn't they leave?"

He'd wondered the same thing himself. "Perhaps they wished to ensure I had indeed died."

"If not captured, they would have probably returned to kill you. Think about it Thomas. I know it's hard. Father Matthews told us you've known them since childhood. I cannot imagine how you feel."

Thomas studied Mary. "You are so different from any other woman I've met. Intelligent, well-spoken and kind."

"Thank you," Mary replied, her cheeks reddening. "Now you should get some rest."

"I don't deserve to even ask, but would you consider the possibility of me courting you?"

Her eyes rounded and mouth fell open. "I thought..."

Before she could finish the thought, Thomas pulled her against him, once again taking her mouth with his. The bandaging of his jaw annoying him because it kept him from kissing her in a way to let her understand his desire. Soon it became painful, so he pulled back just a bit so to not moan in pain and break the spell of how wonderful she felt against him.

Her arms circled his waist, and she pressed her forehead to his chest. "I would very much like to get to know you better."

After pressing another light kiss to her lips, Thomas released her. "I suppose it won't do for someone to walk in and find us together."

She gave him a playful smirk. "Especially Father Matthews."

At the mention of the priest's name, Thomas winced. "I must speak to him first thing in the morning."

WHEN MORNING CAME, Thomas was glad to have rested the night before. He'd tired himself out and had slept soundly all night. When sitting up, he grimaced when his ribs protested, but he managed to do it alone. He studied his bandaged and splinted fingers and attempted to flex them. His left hand was healing quickly, most of the fingers did not pain him.

The right hand however still hurt. Nonetheless, he managed to dress himself, but gave up at combing his hair the comb kept slipping from his fingers. Feeling somewhat presentable, he neared the mirror to study his face.

There was purpling around his eyes, although the swelling was now minimal. The bandage wrapped around his face keeping his chin in place was neatly done and did not distract too much. Other than a somewhat swollen left side of his face, not much more was visible.

There was plenty of bruising around his chest and sides, but thankfully those could be hidden by clothing.

After a slow but productive morning, Thomas walked with measured steps to the kitchen and entered finding that Harold and Moira sat at the table, while Mary and Lottie cooked.

"Sit, I will fetch your tea," Lottie called out shaking a spoon at him.

Mary looked over her shoulder, her eyes softening at meeting his. "We're making steamed pudding."

"It smells very good," he said then thanked Lottie for the tea. "How much longer?"

"Any moment now," Moira replied with a gleeful rubbing of hands. "I was promised first taste."

"If it is Mary's famous plum pudding, then I demand the second serving," Mrs. Yarnsby pronounced entering. "Mary, you haven't made it in a long time."

Mary and Mrs. Yarnsby giggled, seeming to share a secret, while Moira turned to him and narrowed her eyes.

"Something is afoot," Moira pronounced. "I intend to find out what it is."

Lottie hurried over. "What happens? What am I missing?"

Mrs. Yarnsby came to the table with two bowls of pudding with warm cream poured over them. "Everyone must try it. You will think to be in heaven."

She slid a plate in front of him and Thomas thanked her. "I'm sorry Mrs. Yarnsby," he scrambled to stand grimacing at the pain the sudden movement caused."

"No-no-no," Mrs. Yarnsby cried out. "You mustn't hurt yourself."

Once everyone had a bowl, they began to eat. It was like Mrs. Yarnsby had said, the pudding was absolutely delicious.

"I best get breakfast ready," Moira said after emptying her bowl. "Mrs. Yarnsby, let me get that for you." She took a tea kettle from the woman and poured it into a different cup than the one Mrs. Yarnsby had retrieved.

Poor Moira was either overly tired, or excited about the prospect of a second helping of pudding.

Clark, the gardener, came to the doorway. "Someone comes." He looked to the table with longing.

"I will save you some, don't fret," Mary assured him.

Right before anyone could move, Mr. Yarnsby entered the kitchen and went directly to the counter to be served pudding from Mary.

Mr. Yarnsby looked out the window and then to Thomas. "When you were still very injured, I sent for your parents. That is probably them arriving."

At first he couldn't quite understand clearly what the man said. It took several minutes for him to realize everyone stared at him. "My parents?"

Clark went to stand by the side of the house to await the arrival of the carriage, while Thomas gawked in the doorway without speaking. He'd not seen any of his family since leaving his home, and he'd missed them dearly.

Not wishing to make a fool out of himself in front of Mary, he walked out to stand next to the gardener and was joined by Harold, who had followed him out.

In the doorway stood Lottie and Mary, through the window, Mr. and Mrs. Yarnsby peered out. Moira must have been fretting over what to cook, much too busy to look like the rest of them.

Finally, the carriage came to a stop. His father exited and waved to him, he hobbled over, doing his best not to breathe too deeply. Just then, his mother's sweet face appeared, already crying, she hurried down and tentatively hugged him.

"Oh dear, dear me. You look horrible darling." She wiped at tears and attempted to smile. "I have missed you so."

He hugged his mother close, not caring that the action hurt.

"Please come in and get out of the cold," Mrs. Yarnsby waved for them to enter. Once in the house, they went to the parlor, where his parents were shocked at being asked to sit and rest. His mother gave him a quizzical look but after a few moments began to tell the others about their travel and to his horror began sharing stories of his childhood.

It was obvious by the way Mary pressed her lips together, that she did so to keep from smiling, her gaze moving from his mother to him.

Thankfully, when his father's head bobbed, he and Thomas' mother were ushered into the kitchen for a quick meal before heading to bed to rest.

"Has Mr. Yarnsby always been so kind to his staff?" Thomas asked Moira when he caught her alone in the kitchen. "I cannot believe my parents are here."

Moira nodded. "Yes, he has always ensured to take care of us. Mr. Yarnsby didn't have a close-knit family. It's evident he treasures families. I can't wait for them to have their own children. This will be a house filled with love."

Before going to his bedroom, Thomas stopped at the door where his parents were invited to stay. It was a guest room, not as grand as the ones on the second floor, but much nicer than staff was used to. Even the rooms where he, Moira, Lottie and Harold slept in were well appointed with quality furniture.

"I am so happy to be here," his mother said hurrying to him and tugging him into the room. "Please sit with me for a moment. Your father is already half asleep," she said motioning to the bed.

When Thomas sat, his mother met his gaze squarely. "Thomas, there is something you must know. It is about the girl, Catherine, who drowned."

His stomach sank at hearing the words. "What is it?"

"Bernard Anderson killed her."

"What?"

"It so happens that some boys were at the river fishing. When Bernard and Catherine came to view. The boys hid, thinking to spy on lovers. The couple argued upon her telling him she was with child. He threw her to the ground and held her head under water until she died."

"Why did they not say anything right away?"

"I was told one of the boys did, but because Bernard is a good friend of the Constable, his parents told him to stay quiet."

Thomas sat back exhaling. "How did it all come to light?"

"The boys finally spoke out, together. At hearing about it, Bernard's wife admitted to knowing about Catherine and him. Before anyone could approach Bernard, he hung himself in the barn."

"I suppose her brothers were never told?"

"They must have known, because they burned down the Anderson's house and barn. Poor Mrs. Anderson moved away to live with her parents. I believe her brothers wanted to take their ire out on you as well. And now they will hang for it."

"They won't hang. I asked for clemency. They will be jailed for years, but won't die by my hand," Thomas informed her. "It is time the healing begin."

His mother looked to her husband. "We are so very proud of you Thomas."

CHAPTER FIVE

L ike most afternoons, Mary sat in the sitting room with Vivian. Together they worked on gifts for Clara's child. The babe was not to be born for several months and by the time it did, they'd have enough items to fill the entire nursery.

While Vivian knitted a blanket, Mary embroidered the edges on a gown that Thomas' mother helped her make.

The older couple was to leave soon, they'd extended their visit and had stayed a few additional days, and that seemed to please Thomas to no end. He spent many hours with them, mostly in the evenings.

During the days, Mary had gotten to know Mrs. Sullivan. The woman was plump, with graying hair and a sprinkling of freckles across her nose. Although the woman was slow to warm to Mary, soon they spent many hours in the garden, which was almost ready for spring planting.

Thomas had split his time between his parents and Mary; however, they'd yet to announce their relationship. The only person Mary had shared about her interactions with Thomas, was to Vivian.

"Are you spinning wool while you embroider?" Vivian asked with a smile.

Mary shook her head. "I was thinking about the fact Thomas has not told his parents about us. Should I confront him about it?"

"I am not sure what the proper timing is," Vivian said tapping a finger to her chin. "I supposed he was waiting for the perfect time."

"They are about to leave," Mary pressed. "I don't wish him to tell them just as they get on the carriage to head home."

As much as she didn't want to consider it, she wondered if Thomas had changed his mind about her since spending time with his family. Or perhaps he had told them, and they didn't approve of her, and he'd not told her to spare her feelings.

"Perhaps he wishes to invite them to move closer. He spoke to Alexander about the availability of cottages on the estate," Vivian said, and continued. "I love Alexander's parents, so I am fortunate. Thomas' parents are more reserved, aren't they?"

"Yes, they are, especially his father. I wonder if it has to do with my background, the fact that I am not fully English."

Vivian's eyes rounded. "I most certainly hope not. If so, then they will never be allowed here again." Vivian had always been protective of her, which meant she'd never been slighted in the least by Vivian's friends. Although she was just a companion, many times she'd been invited to outings, which had given her privileges others who looked like her never received. Perhaps because of it, she rarely considered how new acquaintances saw her.

"I will speak to Thomas. It's time I find out where he stands," Mary proclaimed.

THE NEXT AFTERNOON, only Moira and Lottie were in the kitchen when Mary entered..

"Thomas' parents are entertaining Father Matthews in the sitting room," Lottie informed her. "He arrived just a few moments ago."

"I need to speak to Thomas," Mary said standing up. "Do you think he's in the stables?"

Lottie nodded. "I saw him headed that way a bit ago." Both looked to Mary waiting for her to explain. As much as she wanted to share things with them, if the conversation with Thomas didn't go as she hoped, then it was best not to divulge any thing at the moment.

Deciding it was best to give them an excuse, so they'd stop staring at her Mary came up with a white lie. "I need to know when he will be going to the village. Mrs. Yarnsby wishes for the seamstress to come to take measurements for dresses."

She hurried from the room before they could ask anything else. Outside sunshine greeted her, it was a beautiful day. Yet, despite a promise of spring by the lengthening of the days, the wind remained chilly and Mary pulled her shawl close around her shoulders.

The stables were warmer as the wind was blocked and the animals within provided some warmth.

With a thick coat on, leather gloves and his pants tucked into knee-high boots, Thomas raked hay in a far stall.

"Thomas," she said in soft voice. "You didn't come inside for breakfast. It is late now, you must be hungry."

He straightened, and upon meeting her gaze, his expression softened. "I am, but I won't be eating until I can wash up. I smell pretty badly right now." Holding the pitchfork with his left hand, he held out the right one. "Don't come too close."

"Should you be doing that. Your hands have just recently healed," Mary admonished him. "I am sure the doctor would be cross to see you doing so much."

"I have a job to do," Thomas said and wiped at his face with a cloth that he'd pulled from his back pocket. "Mr. Yarnsby has continued to pay me and for it I am thankful, however, I will not take advantage of his good will."

Despite his warning, she walked closer. The horse in the nearest stall peered out, and once she stroked its long nose, it turned away, satisfied.

"Thomas have you told your parents about me?"

He gave her a surprised look. "Of course, I have. I told them I was courting you for marriage."

"For marriage?" Mary's eyebrows lifted as she held back a smile.

At his chagrined expression, she gave him a pointed look.

"I just told them the day before yesterday, when the three of us went to town," he admitted.

"How did they take it?" Her voice shook just a bit at the real-ization that if his parents did not accept her, she would not marry Thomas. Her father's parents had never accepted the fact he'd married a black woman. Holding firm until their death, her father had never seen them again. She'd witnessed first-hand his sadness at their continued refusals to visit and the returned correspondence.

Not meeting her grandparents, herself, was something she would not subject her own children to. Mary braced herself for his reply, her mind awhirl.

It was obvious Thomas cherished his parents and she did not wish him to lose that relationship.

"I'm sorry to have waited so long to speak to them and then not talking to you about it," Thomas deflected. "I was hoping to get you alone for a few moments. But it's been so busy..."

Her breath caught. "They are not happy about it then?"

Thomas let out a breath and seemed to steel himself for her reaction. "Mother thinks you are too elevated in status and used to much finer things that I could never provide. Both think very highly of you, but Mother says I am reaching above my social status with you."

She almost laughed. Thomas' parents considered that it was he who was not good enough for her. Laughter bubbled. "Oh dear, that is not what I was expecting."

"What do you mean? Did you expect them to rebuff you because of the color of your skin?"

Mary nodded. "Yes, that is exactly what I expected, and feared actually."

"My mother is correct," Thomas said, his tone somber. "I cannot possibly provide you with the life you've become accustomed to. You should think about it. With me as your husband, you would give up many things."

As much as she wanted to think it didn't matter, Mary had to accept she'd not considered the vast changes to her life if she married Thomas. What if he decided they would leave and take her away from Vivian? Then she'd have to go with him, of course. "I hope that we would remain in the Yarnsby's service. I do not wish to be away from Vivian."

"I would not ever take you from here," Thomas assured her.

Mary relaxed. "Then I see no reason for us to worry about lifestyle. My father provided a comfortable sum for my needs that I have yet to touch. He and mother have a very nice home in London. I confess to being spoiled a bit upon coming to live with the Humphries. However, I have always hoped to one day live in a small cottage that is all my own."

"A cottage I can provide," Thomas said with a grin. There was warmth in his expression as he looked at her. "I wish I could hug you right now."

"Don't you dare," Mary said holding her hands out.

Lottie walked in. "What is he threatening to do?" She asked smiling.

"To come closer," Mary said.

"I don't blame you for telling him to stay away," Lottie

replied. "Moira is threatening to come after both of you. Her meat pies are cooling."

Thomas closed the stall door and put the pitchfork against the wall. "I will be there promptly. I have to wash up."

MARY AND LOTTIE walked back to the kitchen. Lottie weaved her arm through hers. "When are you two formally announcing your courtship?"

"You know?" Mary's cheeks heated.

"Ha," Lottie laughed. "We've all known for a long time. Harold saw you kissing when Thomas was injured."

Her eyes rounded. "Oh dear. I'm not sure I can face him again."

"Don't be silly," Lottie said. "That was almost two months ago, wasn't it?"

"Oh dear," Mary repeated and let out a long sigh. In the kitchen the table set for two along with two goblets and the meat pies.

"Enjoy," Lottie said and walked away.

When Thomas entered, Mary was drinking from the goblet. It was a sweet wine that she was sure Vivian had something to do with.

"What is this?" Thomas asked looking toward the corridor. "Where is everyone?"

"They've eaten. Moira and Lottie did this for us. I believe everyone else in the household has been warned to stay away."

His lips curved. "Ah."

Mary's eyes widened. "You told them didn't you?"

"I admitted to it when Harold confessed to spying us kissing. I asked them not to say anything to you until you were ready to share. I supposed they gave up."

After holding the chair for her to sit, he then sat across the table from her and extended his hand, which she accepted. "I wish to marry you soon, Mary. I hope you will not make me wait long."

Warmth filled her and she lost all interest in the meal. However, when Thomas began to eat with gusto, she did as well. They didn't have a conversation, it was more about companionship and time alone. With so many about in the house, it was rare to steal a moment or two by themselves.

"Tell me," Thomas began. "When would you like to speak with my parents?"

Despite his assurances, Mary was nervous. "Perhaps tomorrow?"

He must have seen her worry because he squeezed her hand. "That I care for you is enough for them to as well."

Only once had she been in a relationship. The courtship had abruptly ended when the man's mother caught sight of her. Despite reassuring her, it had nothing to do with his mother, the man in question had ended things between them immediately thereafter.

Thomas reached for her hand. "Thank you, Mary."

"For?"

"Accepting me."

How she wanted to hold him and be kissed by him in that moment.

Seeming to read her mind, he stood and rounded the table. "Would you like to walk outside a bit. I ate too much." He lifted her shawl and wrapped it around her shoulders.

The chilly air brushing over her face, helped dispel the heat that infused her face at the thought of time alone with Thomas.

Just as they rounded the corner into the walled garden, Thomas pulled her into his arms, his mouth taking hers. Since his jaw healed, Mary discovered kissing him was so much more delightful. His lips pressed against her, tongue probing until she parted her lips and allowed him access. Mary held on to his shoulders, then wrapped her arms around his neck and lifted to her toes. If only time would remain still, she'd be forever grateful.

"I can't wait to marry you," Thomas murmured, trailing kisses down the side of her jawline to her throat. "I want you so much."

It would be almost impossible for them to wait until their wedding night. Mary considered how both Vivian and Clara had married without fanfare. Perhaps it was to become a tradition, because as much as she wanted to have a wedding, what she really wished for was to be Thomas' wife.

Her breathing hitched when his tongue circled at the base of her neck. The man definitely knew how to take prohibitions away. "Oh Thomas," Mary murmured, pulling him closer. "We mustn't."

Unable to move away, she feebly attempted to push him, but then she pulled his face to hers taking his mouth again. His hands slid down her back cupping her bottom and pulling her against the hardness of his sex. Instinctively she knew if they didn't stop then, she'd drag him to her bedroom.

Sounds of the night emerged past their heavy breathing. In the distance owls sang their sad songs, while horses neighed just before ending their vigil. Mary broke the kiss and pressed her forehead to his chin. "We should go inside."

"There is something I must ask you," Thomas said. "I've taken it for granted but have yet to do."

Mary frowned. "What is it?"

"Will you marry me," Thomas lowered to one knee. "I love you Mary Asher, and nothing would make me happier than if you accept me as your husband."

Her breath caught. Although he'd mentioned wishing to marry her, he'd not formally proposed.

"Yes. Of course, I will marry you," Mary exclaimed with half a cry. "I hate that I'm about to cry."

The sight of Thomas' handsome face grew out of focus as happy tears slipped down her cheeks. They hugged and he pressed a kiss to her temple. "Don't cry."

"I'm happy. To be honest, didn't expect to ever marry at all. Even though I wished it."

Thomas chuckled. "I didn't expect to marry either. Father Matthews will be disappointed when we go ask that he marry us."

Dislodging from his embrace, she took his hands and Mary looked up at him. "He may not marry us. I am not catholic."

Thomas frowned. "I'd not considered it. We will have to convince him."

"I must write my parents," Mary said. "You will have to speak to my father."

"Yes, of course."

He took her hand and guided her away from the garden and toward the front of the house. Mary took in the grand estate and sighed. "This house for some reason reminds me of attending Vauxhall with Vivian, it was in June, just last year."

Thomas looked to the building. "Tell me about it."

"It was a grand celebration, a masquerade and reconstruction of the battle of Waterloo. I have never seen so many grand costumes, so many beautiful displays and so much desperation. The debutants out to find husbands, while pretending to be shy, while the mothers did their best to shove them in front of eligible bachelors.

"Did the Humphries ladies not suffer the same fate?"

"Oh no," Mary replied with a soft chuckle. "Mrs. Humphries took ill, so their father and cousin Todd Humphries escorted them. Much to their delight, the men were too overwhelmed with all the happenings, they totally forgot to attempt matchmaking."

Thomas laughed. "I bet it didn't go well with Mrs. Humphries."

"Not at all," Mary replied. "However, she was mollified by our stories of what a wonderful time we all had."

"You have had a good life," Thomas said quietly.

"And it is about to get even better," Mary replied and kissed his jaw. "Shall we go inside?"

THE FOLLOWING morning Mary woke with a smile. It could have been storming outside and she would have seen rainbows and sunshine. As she walked into the kitchen, Moira was alone.

"You are up very early," the woman said motioning to the stove. "There is plenty of hot water in the kettle."

Already bread was baking, the aroma filling the room. Mary prepared tea while telling Moira of her plans for the day.

Thomas appeared in the doorway and her stomach did funny things at seeing him. "Would you like to take breakfast with my parents and I?"

She followed him to the small staff combination sitting and dining room, where the older couple sat with cups in hand and plates before them on a table that seated eight.

Both looked up and smiled warmly as they walked in.

"Good morning," Mary murmured settling into the chair Thomas held out for her.

"Good morning, Dear," his mother replied. "You look absolutely splendid, as always."

It had not occurred to Mary that she wore clothing of the same fabrics that Vivian did. Vivian had always insisted the seamstresses make dresses for her whenever they came to measure her. Although she would only get one, and Vivian three or four, it had allowed her to compile a varied and beautiful wardrobe.

"Thank you, I am very fortunate to have a generous

employer, who considers me a friend," Mary explained. "It is truly a blessing to have come to be Mrs. Yarnsby's companion."

Thomas cleared his throat and reached for her hand. Mary's eyes widened as he spoke. "I have asked Mary to marry me and she's accepted."

His parents exchanged a look, and his father chuckled. "We hoped you would before we left."

Mrs. Sullivan stood and reached for Mary's other hand. "I am very pleased. I am sure you will make Thomas very happy."

"We have raised our son to be a good man, I have no doubt he will make you a good husband, young lady," Mr. Sullivan added, his eyes shiny with emotion.

Mary's heart leaped with joy and she let out a long breath. "I love him very much. I am very fortunate to have met your son."

A COUPLE DAYS LATER, as she walked through the house, Mary mentally inventoried chores that had to be completed upon her return from Lark's Song. With only the Yarnsby's in residence now, the house seemed very empty. Thomas' parents had left the day before with promises to return for their wedding.

"Miss Vivian and I are going to Lark's Song and join Mr. Yarnsby. We are to stay for a few days," Mary announced entering the kitchen. "You will have time to rest, Moira."

"Nonsense," Moira replied. "I plan to scrub the entire kitchen and Lottie will take advantage and clean the sitting area."

Mary laughed. "I hope you will take some time. You deserve it."

I have been to Lark's Song, it is quite a beautiful estate," Moira said ignoring her comment. "Unlike this house, it's a perfect size."

"True," Mary replied. "This house is much too large. Even with a big family and staff, I cannot imagine it ever being filled."

Alexander Yarnsby was already at Lark's Song since he worked with William Torrington. Together the men managed their holdings and investments and were rarely apart for more than a couple days.

Thomas drove them to the Torrington estate and was to remain there, so he could drive them back.

When she and Vivian exited from the coach, Clara Torrington and her companion, Molly, rushed to greet them. After living together since very young, it was an adjustment for all of them not to see each other daily.

"I am so happy you will be staying for a few days," Clara exclaimed, hugging her sister. She then came to Mary and hugged her tightly. "I miss you both and Penelope so much," she said referring to the third and youngest sister, who remained in London.

As they made their way to the front door, Mary looked over her shoulder to see that Thomas spoke with Mr. Yarnsby. She tried to catch his eye, but she was pulled into the house by Molly.

"A letter came for you yesterday," Molly said. "I know you'd want to know right away. It's from your father."

"Oh?" Mary was confused. "Most of her correspondence was always with her mother. "That's odd. Can I see it?"

She hurried with Molly to a small sitting room just outside the kitchen. It was where the staff spent their evenings before retiring for the night. Molly went to a drawer and pulled the letter out. "Here you go. I'll leave you to read."

At her father's perfect penmanship her lips curved. She'd always aspired to write like him and had spent hours practicing. Although her handwriting was nice, it was not as beautiful as his.

She opened the letter and lowered to a chair.

Dearest Mary Elisabeth,

I pray this letter finds you in good health and happy. Your mother and I miss you terribly.

I do not wish to worry you but am hopeful that you can travel to London soon. Your mother has taken a fall and is abed. She's become melancholy since she's unable to go anywhere at the moment. She would be so delighted to see you.

Her birthday is soon, I ask that you consider gifting her with your presence.

Warmest regards, your loving father.

Her heart sank. She'd hoped to spend her time at Lark's Song discussing her upcoming wedding as neither she or Thomas wished to wait long.

Now she had to leave immediately so that she'd arrive in time for her mother's birthday the following day. She leaned back and closed her eyes for a moment before racing from the room and out in hopes of finding Thomas.

"Whatever is the matter?" Molly asked. "Is its bad news?"

Mary stepped outside the front door and looked around, thankfully the carriage remained hitched.

"Somewhat. I must go to London. My mother has taken a fall..." Just then Thomas appeared from the opposite side of the carriage. "Will you excuse me Molly. I must speak to Thomas."

"Yes of course."

When Thomas looked to her, he must have read something in her expression, because he hurried to her. "Is something wrong?"

She led him away from the front of the house. "My mother is not well. She fell. I must go to London immediately."

"I can take you," he said taking her hands. "Don't worry. I will speak to Mr. Yarnsby and I am sure he will agree to it."

"You drove us here. I fear you are too exhausted to make the long ride to London."

He took her face in both hands and kissed her lips. "I'll be fine."

"I will speak to Miss Vivian." She let out a long sigh. "I would prefer to leave within a couple of hours so we can arrive in London before dark."

"I will alert Mr. Yarnsby."

They went inside, Thomas to find Mr. Yarnsby and she to find Vivian.

Upon entering the parlor, it was obvious Molly had already told the others what occurred because Vivian came to her. "You must go immediately."

Clara came up beside her sister. "If Thomas is too tired to take you, our driver can take you."

"He wishes to take me," Mary replied, not sure why, but began to cry. "She is not so ill that I have to worry. However, father wishes for me to come for her birthday."

Vivian hugged her. "I think it is a marvelous idea."

"Are you sure it's prudent for you to travel alone with Thomas?" Clara asked with a gleam in her eye. "That is a long time to be unchaperoned."

Mary couldn't help but allow the moment of levity to entice a smile. "I will be the picture of utter decorum."

"I wouldn't be," Clara admitted. "I bet Vivian would."

Vivian laughed. "Don't be so sure, sister."

She was grateful for the banter as it gave her an opportunity to gather her wits. "Thankfully I am already packed. Which carriage can we take?"

"Ours," Vivian said. "I can return to Woodhall with Alexander in one of the Torrington carriages."

"Thank you," Mary hugged Vivian and then accepted hugs from Clara and Molly. "I plan to remain just a few days."

Vivian hugged her. "You can return with Penelope. She plans to come for the gathering in a couple weeks."

Together they went to find the men and shortly thereafter, Mary found herself on the road again, this time alone.

IT WAS the first time she'd traveled so far alone. Although Thomas was with her, he drove the closed carriage, so it was impossible to hold a conversation with him. If she knocked on the side of it, for him to stop, it would only be for a good reason.

Her mind kept going to her mother. It wasn't like the forever cheery woman to be forlorn for any reason. Always, keeping busy, visiting people and attending to the needs of the elderly in her neighborhood her mother was quite active. It was probably having to remain in bed for an extended time that brought her to be sad.

The letter had been written a week earlier. Hopefully by the time she arrived, her mother would be in better spirits and it would be a wonderful visit.

Mary peered out the window at the passing landscape. They were about halfway to London, soon the outskirts of the huge city would come into view.

They came to a stop and she was glad for it. No doubt Thomas had to relieve himself. Her lips curved as an idea came to mind. This would be a perfect time for privacy and time together. As much as she'd grown to enjoy their little escapades for a kiss here and there, the prospect of not having to worry about someone happening upon them, was enticing.

"Would you like to come out and stretch your legs," Thomas asked when he opened the door.

"Yes, go see about your needs," Mary replied. "Perhaps we can chat when you return."

He hurried to a cusp of trees and Mary sprang into action, grabbing the thick blankets she'd brought to keep warm on the trip. She went just short distance from where the carriage was and spread the blankets, then hurried back for the pillows.

"Mary?" Thomas called out and she giggled softly.

Thinking she was seeing about her needs, he would not

HILDIE MCQUEEN

come right away. She settled down into the blanket and let out a shaky sigh. A soft breeze blew across her heated face, fanning away any doubts about the man she loved.

"Thomas, can you please come here?"

His eyebrows shot up when he neared. "What are you doing?"

"Come closer," Mary beckoned, feeling like a temptress. "For the first time since meeting, we have privacy. I want to steal a few moments with you."

He lowered to the blankets without hesitation. "Of course, I understand." He pressed a kiss to her lips and then promptly rolled onto his back, placed his hands beneath his head and stared up at the sky. "What should we talk about?"

Talking was not exactly what Mary had in mind. Since she was not practiced in the art of seduction, she wondered if perhaps she'd be able to go through with it.

"Thomas," she began trailing a finger down the side of his face. "Talking is not at all what I had in mind."

He lifted up to sit and looked toward the carriage. "Someone could come upon us. It would be..."

Grabbing his lapels, Mary yanked him down and took his mouth with hers. He responded, intensifying the kiss, his arms circling her and bringing her against his chest.

While his mouth traveled down the side of her neck and licked a path down the center of her breasts, he inched her skirts up, and slid his hands up her leg.

Immediately her senses went on high alert, the harshness of their breathing amplified and the scent of him filled her.

"Unbutton your bodice for me." Thomas continued the delicious task of licking circles between her breasts, while his right hand mimicked the patterns on her thigh.

Thoughts evaporated as he took to her exposed breasts, suckling on one tip and then the other. Mary's head fell back, and her eyes fluttered closed.

138

Lifting up, he met her gaze. "I want to make you mine Mary. I desire you so much."

"And I you," Mary replied, her voice breathless.

Once again, he pressed his lips to hers, using both hands to lift her skirts up past her waist. The exposure brought shivers of anticipation and heat pooled between her legs. Mary gasped when Thomas rose to his knees and spread her legs apart.

Thomas lowered, disappearing from her view, blocked by the bunched-up skirts.

When his mouth covered he sex, Mary let out a gasp. "What? ... ohhh." His tongue delved down the center of her nether lips sending quivers of pleasure down her legs and up to her stomach.

When Thomas suckled the tiny nub between her legs, Mary shuddered in response. Never had she felt such sensations.

"Oh. Oh," Mary repeated, her fingers digging into the blanket as waves of pleasure overtook. She lifted her hips up into his mouth, needing more, but at the same time, she feared what would happen. This experience was nothing like the awkward fumbles with her one lover. There had only been a quick joining until he found release.

With Thomas, it was so very different. Beautifully different.

"Ah!" Mary exclaimed when Thomas circled the nub with his tongue and then flicked it up and down, sending even harder jolts through her body. "I... can't...remain..." Mary wasn't sure what she wanted to say and left the sentence unfinished.

The intrusion of his finger into her sex, whilst his mouth continued its wonderful assault, broke every resolve, and Mary lost all control. Her body shuddered in a hard release as she let out a long moan. "Oh, Thomas..."

He came over her, his handsome face hovering with a crooked smile. "Are you sure you wish this to happen?"

"Yes," Mary replied with conviction, not wishing to lose the euphoria of want and passion. "Hurry please."

When his sex pressed against hers, she took Thomas' face in her hands wanting to see every expression.

Thomas' eyes fluttered close as he thrust his thick shaft fully into her. Mary gasped at the wonderful intrusion but forced herself to keep her eyes open.

Her love was absolutely beautiful as he began to move. Lips parted, a burrow between his brows and the tight cordons on his neck tense, he was a masterpiece.

Driving in and out of her, with their mouths joined and hands exploring each other, they fought to keep control. At the same time, while chasing the culmination that would bring a wonderful release.

Mary's entire being seemed to explode, while Thomas continued driving in and out of her, his movements becoming more and more frantic. She'd given up on keeping her gaze on him, losing all focus as she floated into the air.

"Mary," Thomas called out, his body shaking with his release just as he suddenly pulled out of her and spilled onto the blanket. "I love you," he managed to say before collapsing over her.

It was a while before Thomas walked her back to the carriage. He kissed her soundly on the lips. "I will remain at the Humphries estate until I hear from you. Then I must come and speak to your father. We must marry soon."

Mary blushed. "Have I been to brazen?"

To her delight, Thomas smiled brightly. "I would have it no other way. I wish you to be brazen, carefree and explore love in every single way with me."

"Honestly darling, there was no need for your father to insist that you come see about me," her mother insisted. "I am much better now."

Mary gave her an indulgent look. "Can I then presume you are not happy to see my mother?"

Having to use a cane for balance, her mother hobbled to a chair in the parlor. "On the contrary, I am beyond delighted. Now that you've moved outside of London, I will treasure your visits."

After being there a week, her mother left the bed and was now planning to entertain. She'd invited several ladies over for tea. "You are to be my surprise guest today. The ladies will be delighted."

"And I to see them and answer all their questions about the Humphries sisters."

The real reason for teas was to exchange news and to Mary it was always interesting to hear what happened in other households. Despite it being perhaps wicked of her, she did enjoy a bit of gossip.

Her father entered the parlor and immediately his face lit up at seeing her mother. There's was a love match and a somewhat perplexing one. The austere Frederick Asher, an archeologist who visited Jamaica as part of an expedition falling for Amancia Brown, a young outgoing Jamaican woman.

Now with silver-streaked sideburns, dressed head to toe in dark colors, her father continued to be the picture of austerity. "My two beautiful women. It does my heart and soul good to see you." He walked to them and placed a kiss first on his wife's lips and then on Mary's brow.

"I see there's activity. Am I to presume there will be visitors?"

Her mother chuckled. "Yes, so go ahead and plan your hiding strategy dear."

When her father walked away, probably to the kitchen to secure food and a beverage to assist in his seclusion in the study, her mother gave Mary a pointed look. "Who is the young man who has you blushing constantly?"

"I am not blushing mother," Mary said but her face burned, so she knew it turned red.

Her mother lifted a brow. "You have never lied to me, do not start now."

"I had planned to tell you about him. His name is Thomas, he is a coachman." Mary braced for what was sure to be a negative reaction. Her mother, however, waited for her to continue with an unreadable expression.

"He is a good man, a hardworking man. Mr. Yarnsby and Vivian consider him of good character. I know he is but a coachman, but..." She blew out a breath. "Mother say something."

Finally, her mother's lips curved. "How does he treat you?"

Thoughts of what had occurred on the roadside made Mary sigh, but she could never tell her mother about it. "He is kind, respectful."

"Has the young man declared his intentions?"

"He has asked to me to marry him" Mary met her mother's eyes to see tears brimming. Her own stung with unshed tears. "I love him so mother."

"Why did he not come here to speak to your father?"

Mary cleared her throat. "I told him to wait. He is at the Humphries home. Will come when I send word. Of course."

"Then send word, make haste, we must meet him immediately."

Her mother opened her arms and Mary fell against the warm familiar embrace. "I am so happy for you darling girl."

"I am as well," Mary replied with a sniff.

"WHATEVER IS TAKING SO LONG?" Mary asked as she paced the parlor and once again looked to the doorway. "Father and Thomas have been in his study for almost an hour."

Her mother didn't seem as fazed. As a matter of fact, she was much more interested in the tray of sweets, the maid had just placed on a small table in front of her. "They are probably talking of your father's latest project. You know how he can go on."

"They are away we are waiting."

"Come sit," her mother patted the seat next to her. "Let us discuss your wedding."

Mary looked to the closed study door once again and crossed the room to where her mother sat. "I would like it to be at the Yarnsby's estate."

"What of your dress? Have you any particular styles in mind?"

Just then her father and Thomas, who looked a bit unsteady entered the room.

"Your father and I tasted his brandy collection," Thomas explained, his face a bit flushed. "It is rather large."

Her father chuckled. "An Irishman's constitution may be more amenable to whisky, but you must admit, brandy has its merits." Frederick Asher hesitated at seeing both Mary and his wife staring at him waiting for what he was to announce.

"Oh, yes well. Mary, I will allow the marriage between you and Mr. Sullivan."

"Thank you father," Mary jumped to her feet and rushed to her father. He accepted her hug and kissed her indulgently on the brow. "Now, now go on and visit. I must see about something." She caught a shiny glance before he turned away.

"I will go with you dear," her mother said accepting Thomas' help to stand.

Once alone, Thomas pulled Mary against him. The steady beat of his heart against her ear was reassuring and she wished more than anything time would fly so that she could listen to it every single night.

"I love you," he murmured.

CHAPTER SIX

Thomas trudged to the kitchen, only to be sent to sit in the adjoining dining room, to await his meal. The preparations for an upcoming family celebration had everyone in the kitchen in a tizzy. Moira, and her new staff of two, hurried to and fro, stirring, chopping and whipping food and themselves into a frenzy.

"Here you go," Lottie said plopping a plate in front of him. She lowered to a chair and let out a breath. "The new chamber maid won't last long. The girl is daft and slow." Lottie met his gaze. "Still looking glum, I see."

"I am not glum. Just tired."

Lottie huffed. "You miss Mary. We all do. I keep expecting her to walk in the door at any moment."

He did as well. However, in her last letter, Mary had informed him that her mother continued in a bad frame of mind. Because of it, Mary extended her stay. She'd not given him a specific time frame and he could not demand it. It was her mother, after-all.

"Good morning." Mrs. Yarnsby waltzed into the room, a soft smile on her face. "Thomas, I was looking for you. Go to the seamstress at the village and purchase at least two suits on our account. She has some readymade, just ensure they are tailored for you. With your new responsibilities as steward, you must dress the part."

"Of course, Ma'am." Thomas wanted to ask if she'd heard from Mary, but felt it was not his place to inquire into his employer's correspondence.

"I am hopeful Mary will return in time for the festivities. She's always enjoyed them tremendously." She waved her hand in the air as if not worried. "My parents and sister will be coming, so I am sure she will return with them."

He wanted to grin but managed to keep a straight face. "I hope so as well, Ma'am."

After a soft smile, the woman walked out, seeming to be considering something he was not privy to.

When he took his empty dishes into the kitchen, Moira turned to him and shook her head. "They were supposed to get the dishes," she gave the new kitchen maids a stern look, which they seemed to not notice.

Moira sighed. "The household is growing, and I am not sure to be prepared for it." She motioned with her head to two women and shook her head. "Here is the list of things to retrieve from the market, Thomas," she added, handing him a piece of brown paper.

IT WAS late in the day by the time he'd returned to the estate from the village. Thankfully, the seamstress had a suit that fit almost perfectly, the other two had to be adjusted. He hung the suit in his room and then went to the kitchen.

His heart leapt at seeing Mary sitting at the table speaking with Moira. Her cheeks colored upon seeing him, and he had to keep from rushing to her.

"When did you arrive?" He asked.

"Just a few moments ago. I was famished, so I hurried in here," Mary said giving him a warm smile.

Moira and Lottie pretended to be busy by the stove as he neared and placed a soft kiss to her lips. "I missed you," he whispered into her ear.

"And I you," Mary replied her gaze meeting his and lowering to his lips.

Thomas had to swallow to keep from touching her. "How is your mother?"

"She and father are here, they returned to Berkhamsted with me," Mary informed. "Both are resting now, upstairs."

"The house is going to be full, tomorrow," Moira exclaimed.

"Who else is here?" Thomas asked.

"The Humphries, Mr. and Mrs. Humphries and Miss Penelope, as well as her cousin Miss Edna," Mary informed him.

Then she smiled broadly. "I am so very happy to be back with you," she met his gaze and then looked to Moira, "You and Lottie as well."

"Don't forget Harold," Moira added, with a chuckle.

"Of course."

A thought crossed Thomas' mind. "Mary?"

She turned to him and he lost his ability to think straight. She was so utterly beautiful. How was it possible for her to accept him as husband? "We could get married while everyone is here."

"What a grand idea." A younger version of Mrs. Yarnsby strolled in. Her face bright. "Hello Thomas, I'm Penelope Humphries." She held her hand out, and he shook it.

"Very nice to meet you Miss Humphries."

"A wedding, how very exciting, I must tell Vivian at once." She flew from the room. Mary gave him a quizzical look and then hurried after her.

Moira motioned for him to sit. "May as well eat. Now you've done it. You're getting married within a day or two at the most."

THE WEDDING WAS SET for the following day.

THE DAY FLEW by as everyone prepared the house and food for the celebration. They were to entertain the Duke and Lady of Barrow as well as, Lord and Lady Torrington, Mr. Yarnsby's adopted parents.

Thomas kept busy with his new duties. New staff had been hired and he'd spent most of the day at the stables and the corral with a new driver and another man who was to take over care of the horses.

It had been announced that the Yarnsby's were to move soon, closer to Lark's Song and the estate was to be used for hospitality.

Apparently Mr. Yarnsby and Lord Torrington had been working on the plan for several months. With Mary's travel to London, she'd been informed of the upcoming move just the day before and was thrilled at the prospect.

Standing near the corrals, he turned to the estate and studied the grand home. In truth, it was much too large for a single-family and he understood the Yarnsby's wishing to be closer to family.

When Mary appeared through the kitchen door and looked over, her face softening at spotting him, he waved to her.

She walked to him and he didn't move, content to study his soon to be wife as she neared. Mary had a way about her that made one take notice. She was lovely.

"You seem deep in thought," she said, accepting a kiss to her cheek. "I hope you're not troubled about anything."

He shook his head. "Considering we will be married tomorrow and that I will be moving into your bedchamber is giving me pause. What will happen when we relocate?"

Pursing her lips, she studied him for a moment. "Mr. Yarnsby has already promised us a charming cottage. I am so excited about you overseeing the construction of it." She clapped her hands over her chest. "It will have to be perfect."

"It will not be our land, or our home. If anything were to happen, we could be tossed out without any recourse."

He hated to dampen her happiness, but it was true. Only a landowner could be secure in where he lived.

"That would never happen," Mary said giving him an incredulous look. "Why would you think Vivian would ever send me away?"

When he reached to touch her arm, she leaned away, and he met her gaze. "I know she would not. However, futures are not guaranteed."

"How about we go forward as planned. Let us offer to purchase land from Mr. Yarnsby and build on that. Would that sooth your worries?" Mary studied him waiting for his reply.

There wasn't any doubt that because of the high regard the family had for Mary, they would not hesitate to offer the land free of charge. He would not accept the terms and insist on paying for it. It was more than he could have ever hoped for, land of his own. The thought of owning land and his own home filled him with anticipation and pride.

"Very well. Once our wedding day and all the celebrations are over, I will speak to Mr. Yarnsby. Don't you dare speak to him first."

It was obvious by the way she looked to the side it was exactly what she'd planned to do. "Very... well," she replied, with hesitation.

Mary placed a hand on the center of his chest. "I am so

fortunate to have met you Thomas. I cannot wait to be your wife and spend the rest of our lives together."

The way she looked up at him made Thomas feel as if he could move mountains with his bare hands. Never before had a woman looked at him the way she did. Perhaps there had been adoring looks, but none had brought out the response in him like Mary did.

"Thomas," Harold walked toward them with a rope in one hand. "Where should we put the new horses?"

Mr. Yarnsby had purchased a team of very expensive horses, which were to be housed in a not yet built larger stable.

Thomas blew out a breath. "Since this is being done backwards, we will have to leave some of the other horses in the corral overnight."

"Good thing the weather's warmer," Harold replied with a chuckle. "I do believe our employer is overly excited about his new venture."

"I best let you go. I have much to do myself," Mary said and pressed a kiss to his cheek. She went to Harold and gave him a stern look. "Ensure you do not overstress yourself. Moira will be very cross with you if you don't dance with her tomorrow."

Harold chuckled, his cheeks coloring. "I will do my best to allow the younger men to do all the heavy work."

Along with the older man, Thomas walked to where men had arrived with the horses. The animals were beautiful and quite restless. It took time to get them brushed down, watered, fed and in stalls. Later that day, the animals would be loosed into a corral until the night.

One of the newly hired stable men led one of the horses into the stable. Thomas looked on as the man brushed the animal down. The man looked up, meeting his gaze. "Who is that dark woman to you?"

Thomas did his best to keep a flat expression. "Why do you ask?"

The man shrugged. "Looks different. Seems strange that she's allowed so much liberty."

"Measure your words."

Unperturbed, the idiot continued undeterred. "I'm sure you agree with me that no one wants her kind about."

"She's the mistresses' companion and close friend..." Thomas started closing the distance between them until they were nose to nose. "She will be my wife tomorrow."

The man's eyes widened as he realized the huge mistake he'd made during his first week of employment. "I didn't mean..."

"Pack your belongings. I will see about what you're owed. It won't be much."

"Sir, please. I need this job, I have a wife..."

Thomas could barely keep from slamming his fist into the man's face. "I am sorry for your wife, to have a man like you for a husband."

"Thomas?" Harold entered the stables looking from one to the other.

The imbecile turned away to appeal to the older man. "Thomas is firing me. Does he have the authority to do so? I said something, I didn't mean anything by it, I swear."

"What did you say?" Harold said pinning the man with a hard look.

The man looked to the ground. "Just asking about the dark-skinned woman. Why she was about."

"I agree with Thomas. Your services are no longer required." Harold looked to Thomas. "The men who delivered the horses need to be paid. They are about to go to the village to find a bed for the night."

Harold usually handled the payments and ensured anyone who came to the estate was given a small meal before going on their way. Obviously, he wanted Thomas to go and not end up in a fight the day before his wedding.

Moment later, his ire must have still been evident because

while the men, who'd brought the horses, ate, Moira pulled him aside. "What happened?"

Having to repeat the idiot's words made him angrier, but he managed it.

Moira rolled her eyes and huffed. "Do not allow an imbecile like that to ruin things for you. Mary is a beautiful and kind woman. There will be other times when you will face judgement because of the color of her skin. I am not saying to get used to it, but to accept that it will happen."

"I am not sure how to react, other than to get angry and defend her."

Moira sighed and nodded. "There is no better reaction than to love your wife and show judgmental people their opinions don't matter at all."

"This is the first of many, I suppose."

"Yes it is. Local people will come to know her and become aware that she is considered part of the family. They will think twice before insulting her, because it would mean losing access to the most prominent families in the area."

THE NEXT DAY came and Thomas was much too busy to consider it was his wedding day. Mary was conspicuously absent, which he was a bit thankful for as he didn't have time for the distraction her presence brought.

As the visitors arrived, the newly hired coachmen took their carriages away to where the stable workers would handle the care of the horses. Everything went smoothly, and Thomas had to admit, he enjoyed the duties as steward.

He peered out from his position by the door noting there were no carriages on the horizon. Mentally, he went over who was yet to arrive, noting only one set of people had not come.

In the large parlor, everyone mingled, the voices loud and

merry, most excited at the prospect of spending an evening at the estate. The invitation to remain had been done purposefully by the Yarnsby's, so that the guests could properly recommend it to their extended connections in London.

"How are you doing Thomas?" Lottie, dressed in her new starched black and white frock, came to stand next to him. "Isn't this exciting?"

Like him, she'd also been promoted. Lottie was now the housekeeper. Lottie, along with Moira and Harold, had all decided they'd remain behind at the estate. Moira as head cook and Harold as the estate's steward.

"The last of the guests arrive," Lottie said looking into the horizon.

Thomas nodded and took a breath. In just a few hours, he and Mary would be married. Every guest in attendance a witness to their declarations of love.

"MY WEDDING IS FAR TOO LARGE," Mary complained as her mother fussed with her hair. "This is really uncalled for. I am part of the staff." She batted her mother's hands away.

Penelope grinned at her. "I think the family deserves a large wedding since my sisters cheated all of us out of one."

Both Clara and Vivian had impromptu weddings, which although lovely, had been last minute and with only minimal attendance.

Of course, Mary loved to be considered part of the family and that they included her and Thomas' marriage as part of the planned event. The sisters had all insisted she had to have a beautiful wedding. Nonetheless, Mary wasn't sure what kind of impression it would make on the guests.

Mrs. Humphries entered the room and immediately hugged her. "This is all so wonderful. I am so blessed to see all of you get married. You look absolutely beautiful, Mary." She wiped at tears daintily with her handkerchief.

Mrs. Humphries then whirled to Penelope. "You will also have a large wedding. No last-minute dash for you, young lady."

"I agree," Mary said with a grin. "Yours should be the grandest of all."

Penelope grinned and whirled, arms outstretched. "Of course, mother, Tommy and I will have the grandest wedding of the year." She stopped and frowned. "Once he proposes, that is."

As always, there was an awkward silence at the mention of Penelope's childhood friend who showed no interest in her, past a friendship.

"I so love the bride's dressing ritual," Lady Barrow entered the room with Lady Torrington, both neared and looked over Mary.

"You look radiant darling," Lady Torrington said, and then picked up a mirror and held it up for Mary to look at herself.

Barely able to recognize herself in the reflection. Bright eyes looked back at her and Mary was struck speechless and then tears spilled down her cheeks. "I am the most fortunate girl in the world."

"D-don't cry," Vivian said with sniff. "Y-you'll make me start crying."

"Stop at once," her mother's strong accent made Mary sit up straighter and sniff one last time. "This is a joyous occasion, is it not?" Everyone nodded. "Very well."

She took in the room. "Indeed, my daughter is very blessed to be surrounded by all of you. I am grateful for how you've accepted her into your family with so much love."

"I believe there is a wedding to get to," Lady Barrow said, a tell-tale tinge of red on the tip of her nose. "We are all blessed to be part of the Humphries' family."

On the first floor, the murmuring of voices ceased when Mary began her descent down the stairwell. Her heart hammered wildly at the sea of faces looking up to her. Everyone seemed enthralled, following her movements.

Of course, some were there to attest to the fact that the estate would be a perfect place to have a wedding and host guests at the same time, but still, the moment was more than magical.

When she reached the bottom step, her father took her hand and weaved it through his arm. He pressed a kiss to her temple. "You are the most beautiful bride, aside from your mother, that I've ever had the privilege of seeing."

Mary inhaled to keep from openly weeping and kept her gaze forward to where Father Matthews and Thomas stood.

Next to Thomas, who looked so very handsome, stood Harold, who was to be the best man. She'd chosen Vivian to be her maid of honor, however, she was quickly joined by her sisters, and all three took their places on the priest's opposite side.

She had to smile at the three having appointed themselves a trio of maids, for she'd not have it any other way.

As Mary stood next to the love of her life, she repeated the vows and focused on Thomas. At looking up into his eyes, the entire room disappeared and except for Father Matthews' words that they repeated, nothing else existed.

Upon kissing to seal their marriage vows, the room erupted into applause. When they turned to face the room, maids and valets appeared with flutes of champagne so that everyone could toast their nuptials.

The rest of the evening, although magical, had very little to do with them. Thomas and Mary sat at a table to the side of the room, while Duke and Lady Torrington along with the Yarnsby's sat at the head table entertaining the guests.

A harpist and flutist played beautiful songs that Mary committed to memory. The Humphries were well aware of her favorites and the player ensured to play them. It was a beautiful evening and soon Mary could not keep from yawning.

She leaned into Thomas' ear. "I am so glad the focus is not on us so we can escape soon."

"I was thinking the same." He squeezed her hand, the intimate touch as he slid his fingers up the back of it to her forearm sent chills of anticipation up her arm.

A waltz began and they were encouraged to dance. Mary an accomplished dancer, as she'd attended classes with Vivian, worried about Thomas.

However, much to her surprise and elation of those in attendance, he guided her around the room with ease. Soon they were joined by the other couples, the room filling with music and chatter as everyone glided in circles a display of colorful skirts moving in sync.

It was not much later that Thomas guided them to the bottom of the stairs, then taking her hand, pulled her forward. They hurried the rest of the way and escaped to begin a future that Mary knew would be utterly wonderful.

CHAPTER SEVEN

Her bedroom seemed too virginal, Mary thought as they crossed the threshold into it. Thomas didn't glance anywhere, his attention solely on her. Shivers traveled through her, sudden nervousness taking hold. They'd been intimate just once before, however, this felt like the first time. In truth, it was the first time as husband and wife.

All memories of their time on the road to London, dimmed and Mary could barely keep from allowing the weakness in her knees to take over.

"I am very nervous," she admitted. "Thomas, what if you..."

He kissed Mary, quieting all her doubts especially when he intensified the kiss. The strength and hardness of his chest were so very comforting when he pulled her against it.

His mouth never left hers, Thomas continued pressing kisses across her lips. To her delight his tongue pushed against her mouth, requesting permission and she parted her lips, glad to take it in.

After she wrapped her arms around his neck, she lifted to her toes so to fit better against him. A deep moan seared her senses, the handsome man was all hers to have from that day forward and yet this moment, this one evening, she wanted to freeze in time.

Thomas worked with deft fingers to unfasten the long string of buttons down her back, allowing the cool air to caress her overheated skin.

As the folds of fabric flowed from her shoulders to her waist until finally sliding to a satiny heap around her feet, Thomas touched her skin with featherlike caresses.

She shook with want and still could not bring herself to break the kiss, needing to taste him and capture it forever.

When he broke the kiss and stepped back to remove his coat, she focused solely on him. The sight of his body exposed with each layer of clothing Thomas removed, stole any thought of awkwardness.

He was stunning, broad-shouldered, well-formed wide chest with a flat stomach. His legs were muscular and long, and his sex, most definitely expressing his arousal.

"Goodness," Mary exclaimed turning away and pressing both hands to her cheeks. "I didn't mean to stare."

Thomas came up behind her. "I don't mind. We are to be lovers for the rest of our lives and should be familiar with each other's bodies."

When he turned her back to face him, she smiled up at him. "You are very pleasing to look upon."

"Thank you," Thomas gave her a crooked grin. "I assure you to never tire at seeing you bereft of clothing either."

He lifted her up into his arms and walked to the bed. A bed that seemed much too small for the both of them. Thomas didn't seem to mind, placing her down and then climbing in next to her.

After pulling her into his arms, once again, he took her mouth. Mary responded to the kiss thoroughly loving the feel of their skin touching. The longer they kissed the harder she pressed against him. Thomas lifted her left leg over his hip pulling her forward, so that their sexes aligned.

The movement of his hips causing their bodies to rub together brought her to dizzying heights. At the same time, every inch of her body grew hotter as the friction of his staff against her sex continued.

"Oh Thomas, please," she pleaded, needing him to take her fully. The sense of losing control just beyond reach became maddening.

When he reached between them and guided himself to her entrance, she could've cried with joy.

With one quick thrust Thomas entered her and then stilled as the action made Mary gasp loudly.

"Move," Mary demanded. "Hurry."

His chuckle did nothing to keep her from pulling at his thigh. "Thomas, I mean it."

The next plunge was hard, filling her completely, then he withdrew and dove in again and again.

As her climax neared, Mary grabbed Thomas' face and brought his mouth to hers. She kissed him with fervor, needing more contact as her body began to shudder. At the sensation of losing control, she trailed her mouth to his throat and bit at the soft flesh gently.

He continued driving and withdrawing, his movements harder and faster until they were both drenched in sweat. The slickness of their bodies only added to the wonderful joining experience.

"Let go beauty," Thomas urged.

At the words, Mary's sex tightened around his staff and she cried out as her release came so hard, she could barely keep from fainting.

Her husband continued his quest. He rolled her onto her back, lifted her hips with both hands and continued to drive. His movements harder and with less control.

Once again, Mary's body responded seeking release. This time she wasn't sure to survive so many sensations.

"Oh. Oh. Oh," she repeated over and over as heat pooled in her core threatening to consume.

And then, everything burst into hundreds of pieces. Mary lost the ability to comprehend what exactly happened. Everything turned into bright bursts of color that exploded one after the other. Her muffled cries were joined by Thomas', deeper huskier ones as he finally allowed himself release.

"MARY." Thomas' voice permeated through the wonderful fog that surrounded her. She wasn't ready to open her eyes.

"Mmm?"

Thomas shook her. "How do you feel?"

"Absolutely wonderful," Mary said opening her eyes. "Will it be like that always?"

He grinned. "I hope so." Pressing a kiss to her lips, he whispered a soft "I love you," and then rolled to his side pulling her against him.

"I am not in the least bit sleepy now," Mary insisted and then attempted to hide a yawn.

"Me either."

THE HOUSE WAS alive with activity as Mary entered one of two dining rooms where she was to meet the women for breakfast the next morning.

It had been decided to separate the women and men for morning meals to test how everyone would like it. The room was abuzz as soon as she entered, everyone telling her how wonderful the wedding had been.

Although Mary and Thomas were to go away for a few days to spend time in one of the cottages on the estate, both had insisted on remaining in the house until after the guests left. For one thing, Mary wasn't entirely sure she could stand missing everything that happened.

Then, there was the fact of her parents, and the Humphries visited from London. They'd all agreed to remain for the rest of the week and would be leaving in four days, which gave her plenty of time to spend with each of them.

Once everyone headed home, she'd be able to delight in long lazy days with Thomas in the cottage.

"I can't wait to have my own wedding night," Penelope whispered. "I am sure it will leave me glowing like you."

Mary's eyes widened. "What do you mean?"

"You are absolutely luminous," said Penelope, who had a penchant for using flowery words proclaimed. "Every inch of your face radiates with love."

"Goodness, you make it sound almost unnatural," Mary replied and then smiled. "I must admit to feeling as if I am floating."

Vivian leaned closer. "As well you should." She patted her hand. "Eat. If Thomas is anything like Alexander, you will not have a reprieve for many nights to come."

The three giggled until Mrs. Humphries gave them a pointed look.

"Perhaps you could share what you find so comical," Lady Barrows said, looking around to the nodding heads. "What has you three, so entertained?"

Mary exchanged alarmed looks with Penelope and Vivian. It was Vivian, always the level-headed one, and quick to think, who replied. "We were sharing antidotes of when young and the mischief we often got ourselves into."

It was then Penelope piped in. "We once snuck into a ball at your house, Lady Barrow. We went upstairs so that we could peer down from the alcove. We were discovered by that dreadful Mrs. Goathead, who pinched our ears and made us stay in the library for hours."

"Her name was Mrs. Bankhead, and I was glad she often caught you girls and kept you out of trouble," Lady Barrow replied with a chuckle. "I wonder if it was all your mischief that finally drove her away."

Both Lady Barrow and Mrs. Humphries told of other adventures they'd had as children, which thankfully drew attention away from what they'd actually been talking about.

The rest of the day was filled with card games, an excursion to the village, and time in the parlor where the guests mingled and nibbled on appetizers.

Late that night, only a couple of guests still remained in the sitting room, but most had gone to bed.

It was past midnight that Mary finally trudged to the bedroom. After using a cloth and water from the basin to wash up, she slid on her nightgown. Unsure how long it would be before Thomas joined her, she settled into a chair with her journal.

The candlelight dance across her paper as she noted her thoughts. Lips curving, she did her best to describe the wedding just as the door opened.

Thomas entered and neared to press a kiss to her lips. "It was a long day," he said. "You shouldn't have waited up for me."

Mary bit her bottom lip. Was Thomas not to be like Mr. Yarnsby and not seek her in bed that night?

"We've barely spoken today. I wished to see you alone..." she gave up and stood. "You're right, I should let you rest."

Thomas took her shoulders and gave her a playful look. "I will rest, but not until after I thoroughly ravish my beautiful wife."

MARY WAS INTRIGUED that each time they made love, it was so very different. She wondered if the lovemaking would depend on their mood.

This time, they took turns, overtaking one another. Thomas taught her how to be in control, to come over him and take him. Although a bit tentative at first, the exciting sensation soon removed her inhibitions.

Much later as they lay on the bed, she with her leg across his midsection and head on his shoulder, Mary listened to his even breathing.

He barely moved when she rose up and straightened his arm. Then she pulled the blankets over them and nestled against his warmth.

THREE MONTHS LATER...

The sound of birdsong alerted Mary it was time to rise. The sun was not quite up over the horizon yet as she finished dressing and hurried into their small kitchen. Thomas, who looked to have been up for a while, was fully dressed and sat at the table drinking tea.

In the mornings, they ate breakfast at the main house every day. The new cook was wonderful. To everyone's delight, she'd trained with the Humphries' cook in London, so was familiar with the family favorites.

"We are spoiled," Mary said, nearing and kissing Thomas on the jaw. "To not have to cook our meals before our duties begin."

Thomas nodded. "I agree." His warm gaze moving over her. "If I recall, you and Mrs. Yarnsby will be gone most of the day today."

A large group had booked the estate for a family gathering

and Vivian insisted on attending at least one event to ensure everyone felt welcome.

So far, the venture was turning out quite well, the staff at the estate barely having time to clean and organize everything before the next group arrived.

"I look forward to going, although it is a family who thrives on melodrama," Mary said with a chuckle. "Be prepared for entertaining stories upon my return."

Just as they were to head out, they spotted a small carriage arriving. Mary immediately recognized the Yarnsby emblem on the door and knew who it was.

Lady Yarnsby.

It was a rare visit since Mr. Yarnsby's mother, preferred her pampered life in the city. The entire time she visited, the woman spent most of her time complaining of boredom.

"There may be a change in plans," Thomas said in a dry tone. "Lady Yarnsby must have left in the dark to have arrived this early.

"If I know her, she probably left from a ball and is still in her cups. Hurry," Mary tugged his arm and they raced to the back entrance of the main house.

"Fix a basket of food for Mrs. Yarnsby and myself, we must leave at once," Mary called out as she hurried past the startled kitchen staff up the stairs and rapped on Vivian and Alexander's bedroom door."

"What's the matter?" Alexander opened the door and she had to look away as he was shirtless. "Your mother is here."

"Oh no," Vivian exclaimed from inside. "Alexander, you must find a way to keep her busy until I can escape."

Mr. Yarnsby gave Mary a bored look. "Is this necessary? I am sure she will insist on promptly going to bed."

"Please," Vivian said taking Mary's hand and yanking her inside while managing to throw a robe at her husband.

When he staggered away sleepily, both she and Vivian began

giggling. "Help me dress. Did you ask Thomas to prepare a carriage?"

"Yes, of course. Also asked for a basket of food to be prepared."

Within minutes, they hurried out to the top of the stairs, where they stopped and listened. Below, Mr. Yarnsby guided his mother to the small sitting room to give them an opportunity to make it to the kitchen without being seen.

They hurried past the doorway and into the kitchen, where the cook gave them a questioning look.

"There's ham, bread and..."

"Thank you so much, Mrs. Smith," Mary interrupted, grabbing the basket. Together she and Vivian went out to find a carriage ready for them. Thomas stood by the door, holding it open with a resigned look.

"Don't look at us like that," Vivian said. "Alexander's mother would have insisted on coming to the estate, which would be disastrous."

It was obvious he tried to keep from chuckling. "Understood, Ma'am," he said with a stern expression.

"Are you taking us?" Mary asked. "I didn't expect you to."

"No one else is awake," he answered and took the basket of food. "In you go."

As the carriage jolted forward and they were on their way, Vivian elbowed Mary. "Where is our breakfast?"

"Thomas took it."

"I suppose we didn't give him an opportunity to eat," Vivian said.

"That does not excuse him taking our food," Mary complained. "I'm hungry." She knocked on the roof and stuck her head out the window. "You forgot to give us our basket."

"I will give it back to you when we stop to rest."

Mary sat back down. "I think we will have to wait until getting there to eat."

"No matter," Vivian answered. "I'd much rather starve, than spend the day keeping my mother-in-law from bragging to the guests, about a son she didn't have a hand in raising. She'll also insist on being the center of attention."

Once again Mary stuck her head out the window. "Mrs. Yarnsby insists you return the basket."

"No, she doesn't," Thomas replied.

Vivian giggled.

"He is being insubordinate. I am so very embarrassed. Please do not fire him." Mary snapped.

Vivian pulled out a bundle and opened it. In it were ham and bread. "Mrs. Smith gave me this for Thomas. I suppose we will have to share it."

Mary stuck her head out of the window again. "We are going to eat your breakfast."

"I am eating yours, which I'm sure is much better," he called back.

"The nerve of him," Mary said with a huff.

"He's the perfect match for you," Vivian replied. "I like him very much."

THAT NIGHT MARY joined the staff for dinner since the Yarnsby's had gone to the Torrington's for a family meal. Mary was glad for the reprieve, but she felt sorry for Vivian, who had to spend the evening and next day with Lady Yarnsby.

"I'm glad to see you enjoyed my stew," Mrs. Smith said with a bright smile. "Help yourself to a third helping. A woman in your condition should eat well."

Mary laughed. "Do you mean tired and hungry all day, because her husband ate her breakfast?"

Mrs. Smith gave Thomas a pointed look. "You should ensure

Mary eats regularly. You don't want the child to be compromised in any way."

"What child?" both Mary and Thomas asked.

"How can you not know?" Mrs. Smith gave Mary an incredulous look. "You are with child. The last weeks, you've barely eaten, had an upset stomach all the time, and now you are eating as if famished."

Mary blinked and looked at Thomas, whose eyes were wide like saucers.

"I have felt rather oddly," she finally admitted mentally calculating the last time she'd run her courses. "It's been a long time since..." she left the words hanging, her mouth falling open.

"Oh, my goodness," Mrs. Smith said with a smile. "You certainly are with child."

A huge grin split Thomas' face and he lifted her hand to his lips. "I can't believe it." He pressed a kiss to the back of her hand while Mary was torn between wanting to cry or laugh.

So then, she did both.

ABOUT THE AUTHOR

Enticing. Engaging. Romance.

USA Today Bestselling Author Hildie McQueen writes Medieval Scottish Romance, Regency, and American Historical Romance. If you like stories with a mixture of passion, drama and humor, you will love Hildie's storytelling. Strong alpha heroes meet their match and fall in love every time in Hildie's books.

A fan of all things pink, Paris, and four legged creatures, Hildie resides in eastern Georgia, USA, with her super-hero husband Kurt and three little yappy dogs.

Visit her website at www.hildiemcqueen.com

ONE NIGHT ONLY

ELISE MARION

Thalia Ramsey has resigned herself to a quiet life running a respectable book shop in London's West End. Nothing exciting ever happens in her world...until Stephen Dryden, His Grace the Duke of Westerfield, begins patronizing her establishment. Her girlish infatuation is completely ridiculous, and nothing will ever come of it. Yet, a heart's hope is not so easily broken, especially when a chance encounter during a Vauxhall Gardens masquerade brings Thalia face-to-face with the duke.

A night of passionate romance is more than she could have hoped for, but once the night is over, will there be a chance for more?

CHAPTER ONE

LONDON, 1817

Thalia squinted through the dust mites floating on the brightly-lit air, raising up on tiptoe to reach the shelf nearly a foot over her head. The step-stool adding a few inches to her height wobbled, making her heart lurch into her throat. She tightened one hand around the heavy book waiting to be shelved, and the other on the edge of a shelf, regaining her precarious balance.

Where was her assistant when she needed him? Joseph Hyde stood an impressive five feet and ten inches, and could reach every shelf without trouble. Thalia could shelve and procure books with her stool, but only with a great deal of effort for the top shelves—something she wasn't forced to do when Joseph was about. With a decidedly un-ladylike grunt, she heaved the book onto the shelf, one leg kicking out like a ballerina as she gave it a little shove, wedging it between two others.

Thalia's grin of satisfaction lasted until she tried to step down, her foot catching in the hem of her skirts. Arms wheeling, Thalia went backward with a startled yelp, her back hitting the shelves opposite before she slumped in a graceless heap on the floor.

"Bloody hell," she muttered, swiping a dark, loose coil of hair out of her eyes.

"Tsk, tsk, Miss Ramsey," chided a deep, masculine voice from the top of the aisle.

Humiliation heated Thalia's face as she glanced up to discover the last person she would have wanted to catch her in such a position. His Grace Stephen Dryden, Duke of Wester-field, stood before her, an amused grin curving the corners of his sumptuous mouth. Thalia's ribs constricted around her lungs, robbing her of breath at the sight of one of her most dedicated customers. As well, he was the one man who made her heart flutter madly in her chest and her stomach turn wild somersaults.

The duke was immaculately dressed, a bottle-green coat and stark white cravat accentuating the burnished bronze hue of his skin—which he had inherited from an Indian mother. His hair was as black as pitch, gleaming in the sunlight filtering through the large front windows. At first glance his eyes appeared just as black, but when one stood close enough, shades of amber and cognac could be found within the prisms of soft brown eyes fringed by heavy, sooty lashes. Not that Thalia had been close to the man very often. There had only been the one time—as she'd opened a particular book to display the lovely frontispiece—only for His Grace to lean in to study it. The light had touched his eyes in the exact right spot to display the variegated hues, and the circulating spring air coming through the open door had sent the scents of sandalwood and bergamot up her nostrils.

There was no spring breeze today, and her door was closed against the humidity of a summer afternoon. Adding insult to injury, she was heaped on the floor like a rag doll, her skirts hiked up to bare her calves. One of her slippers had fallen off and her fichu was knocked askew, displaying far more skin than was appropriate.

"Your Grace!" Thalia exclaimed, pushing down her skirts and righting her fichu—both of which seemed of more importance than her foul language or her position on the floor. "I beg your pardon, I ... took a little tumble, but ..."

Her stammering trailed off as Westerfield approached, crouching along the way to retrieve her slipper. "Think nothing of it, Miss Ramsey. Are you hurt?"

Thalia's tongue refused to move, her mouth gaping like that of a fish out of water as she stared at the duke, experiencing the heady fragrance of him—both woodsy and citrusy at once. "N-No," she managed. "Only my pride has been injured."

The duke chuckled, gently retrieving her foot and replacing her slipper. Thalia's skin came alive with gooseflesh and shivers, and a dozen other sensations she could not name. All too soon, his hand was gone, leaving her bereft.

"Well, thank goodness no one was here to witness it," he murmured.

"Except you," she pointed out as he offered her a hand up.

"Except for me," he agreed. "And I swear upon my honor that I will never breathe a word to anyone."

As if anyone who ran in the same lofty circles as a duke would care about a nobody bookshop owner who had fallen off a stool. Yet, there was no teasing in Westerfield's voice or on his face—only an earnestness she found as charming as his smiles.

Clearing her throat, Thalia smoothed both hands over her skirts and then adjusted her spectacles. "I had not expected to see you today," she remarked, while resuming her place behind the polished oak counter.

Instead of moving on to peruse the shelves, the duke followed, casually leaning against the edge of the counter. "Really? Why is that?"

Thalia busied herself tidying her surroundings—even

though the remaining books to be shelved were already efficiently sorted and stacked. She needed to do something with her hands to keep from making a cake of herself. "The Vauxhall masquerade is tonight. I would have thought you'd be too busy preparing for it to visit today."

"It is Saturday, is it not?" he said, shrugging one shoulder. "Besides, there is very little for a man to do in preparation for a masquerade. At least, in comparison to the efforts of a lady."

"Especially when said man is a duke with a valet at his disposal," Thalia said.

Westerfield laughed, and the sound warmed Thalia's belly. "Miss Ramsey, are you teasing me?"

Her throat clenched as she realized she might have gone too far, even given their cordial and amiable acquaintance. The man visited her shop every Saturday and was always friendly. But he was still a duke, which placed him so far above her in the social hierarchy that he might as well live in the clouds.

"I beg your pardon, Your Grace," she mumbled, lowering her eyes.

The duke leaned in over the counter, drawing her gaze to one of his winning smiles. "Please, don't beg my pardon. Everyone is too afraid of a duke to tease him properly. I quite enjoy it."

Thalia couldn't help returning his smile, though she was certain hers was nauseatingly simpering, showing her infatuation. "Very well. Then I suppose I ought to ask why a man of your importance makes use of only one valet. I would have assumed you had at least two."

The duke gave her a look that said 'that's the spirit,' before replying. "In truth, Miss Ramsey, I do not have only one valet, or two. No self-respecting duke would go about life with any less than six."

"Please tell me one of them is solely responsible for getting Your Royal Dukeness into his stockings."

A twinkle of humor sparked in his eyes. "But of course. The ducal feet are very important, and all."

They laughed together, his deep baritone combining with her giggle like the strike of drum beneath stringed instruments. Harmony. Perfection.

No.

She couldn't allow herself to grow fanciful, not even when she was alone, but especially when in Westerfield's presence. It wouldn't do for her to delude herself into thinking the man had any interest in her. He was simply easygoing and companionable—the complete opposite of what she expected a duke to be. The thought of a duke conjured the image of a stodgy old man with fuzzy gray side-whiskers and perhaps a portly belly. Tall, strong, and devilishly handsome did not fit into the equation, unless that duke happened to be Westerfield.

However, no matter how handsome or charming he was, Thalia couldn't forget that he was as far out of her reach as the moon was from the sun. If she wasn't careful, she'd find herself chasing him across the sky, endlessly longing for what she could never have.

"What can I do for you today, Your Grace?" she said, adopting her most placid, professional tones. "Have you finished with *Sense and Sensibility* already?"

"I positively devoured it. The author is a most gifted lady."

Thalia pressed her lips together to contain a smile. The duke was not so full of himself that he shunned the enjoyment of novels as many other men did. Westerfield was a voracious reader who delighted in everything from poetry, philosophy and fiction, to science, botany and farming. The latter seemed wise, as he was responsible for one of the largest holdings in the realm, along with several smaller estates. It delighted her to know that he did not shun the work of the author of some of Thalia's favorite books. The anonymous pseudonym, 'A Lady,' graced the title pages of such works as *Sense and Sensibility*, and

Emma. While many of her male patrons scoffed at the mere mention of 'A Lady,' Westerfield had shown an interest in the novels, and Thalia had been happy to present him with a new, pristine copy of *Sense and Sensibility* a few weeks ago.

"I am glad you enjoyed it," she said, skimming her fingers down the stack of books at her side. "If you would like to explore more of A Lady's works, I recommend Mansfield Park. I found it rather diverting. And ... it appears as I only have one copy left. I was just about to place it on the shelf."

"There is no need," he insisted. "I'll take it. As well, I had wondered if you have any copies of *Robinson Crusoe?* My own was irreparably damaged and I need a replacement."

Biting her lip, Thalia gazed down one of the aisles, mentally thumbing through the contents of the shelves. "I believe I do ... if you would give me a moment to search, Your Grace."

"Of course."

Thalia used the time it took to retrieve the book to take a few deep breaths and calm her overwrought nerves. She could do this. She could wrap the duke's purchases and send him off with a cheerful farewell before returning to her mundane life. Oh, Thalia was happy enough and more fortunate than most women like herself. She was lucky that her father's improved circumstances had offered her a life of genteel comfort, if not outright luxury. They hadn't had riches or lofty titles, but they'd been a family—him, her mother, Thalia, and her little sister Theodosia. Ramsey's Books had been left in Thalia's hands, ensuring she would have the means to care for herself and those who depended on her. If there was a lack of excitement in her life, it seemed a small price to pay for security and a full belly. Many women living in London with her dark skin and African features were relegated to deep poverty, most selling their bodies for lack of other means of making money.

It was wrong for her to be ungrateful and long for more.

Thalia told herself this over and over as she located the duke's requested book and walked it back to the front of the shop.

"You are in luck," she told him, lifting the copy of *Robinson Crusoe*.

"Excellent. You are a godsend, Miss Ramsey."

Despite his flattery, Thalia managed to keep a straight face as she began bundling both books together in shop paper and twine.

"Will you attend Vauxhall this evening, Miss Ramsey?"

"Oh, goodness ... I hadn't planned to ... that is ..."

"Whyever not? I hear there are to be fireworks and a hot air balloon ascent. I am not one for stuffy soirées held in ballrooms, but never miss an evening at Vauxhall."

In truth, the event that was being hailed as the grandest of the summer sounded like a wonderful time. People from all walks of life were excited to enjoy the gardens and the fine weather, especially after the dreary Year Without a Summer.

"I must confess to never having visited Vauxhall at night," she said, while snipping at the twine and arranging a perfect bow. "I have heard that it isn't particularly safe after dark— particularly for a lone woman."

"That is true enough, if one veers off the lighted paths. Vauxhall is lit with thousands of lanterns, except for the dark walk. As long as you steer clear of the place, I should think you would be safe enough. Or, perhaps you have a friend or a beau to escort you?"

This time, she couldn't help the little smile that made her left cheek itch. "Your Grace, while I have any number of friends and acquaintances, there is no beau."

Westerfield fell silent a moment, his gaze becoming intent as he stared at her. Thalia fought not to squirm under his perusal, finding it disconcerting.

"That's a shame," he said, his voice so low Thalia had nearly missed what he'd said. Blinking, he looked away and straightened. "At any rate, I do hope you will change your mind. You must experience a night at Vauxhall at least once in your life."

"I will consider it. Thank you, Your Grace."

"Thank *you*," he replied. "You know where to send the receipt."

"Of course."

"I will see you next week ... or tonight, perhaps?"

"Perhaps," she hedged. "Although, it is a masked affair, is it not? You might set eyes on me and not recognize me at all."

"A fair point. Regardless, I hope you have a pleasant evening, Miss Ramsey. Good day."

"Good day, Your Grace."

Thalia slumped once Westerfield was gone, letting out a sigh. She was always on edge following an encounter with the duke, but this felt different. There had been a glimmer of something in his eyes as he'd remarked that it was a shame Thalia had no beau to escort her.

What had it meant?

Nothing, she decided. She was ridiculous for even thinking it. He was simply being kind, as he always was. Still, Thalia allowed herself a moment to think of a night of revelry and fun ... a night under the stars, surrounded by entertainments of all kinds. She hadn't been to a dance in ages, and itched to be partnered on the dance floor—though she wasn't certain the opportunity would present itself. If she wasn't careful, someone might mistake her for a Haymarket strumpet and make untoward advances. It was one of the reasons she had shunned such affairs in the past. Among people like herself—shopkeepers and merchants and such—she was known, she was safe. Many had been acquainted with her father before his death, and were cordial to Thalia and her mother. But mixing with high society was a risk—one that could see her night ruined.

With a shake of her head, Thalia decided it was a decision

best saved for later. It wasn't as if there were numerous options for her in regards to costume—her clothing was well made and adequate, but by no means fine.

One thing was for certain; entertaining the idea of encountering Westerfield at Vauxhall was the height of madness. Thalia would do well to cure herself of such insanity before this evening.

STEPHEN LEANED against the back of his chair, eyes closed as he latched onto the soothing sound of a razor scraping a strop. It reminded him of the waves of the ocean, producing pangs of longing for his estate off the coast of Devon. If it weren't for the need to attend Parliament sessions, he would be there now, walking along the rocky shore and breathing in the salty air. Instead, he was forced to inhabit one of his London residences and endure the filth and smog along with the stifling humidity of summer.

He supposed he ought not complain, even in his own mind. Last year, the unusual temperatures had subjected all of England to an endless winter. Besides, being in London was worth it for the chance to step foot in Vauxhall again. He hadn't attended a masquerade there in years, and was determined not to miss this one. Ever since his ascension to the title, duty and responsibility had steered his every move, forming the majority of his decisions. Attending the revel tonight would be the first time Stephen had chosen personal enjoyment over the needs of the dukedom. It would all be waiting for him in the morning, and he deserved a respite, however short it might be. He had been in earnest when telling Miss Ramsey that attending a Vauxhall affair was a wondrous experience.

Stephen chuckled at the thought of the witty bookshop

owner, snatches of their earlier conversation coming back to him.

"Is something funny, *Sahib?*"

Stephen cracked an eye open to find his valet standing over him. Pavan was a tall, wiry Indian man with a severe face and piercing eyes as black as the night. He dressed in traditional *kurta* and *jodhpur* breeches, his silk, beaded slippers a match for a rich, royal purple turban. The man had been brought to England, along with a newborn Stephen by his father the duke, and his mother—an Indian noblewoman—on their return from Delhi. At the time he had served as valet for the former duke. Upon his death, Stephen had inherited Pavan along with every-thing else connected to the Westerfield title.

"I was only thinking, Pavan," Stephen replied as the valet began preparing a hot towel. "Perhaps I ought to enlist more valets ... five more, I think. And one could be dedicated solely to getting me into my stockings."

Stephen's shoulders quivered with laughter, snorts and chuckles slipped out from between his lips. Meanwhile, Pavan's only change in expression came in the slight narrowing of his eyes.

"What is this talk of stockings?" Pavan replied, his accent thickened by irritability. "Does *Sahib* not approve of the way I tend to his feet?"

Stephen was hopeless, rocking in his chair as he gave in to belly-quivering laughter. "Of course, Pavan ... but if someone else tends the ducal feet, it will free you to pay better attention to my hair."

Pavan pushed him—not gently—against the back of the chair and draped his face in the hot towel. "Perhaps I should merely shave your head and cut out the need for another valet."

Stephen could well imagine Pavan shearing him of his dark, silken locks, and it only made him laugh harder. "Forget I said anything. You have the ingenuity of ten valets, and I value you."

Pavan made a low sound in the back of his throat but said nothing else. Stephen knew the man well enough. Just now, Pavan was beaming with pride. The man had been not only a servant to Stephen's father, but a friend and adviser. Pavan had spent his youth in the royal courts of Indian nobility. The machinations of ruling were known to him, and he'd helped the former Westerfield make a number of important decisions. Now that his father was gone, Stephen had come to rely on Pavan as a fatherly figure.

"All is in readiness for your costume, *Sahib*. I added a bit more beadwork on the lapels. You will look like the nobleman that you are."

Stephen had selected opulent Indian garb for the evening, complete with headwear and a matching mask. It wasn't often he was able to don the dress of his mother's homeland. "Very good, Pavan."

"How long will we remain in Westerfield House, Sahib?" Pavan asked, quickly changing the subject. He was always shy about basking in praise.

"A few more days," Stephen replied. "Mother craves my company, and I owe her that. I've spent so much time in sessions and debating politics at my club that I haven't had much time for her. My time in London is dear, but I will always find some to spare for her."

"You are a good son."

Stephen grinned as the towel was removed from his face. "I like to think I am. I look forward to taking her to Vauxhall tonight. She seems to get along better when she's been out."

"Yes," Pavan agreed. "It is good for her to be social again. To leave this house."

His mother had eschewed English standards of mourning, only recently shedding her black widow's weeds. Four years was a long time to close oneself away from the world, but Stephen's parents had loved one another dearly. Having never been in love, he couldn't fathom feeling so intensely about another person. He loved his family dearly, small as it was, but knew nothing of passionate love. The pain still lingered in his mother's eyes, but she'd begun to smile again and ask him to escort her about. He would attend a ball every night if only to see her take in the beauty of marble floors and crystal chandeliers, and smile.

"She will enjoy the evening, I think," Stephen mused. "That is, if I can keep her and Uncle Philip from murdering one another."

Pavan issued a low snort. "I will pray for you, *Sahib*."

Stephen pinched his lips to keep from laughing as Pavan coated his jaw in shaving balm. His father's brother, Philip, had become a resident of Westerfield House following the death of his wife. The man was loved by all who knew him for his quick wit, easy smiles, and engaging personality. Only the dowager duchess seemed none-too-amused by him. Yet, when at home they were often in each other's company—griping at one another in a way that only old friends could.

"Perhaps you should be glad for your mother to be occupied with Mr. Dryden, for then she will forget to pester you about selecting a duchess."

Stephen groaned as Pavan began meticulously scraping the stubble from his face. "Don't remind me. I am not averse to the idea of marriage. On the contrary, I look forward to being wed —but to the right woman of my choosing, at the right time. Mother means well, but her ideas of what constitutes the perfect bride differ from my own."

"She simply wishes for your duchess to live up to the Westerfield legacy. One scandalous marriage in the line of succession is quite enough, to her mind."

Annoyance lanced through Stephen at Pavan's reminder at what was at stake in his choice of bride. Since becoming a duchess herself and carrying one of the oldest and most illustrious titles in the empire, Sunita Dryden had made it her mission to represent her new name well. She dressed as an Englishwoman always, save for the opulent gold and gems passed down through generations of Indian royalty. Over the years, her accent had grown less and less noticeable, thanks to the efforts of a tutor through elocution lessons. She had borne her husband an heir, as required, though lamented she had been unable to provide the duke with more children.

Stephen's childhood and education had been rigorous, his mother determined for him to become the perfect English gentleman—one worthy of carrying on the Westerfield title and living up to his father's legacy.

And now, it was his turn to do what was necessary for the sake of the dukedom. Only, Stephen was of the opinion the one thing that ought to be decided with no thought to the title was his choice of bride. He had already been asked to give so much of himself to crown and country. Sacrifices must be made, and Stephen had made his peace with that.

However, a man's wife wasn't only a polished gem to be flaunted on his arm, or a broodmare for the sake of an heir. His duchess would be a constant companion, as he had no desire to live a separate life from his wife. Stephen wanted someone he could laugh with and feel comfortable being himself around. He wanted no stiff formality—no lady bowing her head and calling him 'Your Grace.' With her—whoever she might be—he would simply be Stephen, and she would know him like no one else did.

In essence, he wanted what his parents had shared. He wanted love and passion, and for that Stephen must be allowed to choose on his own terms. No matter how many young, pale debutantes his mother paraded before him, Stephen would not have his hand forced.

"She only wants the best for you, *Sahib*," Pavan murmured, as if having read Stephen's thoughts.

"I know," Stephen said with a sigh. "Perhaps I could apply myself a bit more to the wife hunt. It will please her."

"Indeed."

They fell into companionable silence through the rest of his toilette—their years together having attuned them well to one another. Within the hour, he was dressed in a heavily beaded and embroidered *sherwani* coat of yellow-gold silk. Pavan's beadwork added dimension to the piece, enlivening the silk with shades of crimson, purple, and royal blue. His *churidars* trousers were a matching shade to the jacket, while his turban was a contrasting shade of blood red. His mask seemed an unnecessary accoutrement—as no one in London could mistake him for anyone else due to his coloring and mode of dress. Still, it felt good to get into the spirit of the evening, tying the ribbons of a golden half-mask over his face.

He suffered through Pavan's fussing—a loose thread snipped here, an imaginary wrinkle smoothed there. Once his valet was satisfied, Stephen was free to go downstairs, where he found his mother and uncle awaiting him.

His mother was a small woman, slender and short of stature. Her coppery skin had begun to show the signs of her age, yet she was as lovely as the portrait of her youthful self which hung in the gallery. Her thick, waist-length hair was arranged in an elegant knot—strands of silver entwining with ebony black. Her eyes were lighter than his own—like warmed honey, and her features were severe yet somehow all the more beautiful because of it.

Uncle Philip offered a sharp contrast to the dowager duchess —with a ruddy complexion, frazzled gray side-whiskers, and a balding pate. The paunch of his belly pressed at the front of his waistcoat, one button threatening to pop free at any moment.

They had shunned the fanciful costumes preferred by the younger crowd, opting for black dominoes with masks.

His mother smiled at the sight of Stephen, coming toward

him with her arms outstretched. "My son ... you look splendid. Does he not look splendid, Philip?"

His uncle raised a quizzing glass to one eye and made a sound of approval at the back of his throat. "Hmm, quite fine indeed. You cut a dashing figure, nephew."

His mother cut her narrowed eyes at Philip and scowled. "You must not address him so informally. *Nephew* ... I cannot believe ... it is *Your Grace!*"

Stephen cut off Philip's coming tirade with a hand his uncle's shoulder. "We are family and in private. I see no need for formality. How do you fare this evening, Uncle? Looking forward to the fireworks?"

Philip's pale blue eyes glimmered with the glee of a young boy as he tugged on one of his whiskers. "Fireworks are all well and good, but I was hoping you might arrange an ascent in the balloon for an old chap. I'd like to know what it's like to taste the air from such a height at least once before I die."

Stephen opened his mouth to respond that of course he would make the arrangements, but his mother was already taking Philip to task.

"He is to enjoy his evening without feeling beholden to either of us," she admonished, with a click of her tongue. "You will survive just fine without setting foot in a hot air balloon. Besides, they are frightfully dangerous things. I've no idea why one would ever wish—"

"Enjoy his evening—bah!" Philip countered, hands on hips. "You aren't fooling me, Sunita. You will do your best to shove every eligible lady into his path!"

Placing a slender hand over her bosom, his mother conjured her best affronted expression. "How dare you imply—"

"Uncle," Stephen cut in, before the spat escalated any further. "I will do my best to ensure you are able to enjoy an ascension in the balloon. Mother, there are sure to be any number of eligible ladies in attendance. I shall arrange introductions to a few of them myself. Who knows? Perhaps the future Duchess of Westerfield is striding through the gates of Vauxhall at this very moment."

Accepting his arm, Stephen's mother offered him a beaming smile. "From your lips to God's ears."

CHAPTER TWO

Thalia gave herself a once-over in the looking glass for the umpteenth time. Her mauve muslin evening gown was a few years out of fashion, but the strategic placement of some delicate lace and a ribbon beneath the bust had breathed new life into it. The paisley shawl hanging from her arms had been a gift from her father on the occasion of her twenty-first birthday. Unbeknownst to Thalia, it was the last gift she would ever receive from him. He had succumbed to a fever a few short months later, leaving her alone with an aging mother and a young, impressionable sister. With the profits from the bookshop and funds her father had tucked away, they were able to keep a comfortable home in the flat above the storefront.

The sister in question had flung herself across Thalia's bed, nose buried in a worn copy of *The Mirror of Graces*. Theodosia peered at Thalia over the pages and smiled. "You look lovely, sister. Though, I do not think it is fashionable for a lady to wear her curling papers in public."

Thalia rolled her eyes. "I was just about to ask you to help me take them out, Theo. I wanted my curls to be fresh."

Setting *The Mirror of Graces* aside, Theodosia stood, pulling her worn dressing gown closed over her night-rail. The etiquette book for young ladies had been her constant companion ever since Theo had been old enough to dream of a world far out of her reach. Thalia had given up trying to talk sense into her, though their mother was never short on practical advice for her youngest daughter.

As she sat on the bed to allow Theo to unravel her hair—smoothed this afternoon with hot tongs—Thalia glimpsed their reflection in the mirror. They were similar in appearance—with the same gleaming dark skin and deep brown eyes as their mother. But Theo had their father's face—round and pleasant, kissed by mischief. A sweet little divot added charm to Theo's chin, and her smile was as sweet as the morning sun. By contrast, Thalia's features were more chiseled, her cheekbones prominent and her cheeks nipping in below them before ending in the point of her chin. Full lips were turned pink by a light application of rouge.

Thalia supposed it wasn't a bad thing for her sister to be so fanciful. She was the younger sibling, and therefore allowed to dream. Theo wasn't irresponsible—she worked as a seamstress at a dress shop just down the lane from the bookshop. But while she hemmed gowns and stitched pleats, Theo's head was in the clouds—where elegant gentleman twirled her about ballrooms, and candlelight turned the whole world into a hazy world of glitz and glamor.

Who was Thalia to tell Theo she couldn't have the better life she dreamed of? Thalia was the one responsible for seeing to their family's livelihood. Any man who might wish to marry her —and in all her twenty-three years there had never been a single one—he would have to understand that her mother and sister came along with her. Few men would want two additional mouths to feed, which was why Thalia had given up on her own dreams of marriage. But Theo ... perhaps someday she could have all the things that Thalia couldn't.

"You're sighing," Theo murmured, her fingers deft and gentle as she eased the papers from Thalia's hair. Fat spirals fell down her neck, one tickling the shell of her ear.

"Am I?" Thalia whispered, blinking. "I hadn't noticed."

"What are you thinking about? The handsome gentlemen who will ask you to dance tonight?"

"I hardly think anyone will be lining up to dance with me."

Theo gave one of her curls a light tug. "Don't be silly. I wish I were going with you. We'd both drive the other women mad with envy, making every eligible man wish to dance with us."

"You are too young!" called their mother's voice through the open door.

Thalia smirked as she glanced up to find their mother in her customary place—a chair near the fire with a blanket draped over her lap, needle in hand, and basket of mending at her feet. Theo pulled a face, which Thalia saw in the mirror, sending her into a fit of muffled giggles.

"I saw that!" their mother bellowed, prompting Theo to gasp.

"You did not!" she accused.

"I did," their mother insisted. "I am your mother, and I say you are too young for a night at Vauxhall."

"I am eight and ten now," Theo argued, her voice taking on a whining edge. "The girls of the *ton* who are my age are being considered for marriage."

"You are not of the *ton*," their mother argued. "You may attend Vauxhall at night when you are one-and-twenty, and not a day before!"

Theo muttered something unintelligible under her breath, and Thalia placed a hand over hers, stilling it. Their eyes met in the mirror.

"Be careful what you wish for, Theo. The world is vast and

beautiful, but it can also be dangerous and difficult to navigate. I want you to be happy, but I do not want you hurt."

Theo sighed. "I'm not a child."

"I know you aren't. You're a young woman now, with so much promise. Mother only wants to protect you."

"From what? A life that is better than this one?"

"Our lives are far better other women like us," Thalia snapped. At times she wearied of what she perceived as Theo's ungratefulness. "Our father was able to apprentice for the previous owner of this book shop, and worked so hard and so diligently that it was left to him. It was better than a monetary inheritance, Theo … it was a way for us to survive without struggle or worry. It was enough to clothe us, feed us, send us both to decent schools. We are learned women with employment and a place to call home. Perhaps the next time you pass a starving beggar on the way to the dress shop each day, you will remember how fortunate we are and count your blessings."

A tense silence fell between them, during which Theo finished removing the curling papers—though her touch was not as gentle as it had been before. Tossing the last of them at Thalia's side, she snatched up her book and crossed the room to her own bed.

"There is nothing wrong with aspiring to more," she muttered. "If you weren't so satisfied with an ordinary life, perhaps you might understand that."

Thalia ignored Theo, not wishing to further sully the evening with a row. It had taken her hours to decide upon attending Vauxhall, and she had even become excited at the prospect of encountering Westerfield. Now, her heart sank into her belly as she realized that she ought to take her own advice. If she happened to come face-to-face with the duke tonight, nothing of any consequence would happen. Her life would go on as before, and Thalia had already decided that she was pleased with things as they were.

Ignoring Theo's pouting, she returned to the mirror and began pinning her hair atop her head. Thalia allowed her coiffure to take shape without much manipulation, arranging the curls in a cluster, then pulling several small spirals free at her temples and brow. A large, thick curl lay against her shoulder, slightly bared by the cut of her bodice.

Her mask was the final touch, a delicate silver filigree half-mask attached to a lorgnette. Thalia had purchased it after closing the shop for the day, spending more than she had on a single item in a long time. If she was to enjoy herself tonight, Thalia supposed she could allow herself the small indulgence. Holding it over her face, she studied her reflection and smiled. There were few occasions for dressing so well, and a part of her felt like a different person entirely.

Theo murmured a half-hearted, "Have a good time," as Thalia exited into the parlor.

Her mother glanced up from her mending, her gaze both approving and criticizing as she looked Thalia over. Thalia could hear her mother's thoughts as if they were her own: her bodice was too low, but her hair was well arranged, and while the shawl was a nice touch, the mask had been an unnecessary expense.

In the end, her mother merely gave a short nod and returned her gaze to the mending. "You will be careful."

It wasn't a question, Thalia realized. Her family knew her well. Thalia was never anything but careful ... practical.

"Of course," she replied. "I will not tarry late. I simply wish to experience the sights and sounds of the garden in the evening."

"I do not like you going alone."

Thalia arranged her reticule to hang from one wrist. "I will be perfectly safe, and as I do not intend to remain late, I am not worried about being alone."

Her mother looked uncertain but said nothing. Once Thalia

ELISE MARION

had reached her majority, her mother had been content to allow her to make her own decisions. It was Theo who gave cause for worry; never Thalia.

"Will you wait up for me?" Thalia asked, pausing at the door.

Her mother smiled, producing deep lines about her eyes and lips. "There will be a pot of tea, hot and ready. We will drink it while you tell us about your evening."

Thalia smiled. "Thank you, Mama."

Her mother waved her off, content to return to her mending.

Thalia's heart began to pound as she rushed down the back stairs and threw open the door that led out onto the street. The sun hadn't yet set, but it was slowly descending, painting the sky in hues of orange and pink. People came and went on foot and in carriages, many dressed in costume and already masked. A festive mood had filled the air, and Thalia had a spring in her step as she moved down the street, eyes sharp for a hackney coach. She couldn't seem to stop smiling as it occurred to her that she had never done anything like this in her life.

For as long as she could remember, her life had been ordered by responsibility and obligation to her family. Only between the pages of her novels did she find adventure and passion. Leaving home dressed in her favorite gown, with her hair whimsically arranged, Thalia felt as if she'd stepped out of reality and onto the fictional pages.

Which meant that anything could happen.

STEPHEN'S CHEEKS had begun to ache, but he kept the forced, genial smile pasted across his face as he walked alongside the Baroness Atherton. The woman had been introduced to him months ago at a soirée, and seemed to have designs on him as a prospective groom for one of her four daughters. Stephen had

192

always gone out of his way to be polite toward everyone who crossed his path—though his mother constantly reminded him that as a duke he was not obligated to pay notice to those beneath him.

However, as a peer of the realm with very few equals, Stephen shunned his mother's philosophy on the matter. It seemed a very lonely way for one to live. Upon the evening of their acquaintance, Stephen had fetched punch for the baroness, who had nearly swooned in reaction to the gesture. He had then danced with each of the woman's daughters—whose names he could not recall, and knew only that they each began with the letter 'A.'

The feathers in the older woman's turban bobbed as she smiled up at him, a cup of arrack punch clutched in a black-gloved hand. She was dressed as a chess piece—the queen—complete with a turban shaped like a crown and adorned with so many feathers and gems that one couldn't miss her if they tried. Despite her mask, he had recognized her by her voice when she'd called out to him moments ago.

Stephen blinked, tearing his gaze away from the dancers and returning his attention to the baroness just in time to catch the tail end of her monologue.

"...and then, she suggested the ghastliest lace in a most unbecoming shade of puce. *Puce,* Your Grace! Have you ever heard of such a thing? My Amelia has not the complexion to carry off such a drab color. Anyone with sense could have seen that. Why, her presentation at court would have been a disaster had she arrived in such a monstrosity of a gown!"

Stephen, who was not well-versed in the complexities of women's clothing and the making of them, merely clicked his tongue and shook his head. "A disgrace, to be sure. Everyone knows white is the only acceptable color for a debutante's presentation. And the number of flounces you mentioned—"

"Eighteen in all, if you can believe it!"

"I cannot," he replied with a shake of his head. Outwardly, he was the very picture of an attentive gentleman. Inside, he was trying to plot an escape that did not entail hurting the woman's feelings. She might be a chatty old bird, but she was not without her charm ... even if she was scheming to match him with one of her daughters.

Stephen's mind wandered yet again as Lady Atherton blabbered on, his gaze flitting about the dizzying display of Vauxhall Gardens. He had arrived less than an hour past, and ever since been overwhelmed by acquaintances and strangers alike. The informality of an evening where the classes mixed in one venue had emboldened many people, who could pretend not to know who he was—freeing them to address him without the benefit of a proper introduction.

Normally, he wouldn't mind the opportunity to meet new people or converse with them, especially on a night such as this. However, there was a baffling sense of restlessness plaguing him this evening, and Stephen couldn't puzzle out why. The back of his neck tingled, and he kept glancing about as if looking for something.

Yet, there was nothing to be found that he hadn't expected. The fairy-like glow of thousands of colored lanterns set the night ablaze, while people in vibrant, outlandish costume enjoyed the entertainments of the evening. The fireworks had not yet begun, but the amusement of the hot-air balloon had enraptured many. Stephen had sent word ahead to smooth the way for his uncle to enjoy an ascent, and was contemplating taking advantage of the privilege for himself later in the evening.

Lively music flowed from the pillared openings of the Gothic Orchestra, and a sea of dancers moved in time with it— much like undulating ocean waves. The various paths leading this way and that offered many options for amusement, but Stephen could not seem to settle on a single one. It was as if he was being torn in many directions at once, unsure of what to do or where to go. His mother and uncle had parted ways with him upon arriving, which left him unable to even rely upon their whims for guidance.

"My darling Agatha did so enjoy her dance with you at the Smythe's ball earlier in the season," Lady Atherton went on, drawing Stephen's fickle attention back to her. "She has not stopped speaking of it, and the two of you did partner so well. Oh, and my dear Anne is quite accomplished on the pianoforte —did I happen to mention that before?"

She had only brought it up seven times, as if the most imperative requirement for a duchess was that she be able to play a decent composition.

"I do not recall," Stephen lied.

"Perhaps you might call upon us next week so that she can play for you. Oh, and you simply *must* see Amelia's brilliant work with watercolors! She's quite the artist."

The woman was shameless, but Stephen suspected she knew that. He wanted to laugh at her aggressive attempts at matchmaking and make some witty quip about being overcome by so much feminine accomplishment—but then, his gaze settled on a woman coming down the Grand Walk, and all power of speech fled him.

She was set aglow by the lamps like some heavenly vision— the flames that cut through prisms of colored glass painting her in rainbow hues. Despite that, Stephen could see that she wore a dusky shade of pink. The gown was by no means fashionable, but fit the woman well and complimented the dark, gleaming hue of her skin. The bodice was just low enough to display the soft swell of a small but pert bosom beneath a graceful neck. She held a silver lorgnette mask over her eyes, and one large spiral curl slid along her collarbone as she turned her head this way and that to take in her surroundings.

There was something familiar about her, yet Stephen

couldn't quite place her. She walked with a brisk, determined stride—nothing like the sedate mimic of a gliding motion so many fine ladies aspired to.

Stephen couldn't understand why she would draw and hold his eye, but he found himself following her progress as she paused to take in a painted screen illuminated by the lamps. The restlessness within him calmed, and he didn't realize he'd come to a stop until the baroness tightened her hand on his arm.

"Your Grace?"

Stephen blinked, opening his eyes to find the vision still before him. It was unpardonably rude, but he couldn't seem to turn away from the mysterious lady to give the baroness his attention.

"Yes … fine … very good," he murmured, slowly disengaging himself from the woman. He patted her hand and murmured something else about paying a call before striding away from her without a look back.

"Looking forward to it, Your Grace!" the baroness called to his retreating back.

Stephen fought the urgency pushing him to rush toward the lady in pink, deciding that it was best to observe her from a distance for a little while. Perhaps she had come to meet a lover, or maybe her husband had slipped away to procure her a drink. Of course, he hoped neither would turn out to be the case.

The lady had moved on from the painting and was simply gazing upward, turning in a slow circle as she took in the lamps hanging from the trees. A wide smile enlivened her face beneath the mask. Stephen knew the look on her face. It was the wonder-filled expression of one who had never taken in the gardens before. He couldn't help but smile to notice how enchanted she seemed as she spun about, waiting for the next consuming feature to catch her eye.

Stephen took slow steps along the path, watching as she

veered toward one of the many pavilions. Stepping up smooth stone steps, she stood among a display of fine paintings in gilt frames. When she turned to view the one closest to her, Stephen caught a glimpse of something behind her mask. Something that reflected light and appeared to rest over the one ear that he could see.

Spectacles.

Furrowing his brow, he approached, lips parting as he realized why this woman had felt so familiar to him. The closer Stephen drew, the more he began to feel like a complete dolt for having not recognized her.

But then, he had never seen her outside of Ramsey's bookshop, and certainly not dressed like *this*.

His foot found the bottom step to the pavilion, then the second. By the time he entered the circle of pillars and archways, she had registered his footsteps and whirled to face him.

He had startled her, and in reaction she had dropped the arm holding up her mask. Wide brown eyes met his, and lips turned pink by rogue stretched into a little 'o' of surprise.

"Your Grace?" she blurted.

Stephen stepped farther into the pavilion and offered her a bow. "Miss Ramsey. I thought you weren't planning to attend this evening."

Fiddling with her lorgnette with both hands, she shrugged one shoulder. "I changed my mind."

Stephen extended a hand toward her before he could think better of it. He wasn't wearing gloves, and neither was she. They had never touched save for the moment he had helped her back into her slipper this afternoon.

But then, he'd never seen her wearing pink or standing beneath the pale glow of the moon and the dazzling array of Vauxhall's lanterns. He'd never seen her without the surroundings of musty books and dusty shelves.

She gave him his hand and he dipped his head over it—though Stephen merely kissed the air above her knuckles. He did not dare press for more. When he glanced up, she was looking at him as if he'd gone completely mad.

"I'm glad you did," he replied.

CHAPTER THREE

Thalia had never seen anything more stunning than Vauxhall Gardens—except, perhaps, for the Duke of Westerfield adorned like a foreign king. He had come to her shop dressed in all manner of finery, each garment tailored to fit his tall, athletic form. However, she could never imagine anything like the splendor standing before her. He looked as if he had been born to wear such clothing—which, in a way, he had. The golden coat he wore clung to his chest and shoulders, the intricate beading doing nothing to detract from his potent masculinity. If anything, it was enhanced. His trousers were a loose fit in the hips, but then tapered close toward the ankles, displaying a fine set of calves.

She only briefly took in the matching slippers on his feet before jerking her gaze back upward. There had to be a law against ogling a duke's calves. He had released her hand, but the skin of her palm still tingled from where he'd touched her. Her knuckles had warmed, as if the phantom touch of his lips had actually landed.

Her heart was lodged in her throat, making speech all but

impossible. She had imagined encountering him here, of course, but Thalia hadn't let herself get her hopes up. There were thousands of people crowding the gardens tonight. What were the chances that she would come face-to-face with him?

Thalia's question was now answered as she sought out the mysterious dark pools of Westerfield's eyes through the slits of his mask. Less than a half hour in the gardens, and she had found him. Or, rather, he had found her.

She cleared her throat, realizing he had asked her a question. "I … I beg your pardon?"

"Are you here alone?" he asked, that charming smile curving his lips—which she could not help but notice looked fuller and softer with the upper half of his face covered.

"I am," she admitted with a sheepish smile. "My mother has arthritic joints and would not enjoy a long promenade down these paths, and my sister has been declared too young to attend a masquerade."

"What a shame," he said, though his tone implicated he did not think it a shame at all. "One cannot enjoy their first evening in the gardens without a proper guide. I volunteer myself for the honor, if you will have me."

Thalia couldn't wipe the look of surprise off her face. "You want to … with me? I mean … I am certain there are many people here you would rather—"

"Miss Ramsey," he cut in.

"Yes?"

"Accept my offer. I promise you an enjoyable evening."

Recovering from her surprise, she raised an eyebrow. "Only enjoyable."

"Fine then," he conceded with a chuckle. "A spectacular evening."

"I accept," she replied.

Thalia felt as if she had fallen into some kind of dream. She was about to enjoy the beautiful and thrilling gardens on the arm of a *duke*.

No, not just a duke but the man of her dreams.

On any other day she might have chastised herself for such thoughts. They were not like her, and went against the rule she had set for herself. It was a very important rule, one that protected her from certain disappointment. *Do Not Long For The Duke.*

However, she had already decided to allow herself this one evening of excitement. Thalia had had so few such occasions in her life. To be free from responsibility and the weight of her family's livelihood. To be enjoy herself without second thought.

Perhaps she could allow herself one night of longing, and nothing more. Whatever happened, she would cherish this night as a fond memory for the rest of her days.

It had to be enough.

"Well, come along, there is much to see." The duke offered his arm "The first rule of a Vauxhall masquerade ... never lower your mask when others can see you. It ruins the mystique of the evening."

Thalia took his arm with one hand, while quickly raising her lorgnette with the other. She wished she had purchased a mask that tied on with ribbons, but could never wear one comfortably over her spectacles. Theo had suggested she go without them, but Thalia had wanted to enjoy the gardens with the full benefit of her eyesight. Without her glasses, the lanterns would be no more than bright smudges against the splotchy backdrop of the trees.

"Now then," Westerfield said, deftly guiding her through and around the groups of people strolling along the paths. "First, the Prince's Pavilion. It was built for the particular use of Fredrick, Prince of Wales."

The duke led her past the elevated orchestra, skirting the

crowd of exuberant dancers. The pavilion in question sat adjacent to the proprietor's house, through which Thalia had entered the gardens. The white stone appeared to glow in the lamplight, its open, airy portico occupied by small clusters of people inspecting its insides. Two flights of steps faced one another over a stone archway, and Thalia held her skirts as they ascended. The portico was framed by four large columns, and several elegant chandeliers hung from its ceiling. A large door led the way into a wide drawing room, which Thalia could see was lit by a chandelier as large as the three outside fixtures combined.

"The prince and his set spent many an evening here," Westerfield said as they approached the doors. "He held court in this very drawing room, and those who were in favor with him enjoyed wine, dinner, dancing, and of course, his illustrious company."

"Is there no Duke's Pavilion?" she teased.

Westerfield snorted. "No, and it surprises me. I have trouble believing that not a single duke in the history of these gardens was pompous enough to demand such a structure be built in his honor."

"Perhaps you will be the first."

The duke glanced at her from the corner of his eye and smirked. "That isn't altogether a bad idea. My building would feature a library, I think. The grandest in all of London."

Thalia gave him a quizzical look as they paused in the center of the room. Westerfield faced her, hands folded behind his back.

"Have I shocked you?" he asked.

"No ... yes. I do know of your love for books, of course, but—"

"You thought a place constructed in my honor ought to be filled with tributes to my own greatness."

"It seems the dukely thing to do."

"Dukely?" he mused, stroking his jaw. "Is that even a word?"

"I am not certain, but it ought to be."

With one hand hovering at her back, he steered her toward a collection of busts and objects d'art. "I think, Miss Ramsey, that you will find I am not very dukely."

She fell silent then, uncertain of how to respond. He might not think himself much like the other peers, and Thalia could at least acknowledge that he didn't look like any of them. But there, the differences ended as far as she was concerned. He had been born of the bluest blood in both England and India, and was as near to royalty as anyone she would ever encounter. He was far too dukely for her.

They perused the prince's monument in comfortable silence before Westerfield led her back to the Grand Walk. He stopped a passing waiter to procure champagne for them both, and Thalia slowly sipped hers as they walked along a colonnade with pillars draped with climbing ivy and blooming summer flowers. Their perfume wafted up her nostrils, sweet and pleasant.

As they cleared the colonnade, Westerfield paused and pointed upward. "Ah, yes. A performance not to be missed."

Thalia craned her neck to follow his gaze and gasped. Above them, a woman seemed to walk upon the air. Upon closer inspection, Thalia realized that what she witnessed was tightrope-walker. Her lips parted in wonder as she watched the woman balance on one foot, arms raised as she executed a graceful pirouette.

"Isn't she magnificent?"

Thalia flinched at the warm current of air against her ear, Westerfield's deep voice sending a jolt of heated electricity through her veins. She turned to find him standing close—far too close—his head lowered toward hers. Her bosom heaved with labored breath as their eyes met and the musky scent of sandalwood permeated her senses.

God, the man was beautiful ... and far too charming for his own good. It was a wonder women weren't swooning along the path with every step he took.

"Yes," she whispered, finally finding her voice. "Magnificent."

He turned his head to gaze up again, as if unaffected by what had just happened. "Her name is Madame Saqui. She rose to fame in France first, but has become quite popular since her Covent Garden Theatre performance last year. Her grand finale will occur when the fireworks are launched—it is quite a feat."

They stood there for a long while, watching Madame Saqui dance upon the precarious tightrope. She procured small spheres from a pocket in her gown and juggled them while walking backwards. She pivoted without a moment's hesitation and increased her pace while balancing a feather on her head—sending gasps rippling through the crowd below.

"What do you suppose it is like to be so extraordinarily gifted?" Thalia wondered aloud.

She hadn't intended to voice the thought, but it had slipped off her tongue.

"Hmm," Westerfield murmured at her side. "That is quite the question. Perhaps we might seek the lady out after her finale and ask. But, in my experience, extraordinary people rarely think themselves extraordinary. Do you think that is what makes them so special?"

Thalia inclined her head, riveted by the sight of Madame Saqui going up on the toes of one foot, while extending her opposite leg out behind her and bending at the waist until she resembled a bird at flight.

"Or," the duke went on. "It could be a simple matter of us all being quite ordinary on the surface, with hidden depths of the exceptional inside of us. The difference between we mere mortals and those who seem to walk on air, is untapped potential."

Thalia stared at his profile until he turned to meet her gaze.

"Too philosophical?" he asked with a wince.

She smiled. "No. It was very well said."

The duke offered his arm again, and they continued on their way with him insisting that they'd never see it all if they didn't keep moving. Thalia rested her hand on his sleeve and gave herself over to his guidance and expertise.

A daunting thought occurred to her as he led her to the next attraction, and it made her chest ache.

She had been infatuated with Westerfield from the start, but the chance to be alone with him in such an intimate setting left room for only one eventuality.

By the end of the night, she was destined to fall head over heels in love with the Duke of Westerfield.

She had told herself it couldn't happen, but he was simply too much. He was too kind and attentive, too handsome and charming. Too perfect.

Thalia stood no chance.

STEPHEN SPENT the entirety of his evening delighting in Miss Ramsey's enjoyment of the gardens. In her eyes, he saw the wonderment and awe that he himself had felt his first time walking these paths. She was so different from every other lady of his acquaintance—but then, they were from two very disparate worlds.

In his circles, women were coy and demure and never smiled with all their teeth. They didn't laugh as freely or walk with such an ambling, purposeful stride. They were like porcelain marionette dolls, their strings manipulated by the teachings of their mothers and society at large. Thalia was the antithesis of everything he'd been taught a lady ought to be, and yet she was the most dignified, regal creature he'd ever laid eyes upon.

She had been captivated by the Rotunda, which was empty of dancers and musicians because of the fine weather. The columns and painted ceiling enclosed them as Stephen told Miss Ramsey of the circus performances and displays of horsemanship.

"The next time such an event is held, you must attend," he said. "With a seat in the audience boxes, you can gaze down and see everything."

Stephen grew silent then, realizing that he would very much like to be the one to escort her to such a performance. It was presumptuous of him to even think such a thing, but once the thought took root, he couldn't pry it out of his mind. He could too easily imagine her gasping and gripping the arms of her chair as she watched daring feats of acrobatics, her smile bright and genuine.

He was a fool. Upon approaching her, Stephen had never considered that the night would take this turn. He hadn't imagined he might find himself loath to leave her company, and craving it with an odd sort of need.

Before tonight, they'd barely known one another. After hours of roaming the gardens, Stephen had learned that Miss Ramsey took milk and lots of sugar in her tea, and that she was fond of daffodils. She preferred sunsets over sunrises, and loved a well-made, spicy curry. She had never been outside London and longed for the sights and fresh air of the sprawling country. The bookshop had been an inheritance passed down from a father who'd had no sons. Despite the insistence of her mother and several acquaintances that as a woman she was not up to the task, Miss Ramsey had kept the shop open, and it continued to flourish. Providing for a small family was her responsibility, one she took quite seriously.

On first glance, the weight on her shoulders seemed a

pittance compared to all the land and people Stephen was beholden to. Yet, Thalia carried her burden with limited resources and the status of being both a blackamoor and female working against her. She was far stronger and capable than he was, yet her head was always held high and the regal dignity in her posture never diminished.

Stephen threw himself into providing an enjoyable evening for her, as she'd confided that she rarely had time for simple, frivolous fun. He walked her through the Chinese temples and arcade, then the Turkish tent—where they'd rested for a while to sample the best coffee Stephen had ever had, and an array of delectable sweets. They wandered and talked of everything and nothing at all, and Stephen was hard-pressed to remember when he'd enjoyed someone's company more.

During their explorations, they had paused to watch the hot-air balloon ascend into the night. The gasps and exclamations of the crowd were nearly deafening, but he and Thalia merely watched the spectacle in silence.

But then, Thalia turned to him with a curious look on her face. "Have you ever done it … ascended in a balloon?"

"I have," he replied. "At an outdoor ball my parents hosted at Westerfield Abbey in Devon years ago."

Her lips turned up. "What was it like?"

"Bracing. Cold. Exhilarating. I could come up with fifty more adjectives and still never fully encompass the experience. It was like being outside of my body. Being so high in the air with the wind in your face … it's one of those experiences that can make you feel larger than life, more than human."

A wistful look overcame her face as she looked back at the floating balloon. "It sounds wonderful."

Just then, Stephen never wanted anything more than to see Thalia step into the basket of a hot-air balloon. To witness the look on her face as it ascended, bobbing and dipping at the mercy of the wind. Perhaps he could arrange a private ascent for the two of them at the end of the night. If Thalia was going to give herself over to a night of whimsy and wonder, a balloon ascent would be the perfect cap to a lovely evening.

Keeping that thought at the back of his mind, he sought another amusement to point out—desperate to keep her in his company. They had toured most of the biggest attractions of the gardens, but Stephen would have shown her every flower, every pillow, every green leaf if it made her smile as she was right now.

At last, they came upon a panorama depicting an exotic painting of an Indian temple framed by a lush pleasure garden. Stephen found himself searching for more time—one more second, another minute. He stood still once they circled to the back of the painting, the thin, painted screen shielding them from others ambling along the path. The lantern light shined through the panorama, casting its variegated colors across her face. He trembled with the desire to taste her lips—plump and sensuous and still slightly pink with rouge.

"You're different," he blurted aloud before thinking of his words. He had to say *something* to keep from hauling her into his arms. "Outside of the book shop, I mean."

A slight smile curved one corner of her mouth as she turned to face him and lowered her mask. "I am a woman as well as a proprietor of a business. When I leave that shop, I am like any other of my sex."

Of course she was. It was his folly that he hadn't seen it until tonight. Stephen didn't think he could ever look at her again without seeing just how magnificent she was.

"You are also different," she added when he didn't reply. "You've always been genial when you visit to purchase your books on Saturdays, but … tonight you seem less a duke and more a man. I suppose it is the atmosphere of the gardens."

"No," he insisted. "It isn't the gardens, but rather the company. I find you easy to talk to."

She sighed and turned away, reaching out to gently caress the petals of a flower. A green vine twined around the pillar of a faux ruin, its blossoms the same hue as her gown. "I suppose that's because I'm not of your world. You needn't worry about expectations or decorum, or that I might try to trap you into an unwanted marriage. There is no need to act courtly toward a woman beneath their station."

Something in her words left a hollow feeling in Stephen's middle. It bothered him to hear her speak that way of herself, but there was only truth in her words.

Stephen approached slowly, not wanting to frighten her. There was too much air between them, a tension created of things unsaid. Things he didn't even understand himself.

He reached over her shoulder to pluck one of the flowers from the vine, before gently gripping her shoulder to turn her back to him. Miss Ramsey's eyes were wide and fathomless, like still waters in the dark of night. She gazed up at him with parted lips, her bodice straining with each labored breath she took.

He could hardly breathe himself, and felt as if he'd stepped outside his body. He wasn't the Duke of Westerfield just now, but simply Stephen—a man with longings and needs that he hadn't realized went unfulfilled.

She drew in a sharp breath when he tucked the flower into her coiffure so that it rested over one ear, just above where her hanging spiral curl fell. The thick, smoothed coils of her hair brushed his knuckles, and he wondered if her skin would feel as soft as those curls.

He couldn't resist. Stephen smoothed his knuckles over her cheek, his fingers tingling at the revelation that her skin was like satin. He rested his palm at her jaw, unwilling to part from her just yet. It stunned him how right it felt to touch her in such a benign way. It might have been an innocent interaction, but Stephen's blood was on fire and rushing away from his brain.

The primal parts of him were coming alive now, begging for more.

"Your Grace," she whispered, a desperate plea in her voice.

"Stephen," he corrected with a smile. "I think it's time you called me by my Christian name."

Her eyes flared wide and she shook her head. "I cannot. It wouldn't be proper."

"No," he agreed. "But you just reminded me that formalities need not exist between us. We are friends of a sort now, I think. We are certainly more than acquaintances."

And yet, a friend was the least of what he wanted to be to this woman. His head spun as he wrestled with what he felt and what it meant. He hardly knew her, but Stephen had learned enough. He had learned that Miss Ramsey was the sort of woman he felt an unusual comfort around. She was someone he didn't have to put on airs with. Someone who could come to know the real him—the man buried beneath the necessary facade of a duke.

"You were wrong about one thing, though," he added. "There is certainly a need to be courtly toward you, Miss Ramsey. You may not have the title of 'lady', but you are one in every sense of the word."

Miss Ramsey met his gaze again, a bit of the unease in her eyes melting away. "You mustn't toy with me, Your Grace. I am as prone to romantic whimsy as any other woman. I have needs and desires, but with a man like you I cannot allow them to override my better judgment."

"*Stephen*," he insisted, strumming his thumb along the edge of her lower lip. "And I would never toy with you."

"No, but you could far too easily break my heart," she murmured. "Then where will you buy your books?"

He chuckled, so thoroughly charmed by her that he couldn't seem to wipe the smile from his face. "It is not my intention to break your heart."

"I believe you, but I foresee it happening all the same. There could never be more than this night between us. Do you understand that?"

Stephen's heart seemed to have stopped. He couldn't feel his legs. What he did feel was a powerful, all-consuming surge of desire. It raced through him, filling every corner of his being until he was desperate to have her against him, her mouth fitting to his.

"Surely that isn't true," he said.

To his surprise, she lifted one hand and laid it on his chest. Through the heavy layers of the fabric covering him, he felt each fingerprint.

"It is," she argued. "I know I shouldn't allow myself to be content with that much, yet I find myself wanting it all the same."

Was she saying what Stephen thought she was saying? There was no reticence in her gaze now; only sheer determination and resolve. He teetered on the line between decency and the urge to give in to what he truly wanted for the first time in his life. Since he'd been old enough to understand what was expected of him, Stephen had pushed all selfish urgings aside. He had thrown himself into his duty, never wanting to let his mother or father down. He lived his life with as much honor and dignity as he could, and though he was not perfect, it wasn't often that he gave himself over to the selfishness of seizing the moment.

There had been a handful of women over the years—widows and actresses and the like. His affairs with them had been short-lived and free of scandal or complication. Each of them had been treated well, and had entered into such arrangements with an understanding of who he was and what their connection would entail.

This was something entirely different. It was mad and perhaps a bit foolish, but Stephen had never wanted anything more in his life.

ELISE MARION

"I know how you feel," he rasped, feeling as if a stone had lodged itself in his throat. "I shouldn't allow you offer me even that much, but I cannot deny what I want ... and what I want is you."

Miss Ramsey closed her eyes, her free hand resting over the one he held against her cheek. "Then we are agreed. One night only."

Stephen wanted to insist that they could have more. Perhaps from her perspective that seemed impossible, but Stephen was accustomed to the privilege that allowed him to do whatever he wished. However, somewhere deep inside he knew that if he pressed her, Miss Ramsey would flee. The last thing he wanted was to watch her walk away. Perhaps if he agreed now, he could convince her later that he was willing and able to give her far more than the limits she had imposed.

Stephen lowered his head until his brow rested against hers. He closed his eyes and took in her scent—clean and simple, intertwined with the softest hint of orange blossoms.

"I agree," he said, tilting her head back so that her mouth was offered to him at the perfect angle. "One night only. But first ... you must stop calling me 'Your Grace.' If we are to have one night, then you will have it with Stephen ... not the Duke of Westerfield."

Her eyelids were lowered and heavy, her mouth a tempting pucker, his for the taking. "Very well."

Stroking the seam of her lips with his thumb, he smirked. "I'm waiting, Miss Ramsey. And while you're at it, perhaps you might give me the honor of your given name. I can hardly go on calling you Miss Ramsey for the rest of the evening."

She grinned. "Thalia ... my name is Thalia."

The perfect name for her. It rang like a heartbeat, steady and beautiful and life-affirming.

"Thalia," he repeated. "It suits you. Now, it's your turn. Say my name."

Her breath hitched as she swayed into him both hands now seeking support against his chest. "Stephen," she breathed, with a small sound of surrender from the back of her throat.

Stephen lost what was left of his control at that single utterance of his name. Wrapping one arm around Thalia, he drew her tight against him and took her mouth in a desperate, ravaging kiss.

CHAPTER FOUR

Thalia was certain she had died and gone to heaven. Sometime after arriving at Vauxhall, she must have stumbled off the path and bashed her head on a stone or some such. Her body lay in the dark, tangled in foliage and brambles, but her soul was in paradise. Surely that must be how she had wound up here, in the arms of the man who inhabited her deepest, most private fantasies.

She was being kissed by a duke. The Duke of Westerfield was kissing her. *Stephen* was devouring her mouth like a starving man, making her dizzy and weak in the knees.

No matter how she rephrased the words in her mind, they all narrowed down to the same wondrous thing. Her dream was coming true, though only for a short time.

It had to be enough. Thalia had realized hours ago that she was already lost. Her prediction had proven true and as the night went on, she fell deeper and deeper in love with the man who brightened her world by simply walking through a door every Saturday afternoon.

The noise of the festivities beyond the screen faded away, though Thalia could imagine that the lighting cast their shadows for any passersby to see. As if he'd had the same thought, Stephen backed her toward darkness—into the circle of crumbled pillars arranged to look like ancient Greek ruins. He pushed her against one of the smooth stones without breaking their kiss, his hands tight at her waist. Thalia melted into the kiss—not the first she had experienced, but certainly the most significant. Despite her lack of knowledge over what would happen next, she felt emboldened to experience all the things she had daydreamed about.

She ran her hands over the bulge of his chest and up his neck. She stroked his jaw, his cheeks, his brow. Stephen snatched his turban way with a rough grunt, and allowed Thalia to untie the ribbons of his mask. Once his entire face was revealed, Thalia leaned back to study him, finding him as magnetic as ever. She traced her fingertips over his thick, inky black eyebrows, then pushed a heavy lock of hair back from his brow. Once she had touched the silken strands, Thalia had to go back for more. She slipped her fingers through his locks, pulling him back to her for another kiss.

Her own mask had fallen to the ground minutes before, forgotten. There were no untruths between them now—no smoke and mirrors tricking them into thinking this was a mere dream or fantasy.

No, Thalia wasn't dead. She was very much alive with both feet planted on the ground, and this was the truest thing she'd ever experienced.

"Thalia," Stephen murmured against her mouth, his hands running up her back, fingers stroking the sensitive nape of her neck. "Thalia."

She had never hoped to hear him utter her name at all, let alone in such a husky voice, heavy with desire. It was more than she'd dreamed, realizing that he wanted her. Was this what it felt like to be the sort of lady he could make a life with? It was an odd feeling, but one she could quickly become drunk on.

Thalia felt beautiful and powerful and worthy in a way she hadn't her entire life.

Stephen bent his knees so he was more level with her, and the firm, masculine planes of his body fit perfectly against her soft swells. Thalia had never given much thought to the parts of a man, but every inch of Stephen felt wondrous and warm. And tonight, he was wholly hers.

Not wanting to waste another moment when she could enjoy the full range of such freedom, Thalia began searching for the fastenings of his coat. Stephen helped her, showing her that the buttons were hidden beneath a flap of fabric. He shrugged out of the coat while Thalia made quick work of his shirt buttons. Together, they eased the garment off over his head.

Thalia was momentarily frozen to the spot as she took in the breadth and sheer might of him. It was easy to see that he was built like a Corinthian when he was fully dressed, but the splendor of his naked torso was enrapturing. His chest heaved with rapid breaths as he took gentle hold of her wrists, guiding her hands to his naked skin. Her fingertips encountered whorls of dark, sleek hair. The skin beneath was hot to the touch and soft over the steely slabs of muscle.

"Touch me, Thalia," he urged, guiding her hands downward. "I've wanted your hands on me all night."

Thalia obeyed, grateful for his direction. Her uncertainty hampered the urges burning through her, filling her with sensations she'd never before experienced. Her pulse thundered against the thin skin of her throat as she explored him, tracing the light grooves between the muscles of his abdomen, skimming over flat nipples that tightened in reaction, trailing through the thicker line of hair arrowing into his breeches.

He murmured unintelligibly but the sound was encouraging, making it easier for Thalia to continue in her quest. Stephen's hands came to her upper arms, slowly smoothing upward and leaving tremors in his wake. One hand moved to her back, releasing the first fastening of her gown. The bodice sagged, and his other hand dragged the cap sleeve down her arm. Thalia gasped when he dipped his head to kiss her bared shoulder toward the strap of her stays. No one had ever touched her there, but as he made his way back toward the curve of her neck, she realized that she'd never really been touched at all. Nerve endings she hadn't realized she possessed sparked to life as he nibbled at her neck and the lobe of her ear, his hand steadily working to loosen her gown.

Thalia clung to Stephen as the frock pooled at her feet, his tongue finding the most delicious spot behind her ear—one that sent a swift lightning strike into her belly and heat suffusing through her core. Their hands met against her bosom, two sets of fingers tearing at the strings of her stays. Thalia finally let her hands fall and allowed Stephen to take over, too overcome to manage it herself. He never took his lips off her, kissing along her collarbone, then dipping his tongue into the hollow between her breasts as he loosened her stays.

Once she wore only her chemise, stockings, and slippers, Stephen gripped her waist and hoisted her up. With a gasp, she grasped his shoulders and let him wrap one leg around his waist. Her other leg followed, ankles crossed at his tailbone as he sought her mouth again. This time, the silky whisper of his tongue pressed to her lower lip, then pressed into her mouth. Thalia nearly swooned from the sensation of his tongue sliding against her own, allowing her own to push against his. They tangled and dueled, swift, heated breaths traded beneath them as Stephen went to his knees on the ground.

He gingerly laid her over his discarded coat, sprawling atop her his elbows supporting some of his weight. The rest of him pressed Thalia into the ground, the feel of him solid and comforting. Despite a niggle of fear at what was to come, Thalia felt safe. She felt treasured.

Tears stung her eyes, though they did not fall as she gazed

into his eyes, finding them darkened and heavy-lidded. Thalia had supposed she might marry someday, and of course knew the basics of what went into siring children. However, she had never imagined that intimacy could be so liberating—so pleasant. She hadn't thought that a man would ever touch her with such reverence or kiss her with such passion. This night would be a gift, despite the years of bereft emptiness stretching beyond it. That wasn't Stephen's problem, though; it was her own. Tomorrow, she would allow herself to mourn what could never be. Tonight, she would take all she could from this one encounter and pray it would be enough.

Stephen kissed his way from her chin to the edge of her chemise, slowly easing the fabric off her shoulders and over the mounds of her breasts. His heavy exhale brushed over the bared peaks, making her nipples furl tight in anticipation.

"Perfect," he whispered as he gently cupped one and gave it a little squeeze. "You are so beautiful, Thalia. I've always thought so."

She wanted to argue that that couldn't be. Surely Stephen had never looked at her and seen anything other than a frumpy bookseller in spectacles. But as he used his other hand to gingerly lift the frames off the bridge of her nose, Thalia believed him. He could have told her that the sky had opened up and begun raining chocolate drops upon them, and Thalia would have taken it as truth.

Stephen kept his gaze on her face as he took her nipple between his first finger and thumb, giving it a light pinch. Thalia whimpered, her hips raising of their own volition to press her tighter against him. His thighs were brawny and thick, pressing against hers, and the hard swell of his arousal had found its target—pressed against her mons through the fabric of her chemise. Stephen pinched her again, a bit harder this time, then bowed his head over her and resumed the ministrations of his mouth.

Thalia floated on clouds of ecstasy as he kissed and nibbled at first one nipple then the other, his tongue warm and slick as it circled each peak. Her fingers tangled in Stephen's hair, holding him close and urging him on. Her insides were a maelstrom, churning and heating and preparing her for something she couldn't yet fathom.

She let her hands follow the sinewy paths of his body, reveling in the strength and control pulling the cords of his arms and shoulders taut. He trembled atop her, and she sensed him holding back. He might have gotten her agreement for the night, then proceeded to throw her down and take what he wanted. Instead, he was taking his time, allowing her to grow used to one intimacy before he moved on to another.

He groaned against her breastbone when her fingers encountered the fastening of his trousers, surging his hips against hers. The press of him against her most secret places sent flutters of delight through her, her gut clenching with the need for more.

She slowly slipped buttons from their holes as he raised one of her knees and then slid her chemise toward her hip. His hand tightened on her thigh as he worked his way steadily upward, pushing the limb open.

Tremors wracked Thalia from head to toe as the heavy organ between his legs fell free of the fabric. He was larger than she had imagined, but then she had no one to compare him to. She caught her lip between her teeth as he silently encouraged her to go on, nudging the weight of his erection into her palm. Thalia skimmed the bulbous head with her fingertips, then traced the length of him, finding a vein that pulsed with his heartbeat.

Her chemise was now hiked to her waist, but Thalia forgot about modesty when Stephen's hand slid down the inside of one thigh. The pulsing and throbbing within her had centered in the place he now touched with gentle control. She threw her head

ELISE MARION

back and choked down moans of delight as he rubbed and
stroked, his touch producing a moisture Thalia would have
found embarrassing if not for his reaction to it. He moaned
against her ear, kissing her cheek and then her lips as he found
the tiny nub of her pleasure and began to rhythmically circle his
thumb over it. Thalia was lost, her fingernails digging into his
biceps, her legs splayed wide and her back arching as he drove
her closer to a coveted precipice. Tension coiled tight in her
middle, and with every pass of his thumb over that bundle of
nerves her urgency increased. A single finger probed into her
opening, easing deeper as she raised her hips.

Thalia gasped as that finger stretched her, sending an ache
through her core but doing nothing to diminish her pleasure.
"Stephen," she gasped out between throaty sounds of pleasure.
"Oh God ... Stephen!"

He clamped his mouth over hers just as he gave her a second
finger, his thumb pressing down on her nub with startling
precision. It was as if he lived inside her head and knew what
she needed when Thalia herself hadn't even known. She fell
apart beneath him, thrashing and bucking and kissing him with
a force born of the need for an outlet of some kind. The perfection of it was almost too much, sending her spiraling upward in
a dizzying maelstrom.

Stephen chased her through her climax until she came
crashing down, limp and shaking and panting beneath him.
Easing his fingers from inside her, he inched closer, the thick tip
of his cock pressed to her opening. He lifted his head to look at
her, appearing almost drunk on the force of what was
happening between them. Thalia didn't feel quite herself either.

"This may hurt at first," he said solemnly, his mouth set in a
grim line.

She ran a hand up and down his back. "I don't care."

He nodded but still looked remorseful about pain he hadn't
yet inflicted. The tension in his face increased as he began

220

pressing into her, sweat glistening along his brow. Thalia tensed as he worked his slow way through her channel, stretching her, invading her. The sharp burn of it took her breath away, while the fullness of it kept her in the moment. Stephen kissed her brow, the bridge of her nose, her lips, his deep groans muffled as he withdrew and plunged, easing farther in. He toyed with a nipple, combating the pain with pleasure. She melted beneath him, forcing her legs wider and clinging to him, accepting all he had to give. Above her, slivers of moonlight cut through the leaves of the treetops, and the stray pinpoint of a star glowed. Her every sense was heightened, overwhelming her with the scent of him, the warmth and solidity of him, the pressure of him taking up space inside her.

Face buried in her shoulder, Stephen began to move, his hips rolling in a rhythm that sent pulses of sensation through her. He was steady and sure, making it easier for her to relax as he found his way as far as he could reach, touching every hidden depth. The burning pain dulled to a throb as another sensation began to emerge, making her raise her hips to match his rhythm.

Overhead, fireworks began to light up the night, the pop and flare of various hues dancing over bare skin. The gasps and cries of delight from the crowd muffled the sounds of their loving, Stephen groaning and Thalia sighing and whimpering as he drove her back toward that daring precipice.

Slipping his hands beneath her, Stephen cupped her buttocks and held her flush to him, each roll of his hips stimulating her hidden pleasure spot. Thalia's thighs clenched around his hips, back bowing as the final cresting swell washed over her, tipping her off the edge. She muffled a shocked cry against the side of his neck as the torrent of ecstasy unfurled from within her, culminating in breathtaking spasms that gripped him tight and rippled with stunning force. Stephen wasn't far behind her, panting and murmuring against her temple as his movements grew sharper, deeper. He kept up his slow rhythm until the finish, only making haste once he jerked free and rolled off her to spill his seed.

Thalia lay back and stared up at the sky, exploding with light and color. Her limbs were like water and the light twinge of soreness lingered between her legs. Stephen turned back to her, fitting his body against her side and draping her in his leg and one arm.

They said nothing, simply breathing as one and holding tight to one another as the finality of what the end of the night would bring. The tears Thalia had been fighting began to spill in a euphoric rush. She closed her eyes and savored their final moments.

Soon, the time would come to say good-bye.

"STEPHEN."

Prying open his tired eyes, Stephen glanced down at Thalia, who rested between his spread legs, her head rested on his chest tipped back to look at him. They had lingered in the ruins for another hour. Once they helped one another get dressed, they had assumed this position against one of the pillars, surrounded by the fading sounds of the masquerade coming to an end.

They had talked for a while, Stephen soaking in every tidbit about her life and history she would offer. He told her of his parents and how they'd come to meet while his father had been in Delhi on behalf of the Crown. His planned stay of a few months had been extended into two years once he had met and fallen in love with the woman who would become his duchess. Stephen had followed less than a year after the wedding.

He had been amused by tales of Thalia's younger sister, a twinge of envy rolling through him. He had always wanted siblings, but his mother had barely survived birthing him. More Dryden children were out of the question.

Stephen had stopped himself short of asking Thalia if she wanted children. They were not yet ready for such talk. First, he had to convince her not to walk away from him now that their one night was coming to an end.

The look on her face was far too serious for his peace of mind.

He forced a smile and kissed the tip of her nose. "Ready for more, my dear?" he teased.

She frowned and pushed away from his chest. "That isn't funny, Stephen."

He took hold of her arm and gave her a tug, so she fell back into him. "I wasn't joking," he murmured, nuzzling the most fascinating patch of skin he'd discovered behind her ear. It made her wriggle in his lap. "Stay."

"I can't. The hour is late, and my family will surely be worried. I've tarried too long already."

Stephen twined her spiral curl around his finger. "Let me see you home. I will walk you to your door."

She knit her brow and goggled at him as if he had suddenly grown a second head. "Are you mad?"

"Yes," he confessed. "And you are to blame. I am not yet ready to lose you, Thalia. I know we agreed to one night, but I cannot fathom we shall never share this again. It was never going to be enough. If I could have this with you every night, I'd die a happy man. Just think of it. I could give you so much, Thalia ... and you could give me so much in return. Let me take care of you."

Thalia didn't respond for a long moment. Her face went completely blank, and she tore her gaze from his, staring off into the dark. Stephen was just about to ask her what was wrong when she sprang to her feet, hands on her hips as she glared down at him.

"How dare you? Do you think that because I agreed to a single night, you can now coax more out of me? And how many illicit encounters would be good enough, *Your Grace*? I am certain it will only be just enough of them for you to grow bored before you discard me."

Stephen stood, but with far less grace than Thalia had. He was so shocked he could barely manage the feat without falling flat on his face. "Thalia, I think you've misunderstood—"

"No, it is you who has misunderstood, and perhaps that is my fault. After all, I was foolish enough to let you raise my skirts and rut on me in the dirt like some common tart!"

Holding his hands defensively before him, Stephen slowly advanced. "That isn't how it happened, and we both know that. What we did ... Thalia, it was beautiful. I have *never* been so free and comfortable with a person in my life. You cannot tell me you didn't feel the same."

Pulling her shawl tighter around her body, she folded her arms over her chest. "It doesn't matter what I felt. I have far more respect for myself than to be coaxed into becoming some man's mistress—even if he is a bloody duke!"

Stephen flinched as if she'd slapped him across the face. His ears rang as the accusatory word penetrated his confused mind. Mistress? He almost laughed aloud. He'd never kept a mistress in his life and didn't intend to start now. "Thalia, listen to me—"

"No, *you* listen!" she exclaimed, giving him a look that would take the steel out of any man's spine. "I might not be one of your high society ladies, and I may not have much to offer a man who owns any and everything money can buy. But I am worth so much more than what you just tried to offer me. I don't care if becoming your kept pet comes with chests of diamonds and gowns spun from gold—I am not an object for you to buy!"

"Thalia, that isn't the way of it," he protested, chasing her as she began backing away from him. She looked like a skittish doe about to bolt, and Stephen couldn't allow her to get away. "If you would just hear me out—"

"I've heard enough," she interjected. "If you come any closer, I will scream, and everyone in London will know you for the licentious rake you are. I thought you were different. I thought I would be able to look back on this night with fond memories. But you have tainted it, and I never want to see you again."

Stephen's mouth opened and closed several times, but the right words weren't forthcoming. He realized now that he'd been too hasty and hadn't collected his thoughts properly before speaking. Now, Thalia had tears racing down her cheeks and he felt like the lowest creature on earth.

"There is an adequate bookshop on Bond Street," she added just before turning away. "The proprietor is an elderly man with porcelain teeth. I doubt you would be able to seduce *him* so easily."

Before Stephen could say another word, she was gone, dashing between the pillars and disappearing from sight. He tried to follow, but was slowed down by the need to retrieve his mask and turban. By the time he reached the path, she was gone altogether, swallowed up by the crowd moving *en masse* toward the exits.

Glancing down, he found that he had stepped on the lorgnette of her mask. She had forgotten it entirely. Bending to pick it up, he studied the silver filigree and inwardly berated himself. This wasn't how he'd thought the evening would pan out, but then he hadn't planned an adequate strategy. He had foolishly put his foot in his mouth and said all the wrong things, giving Thalia the wrong impression.

Thinking over what he'd said, Stephen could understand how she had drawn the wrong conclusion.

If I could have this every night ... Let me take care of you.

For a woman outside his class, the offer would not have sounded like one of marriage. Of course she had reacted to his overture with anger. She could derive no other meaning from what Stephen had said.

Cradling the lorgnette along with his own mask, as well as the turban, he took himself off in the other direction, seeking the Coach Gate off Kennington Lane. He had entered that way earlier in the night, wanting a moment to enjoy the gardens before being overwhelmed by people. His mother and uncle were likely waiting for him there, and he dare not keep them waiting much longer.

As he made his way, Stephen realized he had never arranged the balloon ascent. He had so badly wanted the experience for Thalia.

Stephen squared his shoulders and told himself this wasn't over yet. He had to ensure she knew his heart … and that he fulfilled every last one of her dreams. He knew where to find her, and this time she would hear him out. This time, he would tell her what he'd really wanted to say, and ensure she understood just what he was asking for.

Her heart. Her soul. Her hand in marriage.

CHAPTER FIVE

Within one week following the masquerade, Stephen's confidence had been shot to hell. Every morning he visited Ramsey's Books, and every morning he was greeting by the male shop assistant who informed him that Miss Ramsey was indisposed. He had returned a few times in the afternoon, only to be greeted by the same young man who informed him that Miss Ramsey would continue to be indisposed indefinitely.

He had tried everything he could think of to smooth the way back into her good graces. He had penned notes only to have them returned unopened. He'd sent flowers and the finest sweets London had to offer—chocolates, marzipan, lemon drops. She kept the bouquets and the sweets, but remained frustratingly silent and unseen. He sent other gifts—kid gloves, shawls, a music box, a painted fan. Those also remained in her possession, but she never sent word that she wished to see or speak to him, and when he walked through the door of the bookshop, she was nowhere to be found. He knew she lived in the rooms above the shop—she had told him as much—but he was reluctant to intrude upon her privacy. However, short of marching up the back stairs and pounding at her door, Stephen was at a loss. He was running out of ideas.

He was also running out of hope.

His family sensed a change in him, and he often caught his mother watching him with confusion all over her face. He barely spoke, picked at his food during mealtimes, and only offered half-hearted responses when spoken to.

Was this what it felt like to have a broken heart? Now he better understood his mother's behavior following his father's death. He didn't want to see anyone but her, talk to anyone but her. Food tasted bland and wine might as well have been water.

The rub was that Thalia was very much alive, and seemingly within reach. Yet she might as well have lived on another planet for how far away she felt.

"All right, I have had enough of this," his mother said on the eighth day following the masquerade. They were having dinner —he, his mother, and his uncle—and Stephen hadn't touched his fish course and was busy pushing his soup course listlessly about his bowl. "Something is wrong with you, Stephen. You haven't been yourself this past week."

"Leave the man alone, Sunita," Philip chided, giving her a narrow-eyed look. "He is a duke with much responsibility. Perhaps there is simply a lot on his mind."

"Nonsense," his mother said with a sniff. "I know my son. This is more than that."

Stephen stared at them both with bleary eyes. He hadn't slept a wink last night and felt weary down to his bones. "It is nothing. I'll be fine."

His mother set her spoon in her bowl and speared him with one of her 'looks.' He knew what that look meant—had been on the other end of it many times.

"Stephen Alexander Warwick Conrad Dryden!"

Stephen groaned. She had used every one of his names—

even the most ridiculous one, Conrad, which he loathed. There was no putting her off now. "Mother—"

"Don't give me that tone. I know my son. Something is wrong with you. Are you ill? Shall I send for Dr. Hunter?"

"I don't need a doctor, I'm in ridiculously good health."

"Then something is troubling you."

Issuing a sigh, Stephen pinched the bridge of his nose. Philip was watching him with concern knitting his brow. The man wasn't as pushy as his mother, but he was definitely concerned.

"Fine," he snapped. "You want to know what's wrong with me? I met the perfect woman—the one I want to be my duchess."

His mother's face lit up, a wide smile crossing her face. She practically bounced in her chair while clapping her hands in delight. "Well, that is wonderful news. Who is she? Do I know her? Is she one of the baroness's daughters?"

Stephen gave a dry snort and shook his head. "God, no. You don't know her, but you would love her. She is beautiful, witty, charming … strong. I … I've fallen in love with her."

Philip was smiling now, and his mother looked as if she were about to swoon.

"Don't keep us in suspense," she demanded. "Tell us who she is? Have you proposed marriage yet? Of course you haven't, I would know if you had. All of London would know. Oh, Stephen, this is excellent news!"

Stephen sat up straighter in his chair and prepared himself for her reaction to his revelation. "Her name is Miss Thalia Ramsey."

His mother furrowed her brown and stared at the ceiling as if searching for something. "Ramsey … Ramsey? I do not believe I know that family."

"No," Stephen confirmed. "They are not of the *ton*."

His mother's eyes snapped back to him, and confusion gave

way to outrage. "You must be joking. Stephen, please tell me this is some kind of joke."

For the first time in over a week, Stephen grinned. "It isn't. She is the proprietor of my favorite bookshop in Soho Square."

His mother made a choked sound, clutching at the rope of pearls about her neck. "My God, I think I'm going to have a heart attack."

Stephen rolled his eyes. "There is no need for dramatics. She is gracious and educated. Everything else she must know to be a duchess can be taught … just as it was taught to you."

His mother came to her feet. "I was born of nobility and more than fit to become an English duchess. This … this *woman* is so far beneath you it is laughable."

"Have a care," Stephen warned, his voice low. "You're referring to the woman I mean to marry. I would hate for you to say something regrettable … something that would cause me to remove myself from this house and never come back."

The threat sent a look of devastation across his mother's face. It pained him to do it, but she needed to understand how serious he was when it came to marrying Thalia.

"People will talk … they will snub her."

"She will be a duchess. *My* duchess. No one would dare."

"Of course they would dare!" his mother argued. "Have you any idea what the *beau monde* put me through when I first arrived here? Those first years would have been absolutely miserable if not for the love of your father and the gift of my son."

Stephen frowned. "But you endured. You survived it and are better for it. Can you honestly say you regret it?"

Her shoulders sagged, her face melting into an expression of sorrow. "No, I do not regret it. I loved your father with all my heart, and without him I would never had had you."

"Then wasn't it worth it?" Stephen asked. "Of all people, I expected you to understand."

"I do understand," she argued. "It is because I understand that I worry you are making a terrible mistake. Your father and I weren't blind. We knew how difficult it would be to go throughout life as a man from two different worlds. Half-English, Half-Indian ... it would invite so much scrutiny. We loved one another too much to be separated, but that love would not protect us, or you, from scorn."

Stephen chuckled. "I suppose now might be the best time for me to tell you that when I wed Thalia, your grandchildren will be even more variegated than I am. She is black."

His mother pinched her lips together and exhaled slowly through her nose. "I am certain she's a lovely woman. She must be for you to have fallen in love with her. But your father and I did not want you to suffer as we suffered. We didn't want you taking on more hardship than you were already born with."

"What hardship?" Stephen challenged. "I was born an earl. I became a duke a few years ago. People bow and scrape and simper in my presence. The mothers of society throw their daughters in my path—they don't care what I look like or where my mother came from. The most difficult thing I ever endured was a single lad at Eton who didn't want to play with me. He called me a heathen. I blackened his eye and never thought of it again. He now goes out of his way to kiss up to me whenever we cross paths. My life has been privilege heaped upon privilege. I have never wanted for anything ... except love. Would you have me go without it for the sake of avoiding a few stares and whispers?"

His mother slumped back into her chair, her face pensive and her eyes shuttered. "No. I suppose not."

"Good. Because either Thalia will be my duchess, or there will be no duchess at all. I'd rather die alone than choose someone else."

Philip cleared his throat, drawing both their notice. "If that is the case, then why are you here sulking instead of going to Miss Ramsey and asking for her hand?"

Stephen blinked, somehow caught off guard by the question. It was a valid one. What *was* he doing here? Would he lie down and accept defeat because she had returned a handful of notes and wouldn't make herself easily accessible? He would rather face her rejection over and over, in the hopes of getting through to her eventually, than wallow in his pain. She didn't understand what he wanted for them—for her. He would make her understand.

Giving his uncle a smile, he laughed. "You know, Uncle, I have no idea!"

He was on his feet in an instant, determination filling him with energy and excitement. All was not lost. Until Thalia could look him in the eye and tell Stephen she wouldn't marry him, he would not stop.

"If you will excuse me," he said. "This cannot wait."

His uncle nodded and returned his smile. "Good luck, nephew."

"Go," his mother said with a shrug of one shoulder. "She is a fool if she refuses."

Stephen didn't have time to waste. He whirled and fled the room, calling for his carriage to be readied. Along the way to the entrance hall, he raced to his study and opened his hidden safe. Within it were a collection of Westerfield family heirlooms. He had already selected the one he wanted Thalia to have. Placing the small cedar box into his breast pocket, he ran from the house and practically threw himself into the carriage.

THALIA TURNED the page of her book, though she hadn't registered a single word. If she didn't at least appear to be reading, her mother and sister would be concerned. It was bad enough that Stephen had filled their small flat with his numerous gifts. The sitting room still smelled like flowers, though two of the bouquets had long wilted and been done away with. The biggest one—a gigantic vase filled with red hothouse roses—graced the table at the center of the room. The other trinkets and things had been stored in her room, though she was determined not to make use of them. Theo had been begging for the kid gloves and fan all week.

"Someone ought to wear them if you will not," she insisted. "And if you don't want whatever man sent them, perhaps you could arrange an introduction. I'm ready to marry him this instant, sight unseen."

Thalia had merely shaken her head at her young, flighty sister. If not for the fact that she didn't want to crush Theo's dreams, Thalia might have told her just how much it hurt when the veil was ripped from over one's eyes. What had begun as the most romantic night of her life—hell, the *only* romantic night of her life—had ended with a heavy dose of hurtful reality.

When the agreement had been made for a single night, Thalia had thought of it as a gift—as something to be cherished once and never repeated. Stephen—no, *Westerfield*—had a life of his own to live. He had a title and lands to look after, and a real lady to court and eventually make into his duchess. He had an heir to produce. Thalia had her family and Ramsey's Books, and a position in society that meant she must remain in her place.

While she had occasionally hoped for more, she wasn't desperate enough to allow the position of a duke's mistress to be her new place. Every time she thought of Stephen's offer, her chest squeezed tight and her heart throbbed with a pain that hadn't lessened a bit since that night at Vauxhall.

How could she have been so wrong about him? In all the time he had been coming into her shop, Thalia had seen only his charm and the veneer of kindness. She'd been seduced by the way he talked to her as if she were his equal, the way he laughed at her quips. Apparently, Theo wasn't the only one who had a lot to learn about the world. She had been naive, acted rashly, and would now suffer for it.

It didn't matter that she had surrendered her innocence. The choice had been hers, and she supposed the right man wouldn't care that she would come into a marriage having already experienced intercourse. Stephen's thoughtfulness had at least ensured she would not bear his child.

Had she agreed to become his mistress, Thalia might find herself tucked away in some lavish townhouse, raising his illegitimate children while he spent most of his time with the babes his duchess would bear. She would live to await his arrival, desperate for even the smallest shred of his affection.

Perhaps if she were destitute and had no other recourse, Thalia might have been grateful for the offer. She might have accepted it without second thought for the sake of a roof over her head and a bed to sleep in. But her father had provided well, and she had everything she needed to live a contented life.

Except, of course, someone to love. Thalia had thought she loved Stephen. Some nights, when she lay in the dark reliving their passionate moments, she heard a whisper from the recesses of her mind insisting that she still did. She was hurt and she was angry, but Thalia couldn't forget the evening in its entirety. He had charmed and dazzled her in the surroundings of the gardens, making her believe that her dreams could someday be real.

Now she knew better and must move on with her life. It was the only thing to do.

Glancing over the rims of her spectacles, Thalia found Theo watching her from where she sat near the fire, that dratted etiquette book resting in her lap. She had asked about Vauxhall numerous times, but Thalia found it too difficult to speak of without thinking of Stephen, so she had offered only the barest information. Theo seemed to sense that something was wrong, and had been ever since the masquerade. Fortunately, Theo eschewed her usual propensity for meddling, leaving Thalia alone to wallow in her sorrow.

Their mother had dozed off in her favorite chair, a lap rug draped over her lap. Looking at her, Thalia had a moment of regret thinking of all the creature comforts Stephen might have offered them. As his mistress, she could have demanded Theo and their mother be allowed to live with her. Servants could wait on her hand and foot, and she would never have to spend her days cooking, tidying, or sewing for Theo and Thalia ever again.

Shaking her head, Thalia dismissed the thought. She had been diligent with her savings. Perhaps she could hire someone to lend her mother a hand. She would find a way to make that happen without having to sell herself in the process.

A sudden knock on the door jolted their mother out of her sleep, and sent Thalia's book crashing to the floor as she shot to her feet. She traded puzzled glances with Theo, who shrugged as if to indicate she wasn't expecting any visitors.

"Who could that be at this hour?" she murmured while bustling toward the door. Patting her hair, she bemoaned its messy state. She had taken very little care with her appearance this week, simply pinning her hair into haphazard coiffures and wearing her most worn and comfortable gowns.

Swinging the door open, her mouth fell open as she found the last person she would have expected. He looked windblown and rumpled, his cravat askew and his hair tousled. It annoyed her that despite this, he was still the most beautiful man she had ever seen.

"Thalia," he said, bracing a hand on the door before she could slam it in his face. "I regret our misunderstanding. I have tried to give you time, and didn't want to come barging up here to disturb your peace. But I can bear this no longer."

"Stephen, now is not a good time," she whispered.

He glanced past her for the first time, noticing that her mother and sister were staring at him with curious eyes. Clearing his throat, he offered a bow. "I beg your pardon, ladies. I did not mean to interrupt your evening."

Thalia's mother was on her feet, already bustling toward the kitchen. "Nonsense. Thalia, stop being so rude and allow your guest through the door. Theo, help me with the tea tray."

"That won't be necessary, Mama," Thalia said. "This will only take a moment."

"Aren't you going to introduce us?" Theo chimed in, her gaze raking over Stephen with curiosity and interest. She knew an aristocrat when she saw one, and seemed to be mentally planning the rest of her life around Stephen walking through their door.

Thalia sighed, realizing she had no choice. She couldn't allow her mother and sister to know what had happened between them. "Stephen, this is my mother, Mrs. Henrietta Ramsey, and my sister, Miss Theodosia Ramsey. Mother, Theo ... this is Stephen Dryden ... the ... the Duke of Westerfield."

Theo dropped her book and issued a loud gasp, while their mother clapped a hand over her bosom.

Theo recovered first, issuing a curtsy that had taken weeks before a mirror to perfect. "We are honored that you would visit our home, Your Grace."

Her mother snapped out of her silent stupor and quickly followed suit—though her curtsy didn't hold a candle to Theo's. "It is a pleasure to meet you, Your Grace."

Stephen waved a hand. "Please, there is no need for that. Thalia and I are friends of a sort, and I would be delighted if you would call me Stephen."

"No," Thalia protested. "They will not call you Stephen. They will say farewell, and you will leave. Now."

But Stephen was already over the threshold, and Thalia knew she wasn't strong enough to budge him. "Not until you hear me out. You had much to say the last time we saw one another, but I never said my piece. If you still wish to put me out after I am finished, I will accept that. But I cannot leave until I've said what I came to say."

Yet again, Thalia was left with no recourse. They were causing a scene, and soon she wouldn't be able to hide what any of this was about.

"Thalia, what's going on?" her mother asked, her anxious eyes flitting from Thalia to the duke and back again.

"Everything is fine, Mother," Thalia replied. "Would you and Theo excuse us for a moment? The duke and I have something to discuss."

Theo protested, but their mother took her arm and hauled her from the room. They disappeared into the room the two women shared, quickly shutting the door behind them. Thalia could only imagine what was being discussed inside.

She turned to face Stephen, her lips set to give him what for. Before she could make a sound, Stephen was on her, yanking her into his arms and pressing his mouth to hers. She stiffened, but he melted her far too easily. Her lips yielded to his, seeking and searching, tingling with sensation. Her stomach twisted itself in knots, and her heart pounded against her breastbone.

Pushing him away, she drew in a deep breath and steadied herself. "No. This cannot happen. You made your offer and I refused. I have not and will not change my mind. If you wish me to return the gifts you sent, I will gladly gather them for you right now."

"What I gave is yours regardless of what happens here tonight," he said, jaw stubbornly set. "I would give you so much more, Thalia. I would give you the world if you let me."

Anger made her palms itch to strike him and sent heat flaring up from her middle. "I have already told you that I am not an object to be bought!"

"For the love of God, woman, I'm not trying to buy you!" he bellowed. "I'm trying to marry you!"

Deathly silence fell over the flat. Then, through the door, Thalia heard her sister squeal with delight. Shaking her head, Thalia frowned, certain she couldn't have heard him correctly.

"Marry me? But ... but you said ..."

"I phrased my words poorly, and for that I apologize. What I should have said is that the night of the masquerade I realized I am quite madly in love with you."

Thalia's mouth gaped open, and she scrambled for words. "But you can't be ... it was only one night ... we ..."

"Have known one another for years," he said with a smile. "I was too blind to see it, or perhaps I never allowed myself to consider the possibilities because we seemed to be worlds apart. At least, that's what I thought when I considered myself a duke and you a bookshop owner. But my eyes were opened that night, Thalia, and I saw us as we really were—a man and a woman who were made for each other. There are hundreds of bookshops and libraries in London, yet I return to yours week after week, even when your selection isn't as plentiful as the others. Haven't you ever wondered why?"

Thalia felt on the verge of collapse. Her palms had broken into a sweat and now that her anger was dissipating, disbelief was taking over. "I suppose I never thought of it."

Stephen smiled and took hold of both her hands. "It was you. It was your smiles and our witty bantering. It was the sweet way you wrinkle your nose when reading the titles on the spines. It was the way you moved, with grace and poise but also with purpose and strength. It was the way you looked at me, as if you could see past the title. As if you knew me."

She did know him. Thalia had realized the night of the masquerade that they knew each other better than she'd thought. She knew his favorite books and authors, his favorite poem. She knew that he took great care not to damage the spines or covers of his books because he cherished them. She knew that he was averse to daisies, because he'd collapsed into a sneezing fit when a vase of them rested on her counter.

She knew she loved him, and always had.

"Stephen," she whispered. "You cannot truly mean to marry me. If it is because of ..." she lowered her voice and her eyes, face flushing hot. "If it is because of what we did, I can assure you I expect nothing because of it. I made my choice and do not regret it."

"That isn't the reason I want to marry you," Stephen said, raising her hands to his lips and kissing the back of each one with such reverence she nearly wept. "I want to marry you because I love you. Because you are the only person who showed me who she really was instead of presenting what you thought would appeal to a duke. I want to marry you because you make me smile and laugh. I want to marry you because I want you so badly I feel as if I'm burning up from the inside, and I will die if I cannot have you."

Now she really was weeping, tears, sobbing, hiccups—the works. "Stephen ... I love you, too."

He closed his eyes and rested his lips against her brow. "Thank God. I would have worked to earn your heart if you weren't yet prepared to give it. But you love me?"

"I do," she confessed. "I have for a long time."

"Then say yes. Marry me."

Swiping at her tears, she backed away from him. "You cannot make me your duchess. I know nothing of being a lady, and even less about the ways of the nobility. I would be an embarrassment to your family."

"You would be my pride and joy. Besides, being an aristocrat isn't difficult at all. You simply look down your nose at people and raise one eyebrow, perhaps while peering through a quizzing glass ... like this."

Thalia sputtered a giggle as he straightened and tipped his

head, giving her a chilling look down the bridge of his nose. The effect was ruined by the almost maniacal lift one of dark eyebrow, making him look like some caricature of a gothic novel villain.

"See?" he said with a chuckle, using his fingers to dash away one last tear. "I can teach you, and no one would dare speak a word against you. But more important than you being my duchess is the fact that I want you to be my wife. My partner. My lover. The mother of my children. My best friend."

Thalia drew in a sharp breath as he reached into his coat pocket, coming out with a box that fit in the palm of his hand. Her knees went weak as he sank to one knee, and it took every bit of her strength to keep from collapsing.

The ring he revealed was brilliant gold with a large, square-cut ruby as its centerpiece. The tiny diamonds flanking it sparkled in the light of the lamps.

Thalia put a hand over her mouth as she stared at the extravagant ring. She had never seen anything so costly or precious in her life. "Stephen ... my God, it's beautiful."

"It's yours," he said, staring up at her with pleading in his eyes. "And so am I if you will have me. So are all the things I possess—my title, my lands, my heart and soul. Marry me, Thalia. Let me care for you and your family and make you happy for the rest of your days."

Thalia went to her knees with a sob and threw her arms around him. "Yes!"

Stephen embraced her, holding her so tight she could barely breathe. But Thalia didn't need to breathe, for the sweet kiss he bestowed on her provided all the air and light and life she needed.

He helped her to her feet, and they stood there staring at one another and grinning like a pair of imbeciles. Thalia had been about to speak, but a loud crash from the other side of her bedroom door made her nearly jump out of her skin.

The door swung open to reveal Theo, who was grinning from ear to ear. The walls were so thin, Thalia didn't doubt every word had been overheard.

"What was that?" Thalia asked, fingers intertwined with Stephen's. He had placed the ring on her left ring finger, and its weight served as a reminder that this was real.

Theo glanced over her shoulder, then looked back at them with a laugh. "Oh, it's nothing. Mother has fainted."

EPILOGUE

"Will you stop fussing? You look perfect."
Stephen watched as Thalia smoothed her skirts for what had to be the hundredth time. Turning left and right, she squared her shoulders and critically observed her appearance.

"The tiara is too much," she mumbled, touching a finger to the gold and ruby coronet he'd given to her as a wedding gift—along with a matching set of earrings, necklace, and bracelet. They were all a match for her engagement ring. "Don't you think it's too much?"

"You're a duchess," he reminded her, something he found himself doing often. "Nothing is ever too much."

They had been wed two months ago in a lavish wedding at St. George's. Thalia had been terrified to appear before the whole of London nobility as his bride, but the moment they'd stood face-to-face at the altar, the fear had melted from her eyes. They had gazed at one another, and a sense of rightness had fallen between them. She looked at no one else for the rest of their wedding day.

The new Duchess of Westerfield became an overnight sensation. Their surprise union had become the talk of London and

242

beyond, and was being portrayed as whimsically romantic. The handsome duke lifting a spinster bookseller out of the gutter and making her his duchess. It didn't matter that the story was only half-true, when it turned Thalia into the *ton*'s newest darling. If anyone disparaged her in private, the words never reached his ears, or Thalia's.

They had remained in London long enough for Thalia to have her presentation at court and endure the tutelage of his mother in the social graces. Stephen had been anxious to depart for their honeymoon, but his mother had insisted that it was important for Thalia to belong.

"You will have to formally introduce her to the *ton*," she had reminded him. "You cannot throw her into that situation without preparation."

Stephen had grudgingly admitted that his mother was right, and waited impatiently through weeks of Thalia's tutoring in everything from silverware and place settings, to proper forms of address. At last, they were able to leave the city, with Stephen whisking the entire family away to Westerfield Abbey—the ducal seat on the coast of Devon. Once there, Stephen had spent his days stealing Thalia away whenever he could, as his mother had engaged her in planning her first ball.

Thalia had seemed overwhelmed by all the preparations, but she and his mother got along famously. Whenever Stephen entered the salon for Thalia's particular use, she would gaze up from samples of china and silver and smile.

Tonight was the night. All of the *beau monde* had journeyed to Devon to be introduced to the new duchess. Everything was arranged, with Thalia's gown being created over three weeks— it's crimson hue a match for the damask waistcoat he wore.

"Will anyone think poorly of me for wearing red?"

Stephen took her hand and turned her away from the mirror. Her gown was in the latest style, the bodice encrusted with beading and edged in gold thread. A gauze over-skirt dotted with more gems fell over the satin underskirt. White gloves were the perfect contrast, and her jewels sparkled in the candlelight.

"My love, they will think you are a goddess. Red looks so beautiful against your skin. Now ... breathe."

Thalia gripped his hands and took a slow, deep breath. He held her gaze, nodding and smiling when she seemed to relax a bit.

"Now, we are going to go into that ballroom so I can present you to the people who will bow and kiss your slippers whenever you pass from here on out. We will dance, and drink champagne, and eat too much dessert at supper, and have a marvelous time. Then, we will leave for our wedding trip. Oh, but not before I give you one final wedding gift. It's a surprise."

Stephen had planned a months-long expedition for himself and his bride. First, they would visit Ireland and Scotland before leaving England for more exotic locales. He planned to take her to Paris and Rome, Venice, and Athens. They would swim in oceans and explore ancient ruins and eat Parisian cuisine. He would introduce her to the world of wonders she had been missing, living her entire life in London. With the Season at an end, they were free to do what they pleased. Stephen could hardly wait to have her all to himself.

"Yes," she said with a genuine smile. "All those things sound wonderful."

"Good. Now take my arm. Remember not to use your full smile ... your face will begin to ache within an hour. And don't worry about committing any faux pas. Everyone seems to adore you. They will be forgiving."

She pulled in her smile a bit, reining in its wideness but losing none of the charm. "All right. I am ready. And what's this about a surprise? Haven't you given me enough already?"

"Ah-ah," he chided. "It isn't a surprise if I tell you what it is.

And no, I haven't given you enough. The entire world wouldn't be enough for you. No more questions. It's time."

Clinging to his arm, she allowed him to lead her from their shared bedchamber. The attached duchess's suite would continue to go unused, for Stephen could not imagine passing a single night without her in his bed.

As they neared the staircase, she gave him a worried look. "Do you promise to help me keep an eye on Theo? I am worried that she will fall prey to the first man to glance her way."

Stephen had harbored similar concerns about his new sister-in-law. She was lovely and he cared dearly for her, but she was young and naive—much like the parade of debutantes who debuted each Season.

"This is only her first ball, and the only one she will attend until her official coming out," Stephen said, patting Thalia's hand. "I will help you keep watch, and by the time she debuts, she will be better prepared to live amongst society."

"Thank you for all you have done for her and my mother. I've never seen them so happy."

Stephen smiled, thinking of his mother-in-law, who had made fast friends with his own mother. The two drank tea and chatted late into the night after dinner, and took their morning walks together. Theo was busy delighting in all the new things her status now afforded—a fashionable new wardrobe, a horse of her own and someone to teach her how to ride it, jewels, and a room the size of a small palace.

"I am glad. I want them to be happy. I want *you* to be happy."

They had now reached the doors of the ballroom. Two footmen waited to open the doors that would usher them into the next phase of their lives.

Thalia looked up at him with all the love in the world in her eyes, reminding Stephen just how fortunate he was. "I am happier than I ever dreamed, and it's all because of you."

"The feeling is mutual, my love. Now, are you ready?"

"Yes. I'm ready."

The doors swung open, and the music from within the ballroom faded away as several hundred heads swiveled in their direction. The clamor of voices hushed, and one could have heard a pin drop.

Stephen led his bride forward just as they were announced, coming to a stop at the top of the curving stairs leading to marble floors below.

"The Duke and Duchess of Westerfield!"

Heads bowed and skirts spread in curtsies like a rippling ocean wave. Stephen laid a hand over his bride's where it rested in the crook of his elbow. Together, they made their way down the staircase and into the throng.

LATER THAT EVENING, a puzzled Thalia took precarious steps down the back staircase of Westerfield Abbey. Her husband had blindfolded her, leaving Thalia to trust him to guide her. The excited murmurings of half their ball guests followed them into the night, the summer air having given way to the crisp coolness of fall.

"Almost there," Stephen whispered close to her ear. "I hope you enjoy your gift, my love."

Thalia grinned and held tighter to his arm. She would never grow tired of hearing him call her 'my love.' Nor would she ever grow tired of his flair for the romantic and dramatic. From the day of their engagement, he had been spoiling her rotten. Thalia protested, but secretly reveled in his attention.

He had just announced to their guests that he had a spectacular end to the evening planned, and he wanted them all to witness it. So, about one hundred guests had followed them through the French doors and off the back terrace. Her feet found soft grass as they reached the large stretch of lawn leading to the gardens.

Stephen placed a hand at the small of her back to bring her to a halt, then the warmth and solidity of him materialized at her back. His hands found her shoulders, and he kissed her cheek.

"I was unable to make this happen for you at Vauxhall," he said as he untied her blindfold. "But I was determined for you to experience this at least once in your life."

Thalia blinked as the fabric fell away from her eyes—revealing a massive hot-air balloon resting right on the house grounds. She made a small sound of shock and turned to look at Stephen over her shoulder.

"How on earth did you arrange this without my knowledge?"

Stephen grinned and kissed the tip of her nose. "You were too busy making plans with my mother. As well, the balloon didn't arrive until the ball was well underway. You were mingling and did not notice."

"Oh, Stephen!" she exclaimed, throwing her arms around him—much to the delight of the onlookers, who cheered and clapped. "It's wonderful! I ... I'm speechless."

"Well, there's nothing to do now but step inside and take flight."

Trepidation curled in the depths of Thalia's gut. "Is it safe?"

Stephen nudged her forward, and they began the walk toward the balloon. "Mr. Cunningham's design is the safest in England and he is experienced. I wouldn't trust anyone else with your life."

The aforementioned Mr. Cunningham stood beside his balloon with a wide smile as they approached—wearing a great-coat and a plaid cap—a pair of goggles lowered around his neck.

"Good evening Your Graces," he said with a sweeping bow. "Welcome aboard!"

Stephen took Thalia's hand and helped her inside the open basket, which felt surprisingly sturdy beneath her feet.

"Thank you very much, Mr. Cunningham," Thalia said as the man followed them inside. "I am honored to have you take me on my first flight."

"The honor is all mine, Your Grace. Now ... don't be alarmed. The ascent can be a bit shaky, but once we're high enough it's smooth sailing."

Thalia bit her lip, moving into the circle of Stephen's arms as Mr. Cunningham began toying with levers and pulleys. A burst of fire went up into the ignited balloon, causing Thalia to gasp and shrink against Stephen. Her husband chuckled and held her tight as they lifted off the ground. The basket bobbed and dipped precariously, and Thalia closed her eyes, afraid they might go toppling at any moment.

The sensation of being lifted churned her stomach and made her heartbeat accelerate, but she took deep breaths and reminded herself that Stephen had done this before. He wouldn't have planned this if he thought anything could go wrong.

"Open your eyes, my love. You're missing the best part."

Thalia obeyed and pried her eyes open, realizing that the frightening swaying had mostly ceased. She gasped, gripping at the edge of the basket as the vast holding of Westerfield Abbey sprawled out below them—growing smaller by the minute. Cool air whipped against her face and she laughed, delighted by the sensation.

"Oh my God," she shouted to be heard over the wind. "It's incredible."

"I told you," Stephen murmured, dropping a kiss onto her shoulder. "Now you know how it feels to fly."

"The night's perfect for it!" Mr. Cunningham called out, still operating his levers and such. "Relax and enjoy the ride, Your Graces."

"Ah, I almost forgot," Stephen said, moving away from Thalia and crouching to retrieve something.

Thalia smiled as she recognized a silver ice bucket, a bottle of uncorked champagne nestled inside. Stephen produced two flutes, giving them to Thalia so he could pour. The bubbling wine filled both glasses, and Stephen left the bottle inside the bucket and retrieve his drink from Thalia.

Raising his glass, he gave her a look filled with naked devotion. "To my beautiful duchess ... the pride of my heart. And to many years of happiness ... and children. I'm thinking there will be at least six."

Thalia held her glass back before Stephen could complete the toast. "Six?"

Stephen gave a sheepish smile. "It seemed appropriate."

"Hmph," she snorted. "Says the man who will not have to carry and birth them."

"If you were to produce twins it would cut down on the number of pregnancies."

"Stephen Alexander Warwick Conrad Dryden!"

He groaned. "I'm going to strangle Mother for teaching you all of my names."

Thalia wrinkled her nose at them. "I would have read it off the church register when you signed it, anyway. Six children, Stephen? Isn't it ... a bit much?"

He raised his eyebrows at her and shrugged. "We are a duke and duchess. Nothing is ever—"

"Too much," Thalia finished for him. "So I've been told."

"Fine," Stephen relented. "Four children."

"Three."

"Done," he agreed. "Unless, of course ... the twins, you know..."

She slapped playfully at his chest, which prompted Stephen to take advantage of her proximity by grabbing her waist and pulling her closer. He held his glass up.

"You don't have to give me a thing to make me happy. You've already made me the happiest man in the world."

Thalia touched her glass to his. "Still ... six *is* a nice even number."

A wicked grin overtook Stephen's face, then he took a long pull of his champagne. "Then Mr. Cunningham had better land this thing right now or turn his back and cover his ears. I'm ready to begin."

Muffling the hysterical laughter coming from Thalia's throat, Stephen then swooped in and consumed her lips in a fiery kiss.

ABOUT THE AUTHOR

Elise Marion is a lover books and has a special place in her heart for sweet and sensual romance. Writing about love across all walks of life is her passion, as is reaching people through the written word. The Army wife and stay-at-home mother of three spends most of her time taking care of her children. Her second job includes writing stories about characters that people can fall in love with. When the Texas native isn't caring for her family or writing, you can usually find her with her nose in a book, singing loudly, or cooking up something new in the kitchen.

Visit her website at www.elisemarion.com

THE NIGHTINGALE AND THE LARK

JESSICA CALE

After years of failed auditions, rum heiress Andromeda
Archambault gives it one last try at The Crow's Nest in
Shoreditch against her better judgment. She may be a lady, but
to director Frank Creighton, she's the Queen of Night, and she's
perfect for a starring role in his theatre and his life. But Andie
isn't who she says she is, and neither is Frank. Will their
Phantasmagoria be a success, or will the skeletons in their
closets close the show before it begins?

CHAPTER ONE

Four bars into the aria, Andromeda Archambault knew she'd lost them.

Sitting in a box at the back of the Theatre-Royal, the directors paid her no mind as they talked among themselves and shuffled papers. She could barely make out their features from her position behind the stage lamps, but she didn't have to. Six months of training for this audition, and it was over in under a minute.

Heart sinking, she kept singing because she was a professional. Or at least she was trying to be. Every audition was the same—weeks of encouraging correspondence ending in surprised dismay when she finally introduced herself. The Lyceum. Haymarket. The King's Theatre. The Adelphi. The Pantheon. The Olympic.

She'd even tried the Aquatic, for heaven's sake. Surrounded by artificial waterfalls, painted krakens, and a splintering shipwreck, she'd felt more like her namesake than ever before—frustrated, helpless, and waiting to be eaten.

There was no hero swooping in to save her at the Theatre-Royal, but she was no sacrifice. She was a *siren*.

Angry now, she sang louder. Improvising, she added trills Mozart himself had never dreamed of, projecting with such clarity and force, she felt she might collapse in on herself. Let every empty seat vibrate with her passion so that night's audience could still feel it when they sat down. Let the curtains tremble on their rods. Let it change the very air itself until she made the space her own, altered it on a fundamental level because she had been inside it. She wouldn't let anyone present forget her name.

When she finished, the three directors in the box looked largely unaffected. The only indication she had of how well she did was the shock on the cleaner's face, stunned into stillness and holding his broom in mid-air. In a doorway stage left, an actress looked on in wonder, tears streaming down her face.

At least *someone* had enjoyed it.

Only one director stood. "Thank you, Miss Archer. We'll be in touch."

"No, you won't," she muttered. Forgoing the traditional curtsy, she exited stage right before she burst into tears. She wouldn't give them the satisfaction.

As she made it into the chequered hallway leading to the foyer, the rapid click of heels on marble stopped her in her tracks.

Wide-eyed and slightly winded, the actress all but flew around the corner. "Wait!" She skidded to a stop, dashing the tears from her cheeks. "I've never heard anything like that in my life. You're unbelievable."

Warmed by the compliment, she let out a shaking breath. "They don't seem to think so."

The actress rolled her eyes. "No accounting for taste." She thrust out a hand. "I'm Emilia."

She took her hand awkwardly. "Andie."

The door flew open and half a dozen stagehands bustled through, two struggling with a massive gilt harp. Emilia's interest turned to horror as they nearly dropped it. "Careful with that!" Distracted, her gaze kept darting back to them as they rounded the corner. "I carted that thing all the way back from bloody Florence; if they so much as chip a cherub, I'll scream." Her eyes bright, she smiled and refocused on Andie. "I'd love to see you perform again. Where are you based?"

Andie sighed and shook her head. "Nowhere. No one will take me."

Emilia's smile faded. "What do you mean?"

"The last one outright told me he didn't like the image of 'a blackbird among the doves.'" She raised her eyebrows. When she'd first started auditioning, she'd only thought to make it on her own without her family's influence. All her life, people had fallen over themselves to please her, but with a borrowed dress and a borrowed name, the situation was suddenly very different.

Emilia's mouth dropped open. "Afraid you'll sing their actresses off the stage, more like." She shook her head, clearly scandalized. "What bollocks!"

Andie had to agree.

"Have you tried the Lyceum? Sadler's Wells?" Emilia asked, hopeful.

With a sigh, Andie listed the last ten auditions she remembered.

Brittle with barely suppressed rage, Emilia crossed her arms. "The Crow's Nest in Shoreditch. Go right now."

Andie blinked. *The Crow's Nest in Shoreditch.* She didn't know whether to laugh or take offense. "I beg your pardon?"

Emilia waved a hand. "I know, I know, it's hardly got the ring of the 'Theatre-Royal,' but Frank Creighton's worth a dozen of these knobs. He's an odd duck, but he pays on time, and he knows talent when he sees it."

Andie was still stuck on *Shoreditch.* She had been to New York, St. Croix, and all over Europe, but although she'd lived in

London all her life, she'd never been to the East End. "Frank Creighton," she repeated. "The Crow's Nest."

She could remember that. Her mother often attended Lavinia Creighton-Crowley's salons, but Andie very much doubted the dowager Lady Bodmin would appreciate such an association, even an imaginary one. The stately old woman had always treated Andie with detached courtesy, but if she knew what she was about to do, she'd drop her petit fours.

With that image in her head, Andie finally smiled.

WHATEVER ANDIE HAD EXPECTED, this wasn't it.

Across the street from St. Leonard's, The Crow's Nest was an Elizabethan behemoth, six stories high, perhaps thirty feet across, and listing ever-so-slightly to the side. Thinking of the plywood shipwreck at the Aquatic, Andie inspected the splintered wood beams for cannon damage. As the sun set behind it, several dozen crows suddenly swooped off the roof and headed for the churchyard behind her.

Across the front of the building, the gas lamps were already lit, and the diamond-paned windows glowed invitingly. Between them, illustrated playbills advertised upcoming acts in Cruickshank-style caricatures and garish letters. *Maggie the Singing Moll. The Bearded Boy's Nocturnal Orchestra. Somnabule the Hypnotist. Frank's Phantasmagoria of Horror and Mystery.*

Not exactly Handel or Haydn. Andie turned the collar of her spencer against the wind and shivered into her cashmere scarf. Twenty years of music lessons, and here she was—not singing in *Figaro* at the Olympic, but potentially opening for *Prospero Pudding's Talking Poppet.*

She pinched the bridge of her nose. Her mother had offered to pull strings for her. Would it really be so awful to compromise just this once?

Andie sighed. She couldn't. If she let her mother get her a part now, she'd never know if she could have done it on her own. Her tutors had told her she was good and her performances at parties had always been well-received, but singing on stage was different. And if she couldn't out-perform *Winifred and the Winchester Geese,* maybe she *should* give up and get married instead.

"I think not," she said to herself, re-pinning her hair in the reflection of a dark window. After the day she'd had, it looked as if lightning had struck it, her carefully pinned chignon giving way to frizz. She looked tired, and her dress was rumpled but still clean. Smoothing a little rose pomade over her lips, she took a breath and straightened her spine.

Before she could talk herself out of it, she strode through the open door.

The Crow's Nest was surprisingly warm, given its size. It smelled of musty old velvet, fresh tobacco, and oranges. Andie began to relax as she heard a piano playing in the distance. Not exactly the Paris Opera, the wooden floors were covered in rushes, rosemary, and sawdust, and they sloped outward to the wider main hall at the back.

Andie stopped in her tracks when she saw it. There were no seats at all on the ground floor, only an open pit for standing with a long bar to the left. The stage was shallow and high, with trapeze equipment hanging between blue curtains decorated with glittering stars. Six levels of balconies were stacked on top of each other like the layers of cake, the ceiling so high she could barely see it. She couldn't tell if the balconies had seats, but each was lit by half a dozen mismatched chandeliers.

It was a mess, but it was magic.

The piano stopped.

"Are you lost?"

Bristling, Andie turned toward the voice. "I beg your pardon?"

A man stood behind the upright piano and leaned over the top of it. Tall and lanky, he seemed more liquid than man with an easy posture and a lazy smile. "You're not the kind of lady we get around these parts, is all."

Andie folded her arms. She was sick of the implication that she didn't belong. "And what kind of lady is that?"

He cleared his throat for effect. "The, erm...*evening* variety." His smile widened at the play on words as he slunk from behind the piano. "You are very clearly a lady of *quality*. What are you doing in Shoreditch?"

"I've been asking myself that for the last twenty minutes," she admitted, relaxing. He was just a flirt. She took in his light linen shirt—collarless, open, and rolled up the elbows. It was tucked into a pair of smart if faded trousers. A musician of little consequence, he probably tried his luck with every woman who walked through the door, and a fair few would take him up on it too. Though the charcoal of his hair was rapidly giving way to gray ash, his manner and mischievous expression gave him an ageless quality that made her think of the fae kings in her fairy stories. He shouldn't be handsome—his chin was too prominent, his skin too pale, his smile too wide—but she couldn't look away. Worse, his gaze was sharp, focused, and above all, interested. A woman could lose herself in eyes like that.

He knew it too.

Andie looked away with some difficulty. *Get it together. You did not turn down a prince, an earl, and three barons to shag an East End piano player.*

"You will." He shrugged, returning to the piano and shuffling his music.

Blinking, she tried to remember what he was responding to. Surely he couldn't read her mind? *Oh, right. Shoreditch.* Flustered, she followed him. "I'm looking for Frank Creighton. Is he here?"

"Usually." He looked up, raising an eyebrow. "What do you want with Frank?"

Andie fiddled with the bottom button of her spencer. Perhaps she should have written first. What if he didn't like her just turning up out of the blue? It wouldn't do to get off on the wrong foot. "I'm a singer," she said. "I had an audition at the Theatre-Royal this afternoon, and an actress there told me I ought to come here instead. Emilia. Do you know her?"

"Emilia?" The man blinked. "Emilia Virtue? Short, Welsh, says whatever's on her mind faster than you can take it in?"

She smiled in spite of herself. "I believe she plays the harp...?"

"What are you waiting for?" He gestured toward the stage and sat behind the piano. "Sing something."

"Now?" Andie laughed.

"Yes, by God." He played a few notes for emphasis. "Anything you like."

Encouraged and relaxing more by the minute, Andie climbed the few steps to the stage and took in the view. The hall was cramped but beautiful in its way, and the chandeliers glittered like dozens of scattered constellations throughout the cavernous balconies. The audience was less likely to have opera glasses, but they'd be so close, they wouldn't need them. She idly batted the trapeze ring, wondering what to sing.

"All right," she said. "Here goes."

THE MOMENT SHE STARTED SINGING, it was over for Frank.

He would have thought he was dreaming, but his dreams were never this good. A few actresses and dancers made their way in every week, but this woman was something else. Shy but self-assured, she had appeared in his doorway like a mirage, a vision of buttoned-up beauty in a girlish coat and expensive scarf. Though everything about her from her posture to the pins in her hair screamed that she was pure class, she took in her surroundings with an unguarded wonder that made his heart skip. World-weary and unimpressed from birth, London girls didn't look at *anything* like that. When the chandeliers sparkled in her soft brown eyes, he wished he had twice as many.

Frank was no stranger to wonder himself, but this was another experience altogether. He couldn't look away if he tried. She climbed up on stage, opened her mouth, and the world shifted. That was the only he could explain it; he lost all awareness of himself and his surroundings. It was a joyful, note-perfect "Der Hölle Rache" from *The Magic Flute* in the original German, but it was more than that. She *became* the Queen of Night. He had seen the opera plenty of times, but he'd never expected the most convincing rendition of what was essentially a detailed curse to come from a smiling young woman dressed like a love letter in lilac and lace.

It was a disguise, he realized. The violet spencer, the suede gloves, the lip rouge as subtle as pink champagne. Demure had never done it for him, but when she let go, she was anything but. Precise, measured, and a little stiff, yes, but the power and passion and her voice were enough to put the fear of God into any man. More terrifying still, she wasn't even *trying*.

She was *playing* with him.

Frank had never been more frightened in his life.

When she finished, she looked a little surprised by the sudden silence. She gave a perfect curtsy and laughed. Her smile was like someone had ignited the sun.

Stunned, Frank pulled a cigar from behind his sheet music and lit it with a match.

He could see her as the Queen of Night. Not Mozart's, but something better. She could preside over the variety show, or she could be a new heroine in the Phantasmagoria—those always did better with a beautiful woman fleeing the monsters.

THE NIGHTINGALE AND THE LARK

He'd dress her in gold dust and diaphanous silk, Grecian sandals, and a crown—no, a halo of stars. No—

"Was that all right?"

He was startled out of his reverie by a ridiculous question in a honeyed voice. When he looked up, she was sitting in the trapeze hoop, spinning in slow circles like she was sitting in a crescent moon.

Feeling like lightning had struck him between the eyes, he jolted back, then took another puff of his cigar to steady his nerves.

"All right?" He ran a hand through his hair. "'The Wrath of Hell.' Interesting choice."

She sighed. "I had an…unpleasant afternoon."

"Evidently." Frank laughed. His was getting better by the minute. "What's your name?"

"Andie," she said, hopping off the trapeze hoop. "Andie Archer."

Frank nodded. "I'm Frank Creighton."

Andie stopped mid-step. "*You* are?"

"Not what you were expecting?" He stood and shuffled through the music in his bench, brushing fragments of ash away as it fell. It hadn't caught fire yet, but the music was battered enough without adding burns to it. Finding the piece he was looking for, he propped his cigar in the dish on top of the piano and took the music to the stage.

Her eyes bright and her shoulders a good deal stiffer, Andie lamented, "I've made a fool of myself."

"Not at all," he insisted. "That's the most I've enjoyed a performance in years." Well, *ever*, but he didn't want to scare her off. "I would like nothing more than to put you on that stage and let you sing anything that pops into your head, but this isn't exactly an opera house."

Clearly disappointed, she straightened her scarf. "Well, thank you for your time—"

Before she could leave, he threw himself between her and the door. "Don't misunderstand me; I need you—" *Too keen. Scale it back.* "Erm, I want you—" *Goddammit, Frank.* He cleared his throat. "You're too good for me. For us, for this theater. We don't do a lot of opera in the traditional sense, but if you'd be open to singing other parts, they're yours."

Her face lit up, but her immediate joy was quickly replaced with a wariness that wasn't unfounded. "What other parts?"

Bracing for a slap, he handed her the sheet music.

Andie looked over it quickly, focused on the notes. "This looks simple enough..." Then she read the lyrics. *"There was a young girl from Regina, who had an oyster shell for a—"* Her mouth dropped open in shock. "I'm not singing that!"

Frank shrugged. "It's a different audience. The humor's coarser, and everything's a double entendre, if not a single one. Is that a thing? If you can get past that, there's a lot of love in it. We work at it every day, try to make people laugh and forget for a few hours. There's nothing wrong with that."

Andie considered him, unconvinced.

"Come to the show tomorrow at seven," he offered. "Be my guest. I'll give you the best seat in the house. You can watch what we do and decide then. Can't say fairer than that."

She held his gaze for a long moment, and he could only guess what she was thinking. Reserved but determined, Andie didn't look away or back down. She wasn't intimidated by him. Despite her girlish attire, he rather suspected she was older than he'd first thought. But why would a dazzlingly beautiful woman dress like an incognito society miss?

The answer was too simple. She *was* an incognito society miss.

Oh, well. No one was perfect.

Andie was unreasonably close, however, or would be until her father or brother or aristocratic cousin called him out for letting her sing in public. Well and good, that was a risk he was willing to take. If he succeeded, the theater's future would be secured. If he was shot, he'd go down having accompanied a classically trained soprano on a nine-verse ballad about shagging nuns.

Few men were able to choose the manner of their deaths, but Frank reckoned he could do worse.

He blinked first, his gaze briefly flitting lower. "Dear God, you have freckles," he mumbled, forgetting himself and his surroundings as he noticed the constellations across her cheeks, only a shade or two deeper than her golden-brown skin.

Andie's eyebrows drew together in an annoyed frown. "Is that a problem?"

"No," Frank blurted. *Only for my sanity.* "No problem at all."

She wasn't sure about him. He couldn't exactly blame her. Who he was and how he lived his life was unusual, to say the least, and kindred spirits were getting harder to find as the years went by. She could still say no—and likely would if she sat through the entirety of his Phantasmagoria—but if there was any chance of having her on his stage, he'd give the performance of his life.

Finally, she nodded. "Seven it is."

CHAPTER TWO

When Andie arrived home, dinner was just beginning. With a conspiratorial nod to Clement at the front door, she removed her slippers, carrying them with her up the stairs to avoid alarming her mother. She dropped them when a familiar figure appeared on the landing.

Eyes sparkling with mischief, Alexandre posed like Louis XIV and pursed his lips. In his best impression of their father, he quietly demanded, "And where have you been, young la—"

His words were cut off as she launched herself into his arms. Her eldest brother had been gone for more than a year, and she hadn't realized how much she missed him. "Alex, thank God." She pulled back and looked at him properly. His dinner jacket was spotless, and he smelled of lavender and bay laurel. "You just got off a ship and you look better than I do. When did you arrive?"

"Late this morning. I made arrangements for everything to be taken to the warehouse and made it back before tea to surprise you. Father sends his love." He took in her disheveled hair and plain clothes. "You look...different. Where *have* you been?"

"Shoreditch," she said before she thought better of it. "I had an audition."

He opened his mouth, but it was a full five seconds before any sound came out of it. "In Shoreditch?" A sudden understanding lit his eyes. "Wait—is The Crow's Nest still open?"

"That's where—" She broke off, alarmed by the intensity in his expression. "How do you know about The Crow's Nest?"

"I've...been there before, is all." He shrugged. "Is Frank still running it?"

A peculiar heat flooded her chest as she was reminded of that afternoon, sitting beside him on the edge of the stage, surrounded by foil stars and faceted crystal. His curious scrutiny was as bright and warm as a gas lamp, dangerous to sit too close to but undeniably delicious. *Dear God, you have freckles.* She still didn't know his opinion of freckles, but she liked that he'd noticed. "He is."

Alex wasn't buying her feigned nonchalance. He laughed under his breath. "How's that for a lark? Mum's going to love this."

"Andromeda, is that you?" their mother called from the dining room.

Andie closed her eyes, cringing at getting caught coming in late. "Yes, Mother."

"Dress for dinner and come down. Your brother has returned from St. Croix."

Andie stifled a laugh as Alex wiggled his eyebrows. "I'll just be a moment."

With a last smile, Alex jogged down the staircase, sure-footed though he'd just spent a month at sea. Andie envied her brother's easy self-assurance. He was the life of every gathering, comfortable with himself and his place in the world even though their position had changed in his lifetime and, depending on what happened in France, may yet change again.

Born the heir to a marquis with an ancestral chateau in

Chartres, by thirty Alex was all but running the London side of St. Croix Luxury Imports, a business their great-grandfather had established in the 1680s to the horror of the French court. Shunned by Versailles for his race and his working-class wife, Achille had gotten the last laugh; when the revolution began a century later, their family left France but kept St. Croix, surviving the Terror and thriving in England as displaced—yet still staggeringly wealthy—aristocrats.

Alex didn't care about the castle or the lost title. He liked London, and he was happy with his life.

Andie was less certain about where she fit in.

Dressing quickly, Andie wondered how she would tell her mother about The Crow's Nest. Her family had always been supportive of her music, but surely that support would not extend to Shoreditch. She'd never exactly lied to her mother, but she wasn't eager to tell her the entire truth.

Besides, she might not take the job.

Andie snorted, tying her coral necklace and sliding a white camelia into her hair. No, The Crow's Nest was not where she'd imagined herself, but she was oddly drawn to it. It was older, comforting yet oddly seductive, a little broken...kind of like Frank. If nothing else, she wanted to see him again.

But why? In the ten years she'd been out in society, very few men had turned her head, but it wasn't for lack of trying. Far more interested in music than marrying, Andie hadn't encouraged them, knowing full well most wanted a fat fortune and a silent, pretty wife.

Over the years, they had sent her countless bouquets and carefully lettered poetry, but they didn't listen to her. Even the ones who praised her singing talked through her songs. Not one of them had ever really *looked* at her.

Andie studied her reflection in the candlelight, noticing her own freckles for the first time in years.

It was nice to be seen.

THE CROW'S NEST blazed like a bonfire on Friday night.

Dozens of people milled about in the street outside, restless but in good spirits. The crowd was mainly working class, men and women from all parts of London and much further afield if their accents were anything to go by. As she made her way to the door, she overheard bits of Italian, German, and Cockney so broad she didn't immediately realize it was English. She had been a little nervous about coming on her own, but few paid her any mind in her oversized blue coat and dove-gray walking skirt. As strange as the situation was to her, for the first time in a long time, no one was looking at her like she didn't belong.

Andie smiled to herself, breathing deeply of the temperate evening air. The people milled about, talking and laughing. Carriages rolled by slowly, delayed by the crowd and the half dozen food stalls set up in the street. One sold bacon baps and picked eggs, another paper cones of roasted nuts, and a third sold tea in china cups. The tea smelled more like chicory than Darjeeling, but it was hot enough that great clouds of steam billowed into the sky every time a new cup was poured. To Andie's amazement, it was drunk just as quickly, the cups returned to the stall keeper for a quick rinse in hot water before they were passed onto the next customer.

As the sun touched the horizon, a cloud of crows seemed to rise from the churchyard outside St. Leonard's. Dozens if not hundreds of them soared above the crowd, swarming up and up and up until they disappeared over the top of the theater. The crowd tittered, but Andie could only stare, aghast.

"It's not just a clever name."

Andie turned at the sound of Frank's voice behind her. He stood in a side doorway with his arms crossed, unbothered by all the people waiting to get in. In a starched white shirt with a high collar and braces, he looked rather more debonaire than the previous day. He'd shaved and taken such care with his hair that Andie might have mistaken him for a gentleman if not for his sleeves, which were once again rolled up to his elbows. Curiously, she didn't mind the oversight.

"The Crow's Nest. Very clever." She smiled. "Were they already here when you moved in, or...?"

Frank gave an almost imperceptible shake of his head and motioned her closer. "Between you and me?" He lowered his face to hers until she could smell the orange-flower water in his skin. "It's sunflower seeds."

Andie was so unnerved by his nearness that she didn't immediately register what he'd said. "Did you say sunflower seeds?"

He nodded. "Get them at the 'change, cheap as anything. I take out a handful, give them a shake, and—" Frank mimed throwing seeds like he was rolling dice at a gaming table. "Works every time."

Unsure if he was joking, Andie laughed. "You'll have to show me sometimes."

"I've got lots of things to show you. Let's get started." Clearly in his element, Frank pulled himself to full height and spun on his heel. He offered her his arm with all the melodrama of a pantomime. He was playing for cheap laughs. Andie knew that, so she was startled when she heard herself giggle.

Frank led her through the side door and down a twisting corridor of back hallways filled with scattered costumes and performers in various stages of undress. Two men assisted each other with affixing collars while three chorus girls layered garish petticoats over old-fashioned paniers. An older woman hauled an enormous tambourine toward a flight of narrow stairs, a thin cigar clamped between her serious lips. Another man followed with a percussion instrument Andie couldn't identify, then the neck of a gargantuan string instrument appeared like a giraffe charging above the melee.

The woman carrying it was younger and smaller than Andie was. She stopped in front of Frank, almost tripping up a mustachioed gentleman carrying what Andie could only assume was a hurdy-gurdy. When the woman spoke, it was with a thick Spanish accent. "Is it bass tonight or not? Tell me before I haul this bastard up the stairs."

"Theorbo," Frank said, and Andie finally recognized the instrument. She had only ever seen illustrations; she didn't expect them to be so big. "We have a guest tonight. We must show her what we can do. Miss Archer, this is Antonia. Antonia, Miss Andie Archer."

Andie extended her hand. "It's a pleasure to meet you...is it *Mrs.* Creighton?"

Antonia's eyes grew huge, then she let out a laugh an ear-splitting laugh. "Mrs..." She laughed until she wheezed. "No, no, no. I would murder him before lunch. You see what he makes me do?" She hurled the theorbo onto her back, and Andie and Frank both ducked as the neck swung toward him. The whole instrument was easily two yards long. Without ceremony, she headed toward the stairs.

"Thank you, Antonia," he called.

"Bugger yourself, Frank," she answered.

Frank ran a hand through his hair with a laugh. "She loves me really."

A man standing behind Frank with a guitar shook his head at her, and Andie had to stifle a laugh. "Is it always this...chaotic?"

"Chaotic? This is just Friday." They continued through the hall toward a more central set of stairs. "I suppose it would seem chaotic if you weren't accustomed to it. You'll get to know everyone soon enough. I'll introduce you around properly later."

As they passed the main doors, Andie noticed the crowd outside had doubled as well. "How many people work here?"

If Frank noticed the crowd, he ignored them as he led her up the stairs. "The orchestra has twelve at the moment, then there's half a dozen regular performers for the show, not counting guests. Of course, some of the musicians are also performers— Pietro and Lorenzo are acrobats, for example. I'd have them on stage every night, but where would I find another oboe da caccia expert in these parts?" He laughed to himself, and Andie began to wonder if he was quite mad. She knew for certain he was when his gaze fixed on a seemingly empty space and he cried, "Lulu!"

After a moment's pause, a girl peeked out from behind a gold-painted pillar. Younger than the other performers by a good few years, she was perhaps fourteen. Tall for a child, she had olive skin and a pair of huge, oddly solemn dark eyes. "I'm here."

Frank's whole face warmed up when he saw her. As they reached the next floor, he introduced them. "This is Miss Archer, the singer I told you about. Would you be so good as to show her the ropes tonight? Give her the famous Lulu tour?"

The girl smiled shyly, but she nodded.

"Lovely. Miss Archer, this is Lucrezia. She's our costume designer, set designer, crow wrangler, and accounts clerk. She keeps the tomatoes alive—old tomatoes very much included— and incidentally, she is also my daughter." Frank bowed.

Lulu rolled her eyes dramatically but gave a little curtsy. "Miss Archer."

Utterly charmed, Andie couldn't help but grin. "I'm delighted to meet you, Lulu. What will you show me first?"

Lulu looked to her father for guidance.

He shrugged. "I trust you. I'd better be off, but you two sit in the box tonight. I want Miss Archer to have a good view."

"But the bridge...?" Lulu frowned.

"Let's not scare her away just yet." At Andie's questioning look, he explained, "There's a hidden walkway just below the top floor, between the stage and the orchestra's gallery." He lowered his voice and whispered, "It's terrifying. Obviously, it's Lu's favorite spot."

"Obviously," Lulu emphasized.

"The box," Frank repeated. With a wink and a bow, he took his leave. "Enjoy the show."

Frank disappeared in a flurry of activity, the sound of dropped instruments and indistinct shouts echoing in his wake. The hall immediately felt emptier without him in it.

Andie let out a sigh. She had briefly forgotten Lulu was there. Frank was all presence, but Lulu was almost the absence of it—quiet and calm, even her breathing was silent as she studied Andie with an artist's eye. Suddenly wishing she'd worn something less dowdy, Andie smiled awkwardly, only just noticing that the girl appeared to be wearing a sort of Greek dress of violet paisley. It had a fraying ribbon belt and a raw hem, but it was more beautiful than half the things Andie's modiste came up with. "Your dress is remarkable. Do you really design the costumes?"

Lulu nodded. "And the sets, although everybody helps. Sometimes I feed the crows, but that's mostly my dad. He is rather prone to exaggeration. He doesn't need me or anyone to keep him alive. He's less scatter-brained than he seems."

"Does your mother help?"

"My mother?" Lulu wrinkled her nose as if Andie had just enquired about her tobacconist. Her voice dropped as she dead-panned, "She's no longer with us."

Her expression was so straight that Andie couldn't tell if she was joking. "Oh...erm, I'm sorry to hear that."

Lulu shrugged and headed down the hall toward the center of the building. "It's quite all right. This way, Miss Archer."

As fast as Frank was, Lulu was quicker. Over the next twenty minutes, Andie was shown every back corridor, seating area, dressing room, and secret passage. Although the theater itself was indeed Elizabethan, it had been modified by three hundred years of eccentric owners who'd thought to use it for every kind of trade and entertainment under the sun. It had housed a potters' guild during the Civil War—the furnaces of which were still used in the kitchen, now at lower temperatures for daily cooking—then became a temporary shelter for those displaced by the Great Fire. Though the Restoration had brought the return of the theater, the top floor was still fitted with Jacobean apartments. Thinking of her mother's interest in art and architecture, Andie wanted to ask more about those, but Lulu was already halfway up the final set of stairs to the roof.

Six floors up, Andie could see for miles.

She could have stood there for ages, just looking at the city lights, but the sound of a piano playing to roaring applause drew them back inside.

In "the box"—one of many, but the lowest central balcony—Andie finally caught her breath. Sitting beside Lulu on a plush velvet settee, she felt more like royalty than she ever had at the opera. Worn as it was, the sofa was preferable to the hard benches and stools of other theaters. The atmosphere was lively and cheerful, no one was spying on her with opera glasses, and best of all, the stage was so close, she could hear and see everything clearly.

The lamps were lower than they were for most performances, the audience in darkness. The brightest thing in the whole theater was the glittering plaster moon affixed to the trapeze ring, now suspended a little higher over the stage. To the left, a comically large top hat bobbed back and forth behind the piano. There was no light back there—Frank was playing the music by memory, or he was improvising it. A galloping rhythm, it was almost a reel, gathering in speed and intensity with stormy minor chords inserted jarringly into random offbeats. The crowd began to clap along, faster and faster until a curtain dropped, light spilled in, and Frank took the stage.

Andie couldn't help but laugh at the sight of him. In the coat and cravat of a funeral director, he'd powdered his face stark white and lined his eyes in kohl until he was the very image of a gothic villain. Affecting a stagger, he hobbled to the center of the stage and took in the crowd, his every expression sinister and every gesture exaggerated. With a lift of an eyebrow, he had the crowd rolling with laughter.

The audience fell into an uncomfortable silence. Frank let it sit, looking out over their expectant faces. "You again?"

The cheers were thunderous.

Frank let them make all the noise they wanted for a moment, then calmed them with a disgusted shake of his head. "Can't a body enjoy the hereafter in peace?"

All at once, the crowd shouted, "No rest for the wicked!"

Andie jumped. Were they supposed to do that?

Frank nodded, humoring them. "And no one would know better than you lot, hey? When's the last time you slept, Billy boy?" he asked a man to the right of the stage.

"May 1803," came the answer.

The crowd laughed, and though Frank didn't join them, he looked delighted by the clever response. "Could say the same for Old Boney and all." When the cheers died down, he continued, "Speaking of bones..."

As the curtains behind the stage parted, Andie gasped. Above the stage was another balcony directly opposite. Sitting or standing in two rows, a dozen musicians burst into feverish song. They all wore black, and like Frank, their faces were powdered into ghastly shades of gray. They wore various amounts of kohl around their eyes, some having extended it to their noses and the hollows of their cheeks to appear like skeletons or cadavers in various stages of decay. The music was not like anything Andie had heard before—a lively cacophony of unusual instruments, it was more akin to Frank's first reel combined with Bohemian folk music. As an eerie fiddle rent the air, the hair on Andie's neck stood on end. "What am I watching?" she whispered to herself.

Lulu shot her a glance and giggled.

Frank spread his arms and shouted, "Ladies, gentlemen, and *everyone* in between,"—he wiggled his eyebrows at a group of unusually tall ladies to the left of the stage, who whistled and applauded in appreciation—"I'm Frank Creighton, and this is my Phantasmagoria of Horror and Mystery."

BETWEEN INTRODUCING THE VARIOUS ACTS, Frank sat behind his piano and dabbed at his face with a towel. At this rate, he'd sweat all his makeup off before the closing bit. He told himself he wasn't nervous, only that the year had been unseasonably warm and—

He pinched the bridge of his nose. He couldn't lie to himself, even in his own head. The year had been miserable, only marginally better than the previous, and Britain hadn't seen a real summer since 1815. Oh no—he had no one to blame for his stage fright but himself.

Stage fright. You're forty-bloody-two, and you've done this every week for going on fifteen—

Almost missing his cue, he grabbed the horn under the piano and honked it. The crowd laughed.

It was a good lot tonight, full of familiar faces. He always watched the audience to gauge their reaction, but tonight there was only one person he was concerned about.

Sitting in the box with the poise of a visiting dignitary was Andie Archer. Though she watched with rapt attention, there was no telling what she made of it. It was ridiculous. *He* was ridiculous, but he had a good time. Life wasn't all stuffy musicales and tired concertos, was it?

Almost as if she sensed his gaze, Andie looked down, spotting him in the shadows behind his piano. He couldn't look away. The few dim lamps in the box limned her face in gold, highlighting the warmth in her expression and the delicious darkness of her eyes.

For a full minute, the noise that always filled his head stopped.

Without warning, confetti fell like rain over his hat and into his lap. The audience applauded, and Frank realized he'd missed the end of the final act. Flustered, he played a few notes, then leapt up to take his bow with the others. He rushed his conclusion, automatic as it was, and managed to mention that the orchestra would be playing at the Waterloo re-enactment in Vauxhall the following month. At least he hoped that was what he said; he could have invited them all to Westminster as far as he knew. Even when he managed to look away from Andie long enough to address the crowd, he was aware that she was there, so he stood a little straighter and smiled a little more.

Good lord, he was pathetic.

Things progressed as usual; the audience reshuffled, some heading to the bar for one last drink, while others filed out in search of entertainment elsewhere. Frank dashed into the kitchen and washed his face in the sink, hanging up his hat and running cold water through his hair. He pulled off his cravat in a single practiced motion and left his coat on a hook by the door. Without the makeup and few costume components, he looked like anyone else and could blend into the crowd without being stopped by people wanting an encore. He was tempted to pour a drink for himself, but he wouldn't chance missing Andie when she inevitably fled screaming into the night, scandalized by the performance.

Frank took a deep breath, then charged through the door.

The theater was a good deal quieter after the show, only a couple of dozen regulars drinking with the performers while Marcel, Cosimo, and Antonia improvised a little music from the balcony for their own enjoyment as much as anyone else's. Frank looked up toward the box to find it empty, almost stumbling over Andie as she reached the bottom of the stairs.

"Mr. Creighton!" she blurted, as surprised to see him as he was her.

He impulsively grasped her elbows to steady her, his breath catching at the excitement in her face. "You're still here."

Andie laughed, stepping out of the way of a passing group and moving toward the empty center of the room. "Of course I'm still here." She shook her head, not knowing where to look. Her expression lost a little of its mirth as she met his eyes. "You've...erm, washed." She motioned toward her own eyes to indicate kohl.

"Oh!" He glanced down sheepishly, only just noticing the confetti still stuck to his shirt. He tried to brush it off to no avail. "Missed a bit as a well. Don't know why I bother. The whole bloody place is likely three-quarters confetti at this point. It's the only thing holding the old beast together." *Stop talking, Frank.* "Didn't want to scare you, is all. Which I appreciate is ridiculous, given..." He glanced up at the musicians still dressed as skeletons and the plaster graves on the stage.

"I loved it."

He looked up, warming at her praise. "Truly?"

"Truly." She bit her lip, mulling something over. "If I might ask...how did all this come about? It's like *Don Giovanni*, but the whole of it's in hell."

Frank felt his eyebrows shoot into his hairline. "Bugger me, I've never been compared to Mozart before." That wasn't strictly true, but it had been a *while*. "It started out as a variety show to fill the days between acts. The audience always responded better to gore—the bloodier, the better. The horror draws them in and keeps them there, and the laughs are bigger because they're more of a relief. There are theaters all over town singing about coconuts and fishwives and what have you, but some of these people work eighty-hour weeks. They don't want twee songs about courting squires in country lanes. They want to see someone get stabbed."

Andie cocked an eyebrow, a dimple appearing in her cheek with her smirk. "And the giant spider?"

"Well, how could I resist?" Frank spread his arms wide, making her giggle. "He lives on the bridge, by the by, so be warned in case Lulu ever takes you up there. You may come face to face with a six-foot wool tarantula."

"I'm most obliged to you for mentioning." Her smile eased and puckered ever so slightly to the side, and those dimples appeared again. Andie Archer had at least seven different smiles, and each was more glorious than the last. "What I don't understand is how I'll fit into"—she motioned toward the carnage of the stage—"all of this."

"You'll ride the spider, of course," he blurted without thinking, sending her into fits of laughter. "Does that mean you'll come back?"

She bit her lip, considering him. Finally, she nodded. "I'll come back."

He wanted to shout, to dance, to punch the air. Instead, he let out the breath he'd been holding all night and gave her a short bow. "I'm most relieved to hear it."

After a moment's hesitation, Andie extended her hand to shake. "Mr. Creighton."

Frank caught her hand and immediately raised it to his lips, kissing her glove. "Miss Archer."

She left with a smile, her eyes still bright with laughter. "I'll see you Monday."

Frank didn't fully relax until Andie was long gone and the theater was finally closed for the evening. As the sounds of the orchestra carousing on the roof drifted down the stairs with the strains of Matthias's accordion, he checked the locks, turned down the lights, and looked in on Lulu.

JESSICA CALE

He found his daughter in bed, falling asleep over a book. He paused in the doorway for a moment, trying not to laugh as her head dipped toward the pages.

She caught herself drooping and startled awake.

"You should sleep, poppet."

She yawned. "I'm not tired."

"I've heard that one before." Sitting in the chair beside her bed, he held out a hand to take her book. She gave it to him with no further protest. Frank held the cover up to the lamp. *"Alastor; or, The Spirit of Solitude.* Sounds like a right laugh."

"Shelley always is." Lulu studied him carefully. It was still surreal to see his own eyes staring back at him from her sweet face. "Will Miss Archer be singing with us?"

Frank nodded, more excited than he cared to admit. "We're going to give it a try and see how she likes it."

Lulu snuggled deeper into her blankets. "I like her."

"So do I." Frank put out her lamp with a sigh, quickly kissing the top of her head. "Goodnight, poppet."

She yawned again. "Night, Dad."

280

CHAPTER THREE

ll the next day, the household was in a flurry of activity as they prepared for Sidonie Archambault's monthly literary salon. After years of hosting it, her mother had it down to an art: the drawing room was dusted at dawn, set with gilt chairs and fresh flowers before noon, and filled with a veritable banquet of pastries, fruit, and their own luxury chocolates by the time the guests arrived.

Tea and coffee were at the ready—no one ever passed up their coffee—and they would be sipped politely until Claudine Durée inevitably asked if she might beg a dash of rum in place of cream. One dash would lead to another, and the month's designated books would be forgotten as the conversation gave way to gossip and speculation.

Andie's family's rum was famous. In the years since her great-grandfather Achille had started the company, it had grown from an importer of coffee and raw sugar to London's main supplier of high-end rum. Sidonie's pet project had been chocolate; at her behest, they had opened their first sweet shop in Grosvenor Square. Their pink foil-wrapped boxes sold so quickly, a small army of chocolatiers worked around the clock on the premises to keep them filled.

Part of the demand, of course, came not only from the quality of the goods, but from the limited quantities and high prices. It all seemed counterintuitive to Andie, but the rarer and more expensive the items seemed to be, the more the ton wanted them. Alex was happy to allow them to pay through the nose. They wasted more on gambling and horses, he reminded her, so it was better that the money they spent like water should go to pay the laborers on their island proper wages. If valentine boxes and candied violets were the way to do that, so be it.

Of course, their less glamorous yams and cassava had kept many in London from starving during the food shortages of the Year Without a Summer, but people had already forgotten about that. The Dowager Duchess of Bodmin would never eat anything so *common.*

The air changed when the old dowager entered a room. Dressed in black silk, she was a crow among the songbirds chattering happily around the pianoforte. Used to her severity by now, the other matrons nevertheless stiffened as she joined them.

Sensing her disapproval from twenty paces, Andie retreated to the table and poured herself a cup of coffee with fresh cream. Seeing that Lady Bodmin had not immediately been offered one, Andie did the honors. "Lady Bodmin, may I offer you a cup of tea?"

After some hesitation, Lady Bodmin inclined her head. "Thank you, dear. Assam, if you will."

Andie poured a cup of Assam for the dowager and loaded a plate with her customary treats, two petit fours—one rose and one orange blossom—and a rum truffle. When Andie brought them to her, the old woman almost smiled.

Almost.

Retrieving her own coffee, Andie quietly took the chair

beside Lady Bodmin. As prickly as she could be, it would be terrible manners to leave her sitting on her own. At any rate, it was her sister Zélie's first Season, and two of Lady Bodmin's grandsons were about her age. They could be related someday.

Chilled by that thought, Andie smiled politely at the old woman. "I trust you are well, Lady Bodmin?"

"Well enough." The dowager waved a hand. "As you know, my niece Clara was married this week."

Andie had forgotten with all the excitement of the theater. "Of course. I wish Lord and Lady Crawford every happiness."

"Indeed." Lady Bodmin fluttered her eyelids in the way she often did before she was about to say something terse. "As relieved as I am that Clara has made a suitable match, I question the necessity of having to go to Norwich to do it. The return journey took an age, and I thought certain I should perish!" Evidently recovered, she focused her shrewd gaze on Andie. "Do you suppose *this* will be the Season you finally make a match? How many years has it been now?"

The clatter of teacups paused as the other ladies pretended not to listen.

Andie felt her cheeks warm. "Well, I—"

"Andromeda is focusing on her music, Lady Bodmin," her mother explained, sending Andie a sympathetic look. Madame Archambault was a formidable woman. Though their family had given up their titles in the Terror, the English still treated her with all the courtesy and deference due a marchioness. In many ways, she had more real influence. As a prominent member in more than a dozen societies for the arts, no one questioned her indulgence of Andromeda's interest in music.

Well, no one except Lady Bodmin.

"Music," the old dowager repeated, affronted. "Music is a hobby, not a vocation. You must not let it distract you from your duty." She fixed her stare on Andie.

Bristling, Andie spoke up. "In actual fact—"

"But she's so talented, Lady Bodmin!" Claudine Durée interrupted, defending Andie even as she cut her off. "She could be on stage at the Theatre-Royal."

Lady Bodmin sniffed. "I should sincerely hope not. I've seen where that leads." Her gaze grew distant. "No, dear. You simply must marry. You'll run out of chances, you understand."

Andie didn't need to be reminded of her rapidly advancing age. It didn't bother her that she was not yet married, but she had always hoped to sing for Queen Charlotte by the time she was thirty. "I really don't mind—"

"Oh, I shouldn't think so," Lady Martin cut in. "Andromeda is a lovely girl. With her sweet disposition and considerable talents, any gentleman would be most fortunate to have her. Perhaps an older widower with children of his own..."

Andie's eyes widened at the implication that the only man who'd want her would have to be in his dotage. "But I'm only twenty-n—"

"Oh, yes!" Claudine Durée clapped happily. "I've heard Lord Bude is looking again. Why, just last week..."

The rest of her statement cut out as a high-pitched ringing filled Andie's ears. *Is this rage? I think this might be rage.* Lord Bude was eighty if he was a day, and if her mother's friends thought she'd willingly move to Cornwall to play nursemaid to a known pervert—

Sidonie straightened in her seat and raised an eyebrow. "What about one of your sons, Lady Bodmin? You have six; surely you could spare one."

Lady Bodmin's jaw visibly clenched. Her sons were in their forties and fifties with children of their own, uniformly serious and hawkishly handsome. Andie had thought they were all married, but perhaps there *was* a widower among them; the very idea seemed to scandalize the dowager into silence.

Small mercies.

Feeling more cheerful already, Andie rose and took a seat

behind the piano. No matter the situation, people always spoke over her or spoke for her. Living with it day to day was an exercise in frustration. The only time anyone ever listened to her was when she sang.

The world seemed to drift as she found her way through her favorite Beethoven sonata. The conversation turned to her own brothers—Alex, the heir apparent to St. Croix Imports; Raphael, a tireless lawyer; and Toussaint, a naval officer in the West Africa Squadron. They were all working to make the world a better place; it hardly seemed fair that the same society that lauded them expected Andie and Zélie merely to marry and remain indoors.

Dismayed by the injustice of it all, she missed a note. Irritated, Andie let her mind go blank and focused on the music.

The rest of the afternoon melted away. By the time her mother bid the last guest goodbye, Andie had made it through a folio of sheet music and her wrists ached.

Sidonie sat on a stool beside her. "All you all right, darling?"

Andie let out an exasperated breath. "Lord Bude?"

Her mother laughed, pure joy on her face. "Leave them to their useless scheming. I would never permit such a thing. No daughter of mine will ever belong to anyone but herself, and certainly not for the sake of something so ridiculous as *convention*." Sidonie took Andie's hands in hers. "How was your audition? Things have been so busy, I quite forgot to ask."

Andie warmed at her mother's support, desperately wanting to tell her everything but afraid she'd forbid her to return to The Crow's Nest. "They weren't interested."

Sidonie pursed her lips. "Let me have a word."

"Please don't. I couldn't bear it." Andie shuffled the sheet music, needing somewhere else to look. "But it's not all bad. I met an actress there who told me of another theater to try. I auditioned straightaway, and they...they offered me a part."

Her mother clapped with delight. "Oh, darling, that's wonderful! Is it an opera?"

Andie bit her lip. "Not exactly. It's erm…more of a series of musical performances." Her mind returned to the giant spider, the fiddling cadavers, and the acrobats swinging from the moon. And Frank, his eyes sparkling with mischief and his lips on her glove. "We're still discussing particulars."

Sidonie beamed with pride. "I knew you could do it, dear. I can't wait to attend opening night. Where is it?"

"Oh, nowhere you'd know." Andie tensed. "It's a smaller theater." She took a breath. "Alex is fond of it, actually. It's in Shoreditch."

Her mother blinked in confusion. "Shoreditch? Well, I suppose if it's good enough for the Bard…" Her smile faded somewhat. "That must be an awfully long drive. You should take Toussaint's carriage. We've just replaced the wheels, and he won't be back until Christmas."

"You—you don't mind?" Andie couldn't quite believe what she was hearing. "I know it's not the West End…"

Sidonie waved a dismissive hand. "Everyone starts some-where. The Theatre-Royal will eventually see their error, and you can keep up with your music in the meantime." The matter quite settled, her mother stood. "Are you still going by 'Archer?'"

Andie nodded.

"Let's keep it that way for the time being. Zélie does want to marry, so we should keep this quiet. Once she's settled, you can do anything you like, as far as I'm concerned." Sidonie laughed. "Within reason, you understand."

Andie very much doubted Frank's Phantasmagoria would be considered reasonable by any measure, but she'd cross that bridge when she got to it. "Thank you, Mother." Remembering the earlier exchange with Lady Bodmin, Andie asked about something that had been bothering her. "Before I forget—I thought Lady Bodmin only had five sons. Did something happen to the sixth? I didn't want to ask."

Sidonie sighed deeply. "There was a terrible scandal years ago. It was around the time the war started. I believe he returned from an extended Grand Tour and decided he didn't want any part of polite society, so he quite removed himself from it. Lady Bodmin all but disowned him. For years, she told people he had never returned from Italy. We knew better than to pry."

Andie could understand that. As fortunate as they were to live in safety and comfort in London after escaping the Terror, the societal expectations for a family of their class were arbitrary and unforgiving. If she had the chance to remove herself from that for the sake of her music without harming her family or their business, she'd do it. "I can sympathize."

Her mother nodded. "I thought you might."

"That's not to say I'm not appreciative of our place in the world," Andie hastened to add. "It's only that I find the ton's priorities infuriating. It's a society built on false assumptions and wishful thinking. They keep up appearances at the expense of everyone who toils, suffers, and dies to enable them. They have the means to do anything they want, and they make an art of idleness."

Sidonie laughed. No one knew this better than she did. Born to an enslaved mother in Guadalupe, they had escaped together to the safe haven of St. Croix, where Sidonie had grown up in freedom and fallen in love with Boniface, the marquis's war hero son, returned from serving in the Légion Saint-Georges, France's first Black regiment. Three decades, five children, and two wars later, she presided over her empire from a palace in Mayfair. "The people with the fewest limitations do take the most comfort from creating them." She smiled. "I'm so glad I raised my daughters to know better."

Andie rolled her eyes. "Well, one of us."

"Ah, let Zélie have her fairy tale. Marriage does work out for some people, you know." Her mother raised an eyebrow. Andie's parents had been hopelessly in love for as long as she could remember. "After all, your cousin Apollo married his actress, and she continues to perform to this day. Perhaps you'll find that too. And if you don't"—she paused at the door and looked back over her shoulder—"there's always Lord Bude."

Her mother's laugh echoed down the hall as Andie shuffled the sheet music and filed it safely away. She could not be more thankful for her liberty, but how far would it extend?

BY THE END of her first week of rehearsals, Andie had begun to wonder if she'd made a horrible mistake.

Every weekday until four, The Crow's Nest was closed to the public as Frank ran through the new show with the orchestra and all the performers. He had apparently written the whole thing in a burst over a weekend, and as strange as it seemed, Andie had to admit that it was good. There were twenty-two parts, and although it followed the structure of their established Phantasmagoria, every aspect of it was different enough that it all had to be learned again. Five days in, the actors were tearing out their hair.

As Frank stopped them to change the stage directions for a third time that day, Polly Virtue groaned aloud. "What's wrong with the way we had it?"

"It's the light," Frank said. "The lamps will be here and here, and they need to see your face."

Polly put her hands on her hips. "Why not move the lamps?"

Frank pointed at the moon affixed to the trapeze hook. "When the moon comes down, Andie's dress will catch fire."

Andie sat up, alarmed. "I beg your pardon—I'm coming in on the moon?"

"Naturally." Frank smiled at Andie like it was the most obvious thing in the world.

"So move the moon," Polly said. "That thing's only attached to the one pole anyway."

"What?!" Andie blurted.

Frank winked at her. "You'll be safe. Don't worry." He turned back to Polly to explain that if they moved the moon, the acoustics would be off, then James the Third—so called because he was the *third James*—had to hold her back from strangling Frank.

To his credit, Frank was remarkably patient. Most directors threw their weight around and rejected any questions whatsoever, but Frank was happy enough to explain his reasoning, even when it was clearly madness. Despite the confusion of the rehearsals, Andie had to admit that she trusted him. Seeing the Phantasmagoria had been one of the most enjoyable experiences of her life, and it had surely started much like this.

Andie flipped through her music again, looking at the stage directions. There it was—*Enter, Moon.* She looked at the contraption with suspicion. When Pietro had swung around it the previous week, he'd made it look easy, but nothing in her years of training had prepared her for anything like that. "Good heavens."

Though she'd muttered it to herself, Frank heard her. He turned from the conversation he was having and gave her an encouraging smile.

A tingle of awareness crept up her spine. She'd never felt listened to in her life, but Frank seemed to hear everything she said. He'd answered all of her questions, taken her concerns seriously, and supported her every step of the way.

This was a new experience. She wasn't sure how she felt about it.

When Polly and James had finally completed the scene to

JESSICA CALE

Frank's liking, he told everyone to take a break, then came and sat beside Andie on the steps. "How are you getting on?"

Andie stifled a yawn. "I don't understand your time signature. Are these marks for emphasis?"

"Oh, it just means it has a swing to it." He moved to the piano and played a few bars from memory.

Andie tried to follow along. *"I'm with you when you're all alone, I see you..."* She trailed off when he stopped playing. "Honestly, I'm not accustomed to singing in English."

"It's all right. Try this." He started playing again from the next verse. *"Love is patient, but it ain't kind, will break your heart and rob you blind, and still the lovers seem to say, 'I'm loving every single day.' Well, you can run but you can't hide, I'll find your heart and climb inside..."* He hummed the rest, meeting her gaze over the piano. "See what I mean?"

Andie stared in stunned silence. What she didn't realize was that Frank could sing. Not like she could—his voice was more conversational with a noticeable accent. Low and full of gravel, it had a kind of effortless honesty to it. She felt the texture of it through her whole body. Her shoulders seemed to loosen, and she tingled to the arches of her feet.

He narrowed his eyes playfully. "What's that look on your face?"

Arousal. "Confusion," she said. "You sound almost vulnerable. I suppose I'm not used to that. Singing is the only time I feel strong."

"So come at it from a position of strength. Remember—you *are* Love. It's not a complaint, it's a threat. A promise. You see Polly and James walking together and you're going to give them this incredible gift, but you're also going to ruin their lives beyond recognition. They'll still thank you for it, and you know it."

Andie raised her eyebrows, trying not to laugh. "So I'm the villain?"

290

Frank shook his head, grinning. "You're the goddess. You're the whole point. For only Love is stronger than Death, and in the end, I succumb to you as well." His gaze softened. "Are you married? Courting anyone?"

Heat rushed to Andie's cheeks at what he was asking and why he might be asking it. "No."

He looked almost satisfied to hear it. "Have you ever been in love?"

"No," she answered without hesitation.

Frank nodded sagely. "Then I see we have some work to do." He played a few notes, breaking the tension in the room. "Could you stay for the show tonight? It might help."

Cosimo and Alessandra, the Italian percussionists, were trying out a new act with the dancers. Andie didn't know what to expect, but apparently it was some kind of folk dance. She couldn't imagine how it would help, but she liked the idea of spending more time with Frank. "All right." Her driver would be waiting around the corner from St. Leonard's, but she would give him a few hours off and the money for an evening out. She was certain Thomas would be happy enough for the diversion.

CHAPTER FOUR

I t wasn't often Frank got a night off. Or close to it, at any rate.

All he had to was introduce Alessandra and Cosimo, then he was free to find Andie and enjoy the show until he had to close it at the end. After checking on the lads at the doors, Frank put on his coat and took the stage to scattered applause. "I now have the great honor of presenting a new act. All the way from Sicily, I give you *The Spider Dance.*"

Frank exited the stage as the drumming began. As it happened, there was nothing new about the tarantella, but even if his audience had heard one before, they never would have seen it played like this. Leaving his coat on its peg in the kitchen, Frank rolled up his sleeves and retrieved a bottle of rum from the cold cellar. Two clean glasses in hand, he took it behind the bar and met Andie at the foot of the stairs. She watched the stage, enthralled. Frank offered his arm. "Shall we?"

She glanced up at him, obviously alarmed. On the stage, Nyra, Diana, and Polly were just getting started. Draped in colorful scarves, they were fully covered at all times, but their sensual movements gave the impression that their clothes were about to fall off.

Frank mentally kicked himself. It should have occurred to him that Andie was likely more sheltered than she seemed. "I'm sorry, is this a bit much? You don't have to stay."

Andie noticed the bottle in his hand, and an odd resolve settled over her features. He couldn't blame her; it was bloody good rum. "No, I'd like to stay. Where shall we sit?"

With a smile, Frank led her to the highest balcony open to the public. It was empty tonight, and they'd be able to see the show but still talk without disturbing anyone. He motioned toward the pink seashell-shaped sofa overlooking the stage. "How's this? You're not afraid of heights, I hope?"

Andie shook her head, taking in the Moroccan lamps suspended from the star-painted ceiling. "This is perfect."

THE DANCE WAS NOT like anything Andie had seen before. It started with Nyra, Diana, and Polly dancing to the roll of the drums. This was no waltz, but a kind of awakening that seemed to overtake them an inch at a time. Andie had never seen hips move like that, and when they tossed their shoulders and arms into the dance, spinning gossamer veils in the air, she had to catch her breath. It was beautiful.

Frank offered her a glass of rum and she accepted, the familiar burnt-sugar taste as comforting as her great-grandfather's profile on the side of the bottle. How would Achille feel about her being here? A proud and accomplished man, his example inspired everything her family did to this day.

Then again, he himself had married an English barmaid from Southwark, so perhaps he would understand.

Acutely aware of the man beside her, Andie focused on the stage without really seeing it. Sitting next to Frank felt natural, and comfortable in a way she'd never experienced. She didn't have to explain herself or fight to be understood; he saw her and celebrated her the way she was.

Well, as much as he really knew about her, anyway. Would his opinion change if he knew her real name?

The drums sped up, and the dancers moved away from each other. As the song began in earnest, they started to spin, tossing themselves about as if in a storm. They shook and tore at their clothes, warring with the drums for speed. Frank leaned forward on his knees. "This is the tarantella," he said. "Have you ever seen it?"

Andie shook her head, leaning toward him to hear him better. "What is it?"

He licked his lip, excited to explain it. "It's a traditional dance from Taranta that dates all the way back to antiquity. It symbolizes the effects of a venomous spider bite, which in this case is a metaphor for the torture of falling in love. The dance itself is therapeutic; the idea is that if they do it correctly and with enough passion, they can exorcise the venom."

She frowned. "So they're doing it to *not* be in love?"

"Theoretically." Frank shrugged. "I suspect it's that all that pent-up energy just needs somewhere to go."

Andie watched with new insight. The dance was captivating, and the women did indeed look tortured. But as they danced and lost themselves in the music, the anguish took on another quality until the women seemed to enter a state of divine ecstasy. "It's incredible."

"It's for you," Frank said. Clearing his throat, he clarified, "In the show, your character—you're based on these ancient mystery goddesses of love and war."

As she looked down upon the dancers and musicians, she tried to imagine them playing for her favor, and the role did indeed begin to make more sense. If she had the power to heal these women of their affliction, she would. "How do I fix it?"

Frank looked at her askance, the lamps glittering in his eyes. They were as dark as the longest night—clear, endless, and deep enough to fall into. "You don't. You can't cure love," he said quietly, his gaze falling to her lips. "The only way out is through."

Andie's breath caught. They were close enough now that she could smell the ginger in his soap. An odd smell for a man, the heat of it diffused with the warmth of his skin, mixing with the starch in his collar and the spice of the rum. Was he going to kiss her?

She hoped to God he would.

A burst of applause announced the end of the dance, and the moment was lost. Andie finished her drink and leaned against the backrest of the sofa, trying to catch her breath. To her surprise, Pietro, Lorenzo, and Andrei joined the women on the stage. Nyra picked up a set of castanets to add to the percussion as she continued to dance. A new rhythm started, and the whole mood of the theater changed. "What is this?" she asked Frank.

"This is 'through.' The tammorriata." He refilled both of their glasses. "You might need that."

The tammorriata was a couple's dance, seemingly improvised. Taking turns supporting each other's weight, each couple leaned back and forth in impossibly deep dips, swinging and swaying and all but climbing each other on stage. Andie might have been inexperienced, but she knew the dance was meant to mimic making love. The dancers took turns taunting each other, pulling away, then embracing each other once again until Andie was sure the temperature in the theater had risen by at least ten degrees. It drew her in but made her uncomfortable at the same time. "Should we be watching this?"

Frank paused with his glass halfway to his lips. "What, together?"

She swallowed the noise of surprise that rose in her throat and was deeply embarrassed when it still sounded like a muffled quack. Of course he heard it. Frank listened to everything. To his credit, he didn't even smile. Andie clarified, "I mean...this seems...private?"

He waved a dismissive hand. "It's all performance. Take everything you've got and leave it on the stage. Frustrated? You dance the tarantella. Bad day? You walk into my theater and absolutely destroy *Der Hölle Rache*." Frank smiled as she fought the urge to hide her face. "You know, I've never seen anything like that in my life. You singing? I could smell the brimstone."

Andie laughed in spite of herself. "Is that a good thing?"

"It's the best thing." He held her gaze a moment too long, and she felt it.

The spider bite.

Attraction leaked slow and warm into her veins, racing toward her heart. Would she have to dance to expel it, or could she transmute it somehow?

Recognition lit his eyes, and as his expression fell from surprise into a kind of nervous vulnerability, she knew.

He felt it too.

Frank took a deep breath, and it shook as he let it out. "It's getting late. I suppose I should check on Lu."

Andie sat up straighter. "Oh, is she here?"

He blinked, confused. "We live just upstairs—didn't she mention? The door's right around the corner. Do you, erm..." He swallowed. "Would you like to come up for a minute?"

Is this *a proposition?* Frank was unguarded about so many things but oddly awkward in others, and she found she couldn't tell. *He's hardly going to seduce you with his child present, is he?* Feeling silly, Andie finished her rum. Surely there was no harm in seeing it for a moment. "That would be lovely."

Frank stood, straightening his shirt and retrieving the bottle from the floor. With a last look over the balcony to check the progress of the show, he led her to the hall around the corner and up another flight of stairs, pausing to unlock a door at the top. "Lu, are you still awake?"

"Reading, Dad."

Feeling like an intruder, Andie followed him into the space.

She wasn't sure what she'd expected, but it wasn't this. It appeared to be a maze of rooms leading into each other, more akin to the private quarters in a palace than a modern house. The rooms were much smaller, of course, but no less grand. The door led directly into a warm sitting room paneled in intricately carved walnut. Enormous windows with stained-glass flourishes looked out over the city, while a fire burned invitingly in the hearth. The mismatched furniture was upholstered in deep red velvet. It was beautiful.

Frank stepped easily through the space, no longer noticing the historic details or careful decoration. Whoever had done it had a good eye.

Perhaps his wife had done it before she'd passed.

Or perhaps he has a mistress who did it last week.

Reasoning away the unfamiliar spark of envy, Andie followed. On the opposite end of the next room—a cavernous space full of unusual musical instruments and a cabinet stuffed to overflowing with sheet music—a doorway glowed with the light of the lamp inside.

Frank paused in the doorway, his broad shoulders limned in candlelight. "Miss Archer is here. Would you like to say goodnight?"

"Miss Archer?" Lulu stood and peeked around the doorway in a long nightdress and brilliant purple robe. She looked at her father. "You haven't done the washing; you'll frighten her away."

Andie laughed to herself. "You have a beautiful home, Lulu. Perhaps you and your father might visit mine for tea sometime?" The invitation was out before Andie thought better of it. She still wasn't sure how Frank would feel about her living in Mayfair.

Lulu's eyes widened. "Can we?" she asked Frank.

Frank raised his arms, giving up responsibility. "I'll leave that to the two of you to arrange. Now get some rest. We've got the museum in the morning."

"All right." She waved from the doorway. "Good night, Miss Archer."

Andie smiled. "Good night, Lulu."

Frank kissed the top of her head, then gently closed the door behind him as he returned to Andie in the sitting room.

Clearly relieved that his daughter was safe and everything was right with the world, he still looked ill-at-ease as he paused in front of the fireplace. He looked around, blowing out a long breath. "This is it. Probably not what you're used to."

"I love it," she said sincerely.

Frank nodded toward a closed door on the opposite end of the sitting room. "You haven't seen the best part."

Curious, Andie followed him. To her considerable shock, the next room was his bedroom. She hesitated before going inside until he continued through and opened another door on the far wall. Moonlight and cold air spilled into the dark space. "This way."

Feeling braver by the moment, Andie followed him, speaking a glance at his room along the way. The light was too poor to make out much of anything, but he appeared to have an old-fashioned canopy bed. It had probably come with the theater and the corpse of an Elizabethan playwright in it. The wall facing the bed seemed to be made of books—hundreds if not thousands stacked in no apparent order on shelves that extended all the way to the high ceiling. Andie wouldn't have expected an East End musician to have quite so many, but everything about Frank was unexpected.

Closing the door behind her, Andie climbed a narrow set of steps to the roof. It was the same roof Lulu had shown her before, but another way of accessing it. They walked between the chimneys and the edge of the massive thatch roof to the terrace in the center.

Frank took a deep breath of the cool night air and visibly relaxed. "This is my favorite place."

Above them, stars filled the sky like foil confetti. Below, the lights of the city flickered golden paths along the labyrinth of streets. This high up, it was quiet and still, and the air seemed fresher somehow. It was a secluded piece of heaven in the middle of all the madness. "I can see why."

Pouring them another two glasses of rum, Frank tapped on the roof with his foot. "You know, most theaters of this period don't have these. They used to leave the tops open to let in the air and light. The potters kept it that way until it flooded with rain and ruined their clay, so they put up a cheap roof to try to stop it happening. Trouble is, it never really stops raining in these parts, so they didn't stick around long. When the next theater owner bought it back in 1665, he kept it up for the sake of the people staying here after the Great Fire, and he liked it so much that he put in a permanent roof around 1670."

"How do you know all this?" Andie asked as she accepted the glass of rum.

"There was a crack in it when I bought the place."

Almost dropping her glass, Andie took a step back.

Frank put up a reassuring hand and laughed. "Not to worry —we fixed the crack and reinforced the whole thing. I found signatures and dates from the original builders beneath the eaves. They're still there." He smiled as he sipped his rum. "That's when we put in the chandelier."

A few wooden benches were arranged in a loose circle around the middle. Andie picked one and sat facing the full moon. It didn't escape her notice that Frank kept saying "we." She knew she was prying, but she had to ask, "When did Lulu's mother pass?"

"Pass?" Frank sat beside her and set the bottle of rum on the floor. "Is that what Lu told you? Too many gothic novels. Can't imagine where she gets it," he deadpanned. "No, we haven't seen her for years. I have no idea where she is."

Andie's mouth dropped open. "You seem remarkably unbothered for someone with a missing wife."

"We were never married." Frank pulled a thin cigar from behind his ear—when had he picked that up?—and lit it with a match. "I suppose I shouldn't admit that." He cringed and exhaled a plume of smoke away from her face. "She was a dancer I met on tour in Italy. Mira. I was playing with an orchestra at the time, and we weren't there for long. She caught up with me in Frankfurt two years later and dropped Lu in my lap. I offered to marry her—seemed the right thing to do—but she told me to fuck myself and went back to Sienna. She named her Lucrezia; I think she was hoping Lu would poison me."

Andie didn't know what to say. "I'm...erm, I'm sorry."

"Don't be." He took a long drag. "We do all right. Don't let the kohl and the confetti fool you—this isn't some sad story about a clueless father and his poor motherless child. Lu goes to school, she eats properly, and she has everything she needs. Since Mira brought her to me, my daughter has been the center of my universe, and I wouldn't have it any other way."

Andie didn't doubt it. Good fathers were so rare. Though her own had been marvelous, most of her friends' fathers were distant, cold, or outright hostile. It spoke volumes that Frank wasn't like that. If Andie ever had a husband—and she still very much doubted she ever would—she hoped he'd be someone like Frank.

A faint tickle crept up the back of her neck. Another imaginary "spider." She gently scratched it. She wasn't ready to crush the poor thing. "I think that's absolutely wonderful."

He met her gaze. "You do?"

"Of course." She smiled. "Lulu's lucky to have you."

Frank smiled around the cigar, looking at the moon. "I'm

lucky to have her. She's the reason I do this, you realize. The shows. If not for her, I don't think I would have been brave enough to do it for myself."

Andie sipped her rum slowly, enjoying the mellow smell of the tobacco. Up here, Frank was the only warmth in the night, and she found herself leaning a little closer to his shoulder. "Perhaps you're braver than you think." She sighed. "Most of the people I grew up with did the opposite. My closest friends married and had children young, and they gave up their interests and very identities. These are people who have armies of servants, nannies, and governesses at their disposal—they're so restricted by what society expects them to do, expects a mother to be, that they moved out to the country one by one and just... faded away."

Frank didn't say anything for a moment. With a sinking feeling, Andie realized she'd all but admitted her station.

As his shoulders started to shake, Andie realized Frank was laughing. "What?"

"You look so panic-stricken." He smiled at her in the moonlight. "I knew you were a lady the moment you walked in the door."

Oddly, that didn't calm her a single bit. "You did?"

He stopped hiding his laughter. "Obviously. How many fishwives do you think look like you?"

Andie folded her arms. "What do you mean by that?"

Frank snorted. "Beautiful. Elegant. Queenly." He rolled a hand as if making a bow to a monarch. "Your borrowed clothes aren't fooling anyone. I've known opera singers my whole life, and not one of them brought the light with her when she walked into a room like you do."

Her breath caught. "You think I'm pretty?"

This was usually the part when tonnish lords fell all over themselves to quote sonnets and praise her with flowery, impersonal cliches.

"Pretty?" Frank emitted an ungentlemanly snort. "No, darling. I'm saying you're the goddamned sun."

Andie didn't know what to say. No man had ever said anything like that to her and meant it. She'd gotten her fair share of awful poetry over the years—as it happened, *nothing* rhymed with Archambault—but none of it meant half as much as knowing that Frank Creighton saw her like *that*.

"You just swore," she said dumbly, kicking herself as soon as it was out.

"I blame the rum." He stubbed out his cigar. "I blame the rum for this too." Frank stood abruptly and crossed to the other doorway. He opened it a crack, and music from the theater spilled out into the night. He grabbed the bucket beside the door and brought it back to where Andie was sitting. "How do you feel about birds?"

Andie sat back, bewildered. She'd thought he might kiss her, and now he was talking about *birds*. "I beg your pardon?"

Frank finished his rum in a single gulp. "Sunflower seeds." He tipped the bucket in her direction so she could see the contents. It was indeed filled to the brim. "Take a handful. I want to show you something."

She looked at him with suspicion. What was *wrong* with this man? "All right…" She reached into the bucket and filled her hand with seeds.

Satisfied, Frank took two great fistfuls for himself. "Hold your hand a little loose and shake them so they rattle. Are you ready?"

Andie wasn't at all sure about this, but at the joyful urgency in his eyes, she acquiesced. "Ready."

She followed his lead as he shook the seeds for about five seconds, then they both tossed them toward the edge of the roof.

Within seconds, they were surrounded by a whirlwind of black feathers. It was so sudden and overwhelming that Andie screamed. Dozens and dozens of crows swooped around them in circles until they settled on the seeds, seizing them from the floor and picking them out of the thatch.

Andie doubled over in fits of laughter, tears streaming down her cheeks as she struggled to catch her breath. "I thought you were joking!"

Frank chuckled at her response, looking a little too natural surrounded by a hundred crows under the full moon. "I never joke about crows."

Andie playfully swatted his shoulder, and Frank caught her hand and held it to his chest. When she didn't pull away but stepped closer, he wound an arm around the small of her back and led her around the roof in a sort of improvised waltz to the music coming from inside. Her cheeks ached from smiling as he spun her under the moon, crows fluttering away to avoid her feet. As he caught her in his arms, she met his gaze and she knew.

She curled her fingers into his crisp white shirt and whispered, "You are quite mad, Frank Creighton."

His eyebrows drew together, and she was treated to a slow, crooked smile. "You have no idea."

Grasping his collar in her hands, she stood on her tiptoes and kissed him.

It was a bad idea, the *worst* idea—she couldn't have explained why she did it other than that she *had* to. He was the most exhilarating, infuriating, impossible man, and every nerve in her body was screaming at her to kiss his ridiculous face.

Frank didn't seem to mind. Gathering her up in his arms, he returned the favor with interest. His kiss was like his music—instinctive, passionate, and casually skilled. Though Andie had very little experience with men—and certainly no one like Frank—kissing him felt as easy and essential as breathing.

The chill of the night seemed to disappear as she pressed herself against the heat of his chest, burying her fingers into the unruly waves of his hair. He tasted of salt and rum, the heady scent of good tobacco still hanging in the air.

In the back of her mind, she was acutely aware that this was expressly forbidden; ladies of her class had been compelled to marry for less. If anyone caught them up here, her reputation would be ruined along with her sister's marriage prospects. Worse, if things went wrong, her career could be over before it truly started.

She knew. She knew, but for now, just for this moment, none of it mattered.

After a lifetime of sacrificing her own wants for the comfort and convenience of others, kissing Frank Creighton felt like a radical act, the first and only time she had not only expressed what she wanted but had outright *taken* it.

The heavens opened, moonlight spilling over them. She heard the sound of angels' wings—or perhaps that was still the crows—followed by the sudden end to the music and a deafening roar of applause.

It was the applause that finally pulled Frank away. He held her gaze, the dreaminess in his eyes giving way to mortified horror. "Oh, shit."

With one last lightning-fast kiss, Frank took off running. Andie had never seen someone move so fast. He flew down the staircase, jumping over the last several steps, and thundered to the central staircase. Andie followed at a rather more sedate pace, reaching the top balcony just in time to see him skid to a stop on the stage below.

Frank straightened his shirt, pulled a brace back up on his shoulder, and ran a hand through the mess of his hair. "The Spider Dance, everyone!"

Clearly knowing exactly what he'd been up to, the cheer that closed the show was at least half whistles and raucous laughter. Frank made a face and laughed at himself, spreading his arms wide and taking a bow. He looked up and met her gaze, and Andie could see his face was red.

She didn't think it was possible, but she'd managed to fluster Frank Creighton.

FRANK MILLED about downstairs after the close of the show, making small talk and checking in with the bar. Andie stayed upstairs for a time, gradually making her way back down as she tried to inconspicuously neaten her hair. Once most everyone had gone, Frank took her through the side door and walked her through the churchyard at St. Leonard's across the street. As expected, Toussaint's carriage was waiting on the other side.

They avoided each other's gazes, unsure of what to say. Finally, Frank stopped in front of an enormous stone cross near the center and pivoted to face her. "I should apologize," he said, his voice low. "I shouldn't have..." He glanced toward the roof of the playhouse. "Well, you know. People around here tend to do what they like, but I know it's different for the ton. I don't want to make trouble for you."

It was good of him to care. She probably should have, but oddly, she still didn't. She bit her lip, still tasting him there. She wanted to kiss him again. Perhaps it was the rum talking, but she wanted to drag him behind that cross and ride him like the plaster moon.

Instead, she pulled on her gloves and straightened her jacket. "I don't want to cause you trouble either. You or Lulu. I know if this got out...well, I'm sure you don't need that kind of press."

He took a step back, ashamed.

"Will I see you tomorrow?" she asked.

Frank looked up, surprised. "You want to come back?"

Andie laughed under her breath. "To be perfectly honest," she lowered her voice and stepped closer, "I don't want to leave."

His mouth dropped open as understanding lit his eyes. "Why, Miss Archer, that's a most improper thing to say," he teased.

She looked down and smiled, oddly bashful. "May I ask...do you mind? That I'm a lady, that is?"

"Why should I mind?" he frowned.

"No one understands about the music," she confessed, the excitement of the night making it easier to say things she usually kept inside. "They find me strange or cold or stunted in some way. I'm twenty-nine, Frank. Twenty-*nine*. I've forgone marriage and everything society expects of me so I can sing, something ladies are only meant to do in very specific places at very specific times, and then it's usually only to capture the interest of some loathsome gentleman pretending to care, and I just *can't do it.* I'll not marry and let some useless toff take away the voice I worked *so hard to find.*"

Andie closed a hand over her mouth, horrified she'd said so much. Ladies were not supposed to be candid.

Ladies were not supposed to drink three measures of rum and kiss musicians on rooftops either, but in for a penny, in for a pound.

"I apologize," she whispered.

The smile Frank gave her was so patient, so kind, the warmth of it wrapped around her like a blanket and soothed her fractured nerves. "Now, how could I ever disapprove of some-thing like that?" He offered his arm. "I'm forty-two," he said quietly. "I'm probably too old for you."

Andie snorted. "There's no such thing for men. My mother's friends are trying to marry me off to an eighty-year-old earl in Cornwall."

Frank stopped in his tracks. "Why on earth would they want to do that?"

"Because the ton thinks I'm past it." Andie sighed as they

continued walking. "Don't you know women are useless after twenty-two?" She rolled her eyes.

"This is why I don't want Lu anywhere near it," he muttered to himself. "You are *not* past it. You're not past anything. You, darling, are only just beginning."

They stopped talking as they neared the carriage, not wanting her driver Thomas to hear. Poor Thomas had no doubt heard much worse in his time, but it wouldn't do to put him in an awkward position.

Frank tipped his hat to Thomas, then handed her into the carriage with all the gallantry of a gentleman. He softly closed the door behind her and paused at the window, briefly taking her hand in his. "Good night, Miss Archer."

Andie held in her sigh until the carriage turned the corner, replaying the evening in her mind a thousand times on the way home.

What on *earth* was she thinking? Frank was odd as anything, a good deal older than she was, and wholly inappropriate for a woman of her station. He was also a musical genius, a doting father, and so absurdly handsome that even greasepaint and kohl couldn't hide it.

Andie clapped her hands over her mouth, erupting into giggles in the solitude of the carriage. She rarely drank, and here she was, half in love with an East End musician who made sailors laugh *for money*. If Lady Bodmin could see her now, she'd never recover.

For some reason that notion made her laugh harder. Lost to daydreams, the rest of the journey passed in a heartbeat. Thomas helped her from the carriage, not saying a word about her inebriated state. Once inside, Andie floated up the stairs, tiptoeing past her parents' room. She could almost imagine their reprimand if they saw her staggering down the hallway, love drunk and merry with rum. *What would your great-grandfather say?*

Andie closed the door to her room behind her, leaning against it with glee. She whispered to herself, "He would probably say, 'I know how you feel!'"

Biting back her giggles, Andie spun a few crazy circles in her room, imagining they were dancing again. She fell back into her plush bed, and the last thing she saw before she fell asleep was a spider crawling across the ceiling.

Andie smiled into her pillow. "Frank bloody Creighton."

CHAPTER FIVE

The next weeks passed in a blur.

Maintaining the current schedule while rehearsing a new show and the music for the Waterloo re-enactment at Vauxhall Gardens was no mean feat. Every day, Frank rose at dawn, made breakfast, took Lulu to school, came back to wash, shave, and change his clothes, then he rehearsed until it was time to perform in the evening. He barely slept, and some days, he forgot to eat. He'd taken on too much again, but he was determined to make it work.

In any case, Andie made it worth it.

Watching her come into her own in the new style of singing was immensely gratifying. He'd suspected she could do it, but he never could have imagined quite how well. She'd been nervous about the trapeze ring, naturally, but after he'd personally shown her the reinforcements and rode to the ground floor on it himself, she agreed to give it a try as long as it did not go higher than the orchestra's balcony. Within a few days, she got over her nerves, twirling with joy and singing better than ever.

And that was only the half of it.

Though they had agreed it best to maintain a more professional relationship—at least in public—they escaped every chance they got, stealing kisses behind the curtains or sneaking up to the roof. They never got more than a minute or two, but they made those minutes count.

Frank hadn't stopped smiling for a month.

It was the worst-kept secret in Shoreditch that Frank Creighton had finally fallen in love. No one said anything, but they'd have to be stupid to miss the heated looks, the "accidental" contact, and the whispered words. He'd always had an expressive face, and when it came to Andie, he couldn't hide his wonder. She thought herself a misfit, but she didn't realize how much strength, talent, and determination it took to get where she was, to resist society's pressure to conform or be destroyed. Frank knew precisely how difficult that was, and he admired her all the more for it. She wasn't only beautiful, talented, and clever; she was formidable.

Frank played her song one more time after she left for the day, still picturing her sitting in the moon. They had to be more careful. He knew he could ruin her life, but he was damned if he could live without her.

"So this is where you've been hiding."

Frank stopped playing as a familiar voice carried through the empty theater. Over the top of the piano, he saw his eldest brother sweeping in like Galahad in a spotless blue coat, his silver hair gleaming bright as the grail. He looked around the theater with a kind of repulsed fascination, the master of any space he deigned to enter.

"I've only been here for fourteen years." Frank played a couple of notes. "Right here, sitting at this piano, waiting for one of you to come berate me. To what do I owe the pleasure, Lord Bodmin?"

Will rolled his eyes, and it was like they were children again. "Always so dramatic, Franz. Perhaps you should open a theater."

"Perhaps I will, *Wilhelm*." Frank grabbed his emergency cigar from behind his sheet music. "You want a drink?"

"Go on, then." His brother followed him to the bar, inspecting a stool before he reluctantly sat down. "What do you have to drink in this place? Tell me it's not all piss water and blue ruin."

Frank pulled a couple of glasses from under the bar, briefly considering actually pissing into one of them, but perhaps he should hear what his brother had to say first. He could always piss into the second one. Wanting to show Will what was what, he opened a fresh bottle of St. Croix and poured them each a measure.

"I'm impressed." Will raised his glass in salute. "Cheers."

"Cheers." Frank sipped his slowly, wanting to keep his wits about him. He had been close to his brothers once, but it had been a long time, and there was a reason he'd left.

Will nodded toward the bottle. "Quality rum. You know Mother is close with this family. Visits Madame Archambault's salons every month. Rather likes her. The younger daughter's having her first Season. Charming girl. But the elder daughter, well…" He raised his eyebrows in a way Frank hadn't seen in about thirty years. "Just your type, come to think of it."

Frank leaned his elbows on the bar. "I haven't seen you since the war broke out. You didn't come all the way to bloody Shoreditch to talk about society girls. Why are you here?"

"It's Mother's birthday," he explained. "She'll be seventy-five. We're hosting a fete to surprise her, inviting all of her friends."

"Mother has *friends*?" Frank frowned. "She won't want me there."

"Of course she'll want you there," Will insisted. "I know you didn't part on the best of terms—"

"She told me I was a disappointment and she wished I'd disappeared in Rome."

Will cringed. "She loves you really."

Frank crossed his arms, unconvinced. "Is she still telling people I'm dead?"

His brother snickered. "Well, aren't you? In a manner of speaking, that is. Isn't that your whole act?"

"You've seen the show?" Frank blinked, shocked.

Will shrugged. "Of course I have. Got to keep an eye out for my little brother. I've still got your best interests at heart, you understand."

Frank stared.

"She should see her granddaughter," Will reasoned. "How old is Lucrezia now?"

"Old enough that I don't want her anywhere near all that nonsense." Frank clenched the glass so hard he thought it might crack. "Next thing you know, Mother will have her trussed up and playing dumb for careless boys who don't give a toss about women beyond owning them and old men who ought to know better."

Will ignored this assessment. "That's marvelous. We'll give her a proper Season. Marie can sponsor her."

Frank leaned over the bar and got very close to his brother's smug face. "Over my dead, lifeless, rotting body."

Raising an eyebrow, Will pointed out, "Dead and lifeless are synonyms."

"So are knob and prick, and you still manage to be both."

The floor creaked above the bar. Lulu was listening, and she was so interested that she'd forgotten where to step. Frank cringed.

Will saw it. Excited, he leaned back and looked up toward the balcony. "Is that Lucrezia?"

Lulu popped her head over the balcony to peep down, curious.

"It's your uncle Will." He smiled up at her, his arms wide. "The last I saw you, you were only an infant! I still recognize you, though. You look just like your father, you poor thing."

Frank rolled his eyes. "I'm surprised you didn't introduce yourself as the Duke of Bodmin."

Will ignored him. "Come down for a moment, won't you?"

Lulu waited for his permission. When Frank nodded, she started down the stairs.

His brother took in her dress with amusement. "What the devil is she wearing, Frank?"

Frank addressed his daughter. "Why don't you show your uncle your latest creation?"

Lulu wore a pleated gold gown with costume armor on her slight shoulders, joined in the front with a chain. If he knew his daughter, she had a dagger hidden down the back of her sandal. "I'm Athena."

She gave a hesitant spin to show off the new dress she'd made, and Frank caught a glint of steel at her ankle.

That's my girl.

He smothered his smile and returned his attention to his brother. "Lu makes all her own dresses."

Will visibly shuddered. "You should have said if you needed money."

"We don't," Frank snapped.

Lulu lingered in the doorway, listening. "Are we going to the party, Dad?"

"No," Frank said as Will said, "Yes."

She looked at him askance. "Will Grandmother come here to meet me instead?"

And just like that, Frank's heart broke into a million pieces. His mother would never set foot in Shoreditch, even to see her own granddaughter grow up. Oh no—even though she had disowned him, disinherited him, and publicly claimed he was dead, if she wanted to meet Lulu, he'd have to visit her on *her* territory.

Still, he wouldn't have his daughter thinking she wasn't good enough for Lavinia Creighton-Crowley. He'd just have to show Lulu she was worth so much more.

"We'll go," he said quietly. "Why don't you start on a new dress?"

CHAPTER SIX

T he week passed too quickly.

With only six days left before Andie's debut at the Waterloo re-enactment in Vauxhall, his family was the last thing he wanted to think about. He couldn't close the theater on such short notice, so he'd left it in the care of Alessandra and Cosimo. They'd been with him since Naples, and they knew how things were run. Their own house was right next door, though they were rarely in it. He'd reluctantly handed over his keys, feeling like he was parting with a piece of himself.

He hadn't seen Andie all day. She'd said she had some family obligation but promised to return on the weekend to see Lulu about her dress. The dress Lu had imagined for her was so elaborate that they'd hired a local seamstress to put the whole thing together, but his daughter wanted to make a few little adjustments of her own. At fifteen, she was a prodigy. If she kept it up, she'd have her own business by twenty.

Frank smiled at her from the opposite side of the carriage. They walked almost everywhere, so riding in the hired hack was an unusual experience for her. She watched the city roll by with her serious, all-seeing eyes, no doubt cataloging every lane. "Are you all right, Lu?"

She gave him a nod and a small smile.

"Nervous?" he asked.

"A little." Her fine eyebrows drew together. "I knew Grandmother was a duchess, but what I don't understand is why they want to see us now. Why not last year or the year before?"

It was around the time that Lulu turned five that Frank stopped wondering when they were going to visit and started feeling angry about it. There she was, the most precious little girl in the whole world, and they didn't want anything to do with her. He hadn't forgiven them for that. "It's her seventy-fifth birthday. Your uncle Will thinks that's important."

"More important than fifteen?" she asked.

"Absolutely not." He looked out the window, beginning to recognize the houses. He hadn't been this far into the West End for years, but very little had changed. As the houses grew bigger, he wondered if Andie lived in one of them or somewhere closer to him. In all the excitement of the previous month, they still hadn't called on her for tea. "I suspect they're hoping I'll come to my senses and marry some society girl." *Or that Lulu will become one of them.* Frank cringed.

Lulu frowned. "You can't do that. You have to marry Miss Archer."

Frank sat up straighter, startled. "Why would you say that?"

"Because you're in love with her," Lulu said slowly as if he was stupid. "It's all right; she loves you too. She makes this little noise whenever you come out wearing kohl." She made a high-pitched squeak in the back of her throat. "Just like that." She did it again.

"Is there anything you don't notice?" He laughed in spite of himself, then sighed. "Nah, she's too good for me."

Lulu met his eyes, deadly serious. "No one's too good for you, Dad."

The carriage slowed as it turned onto his old street. Up ahead, there were so many carriages lined up outside the house that it would still be several minutes before they reached the door. Frank had loved the house growing up, but he hadn't lived there since he was seventeen. Trying to take his mind off his nerves, he returned to the conversation at hand. "How would you feel about that? If Miss Archer took leave of her senses and came to live with us."

"It only makes sense. She's there every day, and she has an awfully long drive..." Lulu smiled hopefully.

Frank had no idea how she knew what she knew, but he'd long since stopped asking. "You're right about that."

As the carriage finally stopped, Lu gave his hand a little squeeze. "It's going to be all right, Dad."

Nearly moved to tears, he patted her hand back, trying to be strong. "It will. Listen, if your grandmother or anybody else says anything to upset you, you tell me and I'll sort them out."

Lulu nodded sagely. "You too."

Frank grinned to himself. Most would find the idea of a child defending them laughable, but he knew better than to underestimate his daughter. "All right, poppet. Let's go."

THE HOUSE WAS EXACTLY as he'd left it.

The décor hadn't changed in thirty years. Every painting, vase, and candlestick was in its rightful place, just like Will and Marie greeting guests in the foyer. At fifty-four, Will had grown into the perfect duke, correct in all ways with a thriving estate and five children of his own. Frank had last seen Marie when she was only eighteen; she'd seemed so mature when he was a child, but now he realized she hadn't been much older than Lulu was now. She barely acknowledged them before they made their way through to the banquet.

"Franz! Is that really you?"

His second brother, Gustav, was loitering near the pork pies with Fritz, his fourth. Both looked at him as if seeing a ghost. Frank joined them at the table and accepted a glass of sherry. He introduced Lulu before she wandered deeper into the party on her own, distracted by something.

Frank scratched the back of his neck. Anxious, he tried to focus on what they were saying. Now fifty-two and forty-eight respectively, they'd both had decades of adventures of their own they were eager to fill him in on. When he mentioned the theater, they grew quiet. "That's brilliant, Franz, truly," Gus said, not meeting his eyes. "We'd love to come see it, but...erm, you know."

"The children," Fritz interjected.

Frank rolled his eyes. They'd both just finished telling him about how their children were all but grown, so they could surely handle a night without their fathers. Unless a great deal had changed, the both of them likely still spent most nights in the gaming hells anyway. "Where's Mother?" Frank asked, looking around. If the night was going to be awful, he might as well get it over with now.

"With Albert," Fritz supplied, referring to their third brother. "She's dining at his house this evening to give us the chance to set up. Felix should be along anytime."

Frank nodded. The party was well underway already. Dozens of guests in opulent clothing flocked between the rooms. In her new orange and white dress, Lulu was lost among them. "I'd better find my daughter," Frank excused himself.

Walking through the house again was a peculiar experience. Everything looked the same but felt completely different. He no longer recognized anyone. Even his brothers felt like strangers to him.

That was down to them, really. When he'd at last returned from his Grand Tour—which had, admittedly, gone about nine years longer than most—they'd expected him to set his music aside to fulfill his "duty to the family." As the youngest son in a family of six, there was very little "duty" left to be fulfilled. All the others had married and promptly had children, taking their places in society exactly as their mother had instructed them to. Frank too had a child, but not in the right way; his mother expected him to set Lulu aside.

When he'd refused to send her away, his mother had stopped speaking to him. When he used his savings to purchase a disused theater in the East End, she'd started telling people he was dead.

That was when Frank started dressing up as a corpse. Over time, the role had stuck.

I shouldn't be here. This was a mistake.

Then, quite suddenly, he heard it.

It was the opening notes to his favorite aria from Gluck's *Orpheus and Eurydice.* The voice was so clear, it sent a cascade of chills through his body. A string quartet joined the voice, and the guests slowly started to make their way into the music room. The voice stopped him in his tracks, bringing tears to his eyes with its beauty. He stopped in the doorway and just listened.

Every note, every trill was perfection. It almost sounded like—

Oh no.

Afraid to look, he peered around the door. Sure enough, Andie stood at the far end of the room, but this was not Andie as he'd ever seen her before. In a gown of sparkling silver and white, she looked like his every fantasy of a woman come to life. Unlike like borrowed clothes she wore to rehearsals, this dress actually fit her properly, and it skimmed her every curve in a way that made his mouth water. There were three camellias in her artfully arranged hair, and three strings of pearls around her long, graceful neck.

She sang with her eyes closed, almost smiling. She was doing it from memory and loving every second of it.

Frank closed his eyes, letting the music pull him out of himself. For a minute, they were back at the theater, and she was singing just for him. They were at the Theatre-Royal as she opened to a packed house; they were in Paris, Brussels, and Vienna. She could sing anywhere she wanted to, and he would follow her there.

Except they weren't in some distant opera house or empty Elizabethan theater; they were in his brother's house, Frank's childhood home, and he was feeling more out of place by the minute.

Turning to leave, he stopped a passing gentleman. "Say, who is that singing?"

"What, you don't know?" The man snorted a laugh. "That's Andromeda Archambault."

Andie Archer.

Frank could have kicked himself.

Andie wasn't only a lady; she was part of one of the wealthiest and most influential families in the city. Her father Boniface was a legend, a French marquis and war hero who'd fought alongside the Chevalier de Saint-Georges and General Dumas. When Napoleon had attempted to bring back slavery in 1802, he'd reportedly camped out on the beach of St Croix with a cannon for two years until he was certain the threat to his island had passed. One of his sons was an abolitionist, and another captured slavers in the West Africa Squadron. The family would have been more controversial if people didn't like them so very much.

Frank's heart dropped. Disgraced as he was, he'd known he didn't have much of a chance of anything serious with her being lady, but Andie was not just any lady. As far as society was concerned, she was very nearly royalty.

Devastated, Frank left the room and went in search of his late father's liquor.

ANDIE FINISHED the song with her eyes closed, wanting to prolong every perfect moment.

When the audience had responded so positively and settled down to listen, she'd relaxed, singing for the joy of it. The air was charged with a familiar energy that reassured her and made her tingle from the inside out. Closing her eyes, she could almost feel Frank there, watching her with wonder as he often did from behind his piano. She sang it for him, counting the minutes until she could return to The Crow's Nest.

When it came, the applause was louder than she expected. Andie curtsied and went in search of water. Her mother stopped her briefly on the way. "There's a director from the Theatre-Royal here tonight." She nodded toward an elderly man in a powdered wig. "You impressed him."

Andie shared an excited smile with her mother. She'd forgotten all about the Theatre-Royal. As much as she would still like to sing there, she had unfinished business in Shoreditch first.

As she glanced up toward the drinks table, Andie spotted someone out of place.

Lulu was leaning against the wall with a glass of lemonade. She was so still, Andie thought she imagined her.

Andie blinked, but the girl remained. Tonight she was wearing a demure girl's dress in ivory lace with little orange flowers embroidered all over it. Her hair was pinned up in a ladylike chignon, and she watched everything with those haunting brown eyes. "Lulu?"

Spotted, Lulu shot her a mischievous smile and disappeared into the crowd in the hallway. If Lulu was here, surely Frank must be too. Her heart speeding up, Andie went to follow her, but she was stopped by the Duke of Bodmin.

"Your Grace." She curtsied.

Lord Bodmin inclined his head in greeting. "Outstanding performance, Miss Archambault. Quite magnificent."

"M-my thanks, Your Grace," Andie stammered, caught off guard by the praise.

The duke was a distinguished older man, finally growing into his features in his fifties. He shouldn't have been handsome, but oddly he was; he had a certain charisma in spite of having a prominent nose and a jaw like an anvil. She'd seen similar features before, but with his close-set blue eyes and faint brows, she couldn't quite place them.

"If you don't mind, Miss Archambault, there's someone here I'd very much like to introduce you to. He's an accomplished musician himself; I'm sure you'll have much to talk about."

Andie looked over his shoulder, trying to hide her impatience. She wasn't interested in Lord Bodmin's attempts at matchmaking, but it would hardly do to say so. She had a girl to find. "Of course, Your Grace. I'm always happy to discuss music."

"Very good." Lord Bodmin smiled pleasantly. "He was here a moment ago. Now, where's he gone...?"

Several yards away, Andie saw a white skirt with orange flowers move swiftly down the hall. She had to catch up before she lost her again. "I'm certain you will locate him, Your Grace. If you'll excuse me, I find myself in desperate need of a glass of water."

"Certainly, you must protect your voice," he said. "I will find you later this evening."

"Your Grace." Andie curtsied once more, then slipped out of the crowd and down the hall.

Lulu was nowhere to be found. Had Andie imagined her?

The hall seemed to stretch forever, a Baroque tunnel of pale blue plaster and gilt molding. It led past half a dozen parlors and sitting rooms of various sorts and ended in a glass conservatory that opened out into the gardens. Andie was just about to give up when she heard a familiar song drift through the hall.

"Love is patient, but it's unkind..."

Andie's pulse hammered in her throat. It couldn't be. It was impossible that he was here, but that *was* her song she was hearing. And the voice...

"Frank?" she whispered to herself, following the sound.

Not far from the conservatory, she found a private room with the door ajar. In the hall outside, the sound was unmistakable. Frank was playing her song and singing inside.

"It'll break your nose and rob you blind. You'll feel so good, you'll forget the bad, she'll make you want everything you never had..."

He'd changed some words, slowed it down, and played it in minor chords. He sounded battered, his voice mournful and raw.

It was *better*.

Checking that no one could see her, Andie slipped inside and closed the door.

Frank sat behind the piano. The room appeared to be a study, mainly books but with a few older instruments displayed throughout. A single lamp glowed weakly on the wall, filling the room with rose-colored light and shadows. He looked up, the relative darkness making him look like his stage persona for a moment. Her eyes adjusted, and she noticed that he was wearing a sharp jacket with a high collar, silk waistcoat, and elaborately tied cravat. Absurdly handsome by any measure, he'd shaved carefully, and his hair was as neat as it had been her first night at The Crow's Nest.

Suddenly it all made sense.

"Oh, Frank," she sighed. "You had a secret too."

"I didn't. Not really." He played a few notes before nodding in polite greeting. "Miss Archambault."

Andie looked around the room. Lulu was nowhere to be found. The little mischief-maker had led her down here and left.

She sat beside Frank on the long piano bench, her fingers automatically finding a compatible chord. "Frank Creighton-Crowley, is it?"

"It's actually Franz." He took a swig of brandy straight out of a faceted crystal decanter, then offered it to her. "Wilhelm, Gustav, Albert, Felix, Fritz, and Franz. She just stopped trying after number four."

Andie accepted the decanter. It was heavier than it looked, and she had to steady it with both hands. "Is your family German? I thought they came from Cornwall."

Frank kept his gaze on the keys, not meeting her eyes. "My mother was born in Hanover. Seventy-five years ago today, in fact, and Pandora's still trying to get the lid back on the box." His shoulders slumped and expression defeated, Andie had never seen him so dejected. She'd seen him anxious, impatient, and even frustrated, but this was something worse.

He was resigned.

"I should have told you," he said, finally glancing up at her. "It doesn't change anything. I didn't know what to say."

Andie took a deep breath. She knew families were complicated, and titles and property only complicated matters. It was clear his relationship with his family was strained. "Why don't you tell me now?" she asked softly, playing a couple of hopeful high notes. "What happened?"

"I don't know where to start." Frank stared straight ahead. Unconsciously, his hands found the opening chords of the Phantasmagoria, and he gently started to play it a new, pensive pattern, the overture to some tragedy. "I always loved music. It was everything to me. I started with a viola, then cello, then piano, harpsichord..." He let out a long breath. "I set out for my Grand Tour with Felix and Fritz when I was seventeen. Did you or your brothers ever do that? You're meant to ponder ancient ruins and produce mediocre watercolors."

Andie shook her head. "They had other interests. I traveled around to study with various tutors, but I didn't do a lot of drawing."

"Me neither." He moved up a key and continued playing. "I was too young to go, really, but old enough that I knew what I wanted out of life. Then one night in Padua, I got the chance to play with an orchestra, and I found I couldn't stop. By the time my brothers returned, I had joined one and was playing nightly in Rome. I only returned to England when the war broke out. By that time, I was twenty-eight."

Andie's hands paused over the keys. "You were gone for eleven years?"

"Just about." Frank nodded. "My brothers had all grown up and married, and I was alone with a two-year-old daughter. Mother was horrified, naturally." He gave Andie a tight smile. "She couldn't understand why I'd brought Lu back with me at all. She insisted I marry, and I even tried courting for a time, but the ladies were the most wretched..." He stopped himself. "Suffice to say, they weren't anything like you. Few could accept that I already had a child, and those who did insisted I send her away. One even offered to 'keep her on in service,' like it was the most generous notion in the world. Can't get in the way of any legitimate children, you understand." He hit a few low notes, his expression disgusted. "Of course, Mother agreed with them. What would people *think?*"

The notes got brighter as he continued. "I had some money of my own. I'd worked nightly for years and never had time to spend it. It wasn't enough to maintain all of this"—he looked around the room— "but it was enough for a little theater. When I saw the apartment on the top floor, I knew I'd found the right place. Lulu and I moved in that week, and my mother hasn't spoken to me since."

Andie rested her hand over his on the keys. "I'm so sorry."

"Do you think less of me?"

The question broke her heart. "How could I?"

He met her gaze, his eyes filled with the pain of old wounds that still refused to heal. She raised a gloved hand and brushed her fingers through his hair, the silver silk bright in all the dark. He didn't say anything but let her do it, closing his eyes at the sweetness of her touch. This was enough. He was everything she'd been looking for but hadn't known she'd wanted. When he opened his eyes, she saw herself in them, recognizing something she'd only felt hints of before.

They were the same.

They understood each other in a way that no one else ever had, because they'd had the same drive, made similar sacrifices, and faced the same impossible decisions. Frank's decision had ultimately been made for him, but Andie could still choose. She was on the precipice of something irreversible, looking over the edge but still holding on.

She jumped.

Andie kissed him. It was a kiss of understanding, of love, and a promise of the union to come. She had sensed he wasn't telling her everything, but now that he had, there was no more hesitation.

Frank felt it and kissed her back, passion and relief making him careless. In one swift motion, he pulled her onto his lap. Elated and suddenly ravenous, Andie straddled his hips and wrapped her arms around his neck. After weeks of sneaking kisses in a packed playhouse, they were finally, blessedly alone in the dark, and Andie was going to enjoy it as much as she could.

Lost in sensation, she seized his cravat and pulled him closer, a few keys fluttering as her back bumped the piano. Frank pulled her closer, his lips on her throat as his hand slid up her stocking to her bare thigh under her petticoat. Feeling him there was alarming, but she found she didn't mind. She had his cravat untied and two buttons popped before he pulled himself away, drowsy with want. "If anyone found us…"

Andie groaned. "I don't care."

Taking her at her word with a cheeky smile, he grasped her hips, lifted her, and sat her down on the piano keys with a single discordant bang. One hand pinning her petticoat to her hips, the other brushed the heat between her thighs. After weeks of frustrated want, Andie was so aroused, she nearly screamed at the contact. "Tell me to stop," he murmured against her lips.

At the press of his arousal against the inside of her thigh, her legs seemed to open of their own accord. She pulled him closer. "Don't you dare."

Focused on the heat of his mouth and the scent of his skin, the first press of his fingers came as a surprise. She was so wet, they slid inside her easily, teasing her toward breaking point with long, slow strokes. The man really *was* good with his hands. Her heart skipped as the tension built, her breath coming faster and faster under she shuddered, only breaking the kiss as she gasped his name.

She held onto his shoulders for dear life as he briefly let go of her hip and fumbled with his falls. Frustrated as his hand left her, she squirmed on the keys, sending a few scrambled notes into the air. Thank God she'd closed the door.

Suddenly something warm, thick, and very hard was pressing up against her. His nose brushing hers, his breath was shallow as he asked, "You're sure now?"

If Andie was any surer, she'd burst into flame. "For God's sake, Frank, yes!"

He held her gaze as he slid into her, wary of causing her pain. She gasped as she felt it, but the initial discomfort passed as she adjusted to the new sense of fullness. The feeling that took over was nothing but sublime. But it was slow, too slow.

JESSICA CALE

Close, so close to edge, Andie buried her fingers in his hair and dragged his mouth to hers.

Understanding without needing to be told, he braced her lower back with one big hand and hammered into her harder, deeper, and faster, the piano banging louder with every thrust. It was an unholy racket, but Andie had never heard a song she liked quite so much. She wrapped her legs around his waist, and the tension inside her burst, erupting in a scream she muffled in his shoulder.

Undone, Frank withdrew and spent into her petticoat. Not caring a fig for the ruined silk, she kissed him slowly as she came down, needing the moment to last for as long as possible.

It wasn't to be. Frank had barely fastened his trousers when the door opened quite suddenly to the Duke of Bodmin with the dowager duchess on his arm.

Lord Bodmin took one look at them—Andie still sitting on the piano with Frank, disheveled and missing his cravat, standing between her legs—and said, "Ah. I see you've already met."

The dowager duchess fainted.

CHAPTER SEVEN

T he Duke of Bodmin was nothing if not a gentleman.
In the panic caused by the dowager duchess fainting, Andie was able to return to the party without notice as Frank stayed behind and attempted to reattach his collar without a mirror. Once their mother was settled, Will quietly returned to assist him.

"I see nothing's changed," Will said as he took over from Frank, attaching the collar with little trouble.

Impatient to find Andie, Frank retorted, "You're one to talk. You were worse than the rest of us combined."

Will lowered his voice as he handed Frank his rumpled cravat. "I never fucked an heiress on a seventeenth-century fortepiano. You do realize that's the oldest one in the world?"

Of course he did. He was the one who insisted they buy it. "I dimly recalled." Frank took the cravat and rapidly tied it. "How long do you suppose I have before her father shoots me?"

"Months. He's in St. Croix on business, but I'm sure her brother will oblige." Will crossed his arms with a sigh. "Meet me in the study when you've straightened yourself up."

Once Will had left, Frank drank a glass of water and combed

his fingers through his hair. Whatever came next was bound to wretched, but he needed to find Andie first to be sure she was all right.

The party was much as he'd left it. If anything, more people were there, and no one seemed to have any idea that anything out of the ordinary had taken place. He found Andie sitting beside the drinks table with Lulu, happily chatting to his daughter about something he couldn't quite hear. Seeing them sitting together hit him in a way he wasn't expecting; he'd long since accepted he would probably never marry, but the of having a family with Andie and Lulu was too divine to bear.

As if she could hear his thoughts, Andie looked up and smiled.

Frank's view of her was cut off quite suddenly by her brother Alexandre stepping between them. Though he smiled pleasantly, his eyes were intense. "Frank! It's been an age. Let's go talk somewhere a bit more private, shall we?"

Six days.

It had been six days, and Andie hadn't heard a word from anyone.

Alone in her room, she stood by the window, watching the street for any familiar faces. While her mother still didn't know exactly what had happened—Lord Bodmin had only privately told Alex that there was been an indiscretion with his brother, but he thankfully did not go into detail—she thought it best for Andie to remain at home until they had decided on the best course of action.

Apart from Lord Bodmin, no one really knew anything, but speculation could be just as damaging. Fortunately, when the dowager duchess had come to and started muttering about her supposedly dead son and the opera singer, the other guests had simply assumed she'd lost her wits in the fall.

Andie missed Frank. Tonight was supposed to be their first real performance together. He'd arranged for a stage to preview their new show after the military parade that night. Would he find someone to fill in for her, or would he cancel?

"*Love is patient...*" Andie hummed to herself, hearing his voice singing in her head.

A light knock interrupted her thoughts.

Alex came in, an enormous striped hatbox under his arm. He set it on the edge of her bed and joined her at the window. "How are you feeling?"

Andie crossed her arms. "Lonely. Frustrated. I have a show tonight I should be rehearsing for, you realize."

"You don't have to go to that," Alex soothed. "There will be other parts." From the look on his face, it was clear he thought he was being helpful.

"I want this part. I want to see Frank," she insisted. "What exactly did you discuss?"

Alex sat in the chair at her dressing table, clearly uncomfortable. "Bodmin declared that Frank ought to marry you. I said it was quite out of the question. He can't hope to keep you in the manner to which you are accustomed. Naturally, your dowry would be substantial, but that's not the point. We'll not force you to marry a villain who would take advantage of you."

She looked at him, incredulous. "Oh, Alex, what have you done? He didn't take advantage of me; I took advantage of him! I'm in love with him, you idiot!"

Her brother's mouth dropped open. "You can't be serious." He looked at her, trying to ascertain if she was joking. "But he's so...odd."

"So am I!" she shouted. "What did he say to all of this?"

Still dazed, Alex inclined his head and continued. "He said he was more than willing to marry you, but that he appreciated you'd have to give up a great deal. He said he would never ask you to make such a sacrifice, and we considered the matter quite settled. He's not to see you again."

Andie's scream was so loud, it cracked the glass on her dresser.

Alex blinked at her, his hands over his ears. "What was that for?"

"Did it not occur to any one of you to ask *me?*" Andie balled up her fists in frustration. "Frank Creighton is the *only* man I would consider marrying. Do you mean to tell me that you and Mother would support the match if I wanted it?"

"Of course." He shrugged. "It's not ideal, obviously, but he is the Bodmin's brother. If he makes you happy..."

"Deliriously," she snapped. "Now, will you help me fix this?"

"Fine!" Alex threw up his hands in surrender. "But seriously..."

Andie looked at him.

"Frank?" He dodged the pillow she threw at him. "I thought it was just a lark. Isn't he fifty?"

"Forty-two." She finally turned her attention to the striped box. "I'll be thirty in September. I'm not a child anymore, Alex." Andie removed the lid to find a letter sitting on top of several layers of tissue paper. "What is this?"

Alex shook his head. "I have no idea. Clement said it arrived for you this morning."

Flipping the letter over, she popped the sealing wax, and a small metal object fell out. Confused, she read the note.

DEAR MISS ARCHER,

Dad's miserable. Please come back. I'll be at the Vauxhall band-stand tonight at 8. I have enclosed a lockpick in case you need it.

With love,

Lu CC

A LOCKPICK. Lulu had sent her a lockpick.

Andie covered her mouth to suppress her laughter as tears sprung to her eyes.

"Is it from Frank?" Alex asked.

She shook her head, removing the tissue paper. Inside the box was a magnificent midnight-blue gown spangled all over with silver stars. It looked just like Lulu's drawing. Andie gathered it to her chest. "If tonight goes the way I very much hope it will, it's from my daughter."

IN THE END, Andie didn't have to look for Lulu.

Within minutes of arriving at Vauxhall with Alex and her mother, Andie had located the bandstand and was on her way there when a slight figure charged out of the crowd. There were plenty of people in military dress, but no one looked quite like Lulu. Tonight she had accented her gold empire-waist gown with costume armor on her shoulders like a short spencer and a steel helmet with an open face. It was probably left over from a medieval play, but without the visor, it looked Greek from a distance.

Andie had never been so happy to see someone in her life. Lulu rushed to hug her, then paused to take in the dress. "It fits. Good. Come on, we'll have to hurry if you don't want him to see you."

"Aren't you going to introduce us?" her mother asked as she and Alex caught up.

Lulu stopped midstride, taking in the magnificence that was Sidonie Archambault. She was wearing an elaborate gown in the exact shade of pink as their foil-wrapped chocolate boxes. Her hair was styled like Madame Pompadour's. Well out of fashion, yes, but Madame Archambault dressed exactly as she wanted, and when it came to hair, bigger was always better. Lulu gaped, hardly able to take it all in. Awkwardly, she curtsied. "Are you the queen?"

Sidonie laughed, genuinely delighted by the question. "Andromeda, dear, who is your charming friend in the marvelous dress?"

Andie watched the exchange with no little amusement. These two would clearly have much to talk about in the coming years. "Mother, this is Lucrezia Creighton-Crowley, Frank's daughter. Lulu, this is my mother, Madame Archambault, and my brother, Alexandre."

"You must call me Sidonie." Her mother embraced Lulu like a long-lost child. As Lulu led them through the park to a smaller stage, her mother chattered happily about the new shipment of arms and armor they had received at the British Museum, offering to take Lulu as her guest.

Andie smiled at Alex as she took his arm. Her brother only laughed and shook his head.

CHAPTER EIGHT

A
s it happened, Frank *was* miserable.

He should have been happy. He'd gotten his entire orchestra good work for the night at the Vauxhall re-enactment of the Battle of Waterloo. After the parades but before the fireworks, he'd secured one of the smaller stages to put on a preview of his new show to an audience far larger than any he could hope to attract in Shoreditch. The night was warm, clear, and beautiful. They would perform under the stars for thousands of people, and that was a major victory.

Except that Andie wasn't there.

Frank changed his clothes in a small tent set aside for the orchestra. He pulled off the red jacket they'd asked him to wear while conducting and put on his new costume. Though his "character" was much like the undertaker figure he played in his Phantasmagoria, for this one, he'd taken it one step further and played Death, the nemesis to Andie's Love. Eventually, she was meant to triumph over him and end the show with her foot on his chest—he'd rather been looking forward to that part—but without her here, he was just some tosser dressed in black.

His best chance at love, and he'd ruined it.

Putting on his hat, he checked in with the orchestra and had a last look to be sure everything was where it was meant to be. They didn't have anyone who could sing Andie's part, so he was going to end it himself. He preferred to leave the audience on a laugh, but there was nothing they could do about that at this point. He'd depress the crowd, take off his makeup, and go back to Shoreditch.

He just hoped Andie was all right.

She'd wanted it as much as he had, he knew it, but that didn't mean it was a good idea. Perhaps she had come to her senses. He hadn't heard from her all week, and now he likely never would.

Being a shortened version of the show, Frank introduced himself as Death, picking up the thread of the story between three acts. The idea was to follow him through different scenes, loosely tied together. Polly and James did a comedic song and dance about the stages of courtship. Alessandra and Cosimo played an abridged tarantella for Nyra and Diana to dance to, and then Frank would be on.

He and Andie were supposed to argue between the acts over who got to keep which performers. The full show was twelve acts, and it would have been a riot.

Would have been, except now he'd probably have to scrap or rewrite the entire thing.

Frank watched the audience from behind the curtain. It was a good crowd tonight. Quiet, if polite. They didn't really know what to do with him. He didn't know either. He wished he could enjoy it more, but his heart wasn't in it. When it was time for him to go on himself, it was all he could do to make himself smile.

Until he saw Lulu sitting in the front row. She always made him smile.

Next to her, however, was an unexpected face. Unless he was very much mistaken, that was Madame Archambault sitting

336

beside—yes, that was Alexandre. Frowning, Frank crossed the stage. Perhaps Alexandre had changed his mind about not wanting to shoot him. Couldn't blame him, really. If he didn't, Will might yet do the honors himself.

Frank skipped the small talk tonight. He sat behind the piano and started to play.

"Love is patient, but it's unkind. It'll break your heart and rob you blind. She'll hold you close and drive you mad, make you want everything you never had..."

He improvised a little on the piano, singing through verses that felt spectacularly pointless now that he didn't have anyone to sing with. He felt it, though. He felt it more than ever, and it was all he could do to keep the shake out of his voice as he reached the end of the final verse.

An unexpected voice came from the other side of the stage. *"Before you go—don't yet depart! You know Love has a woman's heart..."*

Frank stopped playing, stunned into stillness. Andie crossed the stage before him, looking like his first vision of the Queen of Night in a gown of navy-blue velvet and stars. She raised her eyebrows as if asking if she could continue.

He picked up the melody and nodded enthusiastically.

Andie faced the crowd and projected. *"Since life, long last, began at sea, they cry, they beg, 'move Heaven for me!'"* She turned to Frank, growing serious. *"But never once has anyone heard, my own lament, a single word."*

He stopped breathing as she drew closer, his heart in his throat.

Andie stopped not a yard away from him, holding his gaze. *"The sun itself, the skies of blue, I'd give it all, Frank, to be with you."* Sotto voce, she added with a smile, *"And Lulu."*

The seconds after she finished were quiet. Too quiet. Once again, all the noise in his head had stopped. All that remained was a single thought.

She came back to me.

Frank stood so quickly he almost knocked the piano bench over. He reached for her hands, but she wound her arms around his shoulders and kissed him.

Andromeda Archambault had made her decision and didn't care who knew it. Two thousand people saw it, many of them members of the ton, and all two thousand leapt to their feet and cheered.

"Marry me," he said when they finally pulled apart. "I can't live without you. I love you, Andie."

Andie smiled against his lips. "I asked you first."

The End

ABOUT THE AUTHOR

Jessica Cale is a romance author, editor, and historian based in North Carolina. Originally from Minnesota, she lived in Wales for several years where she earned a BA in History and an MFA in Creative Writing while climbing castles and photographing mines for history magazines. She kidnapped ("married") her very own British prince (close enough) and is enjoying her happily ever after with him in a place where no one understands his accent. She is the editor of Dirty, Sexy History and you can visit her at www.dirtysexyhistory.com

REGENCY IN COLOR, VOL. 2 COMING SOON!

Regency in Color

Thank you reading this collection! We look forward to bringing you more diverse romances set in the Regency era!

Regency in Color Vol. 2 is coming soon. For updates, subscribe to the Regency in Color newsletter. Click here to sign up!

CPSIA information can be obtained
at www.ICGtesting.com
Printed in the USA
LVHW040405060921
697080LV00023B/562